MURDER OF CROWS

MURDER OF CROWS

A NOVEL OF THE OTHERS

ANNE BISHOP

A ROC BOOK

ROC
Published by the Penguin Group
Penguin Group (USA) LLC, 375 Hudson Street,
New York, New York 10014

USA | Canada | UK | Ireland | Australia | New Zealand | India | South Africa | China
penguin.com
A Penguin Random House Company

First published by Roc, an imprint of New American Library,
a division of Penguin Group (USA) LLC

First Printing, March 2014

LIBRARY OF CONGRESS CATALOGING-IN-PUBLICATION DATA:

Bishop, Anne.
Murder of crows: a novel of the Others/Anne Bishop.
pages cm.
ISBN 978-0-451-46526-9
1. Women prophets—Fiction. 2. Werewolves—Fiction. I. Title.
PS3552.I7594M87 2014
813'.54—dc23   2013033927

Printed in the United States of America
10 9 8 7 6 5 4 3 2 1

Set in Albertina MT • Designed by Elke Sigal

*For
Pat*

ACKNOWLEDGMENTS

My thanks to Blair Boone for continuing to be my first reader and for all the information about animals and other things that I absorbed and transformed to suit the Others' world, to Debra Dixon for being second reader, to Doranna Durgin for maintaining the Web site, to Adrienne Roehrich for running the official fan page on Facebook, to Catherine Garcia for telling me about fresh-baked dog cookies, to Charles de Lint for the inspiration of music at World Fantasy (Toronto 2012), to Nadine Fallacaro for information about things medical, to Douglas Burke for answering questions about police (and for not asking what I would do with the information), to Anne Sowards and Jennifer Jackson for all their feedback about the story as well as their enthusiasm for the series, and to Pat Feidner for always being supportive and encouraging.

A special thanks to the following people who loaned their names to characters, knowing that the name would be the only connection between reality and fiction: Bobbie Barber, Elizabeth Bennefeld, Blair Boone, Douglas Burke, Starr Corcoran, Jennifer Crow, Lorna MacDonald Czarnota, Julie Czerneda, Roger Czerneda, Merri Lee Debany, Michael Debany, Skip Denby, Mary Claire Eamer, Sarah Jane Elliott, Chris Fallacaro, Dan Fallacaro, Mike Fallacaro, Nadine Fallacaro, James Alan Gardner, Mantovani "Monty" Gay, Julie Green, Lois Gresh, Ann Hergott, Lara Herrera, Robert Herrera, Danielle Hilborn, Heather Houghton, Lorne Kates, Allison King, Jana Paniccia, Jennifer Margaret Seely, Ruth Stuart, and John Wulf.

NAMID—THE WORLD

CONTINENTS/LANDMASSES

Afrikah

Australis

Brittania/Wild Brittania

Cel-Romano/Cel-Romano Alliance of Nations

Felidae

Fingerbone Islands

Storm Islands

Thaisia

Tokhar-Chin

Zelande

Great Lakes—Superior, Tala, Honon, Etu, and Tahki

Other lakes—Feather Lakes/Finger Lakes

River—Talulah/Talulah Falls

Mountains—Addirondak

Cities and villages—Ferryman's Landing, Hubb NE (aka
    Hubbney), Jerzy, Lakeside, Podunk, Sparkletown, Talulah
    Falls, Toland, Walnut Grove, Wheatfield

DAYS OF THE WEEK

Earthday

Moonsday

Sunsday

Windsday

Thaisday

Firesday

Watersday

© 2012 Anne Bishop

This map was created by a geographically challenged author who put in only the bits she needed for the story.

LAKESIDE COURTYARD

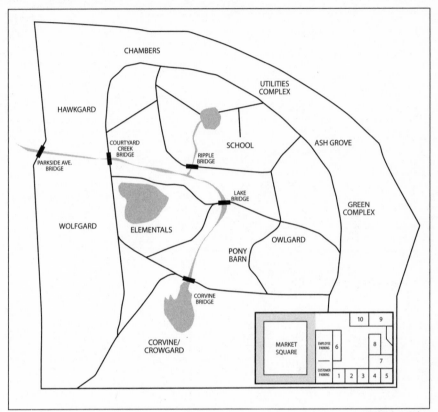

CHAMBERS

UTILITIES COMPLEX

HAWKGARD

ASH GROVE

COURTYARD CREEK BRIDGE

SCHOOL

RIPPLE BRIDGE

PARKSIDE AVE. BRIDGE

LAKE BRIDGE

GREEN COMPLEX

WOLFGARD

ELEMENTALS

OWLGARD

PONY BARN

CORVINE BRIDGE

CORVINE/ CROWGARD

MARKET SQUARE

EMPLOYEE PARKING

CUSTOMER PARKING

10   9

6

8

7

1   2   3   4   5

© 2012 Anne Bishop

1. Seamstress/Tailor & efficiency apartments
2. A Little Bite
3. Howling Good Reads
4. Run & Thump
5. Social Center
6. Garages
7. Earth Native & Henry's Studio
8. Liaison's Office
9. Consulate
10. Three Ps

MURDER OF CROWS

A Brief History of the World

Long ago, Namid gave birth to all kinds of life, including the beings known as humans. She gave the humans fertile pieces of herself, and she gave them good water. Understanding their nature and the nature of her other offspring, she also gave them enough isolation that they would have a chance to survive and grow. And they did.

They learned to build fires and shelters. They learned to farm and build cities. They built boats and fished in the Mediterran and Black seas. They bred and spread throughout their pieces of the world until they pushed into the wild places. That's when they discovered that Namid's other offspring already claimed the rest of the world.

The Others looked at humans and did not see conquerors. They saw a new kind of meat.

Wars were fought to possess the wild places. Sometimes the humans won and spread their seed a little farther. More often, pieces of civilization disappeared, and fearful survivors tried not to shiver when a howl went up in the night or a man, wandering too far from the safety of stout doors and light, was found the next morning drained of blood.

Centuries passed, and the humans built larger ships and sailed across the Atlantik Ocean. When they found virgin land, they built a settlement near the shore. Then they discovered that this land was also claimed by the *terra indigene*, the earth natives. The Others.

The *terra indigene* who ruled the continent called Thaisia became angry when the humans cut down trees and put a plow to land that was not theirs. So the Others ate the settlers and learned the shape of this particular meat, just as they had done many times in the past.

The second wave of explorers and settlers found the abandoned settlement and, once more, tried to claim the land as their own.

The Others ate them too.

The third wave of settlers had a leader who was smarter than his predecessors. He offered the Others warm blankets and lengths of cloth for clothes and interesting bits of shiny in exchange for being allowed to live in the settlement and have enough land to grow crops. The Others thought this was a fair exchange and walked off the boundaries of the land that the humans could use. More gifts were exchanged for hunting and fishing privileges. This arrangement satisfied both sides, even if one side regarded its new neighbors with snarling tolerance and the other side swallowed fear and made sure its people were safely inside the settlement's walls before nightfall.

Years passed and more settlers arrived. Many died, but enough humans prospered. Settlements grew into villages, which grew into towns, which grew into cities. Little by little, humans moved across Thaisia, spreading out as much as they could on the land they were allowed to use.

Centuries passed. Humans were smart. So were the Others. Humans invented electricity and plumbing. The Others controlled all the rivers that could power the generators and all the lakes that supplied fresh drinking water. Humans invented steam engines and central heating. The Others controlled all the fuel needed to run the engines and heat the buildings. Humans invented and manufactured products. The Others controlled all the natural resources, thereby deciding what would and wouldn't be made in their part of the world.

There were collisions, of course, and some places became dark memorials for the dead. Those memorials finally made it clear to human government that the *terra indigene* ruled Thaisia, and nothing short of the end of the world would change that.

So it comes to this current age. Small human villages exist within vast tracts of land that belong to the Others. And in larger human cities, there are fenced parks called Courtyards that are inhabited by the Others who have the task of keeping watch over the city's residents and enforcing the agreements the humans made with the *terra indigene*.

There is still sharp-toothed tolerance on one side and fear of what walks in the dark on the other. But if they are careful, the humans survive.

Most of the time, they survive.

CHAPTER 1

Nudged awake by his bedmate's restless movements, Simon Wolfgard yawned, rolled over on his belly, and studied Meg Corbyn. She'd kicked off most of the covers, which wasn't good for her since she didn't have fur and could end up catching a chill. To a *terra indigene* Wolf, catching something meant you wanted it, and he couldn't think of a single reason a human would want a chill, but apparently humans did and could catch one in cold weather. And even in the last days of Febros, the Northeast Region of Thaisia was plenty cold. Then again, if she started feeling chilly, she'd cuddle up closer to him, which was sensible since he had a good winter coat and, being a Wolf, liked the closeness.

If someone had told him a few weeks ago that he would befriend a human and care enough to watch over her at night, he would have laughed his tail off. But here he was, in Meg's apartment in the Green Complex, while his nephew Sam stayed with his sire Elliot at the Wolfgard Complex. Before the attack on the Lakeside Courtyard earlier in the month, he and Sam had cuddled up with Meg to nap or even sleep through the night. But things had happened that night when men had come to abduct Meg and Sam. For one thing, Meg had almost died while saving Sam from those men. For another, something had happened to *him* on the way to the hospital, causing him to feel out-of-control anger. He had suspicions about what had happened, which was why Sam, who was still a puppy and lacked self-control, no longer slept with him when he curled up with Meg.

Meg told people her height was sixty-three inches because, she said, that sounded taller than being five feet something. She was twenty-four years old, had weird orange hair that was growing out to its natural black, clear gray eyes like some of the Wolves, and fair skin. Strange and fragile skin that scarred so easily.

She was a *cassandra sangue*, a blood prophet—a female who saw visions and spoke prophecy whenever her skin was cut. Whether it was a formal cut with her special razor or a gash caused by a sharp rock, she saw visions of what could happen in the future.

The Sanguinati referred to females like Meg as sweet blood because, even when they were adults, these women retained the sweetness of a child's heart. And that sweetness, combined with blood swimming with visions, made them not prey. Made them Namid's creation, both wondrous and terrible. Maybe made them something more terrible than the *terra indigene* had imagined.

He would deal with the terrible if and when he had to. For now, Meg was Meg, the Courtyard's Human Liaison and his friend.

She began making noises and pumping her legs as if she were running.

<Meg?> She couldn't hear *terra indigene* speech, but he tried anyway since he didn't think this was a good chase-a-deer dream. Especially when he was suddenly getting a whiff of fear off of her. <Meg?>

Intending to nudge her awake, he pressed his nose under her ear.

In the dream, Meg heard the monster coming closer and closer. A familiar sound, made terrible by the destruction she knew would follow in its wake. She tried to shout a warning, tried to yell for help, tried to run away from the images that filled her mind.

When something poked her under the ear, she flailed and screamed and kicked as hard as she could. Her foot connected with something. Terrified, she kicked again.

Those kicks were followed by a loud yelp and a thump that had her scrambling to turn on the lamp.

Breathing hard, feeling her pulse pounding in her ears, she first noticed that the bedside table matched the image she had of it just before she went to sleep, except the small clock beside the lamp said three o'clock. Comforted by the familiar, she looked around.

She was not in a sterile cell in a compound controlled by a man who cut her skin for profit. She was in her own bedroom, in her own apartment at the Lake-side Courtyard. And she was alone.

But she hadn't been alone when she turned off the light a few hours ago. When she'd gone to sleep, there had been a big furry Wolf stretched out beside her.

Grabbing as much of the covers as she could, she lay down and pulled them up to her chin before whispering, "Simon?"

A grunt that sounded like it came from the floor on the other side of the bed. Then a human head came in sight, and Simon Wolfgard stared at her with amber eyes that held flickers of red—a sure sign he was pissed off.

"You awake now?" he growled.

"Yes," she replied meekly.

"Good."

She had a glimpse of lean muscle and *naked* skin before he scrambled under the covers. She turned away from him, her heart pounding with a different kind of fear.

He *never* slept with her in his human form. What did it mean that he was human now? Did he want . . . *sex?* She wasn't . . . She didn't . . . She wasn't even sure she could with . . . But what if he expected . . . ?

"S-Simon?" A tremble in her voice.

"Meg?" Still plenty of growl in *his* voice.

"You're not a Wolf."

"I'm always a Wolf."

"But you're not a *furry* Wolf."

"No, I'm not. And you're hogging the covers." That said, he grabbed the covers she was clinging to and yanked.

She tumbled into him. Before she could decide what to do, the covers were around both of them, and he had her pinned between his body and the bed.

"Stop squirming," he snapped. "If you bruise more than the hip you kicked, I will bite you."

She stopped squirming, but not because he had threatened to bite her. Prophecies and visions swam in her blood, released when her skin was cut. Simon knew that, so he wouldn't tear her flesh. But in the past couple of weeks, he'd figured out how to nip her through her clothes hard enough to hurt without damaging skin—Wolf discipline adjusted to dealing with her kind of human.

She'd stumbled into the Lakeside Courtyard seven weeks ago, half-frozen and looking for a job. Simon had threatened to eat her on a regular basis those first few days, which wasn't his typical way of dealing with employees since most of them would have responded by writing their resignation as they ran for the door. But when the Others discovered she was a blood prophet on the run from the man who had owned her, they had chosen to treat her as one of their own. And protect her as one of their own, especially after she fell through the ice and almost drowned while leading an enemy away from Simon's nephew Sam. Which was why, since her return from the hospital, she went to sleep every night with Simon curled up beside her, on guard.

She'd be less happy about the lack of nighttime privacy if that furry body didn't make such a difference in keeping her warm.

Was that why her apartment was always chilly, so she wouldn't make a fuss about Simon sleeping with her? It hadn't occurred to her to make a fuss about it because he was a Wolf. Except now he wasn't a wolfy-looking Wolf, and Simon as a human in bed with her felt . . . different. Confusing. Threatening in a way she didn't want to explain.

But furry or not, he was still warm and he wasn't *doing* anything, and it was still too early to think about getting up, so this was something . . . to ponder . . . tomorrow.

She started to drift back to sleep when Simon gave her a little shake and said, "What scared you?"

She should have known he wouldn't let it go. And maybe he was right not to let it go. Her abilities as a prophet had changed since she'd escaped from the compound and ended up living with the Others. She was more sensitive now, to the point where she didn't always need to cut her skin to see visions—especially if they concerned her in some way.

The images were fading. She knew there were already things she'd seen in the dream that she couldn't recall. Would she remember anything by morning? And yet, even the thought of recalling the dream made her shudder.

"It was nothing," she said, wanting to believe it. "Just a dream." Even blood prophets had ordinary dreams. Didn't they?

"It scared you enough that you kicked me off the bed. That's not nothing, Meg." Simon's arm tightened around her. "And just so you know? You may be small, but you kick like a moose. Which is something I'm telling the rest of the Wolves."

Great. Just what she needed. *Yep, that's our Liaison. Meg Moosekicker.*

But the dominant Wolf and leader of the Courtyard was waiting for an answer.

"I heard a sound," she said quietly. "I should know what it is, but I can't identify it."

"A sound from your lessons?" he asked just as quietly, referring to the training she'd received in the compound in order to recognize what she saw or heard in prophecies.

"From the lessons," she agreed, "but from here too. And it's not a single sound, but many things that, combined, have a single meaning."

A moment of thoughtful silence. "All right. What else?"

She shivered. He curled around her in response, and she felt warmer. Safe.

"Blood," she whispered. "It's winter. There's snow on the ground, and that snow is splashed with blood. And I saw feathers." She turned her head to look at him. "That's why I was trying to scream, trying to get someone to listen. I saw broken black feathers stuck in the bloody snow."

Simon studied her. "You could see them? It's not dark out?"

She thought for a moment, then shook her head. "Daylight. Not bright sun, but daylight."

"Did you recognize the place?"

"No. I don't remember anything in the dream that indicated where, except there was snow."

Simon reached across her and turned off the light. "In that case, go back to sleep, Meg. We'll chase this prey in the morning."

He stretched out beside her and fell asleep almost immediately, just like he did when he was in Wolf form. Except he wasn't in Wolf form, and she didn't know how to tell him that having him sleeping beside her, looking and feeling like a human male, had changed something between them.

CHAPTER 2

Parked in front of his best friend Grizzly Man's house, Wild Dog sat in his father's pickup truck with his other best friend, Howler, and waited for the fun to begin. Windsday was trash day in this part of Walnut Grove and the freaking Crows from the Courtyard would be flying in just ahead of the garbage trucks to pick over the trash humans threw out. Every freaking week they came around and poked in the trash cans that were put out at the curb. They poked and pecked and flew off with all kinds of crap because, really, that's all Crows were—crap pickers.

Nothing people could do about it. Government Man said so. Couldn't even take a potshot at the black-feathered thieves because the jail time and fines could ruin a whole family. But Grizzly Man, who knew how to find shit on the computer that you wouldn't want your parents to know about, had learned about a bitching game called Crow Bait and Roadkill. Girly boys could sign up at the site and play the game on the computer, but if you wanted to try the real thing you needed two very special drugs: gone over wolf and feel-good.

It wasn't easy to get your hands on the stuff, and neither drug was cheap. It had taken him, Grizzly Man, and Howler two months of pooling most of their spending money to buy the vials that Howler had acquired from a friend of a friend who knew a guy who knew a guy. Now they were going to find out if the drugs and the game were worth it.

"Come on," Wild Dog muttered. "I've got to get the truck back before the old man wants to leave for work."

Howler rolled down the passenger-side window. "I hear the garbage trucks. They must be on the next block. Is G-Man ready?"

Wild Dog pulled the mobile phone out of his pocket and made the call. "You ready?" he asked when Grizzly Man answered.

"I gave 'em the dosed meat," G-Man replied. "You sure about the dosage?"

Gods below, no, he wasn't sure about the dosage. Last week the three of them had split half the vial of gone over wolf in order to try it out, and he had only the vaguest memory of what happened after they caught up with Priscilla Kees, who had no business walking home alone after dark. But he remembered that he'd felt beyond horny. He'd felt wild and powerful—and he wanted to feel that way again.

But not for a while. Not until things cooled down. Priscilla hadn't come back to school, and he'd overheard his mom tell his grandma that the vicious attack had caused some kind of damage to the girl's innards *down there* and maybe other kinds of damage, and she wasn't letting *her* daughter walk alone even to a friend's house that was six doors down the street. Not until the animals who had done *that* to Priscilla were caught.

It felt weird hearing his mom talk that way, like she wanted to lay on some serious hurt. That scared him some, which was why he was glad they voted to use the rest of the gone over wolf for the game. By the time they could afford another vial of the drug, everything would be back to normal.

"Hey, Wild Dog," G-Man said. "You still there? The dogs are acting funny, and I don't like the way they keep looking at me. It's weirding me out."

"Here they come," Howler said as the Crows flew in. Leaning forward, he rested one hand on the dashboard.

"Come on, you freaks," Wild Dog whispered. "Enjoy some spaghetti and feel-good." He snickered. Take some feel-good, and you'll feel so good you won't feel a thing.

Howler swore the drug was powerful enough to make a full-grown Wolf as helpless as a newborn puppy—or keep all the damn Crows grounded. So yesterday they'd bought a large take-out order of spaghetti. This morning they'd laced the food with feel-good and left handfuls of it next to six garbage cans on the street.

The Crows came in, winging toward the cans that didn't have tightly sealed lids or had items left next to them. As soon as the first Crow spotted the spaghetti, birds came in from everywhere, and Wild Dog couldn't tell if they were Crows or crows. But they were all gobbling the spaghetti.

"Go on, you stupid shits," Wild Dog whispered. "Eat up." He spoke into the mobile phone. "G-Man. Almost time."

"Hey," Howler said. "Who's that?"

They watched the petite black-haired girl walk from house to house, looking into the garbage cans.

"That's perfect," Wild Dog said. "We've got one of the Others in human form."

"Garbage truck will be here any minute," Howler said. "We need to be gone before someone spots us."

"Yeah, yeah." Wild Dog watched the birds for a moment longer. A car coming down the street had to swerve to avoid a bird that didn't even try to get out of the way. Perfect. "G-Man, let the dogs loose."

The two hunting dogs that belonged to G-Man's father ran out of the backyard, spotted the birds, and tore into them with a savagery that made Wild Dog feel excited and a little sick. A couple of the birds flapped their wings in a feeble attempt to escape, which did nothing but draw the dogs' attention to them— and to the girl standing frozen next to a garbage can.

"Oh, shit," Howler said. "I know who that is! It's the new girl at school. Her family just moved here, came all the way from Tokhar-Chin. We've got to stop the dogs!"

"We can't stop them!" Wild Dog grabbed for Howler's coat, but Howler had already half fallen out of the truck and was screaming, "G-Man! Get your dad! Get your dad!"

Nothing to do but go with his friend. Couldn't be seen just sitting there with Howler yelling and the girl screaming and people coming out of their houses, some dressed for work and some still in their bathrobes despite the snow and cold.

Suddenly someone shoved him aside and was yelling at everyone to get out of the damn way, and . . .

Bang. Bang.

That same someone was now yelling at people to call the cops, call for an ambulance, and Wild Dog finally recognized him. Didn't know his name, but knew he was a cop friend of G-Man's father.

The cop was next to the girl now, pressing his hand right against the wound on her neck that just kept bleeding. He looked up at G-Man's father and said, "I'm sorry, Stan, but I had to shoot them."

"Is the girl going to be all right?" Stan asked.

The cop paused a moment, then lifted his hand and shook his head. After cleaning his hands with fresh snow, he rose and stared hard at Wild Dog and Howler. "What are you boys doing here?"

Stan just stared at the girl, then at the dogs. "Gods above and below, what got into them? And how did they get out of the yard?"

"We'll take them in, get them tested. Find out if they went crazy for a reason." The cop was talking about the dogs—sure he was—but he kept staring at Wild Dog. Then he looked at the dead birds. "Yeah, we're going to need to do some tests."

Wild Dog tried to field a story about just dropping by to see G-Man for a minute, but suddenly there were all kinds of official vehicles clogging up the street, and there were a lot of cops interested in hearing his story, and they wanted to hear it down at the station with his father present. That was why he ended up riding home in the back of a police car.

And that was why the police were right there with him when he walked into the kitchen and discovered that Priscilla had remembered a lot more about that night last week than he did, and that was why she brought her father's shotgun when she came calling at his house this morning.

CHAPTER 3

ate Windsday morning, Lieutenant Crispin James Montgomery parked the
patrol car in the Courtyard's customer lot, got out, and breathed in air that
still had the bite of deep winter. That wasn't surprising, considering the storm
that had savaged the city of Lakeside at the beginning of the month—a storm
that had proved to everyone living here that the shape-shifters and vampires
who were the public face of the Courtyard were not the most dangerous *terra
indigene* in residence. Enraged by the attack on the Courtyard and the death of
one of their steeds, the Elementals, led by Winter, had unleashed their fury on
the city and its residents in what newspapers and television newscasts had
called the storm of the century.

Some buildings had been damaged or destroyed in that storm. Some people
had been injured and a few had died. Whole sections of the city had been without power for days, and people had struggled to stay warm and fed while Lakeside was locked in by a record snowfall and slabs of ice that blocked all the roads
out of the city.

Having spent every spare moment over the past two weeks reading up on
towns that had been destroyed after a conflict with the Others, Monty knew the
storm and the consequences could have been much, much worse. He wasn't
sure whom Meg Corbyn had talked to or what she'd said, but he would bet a
month's pay that she was the reason the ice slabs simply melted away one night,
allowing needed supplies into the city. She had warned the Others of a poison

that had been intended for the Elementals' steeds. She had saved Simon Wolfgard's nephew Sam during the attack on the Courtyard. She had won the trust
of beings who rarely, if ever, trusted humans.

On the other hand, because she had been the attackers' intended target, she
had been indirectly responsible for the storm that crippled Lakeside, as well as
the deaths of Lakeside's mayor and the governor of the Northeast Region. But
that was something only a handful of people knew. For everyone else, the official story was that a group of outsiders had come to Lakeside with the intention
of stirring up trouble and had provoked the Others' attack when they blew up
part of the Courtyard's Utilities Complex and killed several *terra indigene*. Since
all the news reports made it clear that humans had started the trouble, there had
been a wait-and-see truce between Lakeside's citizens and the Others these past
couple of weeks.

Maybe people were too busy making repairs to their homes and businesses
and just wanted to get back to their lives. Or maybe they were making an effort
to steer clear of the beings who ruled the continent of Thaisia. And not just
Thaisia. The *terra indigene* ruled most of the world. As far as they were concerned,
humans were another kind of meat, and the only difference between people and
deer was that people invented and manufactured products that at least some of
the Others enjoyed having. That was the only reason the Others in Thaisia
leased tracts of land where humans could live and grow food, and supplied people with the resources needed to manufacture products. But people were still
meat the moment they did something the *terra indigene* didn't like.

That wasn't an easy truth to swallow at the best of times, and given the information he was about to share with Simon Wolfgard, today was not going to
be the best of times.

Monty walked past the seamstress/tailor's shop and A Little Bite, the coffee
shop that was one of the few Courtyard stores open to the general human population of Lakeside. When he reached Howling Good Reads, the bookstore run
by Simon Wolfgard and Vladimir Sanguinati, he ignored the Residents Only
sign and rapped on the door.

Simon approached the door and stared at Monty for a little too long, giving
the police officer time to consider the contrast between the two of them. Wolfgard looked like a trim man in his mid-thirties with a handsome face and dark
hair that was cut to match the persona of a business owner. Most of the time, he

easily passed for human. Except for his eyes. The amber eyes never let you forget you were looking at a *terra indigene* Wolf, a predator—especially now that Wolf-gard had given up wearing the wire-rimmed glasses that had been an attempt to make him look less dangerous. Monty, on the other hand, was a dark-skinned human of medium height who stayed trim only with effort. He hadn't reached forty yet, but his short curly hair already showed some gray, and there were lines on his face that hadn't been there a few months ago.

Finally Simon unlocked the door, and Monty slipped inside the store.

"Not open to human customers today?" Monty asked as Simon locked the door again.

"No," Simon replied curtly. He limped over to a cart full of books and began redoing the display table in the front of the store.

Monty nodded to the young woman behind the checkout counter, one of the humans the Courtyard employed. "Ms. Houghton."

"Lieutenant," Heather replied.

She looked scared, and when she tipped her head toward Simon in a "pay attention to him, there's something going on" sort of way, Monty wondered if the Courtyard's residents had already heard the news or if Heather had another reason to be afraid.

After observing Simon for a moment, he said in a conversational tone, "Did you injure your leg?"

Simon slammed a book down on the table and snarled. "She kicked me off the bed! She was having a bad dream, so I tried to wake her up, and *she kicked me off the bed.*"

Monty didn't have to ask who *she* was. He noticed that Heather, now staring at the Wolf with wide eyes, didn't ask either.

"And then she acts and smells all bunny-weird about me being there in human form." Simon dumped more books on the table. One slid off and hit the floor. The Wolf didn't notice. "What difference does it make if I'm furry or not?" He pointed at Heather, and the look in his eyes made it clear he expected an answer.

"Aaaaahhhh," she said, glancing at Monty. "Weeeelllll. When my mom takes a nap, our cat curls up with her, and my dad doesn't care. But I don't think he'd like it if the cat suddenly turned into a man."

"Why?" Simon demanded. "The cat would just be a cat in a different form."

Heather made a funny sound and didn't answer.

Monty quietly cleared his throat before he said, "A form that would be able to have sex with a human female."

"I didn't want sex!" Simon shouted. "I just wanted my share of the covers." A hot and hostile look at Heather. "Females are peculiar."

Oh, geez, Monty thought as he watched Heather's eyes fill with tears.

"I'm going to pull some stock for these orders." Heather sniffed, then hurried toward the stockroom at the back of the store.

"If you try to quit, I will eat you!" Simon yelled.

The only reply was the sound of a door slamming.

Simon stared at the display, which was nothing but a sloppy pile of books. Then he looked at Monty and snarled, "What do you want?"

No, this wasn't the best time for what he'd come to talk about, but he needed any information Wolfgard would give him, and by sharing what he knew, he hoped to spare Lakeside from another display of *terra indigene* rage.

"Have you listened to the radio or television today?" Monty asked. "Have you heard about what happened in Walnut Grove early this morning?"

Simon didn't move, didn't even seem to breathe. "Were Crows murdered?"

"Some birds were killed," Monty replied carefully. "Captain Burke didn't receive many details from his contact in the Walnut Grove police force, so I can't tell you if the birds were crows or Crows." He hesitated. "Ms. Corbyn had a dream about this?" Or had she done more than dream? Had she taken the razor and cut her skin in order to speak words of prophecy?

"She dreamed about blood and broken black feathers in the snow." Simon growled and gave Monty a challenging look. "She didn't make a cut. I would have smelled blood if she'd made a cut."

Were prophetic dreams normal for a blood prophet, or was this a sign that Meg's mental stability was unraveling? Not something he could discuss today. At least, not with Simon Wolfgard.

"Did your Captain Burke hear anything else?" Simon asked.

Are you wondering about something in particular? Monty thought. "It appears two hunting dogs attacked the birds. They might have gotten out of their yard by accident and simply acted on instinct, but a teenage girl was also killed." The mother, father, and younger sister of one of the boys who had been present when the dogs attacked had also been killed. But he didn't think Wolfgard would be interested in a girl shooting a family unless it circled back to whatever had happened to the birds.

Simon stared out the bookstore's front windows. "Haven't seen a Crow this morning. Haven't heard a Crow this morning." Going behind the checkout counter, he picked up the phone and dialed. After a few seconds he muttered, "Busy signal, what a surprise," hung up, and dialed another number. "Jenni? It's Simon. I want to talk to you. *Now*."

Monty could hear Jenni Crowgard's protest from where he stood, so Simon had certainly heard it. The Wolf hung up anyway.

Elliot Wolfgard ran the consulate and was the public face for the Courtyard, the earth native who talked to the mayor and dealt with Lakeside's government. But Simon Wolfgard was the actual leader of this Courtyard, and no one here challenged the leader. Except, perhaps, the Grizzly who also lived here. And the Elementals, who answered to no one.

"You will *not* talk to Meg about this," Simon said. "Not yet."

Monty wanted to ask Meg about her dream before it became fogged by whatever images she heard or saw on the news. But he didn't argue, and he knew he'd made the right choice when he nodded agreement and Simon relaxed a little.

"If any of the Crowgard know anything about the deaths, I'll call you," Simon said.

"Thank you," Monty replied. "The police in Walnut Grove are running tests on the dogs and the birds. It's likely that every police force in the northeastern part of Thaisia will be informed of the results. As soon as I know anything, I will tell you. Frankly, Mr. Wolfgard, we're all hoping the dogs had been riled up and the birds just weren't quick enough to get away." The girl certainly hadn't been quick enough. "If that's not the case . . ." He didn't want to say it.

Simon wasn't hesitant to finish it. "It could be the first sign of sickness in the Northeast Region. It could be the same sickness that caused trouble in the Midwest Region and provoked the fight in Jerzy last month."

Not a sickness but a drug, Monty thought. And *fight* was a small word for the slaughter of one-third of that village's population. But whether it was a sickness or a drug was a subject he would address once the police in Walnut Grove had the test results back, because he was pretty sure Simon had been dosed with the same drug the night of the storm. It was the only thing that could explain the excessive aggression the Wolf had displayed when Meg was brought to the hospital.

"Officer Kowalski was in Run and Thump earlier, running on the treadmill and using some of the weight machines, but I think he went up to the apartments," Simon said.

As thanks for Monty and his team protecting Meg while she was in the hospital, the Others gave the team use of one of the efficiency apartments above the seamstress/tailor's shop. With the water tax being what it was, for someone like Karl Kowalski, taking a shower away from home a couple of times a week was a benefit that couldn't be ignored.

"He doesn't usually use our fitness center in the mornings." Simon gave Monty a questioning look, confirming that the Wolf knew the work schedule of Monty's team almost better than Monty did. It also confirmed that the Others didn't ignore anything that changed the routine of anyone who dealt with them.

"He took a couple of hours' personal time today," Monty said. Wolfgard didn't need to know that Captain Burke considered personal time spent in the Courtyard as on-duty time since dealing with the Others was dangerous even under the best circumstances.

"Dr. Lorenzo is sniffing around the medical office in the Market Square," Simon added.

"Then I'll say hello to the doctor before I pick up Officer Kowalski," Monty said.

Simon returned to the display, acting as if Monty were no longer there. But he said, "Go out the back door. It will be quicker."

Something else Wolfgard wouldn't have considered offering a few weeks ago, Monty thought as he went through the stockroom to HGR's back door. He had no illusions that the Others thought of humans as allies, let alone equals. Humans were still clever meat. But this was the first Courtyard to be so accessible to humans since . . . well, since humans crossed the Atlantik Ocean centuries ago and made their first bargains with the *terra indigene* on this continent.

He just hoped that accessibility remained after Simon figured out he'd been dosed with the drug known as gone over wolf.

Jenni Crowgard walked into the front part of Howling Good Reads wearing nothing but a winter coat that smelled like Heather and covered the Crow's bare legs to midthigh.

Simon studied her. Usually cheerful and curious, she seemed wary this morning.

"You've heard something," he said.

It wasn't a question. Every kind of *terra indigene* had its own strengths. While some called them gossips, few things sent information from one place to another faster than the Crowgard. Even now, the only thing faster than the Crows was the telephone humans had invented a few decades ago. And the computers, since Vlad said you could send the same message to a lot of people.

"Walnut Grove," he prompted, watching her.

Jenni wrapped her arms around herself. "Something bad. Not sure what. Don't know why."

She knew things about the what and the why—things he was sure the human news didn't know yet. Piece by piece, he got it out of her. Fresh food in the snow, a temptation at this time of year. Young crows and Crows flying in to grab a bite. Then dogs and death and many humans.

"Meg had a dream about Crows this morning," he said after Jenni told him what she knew. "It scared her a lot."

Jenni frowned. "Why would our Meg dream about Walnut Grove?"

"No reason for her to dream about the Courtyard there—unless it's a warning for us." He stared at Jenni until she squirmed. "You and your sisters and the rest of the Crowgard in Lakeside need to be careful. Walnut Grove is about one hundred fifty miles south of this city. If the sickness that touched humans and Others in the Midwest and in Jerzy on the West Coast has reached this part of Thaisia, we all need to be careful. It's easy enough to travel to Walnut Grove by train. It's easy enough for the sickness to travel back to Lakeside with someone."

"We'll be careful."

"If you see Meg rubbing her arms the way she does when visions start prickling under her skin, you tell me. And you pay attention to anything she says."

"I'll pay attention," Jenni promised. "Even if what our Meg says isn't about Crows."

Choosing to be satisfied with that, Simon sent her on her way and went back to arranging the display of new books. There had been a noticeable lack of customers since the storm, despite the unprecedented assistance the Others had given to some of the humans who had been stranded.

They'll come back or they won't, Simon thought as he read the back copy on a couple of books and set them aside for himself. *And today we don't want unfamiliar monkeys in the Courtyard anyway.*

Hearing the rattle of wheels, he turned and watched Heather push a cart up to the checkout counter. The Lakeside Courtyard supplied goods to all the *terra indigene* living in the surrounding wild country. What HGR had lacked in human customers lately was more than balanced by the number of book orders sent in from all the settlements.

"You going to work on the orders?" he asked. She'd said she was when she went into the back for stock, so he was just trying to be polite and make up for snarling at her earlier.

Heather didn't answer him. She just gave him A Look.

Grunting, Simon went back to arranging books. A bunny trying to intimidate a Wolf? How ludicrous!

As that thought took hold, he moved so he could watch her while he arranged books. Just how often these days did Heather remind him of a bunny? That comparison had always been there, an assessment of personality as well as how she responded to the Others. But he realized that he thought of her that way more often since the storm.

Something had changed in many of the humans who worked in the Courtyard. Some, like Lorne, who ran the Three Ps—the shop for paper, printing, and postage—went on as they had before. Other humans, like Merri Lee, were showing some Wolf in their personalities and, while still sensibly cautious, were more determined to work with the *terra indigene*. And others, like Heather, had become too aware that they would never be the predators.

He couldn't fire her for being a bunny. Well, he could, but he didn't want to. For one thing, he would lose a good worker. For another, it would be a hardship for her if she couldn't find another job right away, and that would make Meg and the human pack unhappy. He didn't want Meg to be unhappy.

Stifling a sigh, Simon forced his attention back to the display of books.

It didn't matter if he had human customers or not. As long as Meg and her pack were in the Courtyard, he still had plenty of human behavior to study and puzzle over.

Monty found Dominic Lorenzo walking through a first-floor office space in the Market Square.

"Dr. Lorenzo."

"Lieutenant Montgomery."

"So you're serious about opening an office in the Courtyard? I had the impression that you didn't think that well of the Others."

"I'm not sure I do," Lorenzo replied. "But there isn't another doctor anywhere on this continent who has the opportunity to interact this closely with the *terra indigene*. I've checked."

"And being able to interact with a blood prophet?" Monty asked softly.

Lorenzo looked him in the eyes. "That was a big part of the reason I proposed an office here and want to be the doctor in residence, so to speak."

"You're giving up your work at the hospital?"

"No. I talked to the hospital administrators after the Others lifted the water tax as thanks for caring for Meg Corbyn. That's a substantial savings."

Monty nodded. "They lifted the water tax on the Chestnut Street Police Station too."

"While there is plenty of concern about having the Others around sick or injured people, it can't be denied that having a hospital that is willing to provide care to any Courtyard resident could make a big difference for all of us in the future. As you pointed out to me during the storm. Right now I'm proposing to have office hours here a couple of mornings a week."

Winter had made Meg's recovery a condition of the storm ending, and Lorenzo, despite his reservations about the Others, had given the Human Liaison the very best care possible. In a real sense, the doctor's actions had saved everyone in the city.

"Basic medicine," Lorenzo said, sweeping a hand to indicate the office. "The Courtyard's Business Association is willing to purchase any additional equipment that's needed, although I don't think much will be required for the kind of medical care I have in mind. They are being stubborn about my having a nurse to assist or an office manager to help with paperwork." He gave Monty a speculative look. "Anything you could do about that?"

Monty shook his head, then thought about it. "They have some kind of healers here already, don't they? Maybe one of them could assist you and learn a bit about human medicine in the bargain. And isn't there a massage therapist using part of this office space?" He'd seen the Good Hands Massage sign next to the door.

"Yes, she uses one of the rooms for her work. I don't think she has many clients here, so her hours are limited."

"You could inquire how she handles appointments. Maybe the Business Association would agree to hiring one administrative assistant for the two of you, someone to make appointments and handle the paperwork."

"It's a possibility," Lorenzo said. "I'll add that to my notes. I'm making a formal presentation to the Business Association and the consul tomorrow."

Monty finally broached the main reason he'd wanted to see Lorenzo. "You've dealt with *cassandra sangue* before. As soon as you saw Ms. Corbyn's scars, you knew what she was."

"I've seen girls like her before." Lorenzo gave Monty a long look. "Meg Corbyn is healthier and saner than the girls I treated when I was a resident. Wherever she was before she came here, they knew how to take care of girls like her."

"From what I was told, that care included forced lessons, forced cutting, and no chance or choice to experience life. The girls were kept safe, yes, but they were used for someone else's profit."

"I was told pretty much the same thing when the Wolf allowed me to ask Ms. Corbyn a few questions while she was in the hospital," Lorenzo replied. "But even the girls I saw before were in a controlled environment, a privately run house that was an annex to a school. I'm not sure *cassandra sangue* can survive without someone else controlling their lives. Even with supervision, too many of them cut themselves into death or madness." He paused. "There is a group of humans out there who are a danger to themselves, and I want to help. With the kind of care these girls need, *someone* has to know how to handle them and their addiction to cutting. But there is too little information available."

"The lack of information would help discourage people from establishing group homes and trying to cope with the girls," Monty said. "I imagine several good-intentioned facilities have closed down over the years because of deaths caused from cutting." That was something he could check when he returned to the station.

Lorenzo nodded. "Having a chance to interact with Meg Corbyn could be the first step in finding a way for all of these girls to have longer and healthier lives."

After wishing Lorenzo good luck with the meeting tomorrow, Monty took his leave, pulled out his mobile phone, and called Kowalski. After confirming that the younger man would meet him, he headed for the coffee shop.

Using the back entrance, he walked in and greeted Tess, the *terra indigene* who ran A Little Bite. As he watched her arranging plates of cookies and pastries in the glass display case, he wondered if anyone would come in to buy them.

"What happens to the food that's left at the end of the day?" he asked.

"Usually what can't be kept for the next day is passed along," Tess replied. "Meat-n-Greens gets some of it to include in the evening meals served there. The rest is divided among the gards and taken back to the complexes for anyone who wants the food."

Footsteps coming from the back of the store.

Tess lowered her voice. "And on a residents-only day like today, *terra indigene* who have been curious about what it's like to be in a coffee shop will venture in for the experience."

How many of the Others living in the Courtyard wouldn't come to the coffee shop because it was open to humans? Did they resent the human employees who worked in the Market Square and were allowed to shop there? Or was it a case of numbers? A handful of humans posed no danger and therefore could be tolerated, but a shop filled with humans was a place to avoid?

Did the *terra indigene* who lived and worked in the Courtyards feel the pressure of being surrounded by an enemy day after day? Or did they find relief in knowing at least some of their kind would always survive a conflict simply because they were so devastatingly lethal?

And what did that say about Simon Wolfgard's unprecedented decision to allow even a few humans beyond the Human Liaison to interact with the Others living in the Courtyard?

He saw them enter the main part of the coffee shop—six males and two females. Based on general rules of coloring, three males had the amber eyes of the Wolves, one male and one female had the black hair and eyes of the Crows, and he couldn't tell whether the rest were Hawks or Owls or a kind of earth native he hadn't seen before.

"I won't disturb your guests," Monty said quietly. "I'll wait for Officer Kowalski outside."

"Stay," Tess said. It was more command than request.

Monty hesitated a moment, then, with a nod to the group still huddled near the back hallway, he took a seat at a table close to the archway leading into Howling Good Reads.

Tess pointed at the other tables. "Sit."

Wary, always watching him, they split up and sat at tables that were the farthest they could get from him. And all of them chose chairs that kept him in sight.

Kowalski opened the front door and came in. He gave the Others a startled glance, confirming Monty's suspicion that these *terra indigene* weren't usually seen by the humans who were allowed in the Courtyard. Giving them all a nod, Kowalski joined his lieutenant.

Tess brought a tray to their table. She set out two mugs of coffee, along with a small bowl of sugar and a little pitcher of cream. She also gave them silverware and napkins. Then she handed them both a sheet of heavy paper that had a printed menu.

No doubt intending to make a comment about being given a menu, Kowalski opened his mouth, took one look at Tess's hair, which suddenly had green streaks and started curling, and said nothing.

"Our sandwiches today are sliced beef or chicken. I also have a quiche with a side of fresh fruit," Tess said. "Those are in addition to our usual menu."

We're a demonstration, Monty realized. *A live training film showing what to do in a particular situation. That's why Tess wanted us to stay.* "I'll have the quiche and fresh fruit."

When Tess looked at Kowalski, Karl said, "I'd like the beef sandwich."

"Would you like a side of fresh fruit with that?" Tess asked.

"Yes, please."

Merri Lee came out of the back and slipped behind the counter. The human woman looked a little bruised around the eyes. Could be nothing more than lack of sleep. Like Heather Houghton, Merri Lee was a student at Lakeside University, and Monty remembered the late nights of studying for a test or writing a paper that was due the next day.

So it could be nothing more than lack of sleep. Or it could be something else. Since Karl was making an effort not to notice, he would find out later if his officer had heard something.

Tess took the orders from the *terra indigene*, then helped Merri Lee get everyone served.

They watched him, those Wolves and Crows and the rest. They watched how he spread a napkin on his lap, then, after a moment's hesitation, did the same thing. They watched what utensil he used and what, like Karl's sandwich, could be eaten with hands. They watched Merri Lee walking around the tables, refilling coffee mugs and water glasses.

They watched, and as he listened to Karl chatting about the workout equipment at Run & Thump and the new book his fiancée, Ruth, was waiting for, Monty slowly realized these *terra indigene* weren't from the Courtyard. At least, not *this* Courtyard. Maybe they'd made some of the deliveries of meat and produce and had decided to stop in the coffee shop before heading home. Maybe they were here for a meeting with Simon Wolfgard. Maybe they had come in from a settlement in the wild country that had little or no contact with humans.

Whoever they were and wherever they came from, it wasn't just the coffee shop that was a new experience for them. Just being around a human was something they'd never done before. At least, it wasn't something they'd done when they weren't intending to kill and eat the human. Now here they were, drinking coffee and consuming pastries and sandwiches while responding to Merri Lee's friendly comments with stiff, precise words, like travelers who used a foreign-language phrase book to communicate.

Would they go to Howling Good Reads next and purchase books to learn how to use human money?

For the first time since he started coming into A Little Bite, Tess gave them a bill. Feeling more and more like an actor in a play, Monty pulled out his wallet, refusing Kowalski's offer to pay for half. Tess brought back the change, and he and Karl discussed the correct percentage for a tip. They didn't raise their voices. In fact, he spoke more softly than usual. But he knew every one of the *terra indigene* heard what they said and filed it away.

It was a relief to leave and get into the patrol car. Kowalski started the car but didn't put it in gear.

"That was weird," Kowalski said. "I remember my dad taking a bunch of us kids to an ice-cream parlor and doing much the same thing, talking about tips and reminding us of the correct behavior we'd discussed on the way to the shop. Only, none of the kids he was teaching could have bitten his arms off if they didn't like what he said."

"Have you ever wondered how the Others choose the teachers who show them how to be human?" Monty asked.

Karl gave him a wary look. "They're never human, Lieutenant. They just mimic us to get what they want."

Monty nodded. "Yes. They mimic. And you're right. They will never be human. But it occurred to me that who the Others choose as a template determines if they mimic the best or the worst of what it means to be human."

Karl sighed. "I guess that makes us templates."

"Yes, it does," Monty agreed. "And that makes me hopeful for all of us."

As they pulled out of the parking lot and drove toward the Chestnut Street station, Monty wondered if the visitors at the Courtyard were somehow connected to the deaths in Walnut Grove.

Meg gathered the rags, dustpan and broom, and spray bottle of cleaner she needed to tidy up the Liaison's Office. The novelty of cleaning had worn off after the first couple of times she'd done it on her own, but she liked the end result. Besides, a clean office equaled a mouse-free office.

The Liaison's Office was a rectangular building divided into three big rooms. The back room had the bathroom as well as a storage room with bins full of clothes that the Others used when they shifted from fur or feathers to human. It also had a kitchen area and a small round table and two chairs. The middle room was the sorting room. It held the large rectangular table where she sorted the mail and packages that came for the businesses and residents of the Lakeside Courtyard. The front room had a three-sided counter where she talked to deliverymen and accepted packages. It also had two handcarts parked by the delivery door that opened between the front room and the sorting room. And it held Nathan Wolfgard, sprawled on the large dog bed—now called a Wolf bed—that she'd purchased as a friendly gesture toward the Wolf who had been assigned to guard her during working hours.

Meg opened the door marked PRIVATE, which gave her easy access to the front counter when she was working in the sorting room. Setting the broom and dustpan beside the door, she said brightly, "Since I'm not expecting any deliveries this morning, it's a good time to tidy up. Maybe you'd like to take the Wolf bed outside and give it a good shake."

Nathan raised his head just enough to give her a Wolfish stare. Then he yawned and flopped back down on the bed.

He'd do it eventually. And if she didn't nag him about it, he might pull on some pants before he stood in the delivery area and shook out the bed in plain view of anyone walking or driving by. She didn't think anyone actually saw much from the front—at least, Lieutenant Montgomery hadn't called to ask about a naked man—but since the front of the office had two large windows and a glass door, she'd once seen plenty of the back of Nathan's human form.

Based on the training images that had been her reference for the world outside the compound, Nathan had a very nice human form.

And even though she'd had only a quick look before he dove under the covers, Simon felt like he had a very nice human form.

Clean, Meg told herself. *Let the hands work while the mind ponders. That's what Merri Lee said.*

She sprayed the front counter and wiped it down.

Maybe she shouldn't have said anything about Simon being in human form this morning. Well, she hadn't *said* anything. More like babbled for a minute when she dashed into A Little Bite for her morning coffee and a muffin. She wasn't even sure she'd been coherent, but Merri Lee had gotten the gist of it. Hence the suggestion to do some chores while thoughts and feelings sorted themselves out.

She hoped her feelings sorted themselves out. And she hoped when they did, she would still have Simon for a friend even if she decided she didn't want a lover.

And she *didn't* want any kind of a lover right now. Did she?

She rubbed the side of her nose and sucked in a breath at the unexpected pain. Rushing into the bathroom, she studied her face . . . and the split in the skin on the outside of her left nostril.

An hour later, Meg leaned against the sorting room table and flipped through a magazine. When she realized she kept rubbing her arms, she closed the magazine.

Too many images. Too many new things to think about and sort out today. And she was scared that this damage to her skin was a sign of something being terribly wrong. After all, she didn't have any real assurance that *cassandra sangue* could survive outside compounds like the one where she'd been kept for most of her life. Maybe girls like her *couldn't* survive for long.

Don't think about that, she scolded herself, glancing toward the Private door.

Nathan had been suspiciously quiet ever since she dabbed some antiseptic ointment on the split skin and returned to the sorting room. If he'd caught a whiff of the medicine, wouldn't he have howled about it? Wouldn't he have barged into the sorting room to give her a sniff and find out what was wrong? Or had he chosen to be subtle for this hunt?

Many kinds of prey had perfected the art of hiding sickness or injury to avoid being singled out when predators were hunting. *Terra indigene* Wolves had perfected the art of recognizing what prey tried to hide. So Meg wasn't really surprised when Henry Beargard appeared in the doorway between the back room and the sorting room.

Apparently Nathan had decided to tell Henry about the medicine smell rather than howl about it himself.

"How are you, Meg?" Henry asked in his rumbly voice.

"I'm fine," she lied. Wolves could smell fear. So could a Grizzly.

As he crossed the room to stand near the sorting table, he ran a big hand through shoulder-length, shaggy brown hair. The brown eyes that studied her were a reminder that Henry was, among other things, the Courtyard's spirit guide.

He sniffed the air, but he didn't comment about the scent of medicine. Instead, he said, "I heard you kicked Simon out of bed."

She sighed. Since she'd sort of told Merri Lee, she couldn't fault Simon for saying something. But what had felt like a natural friendship a couple of days ago now seemed so complicated. "I had a bad dream. Simon told you about the dream?" She waited for Henry's nod. "I was kicking at something in the dream but Simon got in the way and fell off the bed. But I didn't *deliberately* kick him out of bed. Off the bed. Whatever." She paused. "He's mad about it?"

"He's limping, and everyone asks him why. It's embarrassing for him because it's amusing to the rest of us."

"Well, he shouldn't poke me with his nose when I'm having a bad dream!"

Henry's booming laugh rang out. "I think he's learned that lesson."

At least Simon isn't going around calling me Meg Moosekicker, she thought. *Not yet anyway.*

"Now," Henry said. "Why do you smell of medicine?"

She turned her head and pointed at her nose. "My skin split. I don't know why. I didn't . . . cut it."

"Is that why you had the dream?"

"I don't know. Maybe. It's all different outside the compound. There are so many images, but I can't catalog them and then they get jumbled and don't have labels and sometimes I'll be working and then I'm not working—five or ten minutes will go by while I'm just standing here not seeing anything."

She hadn't meant to say that, hadn't intended to tell anyone about the way her mind sometimes went blank. The Others—Simon especially—wouldn't let her drive a BOW or do things on her own if they knew about the blackouts. And now she'd gone and told Henry, who just stood there looking at her as if she was some strange and curious thing.

"Does Simon know about this?" Henry finally asked.

She shook her head. "Do we have to talk about this now?"

A long look. "There is much to think about, so we can put this aside. For now."

"Thanks." The discussion was postponed, but it wouldn't be forgotten. "Did you just come here to ask about Simon?" She knew Henry had used Simon getting kicked as the excuse to come by and find out why she smelled of medicine.

"The human bodywalker was here, looking at the office in the Market Square," Henry said. "Maybe we should call him back, have him look at your skin."

"Doctor," she said quietly. "He's called a doctor." She shuddered, unable to hold back the fear held in the memories of her old life. "I don't need to see him for this."

"It bothers you to have him here." Henry's voice sounded like thunder that warns of an oncoming storm.

Careful, she thought. "No. Dr. Lorenzo doesn't bother me. He seems like a nice man, and he took good care of me when I was in the hospital."

Henry waited. Meg suspected that he could, and would, wait for hours.

"You're letting in another human because of me. That's why Simon is considering letting Dr. Lorenzo have an office here, isn't it? To take care of me? But he would have access to the Market Square, could observe all of you."

Henry smiled. "As much as humans think they learn about us, we always learn more, Meg."

"Would he treat the other employees?"

"We can discuss that." A silence. Then, "Why don't you want him here?"

"The coat," she blurted out as she tried to scratch her skin through layers of clothing. "The white coat. The Walking Names—the people who took care of the girls at the compound—wore that kind of white coat or white uniforms."

"Then he will not wear a symbol of fear and pain when he is in the Courtyard. Meg!"

Hearing her name roared by a Grizzly startled her enough to stumble away from the table—and that had Nathan leaping up on the counter in the front room, ready to lunge through the Private doorway if she needed him.

"He will not wear the symbol of your enemy," Henry said.

"*Arroooo!*"

Agreement from Nathan. It didn't matter if he'd been paying attention to their conversation or not. No Wolf was going to argue with a Grizzly—especially when he'd called that Grizzly to help with a human.

"It's all right." Something relaxed inside her. Or maybe she was more focused now on saying the right thing so Nathan would get off the counter before he slipped and hurt himself. She looked at Henry, then at the Wolf. "I'm all right."

Crisis resolved, Nathan leaped off the counter and returned to his bed. Henry left after assuring her that white coats would be forbidden.

Meg stood in the sorting room trying to block the memories of her life in the compound and convince herself that she would never have to go back there. During her midday break, she would go to HGR and find one of the horror books written by a *terra indigene*. Those stories scared her enough that she slept with the light on, but she also found it comforting to know how terrifying Wolves could be when they savaged a human they saw as an enemy.

Henry walked over to A Little Bite, grabbed Merri Lee, and hauled her into the back of the shop despite Tess's furious protest.

It took a minute for both females to calm down enough to listen to him, but once they did and Merri Lee understood what he was asking, he felt better and worse. This thing with the skin wasn't about Meg being a blood prophet; it was about Meg being human. But the Others hadn't tried to care for a human before, and even humans found caring for someone like Meg challenging.

How could the *terra indigene* have known that humans had so little instinct left for taking care of themselves?

Although, to be fair, Meg had never been given the chance to care for herself.

Chapped lips. Chapped skin that could split because of cold weather, dry air, and dehydration. Rough cuticles that could split and bleed. Winter was hard on human skin, but there were face and hand creams and body lotions that would help. The brand the Others required their employees to use was available in a few human stores but very expensive, and the lotions and creams weren't sold in the Market Square shops, where they would be more affordable.

Given a choice, Henry would have hugged a porcupine rather than listen to such enthusiasm about lotions and hand creams. Since he hadn't been given a choice, and he *had* asked, he endured Merri Lee's explanations until Tess stopped the girl.

"I'll order enough of the products for all of you if you girls promise to explain to Meg about caring for her skin," Tess said.

"Sure. We can talk after the Quiet Mind class tonight," Merri Lee replied. "Ruthie and Heather will be there too."

"There is another thing," Henry said, looking at Tess. "Our Meg admitted that sometimes she is overwhelmed by images, that her mind goes blank. It frightens her."

"Information overload," Merri Lee said instantly. "When there is too much stimulus, the brain needs a rest. Happens to everyone."

<Doesn't happen to us,> Tess said.

<We are smarter than humans in many ways,> Henry replied. Then he said to Merri Lee, "That is something else to mention to Meg. It is unknown to her, and the experience has been frightening."

After receiving Merri Lee's agreement to tell Meg that overload was a common occurrence among humans, Henry escaped from the coffee shop and headed for the quiet of his studio. As he walked up the path to the studio door, he glanced over the shoulder-high brick wall that separated his yard from the delivery area in front of the Liaison's Office. Then he stopped. The chatter about lotions and creams had been a bewildering distraction, but now he thought about all the other things he had learned that day.

There were no trucks making deliveries at the moment. That wasn't so unusual. There were no Crows on the wall, and that *was* unusual. There had been Crows around the office since Meg started working for the Others. Watchers who announced the arrival of regular deliverymen and warned of the presence of strangers. He didn't always pay attention to them since they tended to chatter as much as human females, but now he felt their absence.

Too restless to work on the wood sculptures and totems, he made a cup of tea and then called Vladimir Sanguinati, the comanager of Howling Good Reads. "Vlad? No, Meg is fine. But when Simon is feeling a little calmer, tell him that she was greatly disturbed when she spoke of doctors and white coats. It's something we should all keep in mind."

And later this evening, he would talk to Simon and Vlad about skin that could split enough to reveal prophecy and yet didn't bleed.

CHAPTER 4

The Controller walked through the corridors of the compound, nodding to his staff as he made his way to one of the prophecy rooms. Dressed in a tailored three-piece suit, crisp shirt, and subtly patterned tie, he looked like a CEO of one of the top businesses on the continent.

In a sense, he was. His great-grandfather had started the family business as an institution for the preservation of an odd branch of humans who could foresee the future when they were injured. The girls could, anyway. The boys carried the seeds of that ability but not the ability itself. So little by little, the institution became a haven for the girls who would otherwise be shunned at best or, at worst, stoned or burned because of fear of what they knew and would say.

Great-grandfather had been praised as a humanitarian by some and condemned as a profiteer by others. But caring for the girls cost money, so what was wrong with using the knowledge that was gained when they deliberately hurt themselves in order to experience euphoria? Especially when that foreknowledge didn't harm anyone else?

Of course, businesses had sometimes soared or crashed depending on whether or not Great-grandfather bought into or sold his shares in a particular company. And yet, overall, little changed in the pieces of the world humans had some control over. Yes, there were inventions, innovations, new skills and technologies. But no matter how fancy it all looked or how large the city, humans were still closing the equivalent of stockade doors at night and shivering in fear of what watched them from the woods and fields.

Great-grandfather had been a humanitarian. Grandfather had been a businessman more interested in profit, and he discovered that a few other families who were saddled with these dependents were also looking to shake off their humanitarian roots and acquire some serious wealth—the kind of wealth that could have an impact on the world.

Laws supporting "benevolent ownership" were passed in the regions where these prophet barons resided. People were hired to teach the girls, look after the girls, even breed the girls and sort the offspring. Benevolence turned into a very profitable business, and the compounds changed into an open secret among wealthy, discreet clients as cutting the girls' skin became a regular, controlled procedure.

But you couldn't breed out all the undesirable tendencies without losing some of the abilities, and it was unfortunately true that intelligence and a tendency toward defiance were linked with the sensitivity to produce the very best prophecies, and none of the efforts of the breeding program had been able to change that. And sometimes fresh blood was needed to revitalize the stock, which was why young girls were occasionally acquired from parents who were frightened by the girls' unnerving addiction to cutting themselves. Sometimes parents gave up a girl willingly, sometimes not. But even if they hadn't been willing, they seldom reported an abduction. After all, if the local government discovered why a girl had been taken, the whole family could be placed under benevolent ownership—for their own good, of course, because that tendency to cut did run in families.

He had expenses and overhead just like any other business. But he no longer had to put down the girls who were difficult to handle and didn't have enough viable skin left to be worth their upkeep. Those girls were now the source of a different kind of product.

Don't always sell the best and use the scrap girls for yourself, his grandfather had said. *Your future is just as important as your clients.*

Sound business advice. Even sound personal advice. That was why twice a month he selected two girls to provide prophecies about his own interests. A year ago, he began hearing the letters *HFL* in those prophecies. Only in the past few months had those letters made sense as talk about the Humans First and

Last movement became included in the background discussions he sometimes had with his more influential clients.

For a man who owned prophets, it wasn't a fluke that becoming aware of the movement coincided with the discovery that there was more swimming in the blood of the *cassandra sangue* than prophecies.

The Controller opened the door to a prophecy room and took his seat as the staff strapped the first girl into the chair.

Opening a notebook, he removed a pen from his inside jacket pocket and said, "My new business venture. What is the next step?"

He repeated the words over and over while the Cutter selected a spot on the left thigh and used the girl's personal razor to slice the fresh skin exactly one-quarter inch from the scar made by a previous cut.

Her face twisted with the terrible pain that came before the first words of prophecy were spoken. Then the girl began to speak, and pain changed to the addictive euphoria that appeared similar to sexual arousal and orgasm.

"Man looking in a mirror. Little bits of paper on his face, spotted red. Fluffy cat clawing a chair cushion. Letters H, F, L." She moaned, her pelvis tipping up in invitation despite the straps holding her to the chair.

So little for a thigh cut, he thought angrily. "Take her back to her cell and prepare the second girl. I'll return in a few minutes."

He went to his office and turned on his computer. While he waited, he made a list of words that were associated with those images. "Cut, scrape, nick" for the first image. "Claw" and "scratch" for the second. Once he got online, he used a search program and played with combinations of the words. Nothing and nothing. Then he typed in "nick," "scratch," and "HFL."

And there it was. Nicholas Scratch. Recently arrived from the Cel-Romano Alliance of Nations. Currently staying in the city of Toland to give several talks about the Humans First and Last movement.

The Controller smiled. Nicholas Scratch wouldn't be easy to reach, but he would reach the man. No matter what face they put on the movement publicly, Humans First and Last was the spearhead for the fight to wrest the world away from the *terra indigene*'s control, and he was the only person who could supply them with ingenious weapons that could make that possible.

For the trial runs, feel-good and gone over wolf were dirty street drugs. But he wouldn't be selling the HFL movement *drugs* for their armies. No, he would provide them with pharmaceutical enhancements that would, on the one hand, soften the enemy and, on the other hand, create a berserk army that wouldn't hesitate to face the *terra indigene* for the glory of the human race.

Yes, contacting Nicholas Scratch was the next step for his new business.

Pleased, the Controller returned to the room for the second prophecy. While technically also a business question, it felt personal because *cs759*, the bitch who called herself Meg Corbyn, was still free. And even though every cut brought them one step closer to dying, blood prophets in the wild could be powerful enemies. That she was speaking prophecies for the Others made her, and them, too dangerous. Especially now. So he needed to reacquire her—or kill her—before she saw a prophecy that exposed his new business and his intended association with the HFL movement.

"Tell me about the Wolf at Lakeside," he said. "What happens to the leader of the Lakeside Courtyard?"

The blood flowed, and the prophecy flowed with it. But this time, instead of speaking, the girl struggled to free herself from the straps and the chair.

"What happens to the Wolf?" the Controller said in a commanding voice. "Tell me about the Wolf!"

The girl looked at him and never stopped screaming.

"That's enough from this one. Patch her up."

"Why are we collecting the nose blood? It's got snot in it."

Sharp, hard laugh. "Who cares? The ones who are going to buy it and swallow a slug of it won't know that. He wants everything from this one. She's the most potent producer we've got. Guess being crazy makes the product even better."

She listened to them talk about her, but the words didn't matter any more than the few pumps it took for them to ejaculate inside her. Sometimes they slapped her, taunted her, pushed her into anger. Other times, they used fists to draw blood from the injuries as well as the cuts. They were cutting her too close to previous scars or cutting across old scars. Either way, whatever she screamed had no meaning to anyone.

Except her.

She didn't fight them when they sealed up the cuts and dealt with the bleeding nose. She was passive now, drained of strength and prophecy.

"See you soon, *cs747*," one of the Walking Names said, giving her an evil leer. "You're still worth a bit of cash, so don't die on us."

I'm not the one who's going to die, she thought as she heard the door of her cell close, heard the key turn in the lock. *I've seen . . . so many things. A white coat who is more than a Walking Name, a man with salt-and-pepper hair. A dark-skinned man riding in a police car. And the Wolf. I've seen Meg's Wolf.*

So many things were going to happen because of Meg and her Wolf.

"I'm not *cs747*," she whispered defiantly as she shifted on her cot in order to lean back against the wall. "My name is Jean."

ate Firesday morning, Vlad looked up from the stack of invoices on the desk, saw Heather and Merri Lee standing in the office doorway, and silently cursed Simon for taking the morning off to sulk or brood or whatever damn thing the Wolf was doing that had left *him* stuck with the bookstore's paperwork and whatever problem these females were about to dump on him. Because it was clear by the look in Merri Lee's eyes and the way she grabbed Heather's wrist and pulled the other girl into the office and up to the desk that at least one of them had something on her mind.

They were good employees. Therefore, they were not edible.

And if they had been considered edible, he suspected even a hungry vampire would find their blood a little too sour this morning.

"What?" he said, trying not to sound wary. Two months ago, there had been no need to be wary. They were humans. If they became troublesome, they were replaceable. Then Merri Lee, Heather, and a few others had befriended Meg Corbyn and morphed into the Courtyard's human pack, and the Business Association was still trying to figure out exactly how that had happened and what it meant and how to explain it to the rest of the *terra indigene* living in the Courtyard, not to mention the rest of the *terra indigene* period.

The Lakeside Courtyard was starting to get visitors coming in for the sole purpose of seeing this strange, inedible human pack. He didn't want to be in the office on the day one of the girls realized the visiting *terra indigene* thought of them as a kind of tourist attraction—not as impressive as Talulah Falls, but more mysterious.

"What?" he said again when they continued to stare at him.

"Nathan needs to leave the Liaison's Office during Meg's midday break," Merri Lee said.

"He usually does leave during the break," Vlad replied.

"But not if Meg stays in. And we're going to have lunch with Meg. In the office."

"So why does he need to leave?"

"It's an intervention," Merri Lee said at the same time Heather mumbled, "It's just girl talk."

"About . . . ?" he prompted when they didn't say anything else.

"Sex," Merri Lee said.

"Maybe sex," Heather said, taking a step away from the desk and giving him what Simon called her bunny look. "I heard Mr. Wolfgard say it wasn't about sex."

"But Meg thinks it is," Merri Lee argued. "Or it might be. Whatever it is, Meg and Simon are acting weird around each other, and they need to sort it out before other people get really upset."

That one isn't a bunny, Vlad thought as he studied the fire in Merri Lee's eyes. *She's got some Wolf in her attitude. Maybe even a touch of Bear.* "If they need to sort it out, why is Meg talking to you? And who are these other people?" And why hadn't he heard about this until now?

"To figure out what she should say!" Merri Lee sounded exasperated by his inability to grasp a simple concept. "As for the other people, someone named Air came into the coffee shop this morning with one of the ponies and told Tess that Spring thought Meg seemed unhappy, and all the girls at the lake want to know why. I got the impression that Tess was concerned about them being interested, and about Air bringing a pony into A Little Bite, so it's time for us girls"—she wagged a finger between herself and Heather—"to help Meg figure this out."

"Which pony?" Vlad asked.

"I don't know. A brown one."

Could have been Earthshaker, Tornado, or Twister. Winter had visited the bookstore's office once, so Vlad appreciated why Tess had been *concerned* about one of the girls paying a visit to the coffee shop for reasons that didn't involve coffee.

He wanted to talk to Nyx, wanted the simplicity of dealing with a female who was a lethal predator and one of his own kind, because these two inedible fluffballs were making him nervous—especially the one who looked about to explode.

Everyone who lived in the Green Complex knew that Meg hadn't spent any time last evening with her Wolf neighbor, which was unusual, and had driven to work by herself today. Also unusual. Even Jester Coyotegard said he didn't want to poke his nose into that emotional porcupine, so the rest of the residents had decided to follow his example, and Vlad would have happily continued to do just that.

On the other hand, it had come to the attention of Grandfather Erebus that the Liaison wasn't exactly speaking to the Wolfgard, and if Grandfather became unhappy because Meg was unhappy, living in the Courtyard could become uncomfortable. If the Elementals were also paying attention now, an uncomfortable situation could change into a dangerous one for all of them.

So maybe the fluffballs had the right idea and could help fix . . . whatever this was.

"Since he guards Meg and not the building, I can get Nathan out of the office but not away from the office," Vlad said. "Why can't he stay in the front room if you're going to be in the back?"

"Because Wolves have excellent hearing," Merri Lee said.

So do the Sanguinati, he thought as he sent out a call. <Nyx? I need to see you at the bookstore.> The Sanguinati's other form was smoke, and smoke could slip into a room through the crack under a door or through a keyhole. Smoke could hide in the shadows of a room. Smoke could listen without anyone realizing someone was there.

"All right," he said. "Nathan will stay outside." He would clear that order with Blair Wolfgard, the Courtyard's main enforcer. And if Blair wouldn't help, he'd call Henry.

He just hoped neither of them asked what a girl-talk intervention involved.

"Go away," he said. "I have work to do."

They hustled out the door in a way that made him think he'd agreed to a lot more than he'd intended.

———————

Heather brought pizza for lunch. Merri Lee brought chocolate and a book called *The Dimwit's Guide to Dating*.

"Thank you." Meg stared at the book for a moment before setting it aside where it wouldn't end up smeared with pizza sauce. "Did you get this at HGR?"

Merri Lee snorted out a laugh. "Gods, no. Yesterday I went to a bookstore near Lakeside University to get that for you. Not that I think you're a dimwit; that's just the name of a whole series of books about various subjects. But I figured this is totally new ground for you, so even basic information might be useful."

"Even if we stocked that book in HGR, which we don't, none of us could have bought it without Mr. Wolfgard being told," Heather said.

Meg's arms began to prickle. She felt like she was hearing one conversation while another one was going on underneath, and it was the one she couldn't hear that held some kind of danger.

"Tess said the order of creams and lotions should come in tomorrow," Merri Lee said as Heather dished out slices of pizza. "And the first supply is free for all of us to try."

"Free?" Heather said. "When I bought the face cream as a gift last year, it cost me half a week's pay! We're getting it *free*?"

"First supply," Merri Lee said. "As a trial run."

Meg's skin buzzed at the words "trial run." Then the feeling faded.

"Why is it so expensive?" she asked.

"Supply and demand," Merri Lee replied. "The *terra indigene* make this line of products mostly for themselves and sell some of it to human stores. Limited supply means it's expensive. There are plenty of the same kind of products being sold, but most have scents added—something most humans don't mind and the Others do."

Meg suddenly remembered a training video of a person being asked a question about one subject and then talking and talking about something else entirely. Like Merri Lee talking about the creams and body lotions, which wasn't why she and Heather were here having lunch.

"You're stalling," Meg said, remembering how the video identified this behavior.

"I guess," Merri Lee admitted. She waited until Heather dished out a second piece for each of them. "So what happened between you and Simon?"

"I don't know what happened," Meg replied. "I don't even know if something *did* happen."

Merri Lee smiled. "Then let's try to figure it out."

They talked for more than an hour while they devoured pizza before switching to chocolate.

"The *terra indigene* shift without thinking about it," Merri Lee said. "At least that's the impression I've had—shifting from one form to the other is no more significant to them than us changing from work clothes to casual, comfy clothes. So maybe it didn't even register with Simon that he had shifted except that he felt cold. You did say he's been sleeping with you since you got home from the hospital."

"Yes, but as a wolf-shaped Wolf," Meg said. "A furry Wolf is warm and cuddly. A people-shaped Wolf is . . . a man." The memories of what happened after a cut were vague, but her *body* had reacted as if there was a reason to be afraid.

"And men like sex," Merri Lee said, giving Meg a measuring look. "Whether or not *you* want sex has to be your choice, same as it is for the rest of us girls."

Choice. Yes. She felt something inside her relax.

"It's kind of romantic," Heather said. "Simon staying with Meg and watching over her. It's like one of the stories where a Wolf or a vampire falls in love with a human girl."

"Those stories are fiction and wishful thinking," Merri Lee said.

"Plenty of *terra indigene* have tried sex with humans," Heather insisted. "Or at least necking. If they weren't interested in having a physical relationship with us, why would Ms. Know-It-All's column in the Courtyard newsletter always have advice about dating and personal interaction between Others and humans?"

"Just because a human guy wants sex doesn't mean he wants a full, committed relationship with every girl who says 'yes,'" Merri Lee countered. "And who knows what the Others really think about it? Does it feel good to them when they're in human form in a way that's commensurate with our experience, or do they view it as an experiment—the equivalent of one of us tonguing the family pet to see what it's like?"

"That's gross!" Heather said.

"And possibly nowhere near the truth," Merri Lee said, giving Meg another measuring look. "I guess our girl-talk intervention didn't help much."

"Not much," Meg admitted. "But Simon getting into bed as a human changed things. I'm not sure why that's true, but it is. I just don't know what to do about it."

Simon sat on a bench in Henry's studio watching the Grizzly touch the totems and other pieces of sculpture that were in various stages of completion. Yes, the Beargard touched the wood, but he didn't pick up any tools—a sign that Henry was too troubled to work.

"The best Nyx could figure out from what she heard is that Meg is worried that I want sex because a human male would have expected it," Simon said.

"Do you?" Henry asked as he turned off the electric teakettle, dropped tea bags into two mugs, and poured boiling water over them. "Did you want sex that morning?"

"No! The room was chilly. I just wanted to get under the covers. I thought me being in human form but still having fur would be upsetting to Meg. I was *trying* to be considerate despite getting kicked off the bed, which wasn't my fault!" Technically, he'd fallen off the bed while dodging that second kick, but no one else had to know that. "And why would Meg think I was looking for sex? She didn't smell lusty the way human females do when they want sex." In fact, she'd smelled nervous, even scared. But he'd thought that was because of the dream. It hadn't occurred to him that it might be a reaction to *him*. He sighed. "I'm confused."

"Where Meg is concerned, you've been confused since you met her." Henry handed one mug to Simon and sat beside him. "And now, my friend, you're a Wolf who has bounded into a pretty meadow and discovered it's full of snakes and steel traps."

He didn't think that was a flattering description of Meg, but he swallowed the impulse to defend her.

"She's not *terra indigene*, Simon," Henry said gently. "She's not one of us. She's human."

"She's not one of us, but she's not one of *them* either," he snapped. "She's Meg."

Henry nodded. "Something new to us and not understood. She came here alone and frightened, with little experience of the world. You gave her a job, gave her a place to live. Became her friend."

"Nothing wrong with being a friend."

"Nothing wrong with having a friend. You just forgot she isn't a Wolf."

Simon sipped his tea and didn't comment. He hadn't forgotten, exactly, but as the days went by it had seemed less and less important. Until Meg got weird about him being in bed with her when he was wearing his human skin.

"You're isolated from your own kind," Henry said.

"Not living in the Wolfgard Complex is my choice."

"It's a good choice for the Courtyard to have the leader living in the multi-species complex, but that doesn't mean it's a good choice for you. Wolves are not happy being solitary for too long."

"I run with some of the pack several times a week, and I have Sam living with me." Or had until he became uneasy about having Meg and Sam together on their own. A simple accident could do so much harm to both woman and pup, but that wasn't something he could explain to them or anyone else. Not yet.

"Now you have Sam," Henry said, nodding. "You used his curiosity about Meg to thaw the fear that had kept him frozen in Wolf form and unable to communicate with any of us. You used Meg."

Simon flinched away from that particular truth. Meg had been used for someone else's benefit all her life. He never wanted to be like those humans and sometimes feared he would need to be. "It helped her too."

"Yes, it did. But if you had done all the things with a female Wolf that you have done with Meg, it would be considered a courtship. You would be presenting yourself as a potential mate."

"I wasn't . . . She didn't . . ." He hadn't been thinking of her like that. But had she been thinking of him that way?

"She isn't one of us, so you didn't consider that the play and grooming and sleeping together would be thought of in that way, especially because she plays with other Wolves. But now that Sam is living with the rest of the Wolfgard, she only sleeps with you, and you were careful to stay in Wolf form. Until yesterday."

"I just wanted to talk to her, to find out about the dream," Simon protested. "She can't communicate the way we do. How else could I talk to her?" When Henry just looked at him, he snarled. "It's the fault of those stories humans write about Wolves and humans mating."

"We have those kinds of stories too," Henry countered. "But they are cautionary tales because they rarely end well for the lovers. And what about offspring?"

"I wasn't planning to mate and have pups while I was leader of a Courtyard." He'd been young when he'd set his sights on running a Courtyard, but even young, he hadn't been foolish. A leader had to stay alert and aware of the enemy who lived all around his people, had to enforce rules and agreements. Had to decide if the humans needed to be exterminated. And a leader ran the risk of absorbing too much that was human, becoming too much like the enemy.

By rights he should be spending this summer in an earth native settlement in another part of Thaisia where he could run and roam and be a Wolf for days on end with no responsibilities. But that wasn't going to happen. Not when the sickness that had touched humans and Others alike had shown up in a town too close to Lakeside.

"What should I do?" he asked.

Henry drank tea and said nothing for a minute. "You can't take back the friendship you've already given without bruising Meg's heart. But you can choose not to go beyond the friendship as it is now. And you *should* choose not to go beyond what has already been done. Meg has been free of her captors for only two months. She is just learning who she is. In that sense, she is a child as young as Sam, despite having an adult female's body." He sighed. "Be careful, Simon. We have contact with humans in ways no other Courtyard does, so what you do with Meg will ripple through the lives of humans and Others alike."

"Can a friendship carry so much weight and survive?"

"I don't know." Henry pulled the mug from Simon's hand. "But it's time for you to find out."

Promptly at four o'clock, Nathan gave Meg an accusing look and slunk out of the office's front door, abandoning his duties as watch Wolf. At the midday break, it had taken Henry coming over and hauling him out by the scruff of the neck to get the Wolf to leave. Now . . . Well, he didn't have his tail between his legs, but it was pretty close.

And that, Meg thought, *means Simon is on his way over.* While she waited, she tidied up the already-tidy sorting room and sharpened a couple of pencils in anticipation of tomorrow's work.

Talking with Merri Lee and Heather had felt good but hadn't provided answers. The person who had the answers was the Wolf who walked in and was now standing on the other side of the sorting table. But after spending an afternoon thinking about males and sex and living in the Courtyard—and remembering some of the bad things that had taken place in the compound—she had an answer. She just wasn't sure how he was going to respond to it.

"I like you," she said quietly. "I like you a lot. And I want to be friends."

He tipped his head and studied her. She hoped he wasn't going to shift his ears. It was always disconcerting when Jester Coyotegard did that because it was hard to remember what you wanted to say when you were watching furry ears attached to a human head.

"But you don't want to have sex," Simon said.

She couldn't find an image from her training that matched the look on his face. Disappointment? Resignation? Relief?

She shook her head. "No, I don't want to have sex. I'm still learning how to be a person for myself. I'm not ready to . . . I'm not ready."

"That's fine," he said quietly.

He gave up awfully quick, Meg thought. *Was this so insignificant to him? Am I the only one struggling with this?* "You've had sex with humans, haven't you?"

Simon shrugged, a dismissive gesture that bit her heart because it made her think that Merri Lee's opinion of how the Others viewed sex with humans was closer to the truth than Heather's. But she didn't want it anyway, so what Simon thought of it shouldn't matter.

"*Terra indigene* females come into season only once or twice a year," he said. "Having sex at other times is enjoyable. But those humans didn't work in the Courtyard or live among us. It amounted to a couple of hours and some fun, and satisfying curiosity on both sides. Nothing more." He paused, then added, "Having you as a friend is more enjoyable."

She wasn't sure she believed him but didn't feel she could ask. Not right now.

"Well, then. I guess that clears things up," Meg said, wanting him to leave. "If you'll excuse me, Simon, I have some deliveries to make, so I'll close up the office now."

"Sure. You need some help loading up the BOW?" The Box on Wheels was a small, electric-powered vehicle that was used inside the Courtyard.

"No, thanks. The packages aren't heavy."

He nodded once, then left by the back door.

Meg stayed in the sorting room until she was sure he was gone—and wondered when she'd started to cry.

––––––––

Simon leaned against the back wall of the Liaison's Office.

Done. Simple enough since Meg had done most of the work of setting boundaries around a friendship that had had none before. He should feel grateful, but what he wanted to do was raise his head and howl the Song of Lonely.

Couldn't do that. Not here. Not today.

Just a misunderstanding. Nothing that was going to stir up the Courtyard or its more dangerous residents. From now on he would keep to the boundaries set by human males and females who were friendly but not friends.

But he would miss curling up with her in bed at night. He would miss that closeness. Would she still play with him, or was this friendship going to be confined to human form from now on? If it was confined to human form, would she let him lick the salt and butter off her fingers from the popcorn she ate on movie nights?

Probably not, and that made him sad because he really did like the way she tasted.

CHAPTER 6

On Moonsday morning, Meg closed her apartment door, then muttered, "Garbage day," and went back in for the paper bag she'd left in the kitchen.

In the compound where she had lived most of her life, garbage was collected by people who worked for the Controller, and the girls' knowledge of how waste products were handled came through photographs or drawings of equipment and activities, or in a training video. Even now, she had only a vague idea of how humans dealt with all the debris that came from day-to-day living. She knew they recycled some things out of necessity, but she didn't think they were as particular about the rest.

The Others wasted almost nothing, so living in the Courtyard meant that sorting garbage was not an all-in-one-bag exercise. Fruit and vegetable waste went in one container. Meat scraps went in another. Bottles were placed in one bin while cans and anything metal went in another. Catalogs that had to be exchanged in order to receive new copies went back to the Liaison's Office, while other kinds of paper went into a *different* bin for recycling.

If they weren't spoiled, cores and other bits of fruit were left on feeders scattered throughout the Courtyard—a food source for birds. If they were spoiled, they went into the compost piles. Edible vegetable bits were scattered on the ground near the feeders for squirrels and rabbits or whatever else liked that kind of food. Meat scraps were distributed in the Hawkgard's area to feed the rats, which, in turn, kept the Hawks supplied with healthy meat since the rats didn't wander into human neighborhoods where the food might be laced with poison.

By the time they were done sorting and recycling, the weekly trash for an entire complex usually fit into a big tote that was picked up and taken to the Utilities Complex for final disposal.

When she'd first moved into the Green Complex, she'd divided her trash into compost, garbage, and recycle. It was only in the past couple of weeks that Simon showed her the holding bins downstairs and gave her *all* the household containers she was now expected to use. At the time, she'd seen that expectation as another sign of acceptance. Now . . .

How do you mend a friendship? she wondered as she locked up her apartment and went down the stairs someone had swept clean of snow so she wouldn't slip.

She deposited her bag of garbage in the big tote that had been placed next to the road, then retraced her steps and went to the garages behind the complex to get her BOW and drive to work.

Spending time with Simon had been so easy. Now just seeing him felt awkward. And yesterday, Earthday, had been downright uncomfortable because she hadn't been invited to go for an afternoon romp with him and Sam. And when Simon invited her over to watch a movie with them in the evening, he had stayed in human form and sat on the other end of the sofa instead of curling up next to her as a Wolf—something he'd done every movie night since the first invitation.

It was Simon as Courtyard leader and business owner being friendly toward an employee rather than Simon spending time with a friend.

And that hurt. It surprised her how much feelings could translate into physical hurt.

"You started this," she muttered as she drove to the office. "You're the one who made a big deal out of . . . something."

But Simon hadn't tried hard—hadn't tried at all, really—to convince her that his being in her bed as a naked human had been totally innocent. If fact, he'd seemed relieved to have an excuse to back away from being friends with her.

"Think of something else." She parked the BOW in the garage behind the office, checking the vehicle's power bar before shutting it off. Didn't need to charge it, so that was one less task to do before she could go inside and open the office in time for the morning deliveries.

Not many deliveries since the storm earlier in the month. Lots of stores were claiming to be out of stock of any item ordered by someone in the Courtyard. Seeing those same items listed on sale in the *Lakeside News* wasn't easing the tension between humans and Others. If human businesses claimed goods were in short supply in order to avoid selling to the *terra indigene*, how long before the *terra indigene* cut off the resources to make those items and turned the short supply into a reality?

If that happened, everyone would be picking through the garbage for anything still usable.

The pins-and-needles feeling filled her arms so suddenly, she dropped her carry bag and purse in order to scrub at her skin through all the layers of clothes. That prickling under her skin used to happen just before she was cut for a prophecy. Now that she was living in the Courtyard, it happened a lot. Sometimes it was a light prickling that went away after a minute. Sometimes it acted like a detector, easing or disappearing altogether when she went into a different room or stepped away from a particular person.

And sometimes the pins-and-needles feeling became a painful buzz that told her *something* was going to happen. And the only way to find out was to cut her skin to see the visions and speak the prophecy.

She stood outside waiting to see if the feeling would fade or intensify.

Then she heard the Crows cawing nearby. Jenni and her sisters, heading out to . . .

She cried out as the prickling became the painful buzz.

"Meg?"

She looked up and saw Vlad leaning out the open window of HGR's upstairs business office. Out of the corner of her eye, she saw Nathan racing around the corner of the Liaison's Office.

"*Meg?*" Smoke flowed out of HGR's window and down the side of the building. Vlad in his other form.

Meg closed her eyes, doing her best to ignore Vlad, who was now flowing toward her, and the Wolf who was crowding her.

In another moment or two, they would both shift to human form and demand to know what was wrong. Before she could tell them, *she* had to figure out what was wrong.

She'd been thinking about garbage, so she began recalling every training image that was related to garbage or collecting garbage or the containers for garbage and recycling. Something about metal garbage cans buried in snow or shiny in the sun? No. The black, wheeled totes like they had in the Courtyard? No, but . . . Garbage truck. The clang of cans, the sound of the brakes or hydraulics or whatever it was that made that distinctive sound you could hear a block away. Feathers and blood in the snow and . . .

"*Jenni!*" Meg screamed. When Vlad, now in human form, grabbed her arms, she grabbed fistfuls of his black turtleneck. "That was the sound. In the dream. The garbage trucks. *That was the sound.* The Crows have to stay away from the garbage cans, the trucks, all of it. If they go near them, they'll die, Vlad. *They'll die!*"

She jolted as Nathan suddenly howled. Moments later, he was answered from the Utilities Complex, from the Wolfgard Complex, from wherever the Wolves were taking care of business in the Courtyard.

"I'll deal with this," Vlad said. "Can you get into the office by yourself?"

"Yes, I—"

"No cutting, Meg. Promise you won't use the razor. *Promise.*"

"I promise. For now."

Not good enough. She saw that in his dark eyes even before he pointed at Nathan and said, "Don't let her out of your sight." Then Vlad ran to A Little Bite's back door. Moments after that, she saw a Hawk flying away from the Courtyard and realized Vlad must have sent Julia Hawkgard to find Jenni.

Nathan bumped his head against her hip. When she didn't move, he clamped his teeth on the sleeve of her coat and started pulling her toward the office.

"All right, all right, let me get my purse," she said. "We can't get inside without keys."

He let her go but didn't stop crowding her until she had unlocked the back door and they were both inside. Even then he stayed close enough to grab an arm or leg if she did anything he considered suspicious.

The prickling remained a torment as she unlocked the office's front door and set up her clipboard for the day's deliveries.

She'd given the warning. The prickling should be fading by now. The fact that it wasn't fading made her wonder if the dream a few nights ago had been a real prophecy. After all, the skin that split along the curve of her nose hadn't bled, and prophecies came from a cut that bled.

And she wondered if, by making that promise to Vlad not to cut her skin, the next warning would come too late.

After dropping Sam and some other pups at the Courtyard school, Simon drove toward HGR. When he heard the howling, he stopped the BOW and rolled down the window to listen as other Wolves took up the song. That first warning howl had come from the direction of the business district. Wasn't likely to be John, so that left the Wolf on guard at the Liaison's Office.

<Nathan?> he called.

<Meg warning! Meg warning!> Nathan howled. <Crows in danger!>

Simon shoved the door open and got out. Smarter to stay in the vehicle if he needed to move quickly, but he couldn't stand being closed in until he understood what they were facing, especially since Wolves all over the Courtyard continued answering Nathan's howl.

<An attack?> he asked.

Before Nathan could reply, Vlad cut in. <Meg says the Crowgard are in danger and have to return to the Courtyard *now*. But it's collection day, and the damn Crows aren't listening! I sent Julia after Jenni and her sisters.>

<How are they in danger?>

<Something about the garbage trucks.>

A chill went through Simon. The Crows who were killed in Walnut Grove had been picking around the garbage when the dogs attacked.

<Jenni!> he shouted. <Get back to the Courtyard now!>

<It's collection day,> she replied in a greedy tone that said she would ignore him for as long as possible. <The humans on this street throw out a lot of good things. And Starr spotted some shiny in one of the cans at the curb.>

No, he thought. *No.* Every week the Crows checked out the neighborhood streets around the Courtyard to see what humans had left at the curb that might strike their fancy. Anyone planning an attack would know where to find them— and what to put out for bait.

Just like someone in Walnut Grove had known what to put out in order to attract the birds.

<Jenni . . . >

<And Crystal found a picture frame she can carry and Jake says there's a box that might have pieces of the building set we—>

<*Jenni!*> Simon shouted. <Meg says you're in danger! All the Crowgard are in danger! You promised to listen, Jenni. You promised!> She'd agreed to pay attention, which wasn't the same thing. Right now, he was hoping she didn't remember that.

<Our Meg says? But . . . *shinies*, Simon.>

<It's bait.> And he was going to find out who had baited those trash cans. <Do you understand, Jenni? It's a trap!> He swore silently and viciously. If he wasn't getting through to Jenni, he wouldn't get through to the rest of the Crowgard. So he'd stop trying to reason with them.

<I am the leader of this Courtyard,> he snarled, sending his words to every *terra indigene* within range. <And I say that any Crow who doesn't return to the Courtyard in the next fifteen minutes will be driven out of Lakeside *forever.*>

<Simon!> Multiple cries now because the Crows knew he meant it. Give up the shinies and other treasures today, or be sent to *terra indigene* settlements in the wild country, where the pickings would be slim. And they knew him well enough to understand that he wouldn't just ban them from Lakeside. If they disobeyed him, he would use his influence with every Courtyard leader in the Northeast Region to ban the Lakeside Crows from *every* human city in this part of Thaisia.

He didn't respond to the arguments or pleas coming from various Crows. He got back in the BOW and drove as fast as he could to HGR. That's where the Crows would expect to find him.

<Julia?> he called.

<Most of the Crows are heading back to the Courtyard,> she replied. <They aren't happy, but they're heading back. I'm in the air, circling. I don't see any danger.>

<Can you see Jenni? Is she heading back with the rest of the Crows?> Shinies and a toy in plain view. How many building sets had the Crowgard ordered from the nearby toy stores in the past month or so? Meg would know, but he suspected there had been enough for humans to guess that at least some of the Crows would be drawn to the box if it was sitting in the open.

After Julia told him which street had drawn more Crows than usual, she added, <Jake was pecking at something near the garbage cans just before you gave your orders and now he isn't flying right. Crystal is helping him get back.

Jenni and Starr want to stay and watch. They promised to perch in the trees. All right?>

He hesitated. Was this a challenge to his authority, an excuse to stay in order to snatch some coveted item, or the Crowgard's need to have a report from one of their own? <As long as they stay in the trees—and you can vouch for them—they can keep watch.>

Besides, he was going to be there too.

As soon as he reached the Courtyard's business district, he parked his BOW near HGR's back door just as Vlad stepped outside. He raised a finger to indicate the vampire should wait, then said, <Blair? I need the passenger van.>

<You need any guards coming with you?> Blair asked.

<Just you. Vlad will come with us.> Satisfied that the Courtyard's dominant enforcer was on the way, Simon turned to the next Wolf on his list. <Nathan? How is Meg?>

<Itchy,> the Wolf replied. <Restless. She tried to step on my foot. On purpose!>

"Did you tell Nathan to stick close to Meg?" he asked Vlad.

"I did."

Since he didn't think Vlad had intended for the Wolf to be underfoot, he said, <Keep out of reach,> then nodded to Tess when she came out of A Little Bite, shoving her arms into her coat. Moments later, Henry opened the wooden gate at the back of his studio's yard and joined them.

Simon told them about the Crows' resistance to giving up this collection day and repeated his ultimatum even though they would have heard that part.

"What do you need?" Henry asked.

Simon looked at Vlad. "I'd like you to come with Blair and me. As a Sanguinati, you might notice something we miss."

"All right," Vlad said. "What about Meg?"

"I'll close A Little Bite and help Nathan watch Meg," Tess said.

Simon shook his head. "Better for you to stay open. If humans are watching to see what we do, let them think we're not aware of the baited street and the trap yet." He thought for a moment. Did Nathan really need someone else in the Liaison's Office to help him watch Meg? Or would having Tess and Henry nearby be enough?

"Henry, I need you to handle the Crows and make sure they all return,"

Simon said. "I gave Jenni and Starr permission to stay and watch the street. Something is wrong with Jake. Crystal is helping him get back to the Crows' complex. Talk to their bodywalker. See if anyone can figure out what happened to him." He looked over his shoulder as Blair pulled up in the small passenger van they used when they needed to travel on human roads.

Blair got out of the van and slipped inside the Liaison's Office. He returned a minute later with an armful of clothes, which he tossed inside the van.

Good idea, Simon thought. That way Jenni, Starr, and Julia could pull on some clothes if they needed to shift and talk to any humans.

Like Lieutenant Crispin James Montgomery? For a moment, Simon wondered if he should call Montgomery and tell him about the baited street.

No. The lieutenant wasn't a hairless gibbering monkey like so many humans were, and he *had* helped protect Meg when she was in the hospital, but that didn't make the man part of the Courtyard. Besides, the Crows had followed orders, so nothing had happened that required the police.

He would go to the baited street first. If he saw something pertinent, then he would call Montgomery.

"Nyx will come up to the office and stay with Meg," Vlad said, breaking into Simon's thoughts. "Grandfather Erebus is concerned about our Liaison. If something is wrong, Meg might tell another female something she wouldn't tell Nathan."

Nothing to be said about that, not even by the leader of the Courtyard. But Simon noticed that Tess's hair had turned solid green and was tightly coiled— a sign she was feeling agitated or uneasy.

Only Henry knew what Tess was, but Simon had his own thoughts about that and was certain having her uneasy about the Sanguinati could be dangerous for everyone. A shape-shifter had little chance of surviving a fight with a Sanguinati. Would a vampire be able to survive a fight with an earth native like Tess?

He hoped that was a question that would never be answered.

"We have to go." As he and Vlad got in the van, Simon heard the bitter cawing of the returning Crows.

A moment after that, Julia Hawkgard screamed, <Simon! Come quick!>

Monty rapped on the doorframe before entering Douglas Burke's office.

The patrol captain of the Chestnut Street station was a big man with neatly trimmed dark hair below a bald pate. His blue eyes, like his smile, usually held a fierce kind of friendliness. Today the smile was absent and the eyes looked sad as he handed a piece of paper to Monty and said, "We got an answer."

Monty read the paragraph, then read it again. "This happened on Trickster Night?"

"Yes," Burke replied. "Months before our friends in the Courtyard gave us that cryptic warning."

Not exactly cryptic. A few weeks ago, Meg Corbyn had cut her skin because she'd sensed something wrong in the back room of the Liaison's Office and couldn't identify the source of her uneasiness. The resulting visions and prophecy had revealed poison in the sugar lumps she usually gave the Courtyard ponies on Moonsday. Among the images she'd seen was a skeleton in a hooded robe, passing out sweets to children, and those children dying in the same way the ponies would have died. Simon Wolfgard had told him what Meg had seen on the chance that the police might find the place and the person in time to save the children.

But it had already happened months ago in another city.

If the police in that city had had access to a *cassandra sangue* like Meg Corbyn, could that tragedy have been averted? Or would a different blood prophet have seen some other prophecy, and the children's deaths would have occurred anyway?

And was justifying the use of one group of humans for the benefit of the rest of them the reason a law supporting benevolent ownership had been passed in the first place? Was the argument that these girls would cut themselves anyway and keep cutting until it killed them sufficient justification for restricting their lives and using this compulsion for the good of government or profit?

Maybe it was better for everyone that the only blood prophet in the city of Lakeside was surrounded by the *terra indigene*.

"Lieutenant?" Burke said.

"Sorry, Captain. My mind wandered." Monty set the paper on Burke's desk.

Sighing, Burke sat back and linked his fingers over his abdomen. "My people immigrated to Thaisia from Brittania a few generations back, and I still have family over there. Went over to visit in my younger years and have kept in touch with some of my relatives, especially the ones who work in law enforcement. Brittania is about one-quarter the size of Wild Brittania, so the people there have few illusions about what watches them on the other side of the agreed-upon boundaries. Those of us living in cities like Lakeside have that in common with them."

Not sure where this was going, Monty just nodded.

"According to my cousin Shady Burke . . ." Burke's smile warmed for a moment. "Shamus David Burke, an officer of the law in Brittania. Usually goes by Shay, but there was already a Shay at his first posting, so my cousin was called Shay D., which quickly became Shady."

"Unusual name for a police officer," Monty said.

"He's quick with his tongue and quick on his feet. Has to be one because of the other." Burke's smile faded. "Anyway, Shady is very good at mixing in where he can hear things of interest. Lately he's been hearing rumors that somewhere in the Cel-Romano Alliance of Nations there is a factory building airplanes—machines that can fly."

Still not sure where the conversation was going, Monty said, "Is that a problem?"

Now Burke gave Monty the typical fierce-friendly smile. "A hardship for the people, I would think, if another industry wants a share of the metal and fuel available to the nations. Shortages and stricter rationing would be just the start of the troubles there."

For a moment, Monty considered the wonder of traveling through the air, high above the ground. The closest thing to air travel in Thaisia was hot-air balloons. Most of the time the balloons remained tethered to prevent them from wandering over land that belonged to the Others. Sometimes photographers or moviemakers were permitted to float over the wild country to take pictures and film herds of animals or places on the continent that humans couldn't see any other way. Those trips were strictly supervised, of course, because the Others would never permit anything on or above their land that might pose a threat to them. "Why didn't the *terra indigene* forbid such a machine from being made in the first place?"

"Cel-Romano is the largest land area in the world that belongs to humans, and those boundaries haven't altered since the first record of human history. Gods below, the boundaries were set even before humans spread out to reach what we call the wild places. The Others understood before we did how much of the world the human race could claim, and they haven't given humans a single acre more. One-third of all the humans on Namid live there. The *terra indigene* don't care what humans do within the boundaries of human land, but the moment human activity touches *their* pieces of the world . . ." Burke gave Monty that fierce-friendly smile again. "Maybe the Others don't know about the airplanes yet. Maybe they know but don't care as long as the flying machines remain within the boundaries of Cel-Romano. But when ships sailing the Mediterran and Black seas can easily provide transport to all the nations, one has to wonder how the manufacturing of airplanes at this time might be connected to the Humans First and Last movement. You remember that slogan, Lieutenant?"

Monty felt a shiver of alarm. "Yes, I remember. Our previous mayor was trying that out as his campaign platform." The mayor had died in the storm that had almost buried Lakeside, but he had died in his bedroom. Winter and some other Elementals had come calling on His Honor. So had the Sanguinati.

"Humans First and Last has become a rallying cry throughout the Cel-Romano Alliance," Burke said. "Speakers are mesmerizing crowds, exciting them with the idea that they can have more. And since the nations in the Alliance have had a habit of expanding their cities and building over good farmland, even the wealthy there can't always buy enough food anymore." Burke's smile faded but the fierceness remained. "That's not a bad incentive if you're looking to start a war."

"War?" Monty groped for the visitor's chair and collapsed into it. "You think there's going to be a war?"

"Shady and some of his contacts believe the Cel-Romano Alliance is heading that way, if for no other reason than to winnow down their population. I just don't think their leaders realize how much winnowing the *terra indigene* can and will do." Burke paused. "There is no indication that the people in Tokhar-Chin or the human sections of Afrikah are aware of what is happening in Cel-Romano . . . or would be willing to risk their own people. And the humans who live in Felidae or Zelande are too far away to become involved in a confrontation with the Others living in the wild country beyond the Mediterran and Black seas."

"What about us?" Monty asked. Gone over wolf was a drug that hyped aggression to the point where self-preservation wasn't a consideration. That wouldn't be a bad drug to have if you were looking to start a war. Was its appearance in some Thaisian towns at a time when trouble was stirring elsewhere in the world just a coincidence, or was Thaisia the testing ground for a bigger conflict?

"For now, war, like the airplane, is just a rumor floating to us from the other side of the Atlantik. Let's hope it remains nothing more than a rumor." Burke rubbed the back of his neck. "Lakeside is in the extraordinary position of actually having a dialogue with the Others who run the Courtyard. As long as we have that, we have a chance of protecting our own city. Maybe protecting even more than that."

Monty felt a weight settling on his shoulders. He and his team were the contacts between the police and the Courtyard's leaders. Elliot Wolfgard, Simon's sire, was the consul who met with human government, but it was Simon who made the decisions that affected humans as well as Others.

"I'll . . ." Monty began.

Kowalski suddenly appeared in the doorway, all the color drained out of his face. "Lieutenant, we've got trouble."

Blood and black feathers in the snow. Broken bodies.

Flanked by Blair and Vlad, Simon walked down the middle of the street and looked at every dead crow.

If not for Meg's warning, many of them would have been Crowgard.

<Jenni and Starr are in that tree up ahead,> Vlad said. <I don't see Julia.>

<She's in the air,> Blair said. <So are a few other Hawkgard.>

Keeping watch. Keeping potential enemies in sight.

<There's a man on the ground near the garbage truck,> Vlad said. <I'll find out why.> He moved toward a crowd of humans while Simon and Blair continued to the end of the block, listening to the sirens coming from several directions.

"It stops here," Simon said.

Blair stared at the next block. "The killing was done on this part of the street, but that doesn't mean the next block wasn't baited too."

"How are we supposed to find out?"

"We don't need to find out. It doesn't matter if the monkeys baited one block or two; the intention was the same." Blair grabbed Simon's arm and pulled him to one side as an ambulance turned the corner and slid to a stop when the driver saw the bodies scattered in the street.

They can't reach the injured human without running over some of the crows, Simon thought. *And they're afraid of what we'll do if they make that choice.*

"That's Lieutenant Montgomery and Officer Kowalski," he said to Blair when he saw the men getting out of one of the cars at the other end of the street. "Tell the lieutenant I'll be with him in a minute."

As Blair ran up the street, Simon looked at the EMTs and twirled a finger to indicate that the man in the passenger seat should roll down his window. "I'll move these bodies out of the way so you can reach your injured."

"Thank you."

Simon nodded, then began moving the dead crows, the ambulance crawling behind him.

Under different circumstances, Hawks and hawks might have snatched up the crows for the meat, and he wouldn't have spent time moving roadkill out of the way of another vehicle. But the humans, not knowing if they were seeing Crows or crows, had stopped, unwilling to drive over the bodies. The least he could do as leader of the Courtyard was show the same respect for Namid's creations—and reinforce that good behavior in the humans. After all, at another time, it *could* be some of the Crowgard lying in the street.

Blair and Kowalski came running back to help while Montgomery headed for the crowd around the injured man. As Blair passed the crowd, he hesitated, drawn by the smell of blood.

When it looked like the ambulance had a clear path, Simon growled, "Enough."

Kowalski looked up, startled. Then he stood and took one careful step away from the Wolves.

"That's enough," Kowalski agreed.

<We have to leave,> Blair said. <I can't stay around wounded prey much longer.>

Simon glanced at his own hands. While handling the crow bodies, his hands had shifted enough to be furry and clawed, but he'd gotten them back to looking human, and he didn't think anything else had shifted. But he doubted he and Blair would pass for human right now.

<Get Jenni and Starr. Meet me at the van.> He looked around and didn't see his other companion. <Vlad?>

<This car that crashed,> Vlad said. <It belongs to some of the attackers. Keep the police busy a minute longer.>

I'm not sure I have a minute. And it wouldn't help matters if his control snapped right now and he ripped out Montgomery's throat.

But he walked up to Montgomery, who moved away from the injured man.

"Lieutenant."

"Mr. Wolfgard." Montgomery's voice held the same quiet courtesy as usual. "Were any of your people injured?"

"No. They returned to the Courtyard before—"

"Is Ms. Corbyn all right?"

Easy enough to understand the question. If the Crowgard escaped the attack that was similar to the one in Walnut Grove, it was because they'd been warned. And only one person in Lakeside could give that kind of warning.

"She's fine." He needed to get back to the Courtyard and confirm that.

"One of the vehicles smashed into trash cans and, as you can see, ended up stuck in the snowbank. The men in the car ran off, but we'll find them and the men who were in the second car. We will find them, Mr. Wolfgard."

"They didn't hurt any *terra indigene*, so it's strictly a human problem."

He said the words. He knew they weren't true. So did Montgomery.

"If any of the Crowgard saw what happened, I'd appreciate the opportunity to talk to them."

"Come by the bookstore in an hour," Simon said. Fur suddenly covered his chest, brushing against the T-shirt he was wearing under a flannel shirt.

Injured prey. Fresh blood. He didn't want to be in this monkey skin a minute longer, but if he shifted to Wolf . . .

"I have to go." He walked away from Montgomery and got in the van. <Vlad?>

The Sanguinati didn't answer—and there was no sign of him on the street.

Meg heard the Crows cawing and felt the awful prickling under her skin start to fade. She sighed with relief, then gave Nathan a tentative smile. "I'm sorry I tried to step on your foot. You were just looking out for me, and I wasn't being nice."

He stared at her with those amber Wolf eyes.

"Would you like a cookie?" Some of the Wolves had decided they liked a cookie that was actually a treat for dogs. They also claimed cookies they bought themselves didn't taste as good as cookies they got from her. She suspected the taste didn't change, but the fun of getting the cookies came from pestering her to pull out the boxes of different flavors and persuade the Wolf to choose two cookies.

Nathan stared at her.

"Two cookies?"

He stared at her.

"Three, and that's my final offer."

"*Arrroooo.*"

She took one cookie from each box. Nope. Too easy. So they went round and round until she correctly deciphered his sounds and the way he thumped the boxes with a paw and gave him three beef-flavored cookies. Which he didn't take to the Wolf bed in the front room as he usually did. No, he sprawled in the most inconvenient spot in the sorting room so that she would spend the morning stepping over him or walking around him. And, oh, how he would howl if she accidentally stepped on him.

Wolves, she was learning, were sneaky when it came to payback.

She made a cup of peppermint tea and finally felt easy again, the prickling in her arms completely gone.

Then Nyx walked into the sorting room.

Vlad flowed just above the snow, searching for signs of the men who had been in the car. In smoke form, the Sanguinati were swift predators. But only when they had some idea of where to find their prey.

Stopping near a tree, he shifted to human form and looked around. If anyone noticed him, they would see a handsome man with an olive complexion and dark hair and eyes, dressed in a black turtleneck, black jeans, and chunky shoes that served as boots. As for what *he* was seeing . . .

Unfamiliar streets. Lakeside was a moderate-size city, and it occurred to him now how little of it the Others actually knew. He'd gotten an address from the car registration he'd found in the abandoned vehicle's glove box, and he'd headed in the same direction as the fresh tire tracks, assuming they had come from the other car that had killed the crows. But the chase had taken him to a street that wasn't in the neighborhoods surrounding the Courtyard or along a route the Others used to reach the things in the city that were of interest to them, like the nearby plaza or the railway station.

Foolish to go chasing blindly after the men who had tried to kill the Crows.

He'd go back to HGR and study a city map, find the street, and *then* do some hunting tonight.

<Vladimir.>

Vlad tensed at the sound of Erebus Sanguinati's voice. <Grandfather?>

<Return to the Courtyard *now*.>

<Has something else happened?>

<Our Meg is upset. You must return.>

<Meg was already upset when I left with Simon and Blair. Why—>

<Everyone else is accounted for, so *you* are the reason the sweet blood still begs for the razor despite having bled.>

She promised me she wouldn't cut, Vlad thought grimly as he shifted to smoke and headed back to the Courtyard. Meg had promised not to cut, and she'd been guarded by Nathan and . . . <Nyx?>

A hesitation before she replied. <Come home as fast as you can. There is something the Sanguinati need to discuss. Henry has summoned the Wolfgard. He's needed here too.>

A chill went through Vlad. What kind of danger had Meg seen that would threaten the Sanguinati? Or, since Simon was also called back to the Courtyard, was the danger to more than one kind of *terra indigene*?

Since the answer was in the Courtyard, he used all the speed he had in this form to reach his people.

<Simon, get back to the Courtyard. There's a potential conflict among the *terra indigene*.>

Simon growled. When Blair glanced at him, he said, "It's Henry." <Trouble because of the Crows?> he asked the Grizzly.

<Conflict between Wolves and the Sanguinati.>

With trouble brewing among the humans, this wasn't the time for two of the strongest groups of predators to be snarling at each other.

"Get us back home," he told Blair, his voice grim. He looked over his shoulder at Jenni, Starr, and Julia. None of them had shifted to human form.

As they pulled into the Main Street entrance that serviced the Liaison's Office, the consulate, and the Market Square, Simon looked in the office window and saw John Wolfgard in human form, leaning against the front counter and chatting with Meg.

<Why aren't you at the bookstore?> Simon asked the other Wolf.

<Henry told me to stay with Meg,> John replied.

<Where's Nathan?>

No answer.

Blair parked the van close to the back entrance of Howling Good Reads. Leaving his enforcer to deal with Julia, Starr, and Jenni, Simon hurried into the store and up the stairs to the Business Association's meeting room. Along with its entryway and coatroom, the meeting room filled half of HGR's second floor and held a ring of wooden chairs set around a low, round sectional table where they sat to talk over Courtyard business. It also had a secretary desk, filing cabinets, and a computer workstation they used for e-mail or placing orders with human companies.

All the *terra indigene* who were present were in human form, and there weren't as many of them as there were sometimes for a business meeting. But everyone was standing and the room felt too crowded, especially with Erebus present and flanked by two male Sanguinati as well as Nyx. Tess stood between the Sanguinati and Nathan, and her hair was completely red and coiling—a sure sign of anger. Even worse, Henry wasn't adjusting his hands to eliminate the Grizzly claws.

Trapped in the small space behind Henry and Tess, Nathan paced and panted, despite being in human form.

"What's going on?" Simon demanded, moving around the low table and the surrounding chairs until he stood closer to Henry than to Erebus.

"That's what we're trying to find out," Tess replied, watching the Sanguinati.

"This one bit the sweet blood." Erebus pointed a finger at Nathan.

"I did *not* bite Meg!" Nathan gave Simon a pleading look. "I was just trying to hold on to her while she was fighting with Nyx, and my teeth slipped."

Before Simon could demand an explanation from Nyx, Vlad arrived, followed by Blair. Blair immediately took a position where he could help defend Simon and Nathan. Vlad carefully took a position between the two groups, not committing himself to either side. That earned him a cold look from Erebus, but Simon felt relieved. Not only did he and Vlad work together at HGR; they were neighbors in the Green Complex.

"Nyx?" Vlad said quietly. "You were at the Liaison's Office helping Nathan guard Meg. Did he bite her?"

After giving Vlad a long stare, Nyx sighed and looked at Erebus. "It wasn't Nathan's fault. When I walked into the sorting room, Meg started screaming. There wasn't any warning or sign of danger. When she pulled the razor out of her pocket, I grabbed her wrists so she couldn't cut herself. But she kept screaming and struggling . . ."

"What was she screaming?" Blair asked.

"That's not important yet," Simon said. "Is it, Nyx?"

"No, it isn't. Not now when . . ." She glanced at Vlad before continuing. "Nathan grabbed one of Meg's ankles to hold her, and she jerked her leg away from him. That's when his teeth—a tooth—scraped her through her sock. We didn't realize anything had changed until she stopped struggling and . . ." Nyx hesitated.

"She started smelling lusty," Nathan said.

Simon snarled, and his canines lengthened as he turned toward the Wolf he had trusted to guard Meg.

"I wasn't *trying* to smell her," Nathan protested.

"She stopped struggling and started saying the same things over and over," Nyx said. "Glass jar. Smoke. Pickles. Hand."

Erebus hissed. The sudden rage filling his old-man face made it terrible to see. As a friendly warning, Vlad had hinted a few times over the years that Erebus ruled more than the Sanguinati in the Lakeside Courtyard. Was, in fact, the dominant vampire in more than the Northeast Region.

For all Simon knew, Erebus could be the one giving orders to every Sanguinati on the whole continent of Thaisia.

"That's all Meg saw?" Vlad asked, sounding puzzled.

"She saw enough," Erebus snarled.

"Wait a minute," Tess said. "I read this. It's a horror story written by one of the *terra indigene*, I think. A Sanguinati goes out hunting one night in his smoke form. As he closes in on his prey, the human swipes at the smoke, traps some of it in a glass jar, and manages to run away. When the Sanguinati shifts back to human form, the smoke in the jar turns into a hand—the same hand the Sanguinati is now missing."

"A truth and a warning hidden as a story," Erebus said.

Everyone froze.

"That's possible?" Simon said, turning toward Vlad, who looked shocked.

Vlad swallowed hard. "A horror novel published last month and written by a human had a similar storyline. I didn't mention the book to any of you because I didn't think such a thing was possible."

"It is possible." Erebus stared at Vlad. "You will give me the name of that human."

"If the human dies suddenly, it will give weight to the story," Simon said.

"You will give me the name of that human," Erebus said again.

Simon looked at Vlad and nodded. The *terra indigene* who lived in the Courtyards were always at risk from the humans they watched. If the human who wrote the story *knew* this was an effective way to harm Sanguinati, he had gotten the information from somewhere or someone. Even if he made it up, there would be humans foolish enough to try to capture a vampire in a jar just to see if it could be done. And if even one human was successful . . . "Vlad and I will look for other books with similar stories—especially anything written by humans."

"Why now?" Tess asked. "Why are stories about trapping Sanguinati being published now?"

"There have always been such stories," Erebus said. "We will deal with this as we have done in the past."

"How is that?" Simon asked.

"By giving humans a reason to tell a different kind of story." Erebus looked at Nathan. "As for the Wolf . . ."

"My decision," Simon said. "And Meg's. If she wants Nathan to remain as the office's watch Wolf, then he'll remain." He met Erebus's eyes, refusing to back down. Erebus might be the leader of all the Sanguinati in this part of Thaisia, but *he* was the leader of *this* Courtyard.

"Yes," Erebus finally said. "I will accept your decision."

More truthful, Erebus felt a mix of wariness and affection for Meg, so he would abide by *her* decision.

"In that case, Lieutenant Montgomery will be here soon to talk to Jenni, Starr, and Julia about what they saw when the humans ran over the crows on the baited street. I'll talk to Meg." Simon took a step toward the door, then stopped. "And everyone in this room is going to think about why Meg went crazy twice in one morning!"

"She did not go crazy, Simon," Henry growled.

"She was grabbing for the razor when she was already out of control," Simon growled in return. "What do *you* call it?"

Not waiting for an answer, he strode out of the room, then rushed to the Liaison's Office. John and Meg were in the sorting room. When Simon walked in, she bristled and said, "It wasn't Nathan's fault."

"Go back to work," Simon told John. He waited for the other Wolf to leave, then took a position on the opposite side of the sorting table from Meg. It occurred to him that they often had the table between them when they had something to discuss.

How many other *terra indigene* instinctively did the same thing in order to avoid touching her skin during a potential argument?

When Simon was sure they were alone, he said, "Let's see the wound."

"It's not a wound. It's barely a scratch." Meg sounded snappish in the way of many small creatures when they were cornered and tried to sound threatening.

"It bled," he snapped in return, showing teeth that were a little too long to be human. "It bled enough for you to slip into speaking prophecy, *so let me see the wound.*"

"Well, you can't see it when you're standing over there." Snappish. Defensive. Scared.

Why scared? He wouldn't hurt her. Okay, he used to threaten to eat her because she annoyed and confused him so much, but that was before she almost died leading the enemy away from Sam. Besides, he'd sensed from the very beginning that she was not prey and, therefore, not edible.

As he walked around the table, she put her right foot on the top step of the step stool she used to reach the higher mail slots in the sorting room's back wall. She pushed down her sock.

He crouched to take a look. She'd smeared her ankle with the stinky ointment humans used when they got hurt. To him, that medicine smell meant *wound.* But the scrape above her ankle bone? She could have done that brushing against a branch or a stone. Definitely not a bite. Just a layer or two of skin stripped off by a tooth. Just enough for blood to replace the missing skin.

Is she really that fragile? Simon thought as he studied the scrape. *Can it take so little to damage her?* Then again, her skin had split just because the winter air was dry.

How could she live among them? How could she play with Sam—or with him? No matter how careful they were, there would be bumps, scrapes, nicks. How long could she survive? It was said the *cassandra sangue*'s body had a thousand cuts. Was that just the cuts with the razor, or did every little scrape count as well?

As soon as he stood, she pulled up her sock and moved away from the step stool.

"It wasn't Nathan's fault," she said. "If it was anyone's fault, it was mine. I needed to cut. Something was going to burst inside me if I couldn't get it out." She wrapped her arms around herself. "Did something happen to one of the Sanguinati?"

"No." But it could have. Vlad had gone off alone without telling anyone anything, not even the direction he was heading. If he hadn't been called back . . . "No, all the Sanguinati are back in the Courtyard." He took a step toward her, immediately stopping when she tensed. "Meg, this isn't good for you. Twice in one day? There has to be something you can do, that we can do."

"What? Put me in a cage?"

He flinched. "I've had enough of cages." He'd kept his nephew Sam in a cage for two years after Daphne was killed. It had been the only way to keep the pup safe. That had been a strain on all the Wolfgard living in the Courtyard. He wasn't going to do it again—even if it meant letting Meg die young. "If you cut when you're out of control, you could kill yourself." He might have to let it happen, but that didn't mean he wouldn't fight against it.

"I know." She hesitated. "I want to think about this for a little bit."

She sounded dismissive. Resentment swelled up inside him.

"Why are you shutting me out?" he shouted.

She jolted, looking as skittish as a lame rabbit. Then her gray eyes lit with anger. "*I'm* shutting *you* out? I tell you I'm not ready to have sex, and you treat me like I'm diseased!"

"*What?*" Shit, fuck, damn. Females! "I thought we settled this. And I *wasn't* treating you like you were diseased. That's ridiculous."

"On Earthday, you didn't invite me to take a walk with you and Sam. And when I came over for movie night, you were so distant, like you didn't want to be bothered with me anymore." Her eyes filled with tears.

Not fair, Meg. That is so not fair! "I wasn't being distant. I was trying to be polite!" He paced for a minute, snarling under his breath. "There are always rules and more rules when it comes to dealing with humans. But I don't know the rules for this because I've never had a human friend. I like spending time with you and playing with you. I like the way the three of us cuddle together on the sofa when we watch a movie. Those things are important to me."

"They're important to me too," Meg said, sniffling as she wiped a tear off her cheek.

"Then why can't we do that?" he asked, trying not to whine.

She looked away, her brow furrowed like she was thinking hard. "The other morning, why did you shift to human and get into bed with me?"

They were back to that? Really? "To *talk* to you. To find out what had scared you so much that you kicked me off the bed." He growled in frustration. "All *I* wanted was my share of the covers."

"But you have fur."

"Not in this form." He waved a hand to indicate his body. "Humans get upset when they see *terra indigene* in between forms, and you were already upset. I keep trying to be polite, and you keep slamming my tail in the door. Not my actual tail but . . . you know." Did she know? With Meg it was hard to tell.

He huffed out a breath. "I just wanted to talk." Human females were supposed to like talking. But Meg hadn't been raised like a typical human female, so maybe this talking wasn't any more natural to her than it was to him.

"You can't communicate the way *terra indigene* can with each other, so I couldn't talk to you in Wolf form," he continued. "That's the only reason I shifted. And I didn't think cuddling for warmth would be a problem when you were okay with it when I was Wolf."

He waited, giving her time to absorb what he'd said. That's what Meg did. She absorbed images, sounds, experiences, and those things became the touchstones she used to convey what she saw in prophecies. But more than that, right now he wanted her to understand for herself why her friendship was important to him.

"A leader needs to look beyond his own kind, needs the obedience of everyone in the Courtyard because we're surrounded by the enemy."

"Who are, in turn, surrounded by the rest of the *terra indigene*," Meg replied thoughtfully.

Simon nodded. "We're here to watch the humans and to acquire the things humans make that we want to have. We may all be earth natives, but we aren't the same kind of earth natives. And although we'll stand together against the common enemy, not all Courtyards are ... pleasant ... places to live. When a leader spends too much time with his own kind, he's not always trusted by the rest of the *terra indigene* living in that Courtyard."

Meg said nothing. Then, "You're lonely, aren't you? But you have friends here, Simon."

"I don't want to cuddle up to Henry. Or Vlad."

He could see her taking that in. Leader. Lonely. But not as lonely since Meg had come to the Courtyard.

"You want to be friends again?" she asked, studying him.

"Being friends isn't a small thing, Meg."

"No, it's not a small thing." She gave him a tentative smile. "But maybe we could have a friend rule to avoid confusion if you need to talk to me."

He hadn't been confused until she started acting weird about his shifting to human the morning she dreamed about the Crows, but he said, "All right. Like what?"

A genuine smile this time. "I don't know. I'll think about that too." The smile faded. "Can Nathan come back and be watch Wolf?"

"Is that what you want?"

"Yes."

"Then I'll tell him he can come back. But, Meg? I want some rules too about you using the razor when you're too upset to think straight."

She hesitated. "It's important for me to have the razor, to be the one who chooses."

"I know that." He hadn't forgotten her telling him she could use anything to cut her skin. At the time it had been a threat to force him to return the razor that had her designation, *cs759*, engraved on one side of the handle. Now, realizing how many things she could use to violate her skin, he saw the razor as a necessary evil—a thin, precise blade honed so sharp it did the least amount of damage.

But every cut brought her closer to the one that would kill her.

<Simon, Lieutenant Montgomery is here,> Vlad said.

"I have to go. The police want to talk to Jenni, Starr, and Julia. I'll send Nathan over."

As he turned to leave, Meg said, "Simon? Nyx didn't mean to hurt me either. Just so you know now and don't get mad about it later."

He turned back and saw her push up her sleeves. He stared at the dark bruises on both of her wrists. Sanguinati were strong. So were Wolves. But Nyx wouldn't have held on with more force than necessary. How hard had Meg struggled to get those kinds of bruises?

"You think hard about why things went out of control today," he said softly. "You think real hard."

And so will I.

CHAPTER 7

"Can you think of anything else?" Monty asked, keeping his eyes focused on his notes to avoid looking at the three females sitting on the other side of the table in the Courtyard's meeting room. What he'd mistaken for oddly styled bangs were actually small feathers that formed a crown at the top of each forehead, rising and flattening in response to his questions.

If anyone needed proof that the Others weren't human, that mix of feathers and hair would do it. And it was an indication of how a loss of composure could affect the *terra indigene*'s ability to hold a human shape.

The two Crows, Jenni and Starr, held hands and huddled as close together as the chairs allowed. The Hawk, Julia, looked like she needed a cuddle but wouldn't ask for one from anyone in the room.

Simon Wolfgard, Blair Wolfgard, Vladimir Sanguinati, and Henry Beargard were in the room as observers. So was Monty's partner, Officer Kowalski.

He'd gone over the Crows' movements. Added to the information he'd received from the trash collectors and the residents on the street, it formed a picture that gave him a feeling of icy sickness. The Crowgard regularly went out on collection day, paying special attention to the upscale neighborhood near Lakeside Park. The heavy-plastic container used for food debris wasn't usually of interest to them because they had plenty of food in the Courtyard, although they often let the crows in the neighborhood know about any available food they spotted. No, the Crowgard were mostly interested in the open metal cans that held all kinds of potential treasures—things the humans were discarding as used up or broken. If a third of the Crows each found one item of interest, they all considered it a successful "hunt."

This morning, several cans had bits and baubles that were sure to catch the eye of a Crow. Much more than usual, Jenni said, even for that street. In fact, the pickings had been so good, Jenni and her sisters had called to the rest of the Crowgard to come over and help them with the bounty. Regular crows were also flocking to that street because of food spilled around the cans.

Jake Crowgard had found an unsoiled piece of pizza between the cans of one house. After consuming a couple of bites, he spotted the box of a building set he liked and left the food for the regular crows.

And then Meg Corbyn became hysterical and Simon threatened all the Crows with expulsion from the Courtyard if they didn't return immediately. So they abandoned their prizes and were heading home when the garbage truck turned the corner.

As the truck came down the street, the crows who had been eating the food dumped around the cans tried to leave. But they kept fluttering and pitching forward, unable to fly away. That's when Jenni and Starr, who had stayed to watch the street, realized there was a real danger. And then two cars came roaring down the street. One of the cars hit a man from the truck and kept going, swerving this way and that in order to run over the most crows—and the birds didn't even try to get out of the way.

"It could have been us," Jenni said, trembling. "Without our Meg giving the warning, it would have been us."

Yes, it would have been, Monty thought grimly. "What about Jake? Is he all right?"

"He will be," Simon said.

Wolfgard's amber eyes had flickers of red, a sign of temper.

"The people who live on that street didn't do this," Monty said. "When questioned, they all thought the food dumped around the cans had been caused by teenagers doing a bit of mischief. But when they saw the items that had been left in their cans as bait, they insisted those weren't things that they had put out."

"Well, they would say that, wouldn't they?" Blair said.

"They're afraid of reprisals. I won't deny that," Monty replied. "And many of them admitted that they put the 'almost usable' discards on top of the rest of the debris because some people who run flea market stalls drive by at night to look for items they can resell. But the items that were left as bait didn't have enough value to be worth the effort of cleaning them up or repairing in order to sell again."

Jenni sniffed. "There were shinies."

Which only proved that whoever had planned this had known what would draw the Crows and keep them around long enough to poke in the cans and eat some of the food so conveniently available.

"I think that's all the questions I have for the ladies," Monty said as he closed his notebook and tucked it in his pocket. "But I would like a word with you, Mr. Wolfgard, if you can spare the time."

"That's fine," Simon said. "I have something to discuss with you too."

Henry Beargard looked at Simon and nodded. Then the Grizzly led the rest of the *terra indigene* out of the room. When Monty made a subtle gesture, Kowalski said, "I'll warm up the car," and left.

Alone with the Wolf, Monty sat back in his chair. "Why would someone target the Crows?"

Simon cocked his head, clearing surprised by the question. "What?"

"Out of all the different kinds of *terra indigene*, why go after the Crows? In Jerzy, the attack took place on a night when the Crowgard were using the house the Others owned in the village. In Walnut Grove, food was used to lure the birds into position to be attacked by the dogs—and the main target was the Crows. And now here, a baited street." Monty leaned forward. "So I'm asking you: What is it about the Crowgard that would make someone feel the need to get them out of the way?"

He had the Wolf's attention. The *terra indigene* must know that Crows died each time there was an attack, but he'd wondered if the more formidable kinds of earth natives had considered that the Crows were the primary target.

"They're curious," Simon finally said. "They pay attention to everything and everyone in their territory. They remember faces that are familiar and know when a stranger shows up. They warn the rest of us when something doesn't look right or someone acts oddly. And they communicate with regular crows."

"The rest of you can't do that?" Monty interrupted. "Communicate with the animals that share your form?"

"How many wolves do you see in a city?" Simon asked dryly. "Or bears?"

"Point taken."

"But the crows are everywhere, and the Crowgard find out about other parts of the city from them." Simon stopped.

Yes, Monty thought. *You've just told both of us why someone wants them dead.* "They see too much," he said quietly. "They pick through the trash, looking for the things that, to them, are little treasures. Which means they might find things the people buying, or selling, drugs like gone over wolf don't want anyone to find."

"They would notice a pattern of activity," Simon said.

He nodded. "But if you murder enough Crows, they'll stop poking through the trash—and secrets will remain secrets."

Simon didn't reply.

"Was there something you wanted to ask me?" Monty asked.

"Dr. Lorenzo. Do you trust him?"

The question took Monty by surprise. "I think he's a good man," he replied cautiously.

"He wants to study *cassandra sangue.* He wants to study Meg. That's why he agreed to supply human healing and medicine."

"I thought you wanted human healing and medicine available in the Courtyard," Monty countered.

Simon looked away.

The leader of a Courtyard looking away first? That couldn't be good. "Did something happen to Ms. Corbyn?"

"A scrape. A nothing sort of scrape that didn't really bleed. But it was enough." Now Simon looked at him. "If that's all it takes for her to see prophecy, why does she need to cut and take the risk of cutting too deep?"

"I don't know." But he was going to call on Dominic Lorenzo and find out. "What did Meg see?"

A hesitation. A reluctance that Monty could feel as a barrier between them.

"The humans who ran away from the damaged car. You know where to find them?" Simon asked.

He nodded. "Officers from that district of Lakeside are looking into it." He studied the Wolf. "What should they be looking for, Mr. Wolfgard?"

Another hesitation. Then, "Jars. Smoke in a jar. A hand . . . or something else."

Gods above and below. "Is anyone missing from the Courtyard?"

"No. Vlad was away from the Courtyard when Meg ... freaked ... even before she spoke prophecy." Simon pulled a folded piece of paper out of his pocket and handed it to Monty. "You might find these stories interesting. But you should be careful who else you tell about them."

The titles weren't familiar to him, but he'd read other books by a couple of the authors. "Do you have any of these books in stock?"

"Some."

The Others didn't admit to vulnerabilities. They didn't willingly share information that could be used against them. For Simon to be pointing him in a particular direction indicated the depth of the Wolf's concern.

"Is Lakeside going to survive whatever's coming?" he asked.

"I hope so," Simon replied. "But if humans declare war on the Sanguinati ..."

"I, and the rest of the Lakeside police force, will do everything we can to prevent that kind of conflict." Suppressing a shiver, Monty stood. "Thank you for your time. I'll go downstairs and pick up those books on my way out."

Monty set two bags of books on the patrol car's backseat. Then he got in and said to Kowalski, "Extra assignment. Pick half the books. I'll take the rest. For now, let's go to Lakeside Hospital. I'd like to catch Dr. Lorenzo before his shift starts."

Kowalski looked at the bags of books, then put the car in gear and drove out of the Courtyard. "If you need information in a hurry, Ruthie could read a third of the books."

"No. You don't need to keep the reading material a secret from her, but I think it's best if Ruth isn't involved in gathering this information."

"Gods below, Lieutenant, what kind of information are we looking for?"

"Anything in those stories about trapping or killing Sanguinati."

Kowalski didn't say anything else during the drive to the hospital.

Monty found Dr. Lorenzo easily enough and noted that the doctor didn't look pleased to see him.

"I'm not on retainer to the Lakeside Police Department," Lorenzo said. "And while I want to establish an office in the Market Square, I'm not on call twenty-four/seven for the Others."

"No, sir, you're not," Monty replied with his usual courtesy. "But you are the doctor who is looking for some inside access to the Courtyard—and a way to study a blood prophet."

Lorenzo bristled. "Is that a threat, Lieutenant? If I'm not available to answer questions whenever you drop by, you'll try to influence Wolfgard's decision about me having an office in the Courtyard?"

Monty shook his head. "The Others—and especially Simon Wolfgard—are still deciding if they're going to trust you. And unless they don't have a choice, they aren't likely to call you here. But I think they gave me some information knowing I would pass it on to you."

Now he had the doctor's attention.

"Did something happen to Meg Corbyn?" Lorenzo asked.

Monty repeated what Simon had told him about the scrape on Meg's ankle. It didn't give him any comfort when Lorenzo looked disturbed.

"Do they have cameras in the Courtyard? Or some kind of ability to make a record of that scrape that I can put in Ms. Corbyn's medical file?"

"It's just a scrape," Monty protested.

"On you and me it would be. But you said she saw things, spoke prophecy. That means that skin has been 'used.' There is speculation that cutting too close to a previous cut can cause mental or emotional complications, maybe even madness."

They looked at each other, remembering the crosshatch of scars on the upper part of Meg Corbyn's left arm.

Lorenzo sighed. "If that scrape wasn't deep enough to leave a scar, I want—and Simon Wolfgard should want—a record of what skin was scraped. It will be important to know, especially if another cut is made around the same area sometime in the future." He hesitated. "Have you heard the slogan Humans First and Last?"

"Doctor, if you're part of that movement, stay away from the Courtyard. For all our sakes."

"I'm not, no. But I was approached at a conference recently by someone who was fishing to see if I was interested in joining the ranks of believers. People talk, Lieutenant. Once it's known that I'm giving any kind of continued assistance to the Courtyard . . . there could be repercussions."

"There could be," Monty agreed. "Especially if people don't stop to realize that helping the Others may prevent minor conflicts from escalating into a war. If you get any odd phone calls or receive any threatening letters, you call me."

Lorenzo nodded. "If that's all, I need to start my shift."

When Monty returned to the patrol car, Kowalski gave him an odd look. "Turn on your mobile phone, Lieutenant. The investigating officers who are tracing the car that struck the city worker want to talk to you."

Monty walked into Captain Burke's office and sat in the visitor's chair without invitation.

Burke folded his hands, placed them on the desk blotter, and leaned forward. "You heard from the officers who were looking for the men driving that car?"

"They found the house . . . and two college boys still hopped up on whatever they had taken before they baited the street and waited for the Crows," Monty said, fighting the sick feeling that had come over him after taking that call. "When the officers searched the house, they found a hand in a jar, most likely pickled in some kind of brine. Supposedly it was a Sanguinati hand. They found eyes. The label claimed they were Wolf eyes, but they weren't amber or gray, so that's unlikely. When the boys were taken into custody, they kept screaming, 'We're going to be the Wolves now.'"

"Where did they get the hand and eyes?" Burke asked.

"An esoteric shop near the university. The front room had the kind of edgy merchandise you would expect to find where a lot of young people are gathered. But the back room . . ." Monty cleared his throat. "Since I could confirm that none of the residents of the Lakeside Courtyard are missing, it's assumed that what the investigating officers found in the back room was brought in from somewhere else. Probably from Toland." The city was a major port for ships that carried passengers and cargo to and from the Cel-Romano Alliance of Nations and other human ports around the world. Easy enough to hide one box of emotionally volatile merchandise among the legitimate cargo in the baggage car of a train traveling between Toland and Lakeside.

Burke sat back. "So the eyes might be human or animal but don't belong to any of our *terra indigene*."

"That's correct," Monty said.

"And the hand? Could it belong to a Sanguinati?"

"Not one from this Courtyard." He hesitated. "Ms. Corbyn had a vision this morning. About jars and hands . . . and the Sanguinati. Captain, if that merchandise came from Toland . . ." He thought of his daughter, Lizzy, living in the Big City with her mother, and fear suddenly made him light-headed.

"The Sanguinati are the dominant earth natives in the Toland Courtyard, backed by the Wolves and whatever else lives there. If any of *them* have gone missing . . ." Burke blew out a sigh. "This just gets better and better. All right, Lieutenant. You keep track of the investigation here. I'll see if I can find someone in the Toland Police Department who doesn't use his brains to wipe his backside." He gave Monty a fierce smile. "I didn't forget that you came from there, but you're not one of them anymore."

"Good to know." Monty pushed out of the chair. Then he stopped. "Should I tell Simon Wolfgard what was found at that house and in the shop?"

"If there were any birds around those places, he probably already knows, so a courtesy call would be prudent." Burke looked uncomfortable. "This isn't the best time for it, but I'd like you to arrange a meeting between me and Mr. Wolfgard at his convenience."

"Why?"

Burke took so long to answer, Monty wasn't sure he would. "I want to ask him for a favor."

CHAPTER 8

Steve Ferryman hustled to reach the passenger ferry before it cast off. He wasn't scheduled to work today, hadn't planned to do anything but watch a movie, do some laundry, and, later, walk over to the island's bookstore and indulge himself with a couple of new novels. But he'd looked out the window when he woke up and felt that familiar, and not always welcome, tightening between his shoulder blades—and had a feeling that he needed to be on the ferry when it made its first run of the day between Great Island and the dock at the mainland half of the village called Ferryman's Landing.

Several Crows huddled together on the deck, black feathers fluffed against the cold.

"Do you want to go inside the cabin?" Steve asked.

After a moment, one Crow shook its head.

"Let me know if you change your mind."

A quick look in the passenger cabin confirmed it was empty. Totally empty. Absolutely, completely empty with no trace that anyone had been in there that morning. Which meant his aunt, Lucinda Fish, wasn't planning to open the ferry's little coffee bar and he would have to do without his morning dose of caffeine.

Sighing, Steve went up to the wheelhouse to see his younger brother, Will, who was the captain today.

"Good morning, Yer Honor," Will said, tugging on his forelock. "I'm surprised to see you up and about so early on your sluggard day. Tell me, sir. Is this a personal trip, or are you traveling on government business?"

"Shut up," Steve muttered.

In looks they were night and day. Steve took after his father, Charles, with dark hair and eyes, sharp features, and a strong but wiry build. Will had the blond hair and blue eyes that he'd inherited from their mother, Rachel, along with the slender grace that was common to all the members of the Fish clan.

"Is that any way to speak to one of your constituents?" Will asked.

"You didn't vote for me," Steve said. "And couldn't, since you're not on the village council."

"And wouldn't have even if I could have, since I know how much you wanted the job," Will replied cheerfully. "Which is not at all."

When it comes to being selected for a thankless job, the man who leaves the room just before the vote is the fool who gets the job, his father often said.

Which was how, by leaving the room to relieve his bladder because he'd thought the council was going to jabber on a while longer, Steve Ferryman had found himself voted in as the new mayor of Ferryman's Landing at the tender age of thirty. The council members must have called for the vote the moment the restroom door closed behind him.

We had a feeling you're what the village needs right now, they'd told him when he tried to decline.

When someone in Ferryman's Landing had a feeling, you paid attention. The Intuits had survived and prospered well enough because they paid attention when someone had a feeling.

He hadn't wanted to be mayor, even if it wasn't a demanding job in a small village like this one. He was a ferryman by birth and by trade, and he'd rather be on the water than anywhere else. But now he was in charge of the island's human government, for better or worse.

"Guess it's good you're not at the wheel today," Will said. "You haven't heard a thing I've said in the past couple of minutes."

"Give me a break," Steve growled. "I barely had time for a shower. Had to give up my morning coffee to get here."

Will gave him an odd look. "Some reason you needed to get here?"

"I had a feeling."

Will said nothing for a moment. Then, "I guess Aunt Lu had a feeling too.

You didn't hear me when I said she brought over an extra thermos of coffee and you're welcome to have some."

Steve spotted the thermos, and just the sight of it had his brain cells firing up enough to create real thoughts.

"May the river bless Aunt Lu," he said, filling a mug. "You want some?"

"I want."

Steve filled another mug and brought it over to his brother. Then he sighed. "Clear skies. Light winds."

"Yep. Going to be a pretty day," Will said. "Why do you sound disappointed?"

"I'm not disappointed. I just . . ." It was still there—that tightness between his shoulder blades was his personal warning sign that he needed to pay attention to *something*. "It feels like a storm is coming."

"Dad didn't say anything." Will studied the sky and then the river. "Neither did Mom or Aunt Lu."

"These feelings aren't always right."

"Yours aren't usually wrong."

No, he wasn't usually wrong. At least, not when it came to the river and the weather. Intuits didn't get feelings about everything, just the things that mattered to them as individuals. So his family had more knowing about water and weather while families like Sledgeman and Liveryman knew about freight and livestock, respectively.

The crossing was uneventful. As soon as the ferry docked, the Crows flew off, splitting up into a handful of small groups that headed in different directions. They would spend the day observing everything and everyone within range, then return in time for a ride back to the island.

After helping Will secure the ferry, Steve headed up to the main street as the mail truck drove down to the dock. Sacks of mail would be offloaded and mail for the island's residents would be loaded. Not many passengers at this time of year—and the fee charged for passage helped discourage tourists.

Clear skies, light winds. Nothing to worry about. Even so, Steve kept looking back at the river.

What was he doing on the mainland side of the village? It was his day off. He could browse in the bookstore over here to pass the time until the ferry made the return trip, but the store on the island carried the same selection. In fact, since the Others purchased books from the island's bookstore, it carried novels by *terra indigene* authors that weren't available in mainland stores that might attract tourists who were visiting the area.

But a book didn't explain the urgency to be on the ferry this morning.

Then he saw Jerry Sledgeman coming out of the drugstore holding a newspaper.

"Jerry!" he called.

Jerry stopped and raised a hand in greeting. "What are you doing here today?"

Jerry was a decade older and had a wife and teenage daughter, as well as two young sons. Despite the difference in years and circumstance, they were friends.

"I'm not sure." Steve looked toward the river. "I just can't shake the feeling that there's a storm coming."

When Steve turned back to look at him, Jerry held out the newspaper and pointed to a story in the *Lakeside News*. Something about birds being run over and a city worker being struck by one of the vehicles.

Not just any kind of birds, Steve realized as he continued reading. Crows. Someone had baited a street and waited for the Crowgard to show up, but only ordinary crows were killed.

Jerry waited for him to finish reading, then said, "Now that you're the mayor, maybe you're developing feelings for a different kind of storm."

Late Sunday morning, Mr. Smith led his first client of the day to the interview room where Daisy waited for them. Unlike some of his associates, he preferred naming his girls rather than assigning them sterile designations. True, designations created a distance between the girls and their handlers, and it reminded the clients that the girls weren't human in the same way *they* were human, making it easier for many clients to justify watching a girl bleed in order for them to receive a prophecy.

He, on the other hand, preferred a softer approach. And clients who wanted the special—and very lucrative—service he sometimes offered afterward found it more satisfying when they could whisper a name while enjoying the thrill of having the commonplace elevated to the exotic. The girls weren't good sex partners. They were too stoned on their own euphoria to even remember if they'd had a penis inside them. But having sex with a blood prophet provided entrée into some social circles. After all, it took more than money to persuade someone like Mr. Smith to grant a client that extra time with a girl. It took ambition and the potential to become a mover and shaker in the highest of human circles.

The client who was about to face Daisy might be such a man. And depending on what the girl said, he might agree that the girl would enjoy a private session since the client had indicated a desire for the experience.

After seating the client in the chair directly in front of the girl, Mr. Smith sat in the chair a little to the side where he could watch client and prophet. The girl was draped with a blanket from neck to knees. Under that blanket she wore nothing but a G-string made of thin material that wouldn't hide the juice brought on by the euphoria.

"Daisy," Mr. Smith said quietly. "This man is running for the office of mayor in his city. He wants to know if using the Humans First and Last platform will help him win. What will the election bring?"

He repeated the same words over and over while the handlers removed the blanket. He'd already had a good idea what this client would ask and had already chosen the skin. A cut along the left side of the belly. The blood trickling from the cut would keep drawing the eyes to the G-string and add another layer of desire for the extra service.

"What will the election bring?" he asked as the handler finished the cut.

Daisy stared at the client, her face filled with the agony that came before the first words of the prophecy were spoken, releasing the addictive euphoria. Their need for that feeling was the reason *cassandra sangue* would cut themselves two or three times a day if they weren't monitored and cut on a schedule.

"Tornado," Daisy said, staring at the client. "Buildings with broken windows. Flowers growing through cracks in pavement. Vines climbing up walls. His face on a piece of paper, and the word 'elect' above the face. Paper blowing down an empty street."

Closing her eyes, she moaned and tipped her pelvis up in invitation as the prophecy ended.

"What does that mean?" the client stammered. "What do any of those images have to do with the election or my chance of winning?"

Hopefully nothing, Mr. Smith thought. "It appears Daisy is experiencing some kind of upset and is unable to offer an accurate prophecy." He rose. Taking a firm grip on the client's arm, he escorted the man out of the room.

"What about my prophecy?" the client demanded. "I paid—"

"You will not be charged for today's session," Mr. Smith interrupted. "We'll make an appointment for you next week with another girl."

"Next week? But I have to make a decision before then!"

Mr. Smith stopped and looked the man in the eyes. "None of my girls are available until next week." Meaning, come back then or find another establishment. Not as easy to do as it sounded. All the men who took care of *cassandra sangue* and sold the girls' abilities recognized the need for some secrecy.

After handing over the client to one of the staff who would escort the man off the grounds, Mr. Smith returned to the interview room and studied Daisy. Her eyes were still glazed, but the euphoria had faded and she was starting to come around.

"Do you want her exercised?" one of the handlers asked.

"No," Mr. Smith said. "Give her some water and a bite to eat, then let her sleep it off."

An hour later, Mr. Smith sat in another interview room with the representative of a farming association that supplied food for several cities in the Midwest Region of Thaisia—an association that wanted to fiddle the books and claim a shortage in order to quietly sell grains to Cel-Romano.

He'd chosen Peaches for this cut. She was the most receptive girl he had for farming prophecies.

"What will grow best on our land this year?" the representative said. "What crops will do well?"

Mr. Smith repeated the questions as the handler made a cut above one of Peaches's ripe breasts.

"Fire." She sighed out the word. "Fire eats and eats. Water swallows. Plate clean. Food all gone."

Mr. Smith walked to his office and closed the door. Then, giving in to the fear that had shuddered through him, he leaned his forehead against the door and closed his eyes. His handlers were experienced professionals and knew the girls. It was possible that they missed some sign that Daisy shouldn't have been put on the roster today, but Daisy *and* Peaches speaking prophecies that had nothing to do with the questions?

Nothing wrong with my girls, Mr. Smith thought. *And that means what they saw did, in fact, answer the questions.*

A city's destruction caused by an election. Fire and flood the only crops a Midwest farming association would harvest this year.

The girls could be wrong. A different decision, a different choice, and what Daisy and Peaches saw today wouldn't happen.

But the people whose choices might make that difference probably were not on his client list. As much as he wanted to believe his movers and shakers were important men and women, they were only big fish in the small pond known as the Midwest Region.

If he wanted to understand why his girls' prophecies were filled with so many images of destruction, he was going to have to seek advice from someone whose client list was more . . . expansive.

He loathed that bastard, but he didn't know who else to call.

Mr. Smith poured himself a stiff drink, then sat at his desk and placed a call to the man known as the Controller.

CHAPTER 9

Meg pulled up in front of the Pony Barn. No Crows or Hawks or Owls around to report that she'd been there. And there was no reason for her to be there—no extra mail or packages to deliver. In fact, she'd ended up here because there was nothing else to deliver but she didn't want to go home yet.

Usually she had the Quiet Mind class on Windsday evening and spent time with Merri Lee, Ruth, and Heather. But *all* the stores were closing at five p.m. because of some special meeting, and Simon had told her not to come back to the Market Square area after she closed the office for the day. Well, now that they were friends again, he *had* made an effort to sound as if he were *asking* her to stay away.

Of course, the word *please* sounded very different when it was snarled. But that was Simon, and friends accepted friends for who they were. She'd read that in a magazine recently.

Ask or order, it amounted to the same thing: the Courtyard's business area was closed to everyone but the members of the Business Association and whoever else was attending the meeting. Even the efficiency apartments were off-limits tonight. Clearly the Others wanted this meeting to remain *private*.

So no Quiet Mind class, no friends, and no one but her at the Green Complex until this meeting was over and the Others returned to their apartments.

She hadn't been alone at the Green Complex since the night men came into the Courtyard and tried to capture her and Sam.

Training images. Empty house with a door hanging off its hinges. Broken windows. Debris blown into the corners of rooms.

Meg shook her head. She wasn't abandoned. Being alone wouldn't precipitate an attack. Would it?

Easy enough to get an answer. One cut to reassure herself that she would be safe until Simon and the rest of the Green's residents came home. Just a small cut.

She looked at how her hands shook as she gripped the steeling wheel. When she was in the hospital, Dr. Lorenzo had said something about post-traumatic stress reactions, but she hadn't paid attention and couldn't recall his words.

Didn't matter if she remembered the words or not. She had enough sense not to open the razor when her hands weren't steady and there wouldn't be anyone around to help her if something went wrong when she cut.

But I can't dither around here all afternoon, she thought. And then, *Too late.*

Jester Coyotegard walked out of the barn and up to the driver's side of the BOW.

"I wasn't expecting a delivery," Jester said, delicately sniffing the air when she rolled down the window to talk to him.

"I don't have one for you," Meg admitted.

A waiting pause. "Something wrong with the BOW?"

"No." She knew that *he* knew there wasn't anything wrong with her Box on Wheels. If there had been, she would have gotten out to ask for help. "It's embarrassing."

"In that case, tell me everything."

He looked so gleeful, she had to laugh. But the amusement faded quickly. "No one else will be home until that meeting is over, and I'm . . . nervous . . . about being in the Green Complex by myself." Darn Coyote must have picked that up with his first sniff and had been playing with her until he found out why she felt nervous. "I can't really visit Sam at the Wolfgard Complex, and I didn't want him to be away from the adult Wolves if something is going on. . . ."

Jester just studied her. If he knew what the meeting was about, he wasn't sharing.

"Have you ever seen the inside of a barn?" he asked.

"Pictures."

He opened the BOW's door and rolled up the window. "Come inside and see the real thing."

If she stayed with Jester and the ponies, she wouldn't be alone.

She shut off the BOW and followed the Coyote.

"You can meet our newest resident if he decides to show himself," Jester said as they reached the barn door. "He hasn't been up to the Liaison's Office yet with the other ponies, so you wouldn't have seen him there. It's unusual for one of his line to be assigned to the Great Lakes area, especially one so young, but the Elementals wanted him here. I have to say, he's settling in remarkably well."

The night of the attack, men had set fire to the Pony Barn and shot old Hurricane while he was in pony form. The Others fixed the Pony Barn before they made any repairs to the other buildings and fences that were damaged during the attack. While the residents of Lakeside had struggled to make repairs to their own buildings in bitingly cold weather, the area around the Pony Barn had enjoyed Spring's delicate touch, making it easier for the workers.

Despite its name, the building fit images of a stable more than a building typically identified as a barn. As she looked around, Meg absorbed what she saw as a connected memory—like a video clip rather than a series of isolated pictures laid out in order. Many of the stalls were empty because the ponies were out in the Courtyard doing whatever ponies did. After looking her fill, she sat on a bale of hay and watched Jester groom Fog. Then she helped him groom Cyclone, enjoying the tactile experience as much as the pony seemed to enjoy it.

And then a white pony stepped out of the last stall, and Meg felt a tingle run under her skin from the soles of her feet to the top of her head. The feeling faded quickly. Almost too quickly, since she stood there and watched him try, and not quite succeed, to match the furry-barrel-with-chubby-legs look of the other ponies. Like a Wolf who couldn't quite hide that he wasn't human, this steed couldn't quite hide the fact that he wasn't really a pony.

Aquamarine, Meg thought, identifying the bluish green of the newcomer's mane and tail. Not a color seen on an ordinary pony.

"Meg," Jester said. "This is Whirlpool."

At 5:15 p.m. on Windsday, Captain Burke turned his black sedan into the Courtyard's Main Street entrance.

"Mr. Wolfgard said to park behind the Liaison's Office," Monty said. He'd made the call and asked for this meeting, but he hadn't expected Simon to agree, especially since he couldn't tell the Wolf why Burke wanted to meet. Which meant the leader of the Lakeside Courtyard had his own reasons for wanting to meet with a police captain.

"I thought we were meeting in the consulate," Burke said as he parked the car. "We are."

"They want the car out of sight?" Burke kept scanning the backs of the buildings, especially the doors and windows.

"More likely, they want it out of the way. But I think the Business Association uses parking as a way to indicate trust."

"Does this mean we're trusted, Lieutenant?"

"Yes, sir, I think it does." *Up to a point,* he added silently.

They walked back up the access way to the consulate. As they waited for someone to answer the door, Monty studied the Liaison's Office. Already closed, with only a dim overnight light in the front room. Too bad Meg Corbyn was gone for the day. He would have liked a chance to check up on her, make sure she'd recovered from the prophecies she'd seen on Moonsday.

The consulate's door opened. Blair Wolfgard stared at them. He wore a mechanic's jumpsuit, which seemed to be his preferred attire when in human form. Behind Blair was a man with thinning hair and the amber eyes of a Wolf. *He* wore a hand-tailored suit of a cut and quality that said "money."

Had to be Elliot Wolfgard. Monty imagined it was unsettling for government officials to realize a Wolf understood human symbols of power and knew how to send an intimidating message before the first word was spoken.

"You can hang up your coats and leave your boots over there," Elliot said, gesturing toward the coat tree and the mat beneath. After they'd dealt with their outer gear, he led them to a meeting room that could have been the boardroom of a major corporation. Big room. Big table. Two big windows covered with wooden blinds.

And three *terra indigene* standing on one side of the table: Simon Wolfgard, Henry Beargard, and Vladimir Sanguinati.

Elliot stepped out of the room and closed the door. Monty wondered if Tess had chosen not to attend this meeting or wasn't invited. Either way, he figured Burke now had confirmation of who gave the orders here in Lakeside.

"I appreciate you seeing me," Burke said.

Simon pulled out a chair and sat down, a signal that the meeting had begun. "Have you found the men who tried to kill the Crows?"

After a moment's hesitation, Burke sat in the chair opposite Simon. Monty sat beside Burke, across from Vlad. Even with the table between them, he wasn't comfortable being that close to the vampire—not when he could still remember the prickling sensation he'd felt when he'd shaken Vlad's hand. That was how he discovered that the Sanguinati could feed by drawing blood through a person's skin.

Henry Beargard sat on the other side of Simon, his chair slightly pushed back from the table and angled in a way that made Monty think he was there as an observer rather than a participant.

"We found two of them," Burke said. "And we found some things in their house that we're investigating."

"Things?" Vlad asked.

"In jars?" Simon asked, staring at Monty.

"Yes, in jars," Monty replied. He kept his eyes on Simon, but he could see Vlad's right hand close into a fist. This wasn't the right time to ask if a severed hand could be dangerous. The novels he and Kowalski had skimmed over the past couple of days made it sound like a body part could survive separation for a long time if the rest of the vampire still lived, but there was no way of knowing if the fiction had been based on any facts. The lab techs were understandably reluctant to open the jars in order to test if the hand or eyes had belonged to a human or one of the *terra indigene* until someone *did* have some facts.

"I don't think the captain is here to talk about the investigation," Henry said, his voice a quiet rumble.

"I'm not here about the investigation," Burke agreed. He linked his fingers and rested his hands on the table. "The son of a good friend of mine was injured in Jerzy last month. Roger was one of the police officers who answered the Crows' call for help. He was shot by the humans who started the attack, but he survived."

Simon said nothing. Monty wished Burke had given him some idea of where this was going.

"Roger is a good police officer, and he's a good man," Burke said. "He'll be ready to return to duty soon, but indications are that it would be prudent for him to relocate."

Simon cocked his head. "Why?"

Vlad gave Burke a chilling smile. "The monkeys blame him, don't they? They think he should have let the Crows in that house die."

Burke barely twitched in response, but Monty didn't doubt the Others saw that twitch.

"Not all the survivors in Jerzy think that Roger is to blame for the fight that came afterward, but enough of them do," Burke replied. "They want to blame someone. Right now, Roger needs to be someplace where the people he's trying to protect don't call him a traitor."

"What do you think would have happened if this Roger had let the Crows die?" Henry asked.

Burke looked the Grizzly in the eyes. "I think if he and the other officers hadn't responded to that call for help, there wouldn't have been any survivors in Jerzy."

Henry dipped his head, an acknowledgment of that truth. "Yes. Those humans are still alive because of him."

"At least for another week or two," Vlad added.

Monty stiffened. "What does that mean?"

Simon ignored the question and focused on Burke. "So you want your friend's pup to relocate to Lakeside?" He shrugged. "You don't need our consent. That's human business."

Now Burke looked uncomfortable. "Roger prefers living in a village—and working for a smaller police force."

Puzzled looks.

"What are you asking us?" Simon finally said.

"I'm asking if you could find a place for Roger on Great Island," Burke said. "I know the island is controlled by the *terra indigene,* but there is a community of Simple Life folks living there, as well as the humans who run the ferry and manage the shops and services on the southern end of the island. I don't know what arrangements Great Island already has, but surely enough humans live on the island to warrant an official police officer or two."

Monty tensed as silence filled the room.

Finally, Henry said, "There is no police force on Great Island. Not like there is in Lakeside. The Intuits who live in Ferryman's Landing aren't the same kind of humans as the Simple Life folk. Or you."

Burke studied the three *terra indigene.* "I've never heard of a race of humans called Intuits."

Henry studied Burke. "In Thaisia, that is what they call themselves. They may have different names in other parts of the world. They are the humans who have a sense of the world the rest of you lack, an ability to feel what is around them and recognize danger or opportunity before it is obvious. They were often killed because other humans believed such an ability must be evil. Even now, they keep to themselves and feel safer living in a human settlement controlled by the *terra indigene* than they do living in a city controlled by your kind." He smiled in a way that seemed a threat. "It would be better if you didn't remember hearing about them."

After a moment, Burke nodded to indicate he understood.

"Letting another human live on Great Island isn't my decision," Simon said. "I don't know if the Intuits at Ferryman's Landing will welcome a human who isn't one of their own. But I will talk to the village leaders about your friend's pup, and they can decide."

"Thank you."

And now a police captain is in debt to the leader of the Courtyard, Monty thought. *Because Simon will make sure Roger is allowed to live on Great Island.* He just hoped that when Wolfgard called in the favor owed, Burke wouldn't choke on it.

"It's for the best this Roger doesn't want to live in Jerzy anymore," Simon said, his tone a little too offhand. "It won't be a human place much longer."

Monty looked at Burke, who held perfectly still. Then he looked at Simon. *This is why he agreed to meet with us. To deliver this message.*

"The lease on the Jerzy farmland expires at the end of next month," Simon said. "The West Coast leaders have decided the lease will not be renewed, and the land will come back to the *terra indigene*. The hamlet's land lease expires at the same time. It, too, will not be renewed."

Burke sucked in a breath but said nothing.

How many people lived in Jerzy? Monty thought. *A few hundred? More? Less?* Stunned, he spoke without thinking. "You're going to evict an entire town? Just like that?"

"Yes, Lieutenant," Simon replied. "Just like that. We may allow you to build on it and use what comes from it, but the land isn't yours. Will never be yours. Humans broke trust with the *terra indigene* who watched over Jerzy. So one way or another, the humans must go."

"But those farms provide food for cities on the West Coast. What are the people in those cities supposed to do for food?"

"Humans can grow food on the farmland they still lease," Simon said, shrugging.

"But . . ."

"Lieutenant," Burke said quietly, a warning that arguing about a decision that was already made on the other side of the continent could be costly to their own city, as well as dangerous to themselves.

As Monty regained control, he caught Vlad looking at him.

The vampire smiled and said, "How will the strong survive?"

Shivering, he looked away, scared sick by the reminder. Vlad had asked him once if stronger humans would justify eating the weak if other food wasn't available. It wouldn't come to that, but he suspected a lot more people all across Thaisia would be trying to grow a little kitchen garden this summer. There had been lean times before. It looked like there would be lean times again. Even now, you needed a ration book for a lot of foodstuffs, like butter and eggs.

"Where are the people in Jerzy supposed to go?" Burke asked, sounding mildly interested. "How are they supposed to transport livestock? *Will* they be allowed to transport livestock?"

"They can take the animals," Simon replied. "They can take whatever was made by humans. But they should take care during their migration. If land or water gets poisoned, if one of the gas stations should explode, if houses should catch fire as people are leaving . . ."

"I understand." Burke's knuckles were white. "What if the people refuse to leave? Some of those families have lived on the farms or in that hamlet for generations."

"Then they should have known what would happen when they attacked the Crows," Simon snarled.

"Where are those people supposed to go?" Monty asked, echoing Burke's question.

"The *terra indigene* leaders on the West Coast and in the Northwest are very angry," Henry said. "They don't care where the Jerzy humans go."

"There is growing unrest in parts of Thaisia, as well as some other places in the world. Evicting the population of an entire hamlet will lend fuel to the Humans First and Last movement," Burke said.

Simon linked his fingers, placed his folded hands on the table, and leaned forward—an exact mirror of Burke's position.

"Namid did not make you from the earth and water of Thaisia. You came to this land from Afrikah and Cel-Romano and Tokhar-Chin and Felidae and the other places where the world made your kind. What you do in your pieces of the world is your concern—until what you do touches us and what is ours. But here? How much of Thaisia we share with you is *our* choice. We learn from other predators. We always have. We've learned enough from you that the *terra indigene* in Thaisia don't need you anymore. You shouldn't forget that."

Burke's face was white, but his voice remained steady. "I didn't come here to fight, Mr. Wolfgard."

Simon sat back and unlinked his fingers. "Nor did I."

Monty stared at Simon's hands. Had he actually seen the fingers resume a more human shape?

No one spoke. Then Vlad stirred. "Did you know that the islands that comprise the western Storm Islands used to be a single body of land that linked Thaisia to Felidae?"

"No, I didn't know that," Monty said. "What happened to it?"

"The humans who lived there began a war with the *terra indigene*. They had been given part of that land as a human cradle. They wanted it all. Now they have less. And every year, the storms sweep in and remind them of why they have less."

"Warn your friend," Simon said, watching Burke. "Jerzy isn't the first human place that was reclaimed by the *terra indigene*. It won't be the last. If humans on the West Coast try to stir up more trouble, your friend might want to find another place to live." He hesitated, then added, "There's nothing I can do about the West Coast. But I would like Lakeside to survive whatever is coming."

"You think there's going to be a fight?" Burke asked.

"Don't you?"

"Not today." Burke pushed his chair back and stood. "And not here. I thank you all for your time."

Monty rose and hoped his legs held. The Others also rose.

"Tell this Roger to travel to Lakeside as soon as he can," Simon said.

Burke nodded and walked out of the room.

Monty hesitated. "Has Ms. Corbyn recovered from Moonsday?"

Simon grunted. Vlad laughed. Henry said, "She is fine. Tomorrow she and the other girls will attend the Quiet Mind class that was canceled this evening."

"How can anything be quiet with the way those females chatter?" Simon grumbled.

The anger and tension that had been in the room had been shaken off by the Others, like water shaken off fur.

Not their fight, Monty thought. *Not yet.* The Others weren't going to forget about the men who had tried to kill the Crows. They had known—or Meg had known—about the body parts in jars, and they weren't going to forget that either.

He bid the Others a good evening and joined Burke. Quickly donning their overcoats and boots, the two men hurried to the car. Relieved that the windows were clear of snow, Monty got in and waited for Burke to start the car. But Burke put the key in the ignition and then just stared out the window.

"Your opinion, Lieutenant?"

"Sir?"

"If the word 'Intuits' was suddenly being bandied about, for whatever reason, what do you think would happen?"

Monty thought for a moment, selecting his words carefully. "I think a freak tornado would appear soon afterward and destroy the Chestnut Street Police Station and everyone inside."

Burke started the car. "Yeah. That's what I think too."

Vlad left the consulate minutes after Burke and Montgomery drove away from the Courtyard. He claimed he was going back to Howling Good Reads to make sure the store was closed up properly. Simon thought it was more likely that Vlad wanted to claim a couple of the new thrillers before putting the rest of the copies on display tomorrow.

Simon, on the other hand, made no move to leave the meeting room. He had still been chewing on the information that had come from the West Coast when he walked into this meeting. Now he studied Henry. "Why did you tell the police about the Intuits? They hide among the *terra indigene* to escape from the humans who hate them."

Henry nodded. "Long ago, they were hated for their abilities. It would be good to know if they still are."

He thought about that. "The West Coast leaders are going to offer the Jerzy land to the Intuits?"

Henry nodded. "It benefits both sides to have some humans living in Jerzy. Some Intuits from several settlements wanted a chance to relocate, and the *terra indigene* agreed to let them try running the businesses and dealing with the other kind of humans who would pass through the hamlet. They won't be hidden in the same way as the settlements located deep in the wild country, but the Intuits on Great Island have successfully hidden in plain sight for many generations."

The Intuits might be human, but their instincts were, in some ways, closer to those of the *terra indigene*. And their ability to sense things before something happened? How did that compare with Meg's ability to speak prophecy? "I wonder if the Intuits know anything about *cassandra sangue*."

"When you escort this Roger to Great Island, you should ask them."

CHAPTER 10

"Phineas Jones is here to see you."

The Controller gathered up the papers on his desk, put them in a folder, and put the folder in the bottom desk drawer before he said, "Send him in."

Phineas Jones was a short man with sandy hair, faded blue eyes, and a sweet smile. He wore an off-the-rack suit with a waistcoat that was a little tight over his rounded belly and one of the bow ties that were his trademark. He looked like he belonged in a sepia print, a photograph of someone who lived a few generations ago. And that was one of his major assets: Phineas Jones looked quaint and harmless. His abilities as a mesmerizer made him the most successful procurer of blood prophets in all of Thaisia.

For more than twenty years, Jones had talked parents into giving up a troubled girl for her own good, and by the time the family realized the contact information they had was bogus and they had no idea where their daughter had gone, Jones had packed up and moved on. And the girl ended up in a compound in some other part of Thaisia.

Even if a family wasn't willing to give up a child, Jones sold the information about the family's location and habits, making a straightforward abduction that much easier.

The Controller didn't like Jones and certainly didn't trust him. But they'd done business on occasion. After all, families who carried the *cassandra sangue* bloodline could be difficult to ferret out—until the girl began cutting and called too much attention to herself.

"I was surprised to hear from you," Jones said as he settled in the visitor's chair. "It's my understanding that you've been running a successful breeding program and would have little use for my services."

"Even the best breeding program benefits from new stock now and then," the Controller replied.

"Is that what you're looking for? New stock? Or perhaps a reacquisition of previously owned property?"

So Jones had heard about *cs759*'s escape and the failure to reacquire her. "New stock. Doesn't have to be prime grade."

"My, my. That wasn't what I expected. Several other gentlemen are looking to acquire new stock. It seems a number of girls have become unreliable all of a sudden. But those men are all looking for the best that's out there."

"I already have the best," the Controller replied. "What I'm looking for is variety."

Jones thought for a moment. "I think I'll poke about in the eastern part of Thaisia. Haven't been there in a while. I've made some excellent finds in some of the sleepy hamlets in the Southeast Region." Then he smiled that sweet smile. "Although with spring so close, the Northeast will be coming into bloom. And I recall there was an incident near Lake Etu last summer. Something about a girl drowning in the river?" He gave the Controller an expectant look.

"I don't recall hearing anything."

"Could be nothing. Accidental drownings happen all the time."

Of course, if it hadn't been an accident, if the girl had jumped into the river to escape the visions she didn't understand . . . Families that had blood prophets either hid among normal humans in solitary fear or gathered together. So a blood prophet in one family could lead to other girls living in the same area who were also *cassandra sangue*.

"Fine," the Controller said. "Go east. See what you can find. I assume you're splitting your expenses among all your potential buyers?"

"For the most part," Jones replied. "Expenses for obtaining a particular girl for a private acquisition would be paid by the buyer."

"Of course." He considered a moment. "Some trouble will be stirring around Lake Etu. Just something to be aware of when you're traveling."

"Trouble tends to stir the pot and bring what is hidden to the surface." Jones stood and tugged his jacket into place. "Well. I must be off. I'll call you when I have a potential delivery."

The Controller watched the man leave the office. He had sent trained fighters to the Lakeside Courtyard to reacquire Meg Corbyn. They had failed. More than failed. Perhaps Phineas Jones's quaint looks and mesmeric abilities could do what guns and explosives could not.

Jean pulled the broken needle out of the seam of her slipper. It wasn't much to work with, but she'd taken it while the Walking Names were distracted by another girl having a fit of hysterics.

No water in the girls' cells. Nothing but a bedpan if a girl couldn't wait for her turn to be taken to the toilet. And with the Walking Names preoccupied by what might be happening outside the compound, they weren't following the schedule as diligently as usual, especially now that some of the girls had seen things so terrible even the euphoria hadn't shielded them completely from the horror.

She knew about terrible things and horror. The wounds that were inflicted on her to harvest her blood produced visions too. But they gagged her because they wanted her pain, so she saw the terrible without anything to shield her mind.

She didn't know if she was halfway crazy or all the way crazy now. Her mind worked. What she overheard, she understood, and she overheard plenty because the Walking Names no longer paid attention to her presence and talked about the other girls they had to deal with—girls who were breaking down mentally because of what they had seen.

Girls talked about cities in ruins, about fields burning, about people killing each other for the last bags of food in a store, about corpses damming a stream that provided the drinking water for a village. They talked about glass jars full of smoke, and a community swimming pool full of severed heads. For the past few days, it didn't matter what the client asked about, whether it was business or politics or the best time to plant crops. The questions didn't matter because *all* the girls were seeing things too terrible to forget.

She'd seen those things too, but the streets and buildings she saw didn't match any of the training images for cities or towns in Thaisia, and the street signs were in a language she didn't recognize.

The Controller and other men like him had set something in motion. They thought prophecies would help them control the world and everything in it. They hadn't considered that they wouldn't be able to control how people felt.

The Others weren't anything close to human, but they had feelings too. They had lots of feelings.

Jean wet a spot on her nightie's hem, then rubbed the needle clean as best she could. Pricking the skin deep enough to draw blood wouldn't give her enough, but a scratch made by a needle would draw attention because the Walking Names would know it wasn't caused by a razor or a beating.

There was one place they wouldn't think to look.

Hooking the side of her mouth with one finger, she put the needle in her mouth and dragged the point along the lower left-hand side of her gum. As the blood welled up, she wiped off the needle and carefully put it back in the slipper, fighting against the building pain and the need to speak. As long as she didn't speak, she would remember the visions, remember the prophecy. But without spoken words, there would be terrible pain instead of the euphoria.

The Walking Names. The ones who touched me today. What is going to happen to them?

She swallowed the blood and the pain . . . and saw the first visions of the prophecy.

Too much. Too terrible.

She grabbed her pillow and covered her face. Then she whispered, describing the images to no one. Euphoria rolled through her body as she spoke, replacing the pain and clouding the images as she described them.

When the prophecy ended, Jean lowered the pillow.

What she'd seen. It was coming here. Maybe not all of it, but enough.

Shivering, she lay down on her narrow bed and pulled up the covers.

She tried not to think about how the Walking Names were going to look one day. Instead she focused on the last image that came to her as the prophecy ended. She had stopped speaking out loud by then, so this image was clear in her memory.

For the rest of the afternoon, she pondered the significance of seeing her own hand holding a jar of honey.

CHAPTER 11

On Earthday morning, Monty left the Universal Temple and walked down Market Street toward home. As he did every Earthday, he stopped at Nadine's Bakery & Café and picked up enough food for the day. Kowalski had invited him over for the midday meal, and he intended to go, but if something came up and he couldn't make it, he wanted a bit of fresh food in the house.

Besides, stopping at Nadine's was a way to feel connected to the people in his neighborhood and hear the gossip on the street.

On Windsday evening, he and Captain Burke were the only people in Lakeside who knew the residents of Jerzy were going to be evicted. By Thaisday, the television news was broadcasting the *terra indigene*'s decision coast to coast. On Firesday, Lakeside radio talk shows were full of outrage that humans could be thrown out of their homes, and did Elliot Wolfgard want to comment.

Elliot Wolfgard's only comment was that, like anyone who rented property to a tenant, the *terra indigene* were within their rights to refuse to renew a lease if the tenants proved themselves to be unsuitable. That caused enough histrionics that Captain Burke put all his men on standby in case a mob formed to move against the Courtyard.

His concern proved unnecessary. As soon as the sun went down on Firesday evening, a storm swept through the city. High winds and sleet encouraged everyone to stay home. Lightning struck with such precision that it *almost* took out all the radio and television stations. The next day there was no mention on the TV news of anything happening outside the Northeast Region of Thaisia, and all radio talk shows were replaced with music.

Warning given. Warning heeded.

So today at the temple and on the street where he'd become a familiar face, several people watched him because they knew he was a policeman, but no one approached and asked him the question that was on everyone's mind: if provoked, would the Others really evict the two hundred thousand people living in Lakeside?

No one had asked the question. Probably because everyone already knew the answer—and feared it.

He left Nadine's with a beef potpie, a container of soup, and a small braid of bread—the kind of food his ex-lover Elayne used to call Bulky Belly. The food probably would put on some bulk, but he craved some physical comfort.

The *terra indigene*'s decision was final, and there was nothing the human government in the West Coast Region could do. One way or another, the humans in Jerzy would be gone by the end of the month.

Monty entered his apartment, toed off his boots, then put the food away before taking off his overcoat. While waiting for his order, he'd overheard two men talking about how rent on apartments all along the West Coast and Northwest had doubled in the past few days. That confirmed what Captain Burke had heard through the police grapevine.

As he hung up his coat, Monty felt grateful to have a one-bedroom apartment with its own bathroom that he didn't have to share with anyone.

Plans for new multistory apartment buildings were being tabled in many cities where government officials suddenly had to consider if the land should be used for farming or grazing in order to feed the people already within the city limits. Efforts to lease more land from the *terra indigene* for new farms or towns had been unsuccessful. And, according to Captain Burke, negotiations to drill new oil wells and gas wells had ended abruptly the day after the attack in Jerzy. So there was no new land for food and no new sources of fuel to heat the houses or supply energy for industries.

Most likely, the small human settlements within the vast tracts of wild country controlled by the Others were Intuit villages. Most people didn't know the particulars about the inhabitants of those settlements, but there was plenty of talk about the places themselves. While not as technology deficient as Simple

Life communities, they weren't *civilized* places to live because they were completely controlled by the *terra indigene*. No human government whatsoever to speak for the human population!

The last new human-controlled village had been built more than a hundred years ago. The Others hadn't given up a single acre of land to humans since then. And now, Monty suspected, angered by the events in Jerzy and the drugs that were harming their own, the *terra indigene* would pounce on every excuse to rid Thaisia of the two-legged pests. Unfortunately, the human-controlled parts of the world that had the same level of technology as the larger Thaisian cities could barely support their own people and had no surplus for outsiders.

Sighing, Monty quickly scanned the *Lakeside News*. The home section had started a series of articles about tub gardens and raised beds for vegetables. He took it as confirmation that, at least for the coming summer, food that couldn't be grown in the Northeast would be expensive—if it was available at all.

Nothing to be done about it today, he thought as he set the newspaper aside and dialed Elayne's phone number. If he timed it right, she and Lizzy should be returning home from temple right about now.

The phone rang four times before he heard his little girl say, "Borden residence. Who's calling?"

He grinned despite the ache in his heart. "Don't you sound grown up."

"Daddy!"

Lizzy's squeal eased the ache a little until he heard Elayne saying something in the background followed by a reply that was definitely a male voice.

"Can I come visit you, Daddy?" Lizzy asked.

"Of course you can, Lizzy girl," he replied.

"Give me the phone," he heard Elayne say harshly. Then Lizzy, now in the background, saying, "Daddy says I can come and visit."

What was he hearing in his daughter's voice? Unhappiness? Or something closer to desperation? What would make a young girl desperate to get away?

"What's going on?" he asked as soon as Elayne came on the phone.

"Don't make this harder," Elayne said, her voice low and fierce. "She's already being difficult about our summer plans, and thinking she can run off to you anytime she doesn't get her way isn't going to help."

"Don't make what harder? What summer plans?" Anger began a slow burn in his chest.

"It's none of your concern," she said, using that dismissive tone of voice she'd been using with him whenever he asked about Lizzy.

"She's my daughter, so it is my concern," Monty replied. "I can't send the support checks if I don't know where Lizzy is."

"You send them here, as usual, and they will be forwarded."

"No, they won't. I send them to where my daughter is residing or I don't send them at all."

"You want me to take you to court over child support?"

"If that's what it takes to get an answer. And then I and a judge and the attorneys will all know about your summer plans."

A startled silence. Then Elayne huffed, "It's not as if I'm doing anything unseemly."

Monty said nothing.

Another huff. And maybe a bit of uneasiness in the sound?

"I met someone, and our relationship is serious."

That was fast, Monty thought. "So he's living with you and Lizzy? Is that what serious means?"

"You're not part of our lives any—"

"Not part of yours, but I am, and always will be, part of Lizzy's life," Monty snapped. "What aren't you saying, Elayne? Not saying is your specialty—you always try to get people to agree to something by omitting the details that would change an agreement to a refusal."

Another silence. "Nicholas is a motivational speaker and very influential in the HFL movement."

HFL? Monty pondered the letters for a moment before shock had him clutching the arm of the chair. "Humans First and Last? You kick *me* out and then take up with someone wearing a target on his back? Do you realize what people spouting Humans First and Last are doing?"

"They're the leaders who will help the rest of us get what we deserve," she replied hotly.

Did it even occur to her that "what we deserve" could have more than one meaning?

"Nicholas came all the way from the Cel-Romano Alliance of Nations to give a series of talks here in Toland," Elayne said, having regained her typical cold dignity. "When he returns to his family's villa, Lizzy and I will be going with him and will be staying with him at least through the summer."

"What's his full name?" Monty asked.

An odd pause. "Scratch. Nicholas Scratch. Of course, that's the alias he uses for his speaking engagements. It's a necessary precaution since his family name is well-known and he has several relatives who are wealthy as well as influential. As is Nicholas."

His anger turned to ash. Anger wouldn't get him anywhere with her, so he would try to appeal to her own self-interest. "Do you understand what's going on in Cel-Romano? The food shortages, the rationing? Things are not good over there, Elayne."

"Don't be ridiculous. Nicholas wouldn't have invited us if that was the case. You're just trying to spoil things for me again."

The reminder that Elayne didn't currently have the kind of social clout that should have attracted an influential man from an influential family had him thinking like a cop instead of a father. A woman desperate to climb the social ladder would be an easy mark for a man who didn't want the expense of living in a hotel for the duration of his speaking engagements. Had Nicholas Scratch come over to Toland at someone's invitation, or had he crossed the Atlantik in the hopes of making some money? Easy enough to say you come from a wealthy family if no one can verify that fact.

"Fine," Monty said. "If you want to go to Cel-Romano with Mr. Scratch, that's your business. Lizzy can stay here with me until you get back."

"I'm not leaving my daughter in a place like *Lakeside*," Elayne said. "Besides, you'll be working all the time. Where could she stay?"

"I'll work it out," Monty insisted.

A different kind of silence. Then, "There's nothing to work out. Lizzy and I are going to Cel-Romano with Nicholas. And we might not be coming back to Toland or even Thaisia. I want my daughter to live in a city that doesn't have shifters and vampires watching her from every corner. Until we can civilize the world, we'll never truly be able to enjoy civilization."

That had to be HFL rhetoric.

No point continuing to talk to her. Tomorrow he would look for an attorney and see what he would need to do to gain custody of his daughter—or, at the very least, stop Elayne from taking Lizzy to another continent.

"Take care of yourself, for Lizzy's sake," he said.

"Why would you say that?" she asked.

"Because, Elayne, if your friend really is trying to stir up the Humans First and Last movement in Toland, there will be shifters and vampires watching his every move and listening to everything he says from now on."

"You're just saying that to scare me."

"No, I'm saying it because it's true."

He knew he'd unnerved her when she let Lizzy come back on the phone and talk to him for a minute before someone took the receiver from his girl and hung up without speaking.

He didn't know what he would do with Lizzy over the summer, but he'd be damned if he let her get on a ship and cross the Atlantik without putting up a fight.

"But *why* do I have to stay here?" Sam asked, pitching his voice to a whine.

Simon gritted his teeth and kept walking back to the Wolfgard Complex. Whines sounded a lot more annoying coming from a human form. Especially puppy whines. "You like staying with Elliot because you get to play with the other pups."

"But I wanna live with you and Meg!"

Especially with Meg, Simon acknowledged silently. Now that the novelty of sleeping in a pile of pups had faded, Sam was campaigning hard to go back to living with Simon, who lived next door to Meg in the Green Complex. He wanted to play with his adventure buddy. He wanted to tell her about school. He wanted to do all the things he'd done before Simon began to appreciate the danger puppy clumsiness and enthusiasm could have for both Sam and Meg.

Wasn't that the reason he and the pup were taking this walk in human form? So they could talk? So he could explain?

"Sam." Simon stopped walking. His sister Daphne had gray eyes, like Elliot. Sam had gray eyes too, but the pup's eyes made him think more of Meg than Daphne. "This isn't a good time for you to be staying with me."

Sam lowered his eyes. "Is Meg sick again?"

So much fear in the pup's voice. Sam had seen his mother die, had watched her bleed out from a gunshot wound. It had taken Meg's unusual way of thinking to bring the traumatized pup back to them.

Simon crouched, the act of a caring uncle rather than the dominant wolf. "Meg is fine. But we've learned some things about her. Her skin . . ." How to explain Meg's strange and fragile skin?

"It smells good," Sam offered.

Good, yes. Intriguing because of her not-prey scent, definitely.

"Yes, it smells good. But it's easy to hurt her."

Sam took a step back, offended. "I wouldn't hurt Meg!"

"Not on purpose, no," Simon agreed. "But even a little scratch is dangerous for her."

"But it wasn't before!"

"Yes, it was. We just didn't know how dangerous. That's what Meg and I are trying to figure out. And there are bad things happening, so I don't want you staying by yourself. That's why I want you with the rest of the Wolfgard."

A different kind of whine now. Softer. Unhappy. The kind of sound that felt like teeth closing around his heart.

"Look," Simon said. "We can't do it this week, but next Earthday, why don't you pick out a couple of movies, and I'll ask Meg to join us for a movie night. All right?"

"Okay." A pause. "Can I get new movies?"

Simon held up two fingers. "Two new movies."

The pup would have settled for one, but until a few weeks ago, Sam had been hiding in a cage, afraid of everything. A little indulgence wouldn't hurt either of them.

A howl that quickly became a chorus.

"Come on," Simon said, heading for the Wolfgard Complex quickly enough that Sam had to run to keep up with him. "It's time to join the others for a hunt."

Simon trotted back to the Green Complex. The hunters had brought down a buck and eaten well before howling the Song of Prey to let the rest of the Wolfgard know there was fresh meat. Sam tore into the kill with the same enthusiasm as the other pups, and all the Wolves viewed it as a good sign.

Having sufficiently socialized with his own kind, Simon felt itchy. He kept thinking about Meg spending Earthday all by herself. Maybe she wanted some solitude. Maybe she had made plans with her human pack that he didn't know about. Maybe, maybe, maybe didn't change the simple fact that he wanted to spend some time with his friend now that they were friends again. Besides, Jester had told him that Meg felt nervous about being too alone. Very Wolfish of her, not wanting to be too alone. He approved.

When he reached his apartment, Simon paused and considered. Human skin or Wolf? Which shape would achieve what he wanted?

Since that answer was easy, he bounded up the stairs to Meg's porch, pressed on the doorbell in a way that made it sound like a demented mechanical squirrel, then gave his fur a good shake while he waited.

Meg opened the door. He gave her a Wolfy grin. When she didn't invite him in, he studied her face, wishing he could step closer for a good sniff without her slamming the door on his nose.

She looked embarrassed, uneasy. Since he didn't understand why she looked that way, he pushed past her, then stopped so he wouldn't track snow all over her floor.

"Simon?" Meg finally said as she closed the door. "Why are you here?"

She was his friend, and he wanted to be with his friend.

"Do you want something?"

A towel to dry his feet would be nice.

She couldn't communicate the way the *terra indigene* did, but she must have figured out why he was waiting near the door because she disappeared for a moment and came back with a towel that she put on the floor so he could press his feet against it.

Must have gotten it from the hamper since it smelled like her.

He pressed his feet into it a few more times before going over to her sofa and getting comfortable. Okay, she hadn't actually invited him to come in and get comfy, but she wasn't screeching for him to get out either.

Meg stood near the sofa instead of sitting down the way she was supposed to.

She said, "I know you prefer to stay in Wolf form on Earthday, but maybe you could shift for a few minutes so you can tell me what you want?"

Oh, no. He was furry, not stupid. The last time he'd shifted from Wolf to human in order to talk to her, she'd gotten all confused and things had gotten strange between them. He wasn't stepping into *that* trap again.

So he just looked at her expectantly.

"If you could just tell me what you want . . ." Her face colored as she glanced at the small clock on the table and then at the television. "It's just . . . I watched a television show last Earthday, and the next segment is on in a few minutes."

He wasn't stopping her from turning on the TV. In fact, he liked this idea. She would sit still and pet him.

He waved the tip of his tail a couple of times to indicate approval.

Meg sighed, turned on the TV, and selected the channel. Then she sat at one end of the sofa, her cheeks still full of color.

Once the show started, Simon intended to reposition himself so that he could rest his head on her thigh the way he used to on movie night. Before he could do that, Meg opened a jar full of thick cream that smelled like the soap and shampoo the *terra indigene* sold in their stores. Propping one foot on her knee, she slathered cream all over that foot, spending extra time on the skin around her toes while she watched the TV show. Then she pulled on a thick sock before doing the same thing to the other foot.

Feeling a quiver of excitement, Simon thought, *Oh. New game!*

The first time Simon prodded her thigh with his paw, she ignored him because the story on TV had reached a tense moment. And she ignored the second poke a minute later. But she squealed when a big paw suddenly appeared in front of her face.

She jerked her head back and yelped, "What?"

He looked at the jar of cream, then held up his paw again.

No, he couldn't mean . . . "You're kidding."

The heroine screamed, pulling Meg's attention back to the story. But she couldn't see what was happening because that big paw appeared in front of her face again.

"All right!" Scooping more cream out of the jar, she carefully rubbed it into the pads of one front paw and then the other, massaging the paws longer than she'd intended because she got caught up in the story.

After she finished the front paws, Simon settled his head on her thigh and closed his eyes.

"Bad Wolf," she muttered. As she burrowed her fingers into his fur, she added, "Hope your front end doesn't go sliding across the floor."

His response was a contented sigh.

A slidy game of chase on the apartment's wood floors might have been fun, but this was very nice too. And he liked how careful she'd been with his paws.

Simon listened to enough of the story to decide it held no interest for him. In fact, he wasn't sure it would hold much interest for any kind of male, and if he'd worn his human skin, it would have been hard not to look bored. And that would have made Meg unhappy. But a Wolf could keep her company and snooze while snuggling up much closer than she would have allowed him to do if he looked human. A furry Wolf was a friend. A human-shaped male was a confusion.

Contentment filled him as he breathed in the scent of her.

He raised his head and gave her hand a couple of licks—and felt a quiet happiness flow through him as he went back to snoozing.

Even with the cream on her skin, he really did like the taste of her.

CHAPTER 12

Monty figured he was in some kind of trouble when Captain Burke summoned him first thing on Windsday morning. Then he walked in and spotted the fax on the desk before Burke folded his hands over it and gave him a smile that was more fierce than friendly.

"Nicholas Scratch," Burke said. "Who is he and why is he of interest to the police?"

Busted. "I'm not sure he is of interest to the police yet," Monty replied cautiously.

"That still leaves the first question. Who is he?"

While he considered his answer, he remembered that Burke understood that sometimes there wasn't much of a line between the job and your personal life. "He's Elayne Borden's new lover. He's a man whose identity can't be confirmed. And he's the man who is living in the same apartment as my daughter, Lizzy."

Burke lifted his chin to indicate the visitor's chair. "Sit."

Monty sat.

"This fax doesn't say much. Did you find out anything else?"

"Only that there's plenty I can't find out about the man. According to Elayne, Scratch comes from the Cel-Romano Alliance of Nations, hails from a wealthy and influential family, uses an alias to protect the other members of said family, and is in Toland as a motivational speaker for the Humans First and Last movement."

Monty clenched his teeth to prevent himself from saying anything more. Two days of hitting walls where Nicholas Scratch was concerned had left him frustrated and angry.

"Can you verify any of that?" Burke asked.

"Scratch is scheduled for several speaking engagements in Toland." He hadn't been able to confirm that personally. He had no allies in the Toland Police Department for the same reason he'd been transferred to Lakeside—he had killed a human to save a young Wolf. So he'd asked Kowalski to make the inquiry. "Either no one knew anything more about him, or no one wanted to share what they knew."

"Understandable if he has some government support and really is over here to stir up the HFL movement," Burke said thoughtfully. "Ms. Borden is Lizzy's mother?"

"Yes."

"Does she understand what Scratch is getting her involved in by association?"

Monty smiled bitterly. "She's rubbing elbows with socially important people. She's quite happy with the association." Since Burke hadn't chewed him out—yet—for using time and resources for something that wasn't work related, he lowered his guard. "She wants to take Lizzy to Cel-Romano this summer. She's talking about not coming back to Toland or even returning to Thaisia. I'm not sure there is anything I can do to stop her."

"We're just a few days into Viridus. Summer is a whole season away, so let's work on the immediate problem, which is finding out about Scratch," Burke said. "I'll ask my cousin Shady to find out what he can, and he'll reach out to other Brittania relatives. It's a long shot, but the ones who work in law enforcement have been keeping a sharp eye on Cel-Romano, so they might have heard a rumor or two."

"Thank you, sir. I appreciate it." Monty pushed to his feet, then remembered the e-mail he'd received that morning from the Courtyard. "Simon Wolfgard and Henry Beargard are going over to Great Island tomorrow. He'll ask whoever runs the island if your friend's son can relocate there."

"I appreciate it."

Not having anything else to say, Monty gave his captain a nod and returned to his own desk to continue searching for information about the man now tangled up in his daughter's life.

Until he—or someone—found that first nugget of real information, Scratch's alias was holding up, keeping even his nation of origin a secret. Had Scratch gone through that much effort to hide from the Others, or did he have a reason to hide from humans as well?

CHAPTER 13

"I appreciate the invitation," Burke said after Simon Wolfgard had been driving north on River Road for several minutes. "It wasn't necessary to have me come along for this meeting."

Simon glanced in the rearview mirror, then fixed his eyes on the road. "You planning to visit your friend's pup if he settles on Great Island?"

"I'd like to, yes."

"Then your coming along is necessary."

Monty glanced at Burke. Nothing showed in the other man's face, but the tension in the vehicle increased a little more. Burke took a proprietary interest in what happened in Lakeside and knew whom to call when he needed information about his city or the human places nearby. But he'd drawn a blank when he tried to find out more about Ferryman's Landing than they'd been told at last week's meeting with Simon Wolfgard.

The Simple Life community was the only acknowledged group of humans on Great Island. Yes, there were some humans who ran a few stores and the island's ferry, but their village, such as it was, wasn't under human control. Like the rest of the island, it belonged to the *terra indigene*. Population, unknown. Level of technology, unknown. Pretty much everything, unknown. Which meant the human governments of Lakeside and Talulah Falls, which were the nearest human-controlled places, didn't know Ferryman's Landing was an Intuit village.

So Burke had to be wondering what he'd gotten his friend's son into.

Simon and Henry weren't big on small talk. They also weren't big on explanations. Wolfgard's call that morning had been unexpected, as was the invitation—demand?—that Monty and Burke come with him and Henry to discuss whether Roger Czerneda would be acceptable as an official police officer for Great Island.

Monty wasn't sure if the short notice—little more than the time it took Wolfgard to drive from the Courtyard to the Chestnut Street Police Station—showed a lack of courtesy or a last-minute decision to include two members of Lakeside's police force so that there was someone available to answer any questions the Great Island residents might have. Either way, every effort Burke had made to find out why they were both invited and unwelcome had been met with silence.

Sitting on the right side of the van behind Henry, Monty couldn't see much of the Talulah River, so he concentrated on the landward side. The moment they passed the sign that read LEAVING LAKESIDE, he saw nothing but brown fields and bare trees. Viridus was the greening month, but nothing was blooming yet. Then he spotted an industrial complex that looked abandoned and houses crowded together on the land that rose behind it. He barely had time to blink when he was looking at open land and stands of trees again. The visual difference was so sharp, it felt like a blow to the senses.

"What kind of businesses were in the buildings we just passed?" he asked.

"Those buildings are closed," Henry replied.

That didn't answer his question. "Closed? Why?"

"They were warned twice about dumping too much badness into the land and water. They were told to find another way to make their products. They didn't listen, so the Others who watch over this piece of Namid said, 'No more,' and the businesses had to leave."

"To go where?"

Henry shrugged. "Into a city where they can dump their badness into land and water the humans use, or to another part of Thaisia that did not already have much badness from what humans made. Either way, they are gone from here, and the water and land do not taste of them anymore."

Burke set his hand on the seat between them and wagged a finger in warning, but Monty couldn't let it go. "What about the people?"

"I think some found other work and still live in the houses. Most moved away," Henry replied.

Only this much land and not an acre more, no matter how cramped and crowded people's living conditions become, Monty thought. *Only this much waste as a by-product of what is made, or even the little bit granted to you will be lost.*

Monty had read the human version of Thaisia's history. He knew that boom-towns could become ghost towns. Even hamlets didn't survive. Look at Jerzy.

Would anyone from Jerzy end up living in one of those empty houses? Would the decision makers on Great Island consider making room for more than one new resident?

Then Monty saw a small sign that read, FERRYMAN'S ORCHARDS NEXT RIGHT.

"We're almost there," Simon said.

Henry turned his head toward the backseat. "The Intuits have a shared use of all this land."

Monty saw Burke's look of surprise before the man regained control.

Open land changed to fenced pastures. Barns and farmhouses. Herds of cows and horses. Some sheep. A silo. A fading sign about picking your own ber-ries. Rural, if Monty correctly understood the word.

Then it all changed again, and they were driving down the main street of a rustic little village. Electrical lines and lights in the windows were indications that this wasn't a Simple Life community. The stores, while basic, were also abundant: grocery store, department store, general store, gas station; a handful of places to eat; a medical center and a dentist's office; hair salon, bookstore, and a theater that offered two movies. And as they passed one of the side streets, he got a glimpse of signs for a bank and post office.

Not all that different from the Lakeside Courtyard's Market Square, but built along the lines of a human business district.

"Ferryman's Landing is divided by the river. This is the mainland half of it," Simon said as he drove toward the water, then turned into a parking area. He shut off the van and got out, leaving the other three to catch up to him as he walked toward the dock.

"This is a marina?" Monty asked, noticing the building that indicated it was a boat repair and storage facility.

"Yes," Henry said. "Some of the boats that dock here belong to families who fish for a living. Some will take visitors for a ride along the river." The Grizzly pointed at a vessel. "And, as you can see, the ferry also runs out of here."

More like a miniature ferry, Monty thought. The ferries he'd seen when he lived in Toland were three times the size of the boat he was looking at now.

One sign near the ferry's dock posted the times. The other sign posted the fees for a round-trip ticket: $10 PER PERSON.

Not a trip anyone would want to do for fun, Monty thought. *Especially with a family.*

Burke pulled out his wallet and said, "Allow me." He handed the man in the kiosk two twenty-dollar bills.

The man in the kiosk studied Simon and Henry. "I was told to expect the Lakeside Wolfgard. Would that be you?"

Simon nodded.

The man folded one of the bills and handed it back to Burke along with four tickets. "Day passes, in case you need to cross more than once during your visit."

After a moment's hesitation, Burke took the twenty and stuffed it into his coat pocket before handing the tickets to Monty, Simon, and Henry.

Only one price listed, and that one high enough to discourage visitors, Monty thought. "What happens if you want to bring a car to the island?" he asked once they boarded the ferry. Simon led them into the cabin, and he was grateful. Despite the sunshine, it didn't feel like spring yet, especially on the water.

"Have to wait for the barge if you want to bring cars or trucks across," Henry replied, taking a seat. "If you need something hauled on water, you call Ferryman. On land, you call Sledgeman Freight. That's their building over there."

Monty looked out the cabin window and studied the sign painted on one of the buildings. "They use horses to haul freight?"

Henry nodded. "They use trucks as well, but they still have working teams of horses on both sides of the river."

Monty glanced at Burke and wondered if the man still wanted his friend's son to relocate to the island.

"Morning." A man wearing the gray uniform of the post office paused instead of walking by. "Saw some blue dancers yesterday."

"Blue dancers?" Burke asked.

"A wildflower," Henry replied. "When you see blue dancers, you know Spring is awake and Winter is yielding."

The postman grinned. "But she never yields until she gives us one or two reminders of who she is before she settles in to sleep." With a casual wave, he moved toward the front of the cabin and took a seat.

"They don't have a full crew today," Simon said, pointing to what looked like a small bar. "Usually they have someone in here selling coffee and sandwiches. In the summer, it's cold drinks and ice cream."

Could be a pleasant trip in the summertime if you could afford it, Monty thought. An afternoon's outing to take the ferry, visit the village on the other side, and be home in time for dinner. Did the ferry run on Earthday if he wanted to take Lizzy, or would he need to arrange a day off?

Assuming he could win enough of a custody battle to keep his daughter on this continent. And assuming visitors were tolerated in the village. That was something he could report to Kowalski since Ruth was keen to visit the Simple Life community on the island but couldn't find any information about a possible place to stay if they wanted to do an overnighter.

The welcoming committee waited for them at the dock—two men and one woman. Monty recognized the feral quality in the woman and one of the men, but he couldn't tell what kind of earth natives had chosen to meet them.

"Mr. Ferryman," Simon said when they stood in front of the Great Islanders.

"Mr. Wolfgard. You've brought guests."

"This is Captain Burke and Lieutenant Montgomery. They need to be here for this discussion." He looked at Burke. "Steve Ferryman is the mayor of Ferryman's Landing."

"Which will teach me not to leave the room just before a vote is about to be taken by the village council." Steve gave them all an easy smile. "Welcome to Great Island and Ferryman's Landing. As you can guess by the name, my family has been working the river since my ancestors came to this part of the Great Lakes. And this is Ming Beargard and Flash Foxgard. They're a couple of the island's peacekeepers. Since Mr. Wolfgard indicated on the phone that you all wanted to talk about the police on the island, I asked Ming and Flash to join us. I also reserved one of the rooms in the government building for us."

Steve waved a hand. A moment later, an open carriage pulled by a horse arrived at the dock. "One of our village taxis."

"We'll meet you there," Ming said, indicating himself and Flash. "Henry? Want to stretch your legs?" When Henry agreed, he and the Great Island earth natives strode off.

Monty and Burke climbed into the forward-facing seat. Simon and Steve took the seat behind the driver, whom Steve introduced as Jerry Sledgeman. As soon as they were seated, Jerry clucked to the horse and the carriage headed away from the dock.

"You don't have cars?" Monty asked.

"Sure we do. But we don't use them much around the village proper," Steve replied.

"We have a regular taxi and a small bus for village stops," Jerry said over his shoulder. "And there's the bus that makes a couple of runs out to the Simple Life folks and the terra indigene complexes each day. It also provides special transportation to the island's athletic and community centers. "

"Since each half of the village is only a few blocks in any direction, those of us who are young enough and fit enough tend to use our own feet to get around," Steve said. "Or we ride bicycles in the summer. Jerry just put away the sleighs that are part of our winter transportation."

This half of Ferryman's Landing was almost identical to the business district on the other side of the river. Most of the same businesses and stores. Monty had the impression this side was a little bigger, had a little more of everything—which made him wonder if the island residents were cut off from the mainland by weather for parts of the year.

"Government building is exactly that," Steve said when Jerry pulled up in front of a long, two-story stone building. "Police and court, what there is of it, on one end. General government in the middle. Post office on the other end."

"That's handy," Burke said politely.

"It is," Steve agreed. "Especially since the post office is the part of the building that gets the most use."

When they walked into the building, Ming, Flash, and Henry were waiting for them. They went upstairs to a room that had a Reserved sign hanging from a hook on the wooden door. Steve removed that sign and replaced it with a Do Not Disturb sign that he took from a rack on the wall.

When they were all seated around a table, Steve looked at Simon and said, "It's your meeting."

"You heard what happened in Jerzy?" Simon asked.

"Everyone has heard what happened in Jerzy," Ming growled. "We received your warning about the sickness and the signs to watch for if it comes to the island."

"That's good," Simon said.

Something's not right between them, Monty thought as he studied Simon and Steve.

"A policeman in Jerzy who came to the aid of the Crowgard has to relocate," Simon said.

"Everyone in Jerzy has to relocate," Steve countered. "At least, that's what we heard on the news."

"This policeman is known to Captain Burke, who says the man would like to relocate here."

"Is this policeman who wants to live here one of us?" Steve asked softly.

"No," Simon replied.

Steve tipped his head to indicate Burke. "Does *he* know what we are?"

"He knows you are Intuit. I don't think he truly appreciates what that means."

Steve studied Burke, then looked at Simon. "Can he be trusted?"

"These two can be trusted," Simon said.

Monty released the breath he hadn't realized he'd been holding.

Steve sat back and gave Burke a sharp smile. "We were persecuted by your kind of humans, driven out of the settlements we helped build when we weren't killed outright. Many generations ago, we fled into the wild country to make our own bargains with the *terra indigene* and build our own communities. We attend your universities and technical colleges for the knowledge, and we risk working for some of your companies for a few years in order to acquire experience and necessary skills that we bring back to our own people. But for the most part, we have kept ourselves apart from you in order to survive. That is still a prudent choice. So, you see, having a non-Intuit human living among us would be . . . unprecedented."

"You have the Simple Life folk living on the island," Burke countered. "How is that different from someone living among you in the village?"

"Simple Life is a chosen way of life," Steve replied. "It doesn't fit with your cities, but it does mesh fairly well with our little villages. The Simple Life folk tolerate our ways, and we tolerate theirs. And the *terra indigene* tolerate the presence of all of us."

"You earn your place here," Ming said.

To Monty, that sounded like high praise coming from a *terra indigene* Bear.

"In Brittania, where my ancestors hail from, I believe your ability would be called second sight," Burke said to Steve. "A knowing that can't be explained. Would that be accurate?"

"Close enough," Steve said.

"Prophecy?" Monty asked.

"*No.*"

The forceful denial startled Monty. But it seemed to confirm something for Simon Wolfgard, who tensed.

"Intuits don't have visions; we don't see images of the future," Steve said, sounding a bit too insistent. "We just get a feeling for good or ill when something is happening around us."

"And now?" Simon asked. "What are you feeling now?"

Wolf and Intuit stared at each other.

Then Steve looked at Burke and Monty. After a moment, he said, "I have a feeling that there's a storm coming, and maybe it would be good to have an official police officer living among us, even if he isn't one of us." A hesitation. "Intuits make use of technology, but we've also made choices that keep us in harmony with the *terra indigene*. Those aren't choices most humans want to make. Would this policeman be easy with that? With us?"

"I think Roger would be able to adjust," Burke said carefully.

Steve sat back. "Does this Roger know how to ride a horse?"

"I don't know. Will he need to?"

"It would be handy. What about sports?"

"He played hockey when he was in school."

"Baseball? Volleyball? Anything like that?"

"I don't know."

"He's supposed to be a police officer, not fill vacancies in your sports teams," Henry said.

"No reason he can't do both," Steve replied. He exchanged a look with Ming and Flash, then nodded. "All right. We won't be able to pay him much, but we'll give Roger a chance to make a place for himself here."

"Thank you," Burke said. "If there is anything I can do to help, let me know."

"Some suggestions for how to purchase an official police car would be helpful. We don't have one." Smiling, Steve pushed back from the table.

Simon gave the table three sharp taps.

Steve settled back in his chair, his smile fading. "Why don't you take a look around the village? Mr. Wolfgard and I will catch up to you."

Monty and Burke followed Henry and Ming out of the room, with Flash bringing up the rear. He looked back as Flash closed the door—and he wondered why seeing Steve and Simon lean toward each other made him uneasy.

"When you sent word the other day, saying you were coming to the island, I wondered if you wanted to get away from the Courtyard for a couple of days," Steve said. "Coming here would be a good choice. It's close but not your responsibility. And you're not opposed to our way of life, which is more than can be said for the Talulah Falls Courtyard."

"That's not why I called," Simon replied. He'd spent the drive up to the island thinking about what he wanted to know and how to ask the questions. Intuits had survived by being very careful. They lived up to the bargains they made with the *terra indigene*, which was why the Others helped them attend colleges in human cities or learn useful trades so that they knew the workings of human businesses. With that knowledge, they were consultants for the *terra indigene* when it came to making bargains with other humans, and their loyalty was well rewarded with land and protection.

"No, that's not why you called," Steve agreed. "You showed up with Lakeside police and this request to bring in an outsider. But that's not why *you're* here."

<Simon,> Henry said. <Everyone is away from the room. Ming, Flash, and I will show Burke and Montgomery around the village.>

<I'll catch up with you when I'm done,> Simon said. He didn't know how long it would take to ask the right question to find out what he needed, so he didn't waste time. "You told Lieutenant Montgomery that you don't see prophecy. But I think the Intuits know about the *cassandra sangue*."

Steve pushed back from the table, looking a little frightened. "Don't go there."

Interesting. And not what he expected. But the response told him how he needed to proceed with this hunt. "I have to go there. Meg is my friend."

"Who is Meg?"

"Our Human Liaison. She's a blood prophet. Being out in the world is causing some . . . reactions."

"Then take her back to her caregivers."

Ignoring the plea in Steve's voice—and the strange, desperate hope—Simon snarled and let his canines lengthen enough that they couldn't be mistaken for human. "Keepers and cages. She said she'd rather die than go back to that place, and she meant it." He waited a moment. "What do you know?"

Steve scrubbed his face with his hands. "It was a dark time in our history, and Intuits still carry the shame of it." He sighed. "All I can offer is old stories that were passed down. But I want your word that you won't say anything about this to Jerry Sledgeman or any of his family."

"Why?"

"Because his niece started cutting herself when she reached puberty. By the time the family realized the cuts were deliberate and she was hiding a lot more than they'd seen, she started going mad—and they started to suspect she might be a *cassandra sangue*. But it's been six, maybe even seven, generations since a blood prophet was born to any of the families on the island. No one knew how to help her. There was talk of finding one of those places that take care of such girls, but Penny, Jerry's wife, was against it. Because of what had happened before. She's the island's historian and has studied Intuit history in Thaisia, so her opinion carried weight."

"Where is the girl?" Simon asked. Meg was learning how to live outside the compound where she'd been held. He thought she did pretty well most days, but she was plagued by the pins-and-needles feeling, as if prophecies were like horseflies always swarming and biting. Still, she could explain some things to a girl who had no understanding of how the visions worked.

"Dead," Steve replied sadly. "She jumped in the river last summer and was swept over the falls before anyone could try to save her."

"I'm sorry." He didn't feel any sorrow or regret for a stranger, but he did understand how the loss of kin hurt. So he knew offering condolences was the proper thing to do.

"Penny's sister hasn't spoken to her since that day."

Words, words, words. And nothing said yet that would help him.

"Meg said the girls were kept in cages. Cells with locked doors. They were tied down and cut when someone paid for a prophecy. Her designation was *cs759*."

Steve stared at him. "Designation?"

"They weren't given names. Property isn't given names." Simon watched anger kindle in Steve's eyes, and used words to lay a trail for this hunt for information. "Meg has a silver razor. The blade's width is a precise measure of how far apart the cuts have to be. Her designation was engraved on one side of the handle."

"Seven five nine. *Seven hundred fifty-nine?* There have been seven hundred fifty-nine girls in that one place?" Steve raked a hand through his hair. "When humans first met the *terra indigene* in other parts of the world, they ignored the boundaries that had been set by Namid itself, and there were great battles. When it looked like they would become purged from the world, Namid gave some of them the gift of knowing that humans call intuition. And the world changed a few humans so that their blood became a window to the future. More than just a knowing. But such a gift always comes at a cost. The women, because the prophets were always women, went mad after a few years.

"Then it was discovered that the blood of the *cassandra sangue* could quiet anger, could take away pain."

"Could make someone so passive they wouldn't fight back even if attacked?" Simon asked.

Steve shrugged. "That wasn't mentioned in the stories, but there are several historical references from the years when settlers first came to Thaisia of how the presence of something the *terra indigene* called sweet blood ended a conflict without a fight. And there were also a few mentions of *terra indigene* lapping up blood and then going mad. Reading between the lines, and given the fact that blood is mentioned in both cases, I'd guess that both those things had something to do with the girls who were prophets."

So this isn't the first time this has happened, Simon thought. Did someone find these historical references? Is that where the idea for making the drugs that are causing the sickness came from? "What does this have to do with the Intuits?"

"The *cassandra sangue* came from us. The special girls. The prophets. But when you're trying to hide in a human village, when you're trying to avoid being branded as having some kind of sorcery or channeling power that belongs to the gods, having a girl in the family who has visions of the future and warns of disasters whenever she gets a cut can be an excuse to hang an entire family. And it was done, Mr. Wolfgard. It was done."

He nodded to indicate he was listening.

"A few generations ago, men started showing up when stories began spreading about a girl. They talked about a special home, a secret place where the girls would be safe, would be cared for without putting their families at risk. Safety for everyone. Family stories always emphasized that parents gave up their daughters to keep the girls safe, to keep the rest of their children safe."

"Maybe it was safer in the beginning," Simon said.

"Maybe. But hunters learn how to find their preferred prey, and soon the special girls, the *cassandra sangue*, had disappeared from Intuit family lines."

"They didn't disappear from all the family lines," Simon said, thinking of Meg's friend Jean, who had been born outside the compound.

"The potential didn't completely disappear, at any rate. But..."—Steve's hand closed into a fist—"those men. They breed the girls now, don't they? Like livestock. Select the specific traits they want in the offspring."

"I think so. Meg doesn't talk about it much, so I don't know for sure. But I think so."

Neither spoke for a few minutes. Simon felt disappointed. He hadn't learned anything that would help Meg.

"I don't want to stir things up in the village by asking too many questions," Steve said. "Is there something specific you want to know about the blood prophets?"

Simon thought for a moment. "Pins and needles. The prickling Meg feels so much of the time. Is that how it always is for a *cassandra sangue* who isn't confined? Is that feeling why they start cutting in the first place?"

"I don't know. I'll talk to Penny, quietly. I think it will help her and her sister to know the river might have been the kinder choice. And I'll contact other Intuit villages and see what I can find out."

"Be careful. The man who held Meg is still trying to get her back. He sent men after her. They killed some of the *terra indigene* in the Courtyard before we destroyed them. And they almost killed Meg."

"That's what provoked the storm that shut down Lakeside?"

Simon nodded.

Putting his hands flat on the table, Steve rose. "All right. I'll find out what I can about blood prophets, and we'll do what we can for your policeman's friend. Like I said before, we can't pay him much, but I can promise food, clothes, and a roof over his head."

"I think for now that will be enough." Simon rose.

Steve studied him for a moment, then gave him an odd smile. "You called her a friend."

"What?"

"Your Meg. You said she was a friend. A Wolf has really made friends with a human?"

He growled. He couldn't help it. "Lakeside has a human pack now because of her. A whole pack of troublesome, not-edible females." All right, the pack was made up of three females plus Meg, but when they ganged up on him, they felt like a lot more.

Steve pressed his lips together and kept blinking like there was something in his eyes.

"What?"

Steve rubbed his eyes and sighed. "Intuits, Simple Life folks, and the *terra indigene* have different tasks, but taken together, those tasks and abilities benefit all of us. And I think we've worked well together for a lot of years. But I don't think Ming or Flash or any other *terra indigene* living here has ever thought of any Intuit as a friend. I have a feeling your Meg has changed things between your kind and mine more than anyone yet realizes."

Simon cocked his head and studied the man. "You have a feeling?"

"Yes. A feeling."

Not a word an Intuit used lightly.

"I'll send word when Roger Czerneda is ready to come to the island."

Steve reached back and rubbed a hand between his shoulders. "Maybe that's part of it. The prickling you said your Meg feels. Intuits do better with a limited number of people. You get used to how people fit into the whole, so you know when something has changed. That's one reason we don't welcome people who find our village while they're visiting Talulah Falls."

Simon waited.

"Every choice changes the future."

"So every time I choose whether or not to have a muffin at breakfast I'm an itch under Meg's skin?"

"No. If that were true, all those girls would be completely insane no matter how few people they came into contact with. But since her kind came from us, once a prophet gets used to her surroundings and the people she usually sees, the day-to-day choices shouldn't affect her anymore."

Steve looked excited. But he hadn't met Meg. Simon didn't share that excitement.

"She's been with us two months now. If she stills gets that prickling feeling several times a day . . . ?"

The excitement faded from Steve's face, and he looked grim. "If that's the case, I have a feeling that your prophet is sensing a whole lot of bad headed your way."

Yeah. That was what worried him. "I'll be in touch."

Steve hesitated. "Would you have any objection to my visiting the Lakeside Courtyard?"

He thought about that for a moment and why Ferryman would be asking now. "You want to get a look at Meg?"

"Yes, I'd like to meet her. But more than that, I'd like her to get a look at me."

He thought about that too—and decided tearing out Steve's throat was an honest response but not an appropriate one. And since he had enough to think about, he wasn't going to ponder why that *was* his response.

He walked out of the room and kept going. He found Henry, Burke, and Montgomery at the ferry, loading jars of jam and honey to take back to the Courtyard.

Steve didn't join them. Simon thought that was for the best.

On the drive back to Lakeside, he expected Burke at least to ask questions about what his friend's pup could anticipate from living on the island. But the two humans were quiet, and he suspected Henry's thoughts were more focused on the honey and jam they were bringing back.

That was fine. He didn't need anyone yipping at him. But his talk with Steve had decided one thing: the next time Meg needed to cut, he was going to be there to confirm or deny his suspicions about the humans Namid made to be both wondrous and terrible.

CHAPTER 14

The following Earthday, as he'd promised, Simon picked up Sam late in the afternoon and prepared for a movie night with Meg. Despite their apartments having access to a common back hallway, which would make it easy to visit, Meg persisted in using the front door when invited over, even though it still meant putting on a winter coat and boots.

Today that suited him. While she shrugged off the winter garments—and tried to avoid clobbering Sam, who bounced around her and jabbered about school, the new movies, the other puppies, and everything else he could manage to say before he had to take a breath—Simon made the popcorn and poured glasses of water for Sam and Meg. And if the popcorn had a little more butter and salt than usual, and if he forgot to bring extra napkins before slipping out of the living room to strip off his clothes and shift, then he'd just have to be polite and help Meg clean her fingers, wouldn't he?

Meg and Sam had started the first movie and each had a helping of popcorn when he returned, so he took his place on the sofa and snuggled up next to Meg.

Adventure movie. Still geared for youngsters Sam's age, but much more interesting than the movies the pup had wanted to watch a couple of months ago. He'd done more growing, both mentally and physically, since Meg coaxed him out of the cage than he'd done during the two years he'd been frozen by the trauma of his mother's death.

Feeling content, Simon stretched out. The movie was interesting, but resting his head in Meg's lap and snoozing was much better.

He wasn't sure when things changed. He must have dozed off more deeply than he'd intended. One moment he was vaguely aware of Meg's hands in his fur, urging him to sit up. The next moment he was being choked.

Fully awake now, he struggled—and the arms tightened. He bared his teeth, prepared to bite, but the only scent surrounding him was Meg's.

<Meg? Let go, Meg. I can't breathe.> Not that she could hear him. He started to jam a paw between her arms and his throat, then remembered what a toenail scrape could do to her. <Meg? MegMegMeg! Ack!>

"Hey, Meg," Sam said, looking over and giggling. "You're choking Uncle Simon."

"Oh! Sorry." Loosening her grip, she gave Simon a couple of thumpy pats and a kiss between the ears.

He would have preferred less thumps and more kisses, but he happily settled for breathing. The next time she closed around him, he managed to get a paw between her arms and his throat to give himself breathing room before she squeezed him again.

Sam glanced at him. <You look funny.>

He growled. <Eat your popcorn.>

Of course he looked funny. Meg had hauled him halfway into her lap and was using him as a furry shield, peering between his ears when she wasn't squeezing him breathless during the movie's scary bits. Problem was, Sam wasn't giving him any clues about what would be considered the scary bits. The pup was bouncing and shouting and cheering and howling as the Wolf Team fulfilled their mission. Whatever it was. The second time he almost poked himself in the eye when Meg squeezed him, he decided to pay more attention to the story. Her breath ruffling his fur was more of a clue than the story, but at least he started to recognize the signs and began to anticipate when to take a deep breath.

By the time they finished the first movie, Sam was bouncing around the living room and Simon had a crick in his back. After getting his hindquarters on the floor, he managed to pull himself out of Meg's arms.

She looked like she'd rubbed her face with flour to erase every bit of color.

"Did you see how the Wolf Team tore up the bad guys?" Sam said, waving his arms. "They tracked 'em and found 'em and—"

"That was so scary!"

"Yeah, it was scary when the Wolf Team almost got caught. But they found the bad guys and—"

<Sam.>

Sam stopped bouncing and looked at Meg.

The pup loves her, Simon thought as he watched Sam absorb Meg's reaction to the movie. *Not like he loved Daphne, but like a sister. Like pack. Like . . . family.*

"Well," Sam said, "I guess it might have been more scary for you because you're a girl."

Simon didn't think it was Meg's being a girl but being human that made the difference, but he didn't correct the pup. <I think that's enough movies for tonight.>

"Wanna play a card game, Meg?" Sam asked.

"O-okay." She reached for the popcorn bowl. "Let me put this in the kitchen and wash my hands."

Sighing at the missed opportunity to get a few licks, Simon hurried out of the room to shift before Meg reached the kitchen. He had his jeans on and was pulling the sweater over his head when she walked in. Her gait wasn't steady. Neither were her hands when she set the bowl on the kitchen table.

"Simon?"

"Meg?"

"Can I stay here tonight?"

That movie really scared her. "Sure. But . . . Sam was going to curl up with me tonight. Is that okay as long as he and I stay in Wolf form?"

She nodded. Then she looked at her hands. "That's a lot of loose fur."

He wasn't sure all that fur had been loose when the evening started. In fact, even in this form, his skin felt a little sore, the way you'd expect it to feel after being plucked.

Busy, nervous fingers. He'd have to remember that.

"Why don't you and Sam start the card game?" he suggested. "I want to make a last walk around the complex."

"Why?" Meg squeaked. "Is something wrong?"

"Nothing's wrong. I do this every night. Remember?"

"Oh. Yes. You do."

Meg wasn't a bunny, but tonight she sure did want a furry, Wolf-size security blanket. Which, considering what had scared her, was kind of funny.

"I won't be gone long," Simon said.

He stopped in the living room to sniff out Sam, who had hidden behind the sofa so he could jump out and growl. Meg's fear of the movie had already bounced right out of the puppy's head. Reminding Sam that Meg wouldn't want to watch movies with them anymore if the pup scared her on purpose, he left the youngster sufficiently settled down and waiting for his adventure buddy.

Simon stepped outside. He swallowed a couple of times to make sure his throat worked, then took a deep breath. He stretched his back, wincing a little. Definitely a crick. The *terra indigene* had given Elizabeth Bennefeld office space in the Market Square, but he didn't think any of the Others had actually tried that massage stuff. However, Meg and the human pack liked it and said it helped sore muscles, so maybe he'd make an appointment. If movie night was going to be like this from now on, his muscles would need some help.

He walked around the interior of the complex, noting who had lights on and whose homes were dark. Then he spotted Henry standing in the archway that provided access to the Green Complex's garages.

"You already watch both movies?" Henry asked.

"One was all Meg could handle," Simon replied.

Henry frowned. "I thought you were going to watch something Sam had selected. Something suitable for a youngster."

"We did. But it was a *terra indigene* movie."

Henry laughed so long and so loud, every resident in the complex looked out a window or opened their doors.

<Henry? Simon?> Vlad called. <What's going on?>

He heard the same question from Jester Coyotegard, Marie Hawkgard, Jenni Crowgard, and Tess.

I'm not going to be the one telling on her, Simon thought as he ignored the queries and hurried back to his apartment. But when he shook his head at Vlad and Jester before dashing into his apartment and locking the door, he knew that, by morning, everyone in the Courtyard would have heard this new tidbit about their Meg.

CHAPTER 15

On Thaisday, Simon unlocked Howling Good Reads' front door, then went about opening the store for business. Not that there was much business. There hadn't been many human customers stopping at HGR or A Little Bite for a while now. There were even fewer since the incident last week when two girls tried to vandalize the bookstore by smearing dog poop on the books.

The girls' stinky perfume had almost masked the scent of poop. They'd gotten past John, who was manning the checkout counter that day, but then they tried to walk past Blair and Nathan. The two enforcers pinned the girls to the shelves before howling for Simon and Vlad.

Human law did not apply in the Courtyard. A few months ago, Blair and Nathan would have killed those girls just for trying to damage the books. But that day, Simon had called Lieutenant Montgomery and demanded that the girls be arrested.

When two patrol cars showed up with lights and sirens going, the girls were stunned. They were going to be arrested? They were going to have a *police record*? They were going to pay fines or go to jail? *But they didn't do anything!*

That's when Blair lost the little tolerance he had for whining, dumb-ass monkeys and snarled that the Wolves were hungry and which of the damn vandals' arms could they rip off for lunch?

It didn't surprise anyone that the girls were suddenly thrilled to be arrested and walked out of the store by armed police officers.

They hadn't had time to damage anything in the store, so there wasn't any evidence of intended vandalism beyond the bags of dog poop found in the girls' day packs, and the cops on TV shows were always growling about needing evidence. So it wasn't likely that human law would do more than give the girls a nip. And that would not sit well with the *terra indigene* living in the Courtyard. Most of them would have preferred Simon giving Montgomery enough of the girls' possessions so that the police could fill out a Deceased, Location Unknown form. Then Boone Hawkgard could put up the sign in the Market Square butcher shop indicating the availability of special meat.

The girls wouldn't understand or appreciate the decision Simon had made, but Montgomery did. The lieutenant's quiet "Thank you" as Kowalski and two other officers escorted the girls out of the store confirmed that the human recognized the call as an effort to keep the peace a little longer—and as an acknowledgment of the efforts the police were making to uphold the agreements between the city of Lakeside and the *terra indigene*.

It had been only a few weeks since Winter had locked the city in a blizzard of rage. Every day the news on the radio whined about the difficulties people were having with getting the building supplies needed to repair the damage done to houses and businesses during that storm.

The humans had no idea how close they had come to being wiped out completely. If Meg had died that night, Winter would have shown no mercy, and Lakeside would have been another human city that disappeared.

Because it hadn't been that long since the storm, and because he hoped Spring's warmth would ease the tension in the city, he was giving the humans some time to use their brains—and giving the police time to shake things out in their own way. Besides, he had other things to think about.

Last week, he had gone to Great Island to talk to Steve Ferryman. Now Ferryman was coming to the Courtyard to meet with Captain Burke and Roger Czerneda. It was sensible to host the meeting since it meant he and Vlad could sit in and listen. But there were two problems with meeting here: one was Roger Czerneda and the other was Steve Ferryman. Both were unattached males, and Ferryman had already indicated an interest in sniffing around his Meg!

Not my Meg, Simon thought, wondering why he'd opened the cash drawer. *Not exactly.* Earth natives in human form could have sex with humans, but they didn't *mate* with humans.

But an Intuit could be a mate for a *cassandra sangue*. So could a regular human.

Fur suddenly covered his chest and shoulders. His hands shifted enough to have fur and claws. He didn't realize he was snarling or that his fangs had lengthened until he heard a gasping squeak.

Heather, the *only* human employee left at HGR, stared at him.

"Should I leave?" she asked.

He shook his head. Damn! He had shifted enough that he didn't have human speech. As he pointed at the register, he wondered what else had shifted, but he didn't think patting his head to find out how much was still human-looking and how much was Wolf would be a good thing to do.

Don't think about human males, or females, or mating, or . . . anything. Just get up to the office before you scare the bunny. Heather. Shit, fuck, damn!

She tensed when the checkout counter was no longer between them, but he kept moving toward the stockroom and the stairs. Except he couldn't stand the thought of being confined in the office. He needed to run!

He stripped off his clothes, leaving them on the floor near HGR's back door. Then he stepped outside, shifted to Wolf, and let out a howl that rang with frustration.

<Simon?> Nathan called.

<Guard Meg,> he said and took off running. He ran away from the Courtyard's business district, ignoring the queries from Elliot and Tess asking what was wrong. Running on clear roads wasn't demanding enough, so he ran across open ground and through the trees, plowing his way through some drifts of snow. It was Spring's official reign now, but reminders of Winter still lingered.

He ran until he was tired enough that his first thought wasn't tearing out Steve Ferryman's throat just for being male. He shouldn't feel that way, didn't understand *why* he felt that way.

Meg had been a source of confusion since he hired her to be the Courtyard's Human Liaison. His response to Ferryman was just another example of how she muddled him up.

He wasn't surprised when Blair joined him as he trotted back toward the business district.

<You all right?> Blair asked.

<Fine,> he grumbled.

<Having second thoughts about the meeting?>

<Not about the meeting.>

They trotted in silence for a couple of minutes. Then Blair said, <Be careful, Simon. You don't want to become too human. We see a few of them differently now, but most of them are still just meat.>

<I know.> It was one thing for an earth native to be able to pass for human. It was quite another thing to start *thinking* like a human.

Blair headed back to the Utilities Complex while Simon continued trotting toward the business district.

Becoming too human was always a danger to *terra indigene* who worked in the Courtyards and kept careful watch over the clever meat. He should go to the wild country for a couple of weeks this summer. He could stay in Wolf form for days at a time and regain his sense of who he was, *what* he was.

But he already knew he wouldn't go to the wild country. Too much unrest rippled throughout Thaisia, as well as right here in Lakeside. Until they figured out who was making the drugs that had reached his piece of the world, there was too much uncertainty.

And there was too much need to stay close to Meg.

Trying to figure that out confused him, and being confused made him angry.

It was unfortunate for the four-footed bunny that it chose that moment to bolt from its hiding place.

Four young men stood across the street from A Little Bite. Tess watched them crowd Merri Lee when she stood at the corner, waiting for the light to change, jostling her until she almost stumbled in front of a car. When she crossed the street and hurried to the coffee shop, the men stayed on the other side, the *human* side. Tess hadn't heard what they said to the girl, but she saw the look on Merri Lee's face—a look that was quickly hidden behind a cheerful mask.

An hour later, they were still there, watching. And Merri Lee watched *them* while she went about her work.

And Tess, being one of Namid's most ferocious predators, knew the difference between a hunter watching and prey watching.

"Do you know them?" Tess asked, tipping her head to indicate the men across the street.

"Not really," Merri Lee replied. "They go to Lakeside University. I think I've had a class with a couple of them." As she wiped off the tables near the windows, the men shouted something.

<What did they say?> Tess asked the Crows who were perched on the roof. They, too, were watching.

<They say the Merri Lee is a Wolf lover and is going to get what she deserves,> Jake replied. <Is the Merri Lee having sex with a Wolf?>

<It wouldn't be Simon,> Jenni said. <Simon likes our Meg.> A pause. <Do Simon and Meg have sex after they play?>

<No,> Tess said firmly. Simon's relationship with Meg was too complex for anything as simple as sex. <And asking about that will upset Meg.>

No response from the Crows. She didn't expect one. They might be willing to poke at a Wolf and say something to get a reaction, but they wouldn't say anything to upset the blood prophet who had saved their lives.

Tess turned her attention back to Merri Lee. "Those men. Do you know their names?"

Merri Lee shook her head. "It's nothing."

Tess let it go. Except for Meg, Merri Lee and Heather were the only humans left who worked in the businesses open to the public. Lorne Kates ran the Three Ps, but the print shop was for Courtyard residents only; Elizabeth Bennefeld, the massage therapist, was an independent contractor who worked in her Market Square office two days a week; and despite some concerns expressed by the administrators of Lakeside Hospital, Dominic Lorenzo was going ahead with his plans to provide care for Courtyard residents and employees. The other humans who worked for some of the Market Square businesses had been calling in sick a lot over the past couple of weeks, and some of them had stopped calling. Even the consulate had lost its human employees.

All of it was a backlash from the storm in early Febros and not unexpected. But it only proved the fleeting nature of human memory. The humans who quit had forgotten that working in the Courtyard was the only thing that made them not edible.

"Why don't you check the storeroom?" Tess told Merri Lee. "See if we're running low on anything."

She waited until the girl was in the back before she walked out the front door. Nothing between her and those four men except pavement. But still too much distance to reveal her true nature. Too much chance of other people looking upon her. If many people became ill while driving past the Courtyard, there would be questions she didn't want asked because she had no intention of letting anyone with answers survive.

At least, no one human. She had revealed her true nature when she killed Asia Crane, the human female who had participated in the attempted abduction of Sam and Meg. Afterward she wondered if Henry or Simon had suspected what kind of *terra indigene* she was, but neither of them said anything. She valued their unspoken acceptance enough that she wouldn't deliberately bring trouble to the Courtyard without good reason.

"See something you like?" Nyx joined her.

Tess glanced toward the Courtyard's customer parking lot. How many Sanguinati were watching from the shadows? "I see a pack of two-legged nuisances."

"Hmm. I see takeout."

Tess laughed, which seemed to enrage the men. One of them pulled a small container out of his coat pocket and waved it at them.

"Come on, then!" he shouted. "Bitch in a jar!"

Nyx's smile didn't change, but Tess's hair turned red with black streaks. Black. The death color. So tempting to let her true nature show when she could feel the effort Nyx was making not to attack.

But in the end, the men weren't tempting enough. Yet.

She went back into the shop. A moment later, still smiling at the men, Nyx went into Howling Good Reads.

Had to make a decision soon. She'd already checked her stockroom and knew what she had to order. It wasn't going to take Merri Lee much more time.

It wasn't the *terra indigene*'s place to protect humans—at least not when they were beyond the Courtyard's boundaries. But she knew one human who would be interested in keeping Merri Lee from harm.

She dialed the number for HGR's office. "Vlad? Tell Simon I want to be at the meeting when he talks to the police."

"You're out of the beef flavored? What about the chicken?" Meg listened to the blustering manager of the Pet Palace and bared her teeth in a smile. She'd read a magazine article the other day about how maintaining a positive attitude produced better results when dealing with someone who forgot the *service* in *customer service*.

Unfortunately, Wolves were much better at discerning attitude than humans. As soon as she bared her teeth, Nathan hurried over, flopped his forelegs on the counter, and pricked his ears to hear the other side of the conversation.

Since she was trying to order more boxes of dog cookies, she was surprised he'd resisted butting in for as long as he had.

"What about the puppy cookies?" Meg asked. "Completely sold out of those too. I see. When do you expect . . . ? Oh. No longer being made? Yes. I'm sure you are sorry."

"*Arrooo?*" Nathan queried softly.

She hung up a little more forcefully than required just as the office door opened and Nathan twisted around to see who was coming in.

Harry from Everywhere Delivery hesitated in the doorway. Then he came in and set his packages on the end of the counter farthest away from them.

"Guess I don't have to ask if you two are having a good morning," he said.

"*Arrooo!*"

Meg blew out a breath and picked up her pen and clipboard. Harry was a darling who chatted about his wife and showed her pictures of his grandchildren. It wasn't fair to be grumpy with him.

"Sorry, Harry. I'm having some trouble getting an order delivered." She began filling out the information on the packages he'd brought.

"Oh? What kind of trouble?" When she didn't answer, he looked at Nathan. "Guess you can't tell me?"

The Wolf leaped over the counter and through the Private doorway into the sorting room.

"Do not shift unless you're going to put on clothes!" Meg yelled when she heard Nathan rummaging around.

He returned with a box of dog cookies and dropped it on the counter.

Harry looked at the package, then raised his eyebrows at Meg.

She sighed. "I called the Pet Palace to have them deliver more boxes of cookies. The manager informed me that they were out of stock, all flavors, all sizes."

"It does happen, Miz Meg," Harry said. "You go into stores the day before the next delivery, and you'll find plenty of empty shelves. And with seasonal items, stores just plain run out for the year."

"I understand that," Meg said. "But that doesn't explain why, when I called Hot Crust yesterday to have a pizza delivered, they told me they didn't make deliveries anymore, and a few minutes later I saw their delivery car drive by!" Since Nathan was crowding her to the point of stepping on her foot, she put her hands over his ears and whispered, "And Julia Hawkgard told me that when the Courtyard bus went to the plaza last Firesday, there were signs in some of the store windows that said Humans Only."

She let go of Nathan's ears in order to dig her fingers through the weave of her sweater and scratch at the pins-and-needles feeling that suddenly filled her right arm.

"Damn fools," Harry muttered. He picked up the box of dog cookies. "This what you want?"

"Yes, but—"

"Don't carry much money on me, but I can swing by that store during my lunch break and pick up a box or two—unless they're telling the truth about being out of stock."

"I have money," Simon said, stepping up to the counter.

She hadn't heard him come in. Nathan squeezed behind her to crowd her on the other side, wedging her between a Wolf in Wolf form and a Wolf in human form. It made her very aware that she was a short human—and it made her aware that the pins-and-needles feeling was quickly fading.

Simon put two twenty-dollar bills on the counter. "People might ask questions if you buy too many. A box of each flavor will be sufficient."

"Fair enough." Harry pocketed the bills. "I'll see what I can do." He tapped a finger to the brim of his cap and left.

"Watch the counter," Simon said, then took Meg by the arm, hauled her into the sorting room, and closed the Private door.

"Nathan can't sign for packages unless he shifts," Meg protested. "And a naked Wolf is *not* going to make deliverymen feel easy."

"This will only take a minute. Why are you scratching your arm?"

"It prickled." When she reached for her right arm again, he grabbed both her wrists and held her hands apart. "Simon!"

"Your skin hasn't been prickling all week. Not here, not at home. And you haven't needed to cut."

He was being careful not to hurt her, so she didn't struggle—especially when she realized he was right about the pins-and-needles feeling. And he was right about the cutting, up to a point. Some days she *wanted* to cut, desperately wanted to feel the euphoria, but she didn't *need* to cut. While everyday activities couldn't match the orgasmic release that came from cutting, they did blunt the need. And being surrounded by neighbors who had a wickedly keen sense of smell meant you couldn't hide even the smallest cut.

"I don't understand," Meg said.

"When I went to that meeting on Great Island? Steve Ferryman said that Intuits live in small communities in order to become attuned with the place where they live and the people around them."

"I've never heard of Intuits."

He looked uncomfortable. "They're a between kind of human."

"Between what?"

"Between a human like Lieutenant Montgomery and a human like you. Most of the Intuits can't see prophecies, but they get feelings about things, for good or bad."

"Most of them?" Meg's heart jumped. "But some of them do see visions, speak prophecies?"

Fur sprang out on Simon's cheeks and hands, then retreated and returned. Involuntary shifting was a sure sign of strong emotions in the Others.

"The *cassandra sangue* originally came from the Intuits," Simon admitted. "At least, that's what I was told."

He didn't want to tell me that, Meg thought. *So why is he telling me now?*

But the wonder of it! Her friend Jean had insisted that girls like them could live outside in the world. Jean had come from a family that had lived outside the control of people who became richer with every scar a girl acquired.

Jean.

Meg cried out and tried to claw at her arms, but Simon still held her wrists.

"Meg!"

Couldn't cut now. Not with Simon holding on to her and Nathan howling in the front room in response to whatever he was sensing. And if Nathan didn't shut up, there would be Wolves and Bears and Sanguinati crowding in and wanting to know what was wrong.

"I'm okay," she gasped. "I'm okay."

"I'll send him away," Simon growled. "I don't care if he wants to meet you. I won't allow him to enter the Courtyard."

"Who? What?" Had to regain control. Couldn't think about Jean or the compound. Concentrate on something new. Intuits. Could they help her understand how to live in the outside world?

"Steve Ferryman," Simon snapped. "He's not even here yet and he upset you!"

"No, he didn't. I was thinking about my friend Jean. You can't blame Mr. Ferryman for that. And I would like to meet him."

"Why? Have you seen him?"

She hadn't known he existed until Simon mentioned him, so where would she see . . . ?

Of course. She could have seen this man in a vision—just as she'd first seen Simon in a vision. But she hadn't seen Steve Ferryman, hadn't known anything about him or humans who were called Intuits.

Did the Controller know about these people?

Focus on Simon. "You said Intuits live in small communities. If blood prophets started out as Intuits, maybe that's also an important thing to know about people like me."

The fur receded from Simon's cheeks. The fingernails were still claws, but he was being careful not to damage her.

"I did wonder if it might be the same for you," Simon said. "Maybe your skin isn't prickling all the time because you've gotten used to us."

She thought about the routine of her days. She opened the Liaison's Office and mostly had Nathan, and sometimes Jake Crowgard, snoozing in the front room in between deliveries. All the deliverymen were people she saw a couple of times a week. She went to the Quiet Mind class with Merri Lee, Heather, and Ruth Stuart. At the Green Complex, she came in daily contact with Henry, Tess, Vlad, Julia Hawkgard, Jester Coyotegard, and Jenni Crowgard and her sisters. And Simon.

There had been little prickles—like the time when Ruth misplaced her keys after class—but she was learning that small things could be dealt with in mundane ways, like having your friends help you look for the keys, so little prickles could be ignored.

"I'll have to think about this some more, pay more attention," she said.

"You haven't been scratching at your skin until today."

"Is something happening today?"

He growled, and she watched his canines lengthen.

"Maybe you need to go outside and run around for a while."

"Did that."

Meg sighed. When she tried to tug her wrists out of his hold, he released her. "Simon, go to your meeting. Try not to bite anyone. And after work, you and Sam and I can go for a walk."

"Okay. Yeah. All right."

He sounded unhappy. He arranged this meeting, so why would he be unhappy? Unless it had something to do with her?

"If it really bothers you, I don't have to meet Mr. Ferryman," she said, trying to interpret his body language and expression.

"You should meet him. Just . . . don't like him too much." He looked toward the front room. "Nathan says the police are here for the meeting, and another car pulled in too."

"Then you should go."

He hesitated, then gave her cheek a quick lick before rushing into the back room and out the door.

Meg stood there trying to sort through it all as she recalled training images of men's faces showing various expressions and emotions. Then she shook her head and opened the Private door to keep Nathan from fretting.

When she spotted *The Dimwit's Guide to Dating*, which she'd left on the counter, she closed her eyes and tried to imagine a series of images that could fit.

Simon coming into the office, thinking about this meeting and having a strange human—Steve Ferryman—in the Courtyard. Simon seeing the book that she'd hidden until now because she didn't want to explain that she was reading a book about humans dating humans in an effort to understand *him*. Simon now wondering about her interest in Steve Ferryman and Ferryman's interest in her. And last, Meg and Simon having this odd conversation.

She had to be mistaken, had to be interpreting the past few minutes incorrectly. After all, this was *Simon*, who was a *terra indigene* Wolf.

But if he'd been human, she would have said he was jealous.

Simon paused outside the Business Association's meeting room and took stock.

Hands? Human. Ears? Human shaped and not furry. Teeth? He growled, "Close enough," and walked into the room.

He'd expected Vlad and Henry to sit in on this meeting even though it didn't have anything to do with the Lakeside Courtyard. But Tess's being there, with her hair red and curling, was an unwelcome surprise.

<Why are you here?> he asked her.

<There is something the police need to know,> she replied.

Steve Ferryman was there, of course. He might know things Meg wanted to learn, but *he* would never be as thorough about cleaning the salt and butter off her hands after movie night.

Picturing Ferryman licking Meg's hands surprised a growl out of Simon. That made everyone else sit up—except Ferryman, who made an effort to look smaller.

<Simon?> Henry asked. Or warned.

Simon blew out a breath and turned toward the other humans in the room. Sitting between Captain Burke and Lieutenant Montgomery was a male he didn't know.

Roger Czerneda was medium height with blond hair and blue eyes. Nothing challenging or aggressive in his demeanor, which would lessen friction when he had to deal with the Others on Great Island. And still healing from the wound he'd received in Jerzy. If the pack was hunting and Roger was in a crowd of humans, they would try to separate him from the rest because he'd be vulnerable and easier to bring down.

An invited guest is not edible, Simon reminded himself as he took a seat. The look Henry gave him had him running his tongue over his teeth to confirm they were still close enough to human.

"We appreciate your hosting this meeting," Captain Burke said, addressing the remark to Simon but managing to include the other three *terra indigene* in the room. "And we appreciate Mr. Ferryman driving down to Lakeside to meet Roger."

"I'm glad to have an opportunity to visit the Lakeside Courtyard," Steve Ferryman said. "And Officer Czerneda should know some things about Ferryman's Landing before he makes a decision." No longer needing to show the Courtyard leader he wasn't issuing a challenge, he leaned back in his chair and crossed his legs at the ankles. "The way things work on Great Island isn't unique in Thaisia, but it's one of the most visible communities where *terra indigene*, Simple Life folks, and Intuits divide tasks between the groups so that all the parts make up the whole. Nobody has a lot in terms of wealth and material goods, but everyone has enough."

Since the outcome didn't affect the Courtyard one way or the other, Simon didn't pay much attention to the "blah, blah, blah" about how the different groups worked together. Ferryman's Landing wasn't the only "human" village that belonged to the *terra indigene*. There were a couple of Intuit and Simple Life communities in the Addirondak Mountains, where products of interest to the Others were made in exchange for the use of land and natural resources. Not that different from other human towns and cities—except Courtyards were surrounded by a city and the humans who lived there, whereas small human settlements were surrounded by the wild country and the *terra indigene* who lived there. That meant the Intuits didn't forget that their survival was, always, dependent on what the Others considered a fair exchange.

And the Others in the wild country didn't forget that humans weren't *terra indigene* and get tangled up in a friendship with one and start caring.

<You might want to pay attention now,> Vlad said. <It sounds like they're finishing up.>

<What did I miss?>

<Roger is going to be the official police officer for Ferryman's Landing. Burke is going to help Steve Ferryman acquire an official patrol car since the village doesn't have one. Flash Foxgard is going to be Roger's partner while he's becoming familiar with the island and both sides of the village.>

<Will anyone tell him to look the other way if a farmer reports some eggs missing from a henhouse?>

<I'm sure the Foxgard can account for any and all eggs.>

"Well," Burke said, shifting in his chair. "I think that concludes—"

"No," Tess said. "There's something you all need to know." She looked at Vlad. "Unless you want to tell them?"

"Tell them what?" Vlad sounded puzzled.

As he listened to Tess's account of the men who were watching Merri Lee, Simon studied Burke and Montgomery. Anger and concern, respectively. The Wolf-lover remark wasn't a surprise to Burke. The question was which group—police or *terra indigene*—was going to curb the trouble before it turned into a full fight. Seeing the look in Vlad's eyes when Tess mentioned the "bitch in a jar" remark, he didn't think the police would have much time to act once Erebus Sanguinati decided how his people would respond.

"I'll have a word with the patrol captain in the university district," Burke said.

"It's not just Lakeside," Ferryman said. "We've heard rumblings about trouble brewing in Talulah Falls. A couple of demonstrations near the Courtyard there, some speeches at the colleges." He paused, then added, "And we had an incident a few nights ago. It's a big reason why we decided to adjust the village budget to hire an official police officer."

"What happened?" Roger asked, looking pale.

"A boat landed on the north end of the island, where most of the Simple Life folks have their farms. Someone tried to set fire to a barn."

"Tried?" Simon said.

"We had a sudden downpour that lasted a couple of hours. The rain put out the fire before the farmer could report it. About the same time the rain started, a heavy fog covered the river. You couldn't have seen your own hand out on the water."

Ah, Simon thought. *Water must have been riding Fog that night.* Not even the rest of the *terra indigene* knew how the Elementals divided the world into territories or even how many of them there were. But he was fairly certain that the Elementals who touched Great Island and Talulah Falls were the ladies who lived in the Lakeside Courtyard.

"Did the police have any luck finding the person responsible?" Burke asked.

Ferryman gave the captain an odd smile. "Thick fog and a fast river leading right to the falls. The morning after the fire, a broken boat and two bodies were pulled from the river."

"Were the bodies drained of blood?" Vlad asked. "I know the Sanguinati who live on the island have been interested in the shore for the past few days. Such interest usually means an incursion of humans who might cause trouble for the island's residents."

Ferryman shrugged. "Those men went over the falls. If they were dead when they went over, the Sanguinati did them a favor."

"Anything else?" Simon asked. When his only answer was several headshakes, he stood.

"Come up to the village whenever you're ready and we'll get you settled in," Ferryman told Roger.

"Mr. Wolfgard," Montgomery said. "If I could have a minute?"

"A minute," Simon agreed.

"I'll wait outside," Ferryman said.

"Why don't I give our guests a quick tour of the Market Square?" Vlad said.

When everyone else left the room, Simon studied Montgomery. Not sick, but the dark skin didn't look as healthy as usual.

"Something wrong with you?" Simon asked.

Montgomery smiled. "Too many sleepless nights lately."

A Wolf would curl up and take a nap, but humans were rarely as sensible.

"I understand a few of your human employees have left recently," Montgomery said.

"Most, actually. Why?"

"Officer MacDonald's cousin is looking for work. She has secretarial and business skills that might be useful to Dr. Lorenzo, if he hasn't already hired someone for the office here."

"Why would she want to work in the Courtyard?"

Montgomery looked uncomfortable. "Theral got out of an abusive relationship a few months ago. She's had two jobs since then and was fired from both of them because her ex-partner showed up at her place of work, making threats and causing trouble. She moved back to Lakeside because she has family here. When Officer MacDonald mentioned that Theral was looking for work, I offered to broach the subject with you, in case you were looking for new employees. If you're interested, she can call and make an appointment for an interview."

Simon scratched behind one ear to give himself a moment to figure out what Montgomery was really trying to tell him. "You think this man will follow her to Lakeside and cause trouble?"

"I hope not."

"But you want us to eat him if he does show up?"

"No, no, nothing like that."

Despite the words, Simon didn't think Montgomery would be too upset if he had to fill out a DLU form for this male who threatened a member of MacDonald's family. "I'll talk to the other members of the Business Association."

"Thank you."

He walked out with Montgomery and wished that Ferryman, who was standing near the back of the Liaison's Office, would make some lame excuse about needing to get home and not having time to meet Meg.

They didn't speak until the police drove away, Henry went back to his studio, and Vlad and Tess went back to their stores. Then Ferryman studied him for a moment. "When you walked into the meeting, I had a feeling that you really didn't want me in your Courtyard. But it's not the whole Courtyard, is it? It's this office."

Simon didn't answer.

"Do you want me to make an excuse and leave?"

"No." That's exactly what he wanted, but he couldn't figure out how to explain Ferryman's departure to Meg. Besides, it was possible Ferryman could help her.

"Do all *terra indigene* react this way to a *cassandra sangue*?" Steve asked.

Simon just opened the back door and walked in. Hearing Nathan's growl, he hurried into the sorting room with Ferryman on his heels.

"Give it back," Meg said, pulling on one end of a catalog as hard as she could while Nathan pulled on the other end. "Give . . . it . . . back!"

"Stop," Simon said. <What are you doing?>

<It made her angry,> Nathan replied. He stopped pulling but didn't let go of his end of the catalog. <I tried to take it away, but Henry said not to pull paper away too fast because it can cut Meg's hands.>

Meg looked over and saw the two men. Blushing, she released the catalog, which Nathan then dropped on the floor.

"Problem?" Simon asked.

"I've been trying to get some orders filled. Stores have the merchandise until they find out I'm placing the order for the Courtyard, and then suddenly they're out of stock!"

"That's a government problem, not yours. Make a list of the stores who are refusing to make deliveries and give it to Elliot. And include that pet store and Hot Crust on that list."

"Why should Elliot have to deal with this?"

"Because there are penalties for refusing to make deliveries to the Courtyard, and it's the government's responsibility to enforce the agreements made between the humans and us."

"There are penalties?" Meg said. "Good!"

See? Simon thought, slanting a look at Ferryman. *She's not a sweet, fluffy bunny. There's a streak of Wolf in her.* "Meg, this is Steve Ferryman, the mayor of Ferryman's Landing. And this is Meg Corbyn."

Ferryman reached out to shake her hand, and it was only Simon's concern that he might miss and nip one of Meg's fingers that kept him from biting Steve.

They barely touched hands before they both pulled back. To his credit, Steve looked concerned when Meg started scratching at her arm. But he looked at the box on the sorting table and said, "What are these?"

"Dog cookies," Meg said at the same time Simon said, "Wolf cookies."

"One of the items that are suddenly not available to Courtyard residents," Meg said with a bitterness that surprised and worried Simon—especially when her fingers dug into her arm. If she scratched any harder, even the sweater wouldn't protect her skin.

Steve picked up the box and shook out a cookie. After examining it, he said, "Do they have to be exactly like this?"

Meg stopped scratching. "Like what?"

Steve held up a cookie. "Like this. We're always looking for ways to help our Great Island community prosper and make sure everyone has work, whether it's Intuit or Simple Life or *terra indigene*. I can think of a few women who might be interested in developing a similar kind of cookie."

"Fresh-baked cookies for Wolves?"

"Why not?"

Simon stepped away from Ferryman. Meg looked too interested in the man, and it was getting harder to remember that Steve wasn't edible.

"I'd like you to look at something," Meg said. She led them into the front room and pointed at the Wolf bed.

After glancing at Simon for permission, Steve crouched beside the bed and examined it. "Do you have a spare one I could take back with me?"

"I think there are a couple left in the general store," Simon replied. "You can have one."

"Thanks." Steve rose and smiled at Meg. Then the smile faded. "When an Intuit gets a feeling, there's always some physical sign—a fluttering in the belly or a particular group of muscles getting tight. But it's so much harder for you, isn't it?"

Simon moved closer to Meg, a protective stance.

"Do you know a blood prophet?" Meg asked. "Is there a girl on the island?"

Steve shook his head. "We couldn't figure out how to help her in time to save her."

"Oh. I'm sorry."

"So am I." Steve looked uncomfortable. "I'd better be going."

"I'll take you over to the general store," Simon said.

"Thanks for your help, Mr. Ferryman," Meg said.

"Steve. No need to be so formal."

She smiled—and Simon swallowed a snarl.

He and Steve walked to the Market Square in silence. In fact, Ferryman didn't say anything until they picked up the Wolf bed and packed it into the back of his car. Then he turned to Simon.

"While I would like to have Ms. Corbyn as a friend, I'm not chasing after your girl, Mr. Wolfgard."

"She's not mine." Since Meg made an excellent squeaky toy, why wouldn't Ferryman want to chase her when it was so much fun?

Steve smiled. "She's the Courtyard's Liaison and you're the Courtyard's leader. In a way, that makes her yours."

He tipped his head to acknowledge that point—and realized that Steve wouldn't come sniffing around Meg. Simon wasn't an Intuit or a blood prophet, but he had good instincts. "You want ties to Lakeside. That's why you're looking for a way to make the cookies and the beds. What are the *terra indigene* on Great Island going to say about that?"

"Something is wrong in Talulah Falls. We feel it; so do the *terra indigene* who live on the island. Ming Beargard has tried to talk to the Others who are in charge of the Talulah Falls Courtyard, but they won't talk to him because they think the island's earth natives are too friendly with humans. Ming was told the Others are supposed to receive goods made by humans, not *help* the humans with the work. I don't think that was always their attitude, but the current rulers of the Talulah Falls Courtyard want as little interaction with humans as possible."

"So Ming wants a bond with the Lakeside Courtyard too?"

Steve nodded. "We used to sell some of our specialty items at shops in Talulah Falls—things the tourists visiting the Falls love taking home with them. When our team of sales representatives drove up to the Falls to talk with the shops and write up orders for the summer tourist season, *none* of those businesses would place an order with us, and a few of them muttered that they wouldn't buy anything from anyone who put humans last. Our team felt a hostility whenever a *terra indigene* and a human came within sight of each other." He paused, as if considering his words carefully. "When things go wrong in Talulah Falls—and I think it's a matter of when and not if—the *terra indigene* who rule the Courtyard there aren't going to talk to the police or give the government a chance to fix things. So, if possible, I would rather do business with you."

Simon wasn't sure he would be any more merciful if too much trouble stirred up the *terra indigene* in Lakeside, but at least, for now, he could take advantage of a business deal that would benefit both sides.

By the time Ferryman drove off, Meg had closed the Liaison's Office for her midday break and gone out to lunch with Heather and Merri Lee. He would have growled about Meg leaving the Courtyard with two females who didn't have a fang between them, but when he walked into Howling Good Reads, John informed him that the girls had gone to the Saucy Plate for lunch, and Henry and Vlad had gone to Hot Crust to pick up pizzas. Since the two places were in the same plaza, the girls would be guarded. And even if the humans at Hot Crust gave Meg a hard time about delivering to the Courtyard, no one but a fool denied food to a Grizzly.

Plenty to think about. Too much to think about and not a lot he could do about any of it right now.

But there was one thing he could do. Picking up the phone, Simon called Dr. Lorenzo to tell him about Officer MacDonald's cousin.

CHAPTER 16

Toward the end of Viridus, the Crows from the Talulah Falls Courtyard flew to the part of town where most of the tourists walked and ate and bought souvenirs at the kiosks. For three days, they watched humans toss sparkly toys into the trash cans—toys that were only a little broken in ways that, for Crows, did not diminish their appeal. They watched humans throw away half a hamburger still in the thin paper wrapping so it wasn't soiled by other debris. They watched little treasures being dropped into the cans—and they watched while city workers emptied the cans and took away that food and those treasures.

And there were bits of shiny nearby, coins that had fallen from pockets and caught the sun, a glittering lure.

For three days, the Crows resisted doing more than keeping watch. But on the fourth day, a few of the adolescent Crows dared to come down from the trees to grab a shiny or snatch a morsel of food or fly off with one of the sparkly toys.

And nothing happened. The humans, who were entranced by the water thundering into the river below, barely noticed them. So on the fifth day, more of the Crows flew down from the trees to snatch a morsel of food or make off with a shiny coin or a little treasure. On the sixth day, even more Crows gathered around the cans, enjoying the hunt for discarded items that sparkled.

On the seventh day, the trash cans that had the choicest morsels of food and the best little treasures exploded, killing Crows and tourists alike.

That night, one of the Sanguinati who had been hunting for the humans responsible for murdering the Crows didn't return to the Talulah Falls Courtyard.

And early the following morning, in Lakeside, Meg Corbyn woke up screaming.

"Meg!" Standing in their common back hallway, Simon pounded on Meg's kitchen door, then paused to pull on the jeans he'd grabbed when he heard her scream. "Meg!" He snarled at the door when it didn't open, when he didn't hear anything.

Jamming his hand in the jeans' pocket, he pulled out the keys to Meg's apartment and turned the lock—and still couldn't get in.

Why did she have to use that slide lock as well as the regular lock? It wasn't like anyone used the kitchen door for visiting. Except him. And Sam when the pup was with him. The common outside door was locked, and he checked it every night before turning in, so she didn't have to worry about an intruder coming in through the back way. He knew she didn't have company, since she'd quietly told him she wanted to sleep alone tonight.

"And that's the last time I listen to you about who sleeps where," he grumbled as he pounded on the door again. "Damn it, Meg. What are you doing that you don't want me to know about?"

The answer to that had him scratching at the door before he remembered he was in human form.

"*Meg!*"

Fur suddenly covered Simon's shoulders and chest as he threw his weight against the door, breaking the wood and the slide lock. He rushed toward Meg's bedroom, but the fresh scent of blood pulled him toward the bathroom. He shoved at the door and Meg cried out, so he squeezed through the narrow opening to avoid ramming her legs again.

She was on the floor, bleeding. The cut ran all the way across her torso just under her breasts. Too long a cut. Too deep a cut. Too much blood.

"Meg." Barely enough room to straddle her legs when he dropped to his knees to reach her.

"Simon," she gasped. "You have to listen."

"Yeah. Sure."

His friend was bleeding. It didn't matter that she was human. His friend Meg was bleeding too much.

He lowered his head, then paused.

It would make him so angry. Like the last time when she fell in the creek and cut her chin and he had to get her to the human bodywalker.

I don't care. She's one of us now. Clean the wound. Get rid of the blood scent and hide the fact that she's vulnerable.

He quickly licked the blood flowing from the cut. Licked and licked to keep it from dripping on the towel Meg had put on the floor to soak it up.

"Simon," Meg moaned. "Simon. I see . . . It's too much. I have to speak. You have to listen."

For a moment he'd been very angry, and now he wasn't. He heard Meg's voice and something changed and he wasn't angry at all.

Lick, lick.

She always tasted good. But this was *wonderful*.

Lick, lick.

He liked the sound of her voice. Even when she was yelling at him. Which she wasn't doing now. She was . . .

The scent of arousal, as alluring as the scent of blood.

He sat back on his heels to bring his face closer to this new, delightful scent. His human body responded with pleasure, responded with a willingness that was hard to ignore.

"*Simon.*"

Something not pleasing in her voice now. Something . . . that should bother him.

"You have to remember," she pleaded.

Remember? Yes. Lick, lick. The wonderful taste of Meg. But no biting. No tearing the flesh because . . . Why? It would feel so good to taste flesh. So very good. But not Meg's flesh. He wouldn't hurt Meg. Would never hurt Meg.

Something he was supposed to remember. Something about Meg talking when there was a cut and blood.

"Have to write it down," he mumbled.

"Yes," she said. "Hurry."

He tried to get up, tried to leave the bathroom and fetch paper and pencil to write down . . . words! Write down words. She smelled *so* good. Tasted even better. Even her hair, still all weird shades of orange and red, didn't stink anymore from whatever she had done to it.

Words. Important to write down Meg's words.

Using the sink for support, Simon struggled to his feet. Maybe his feet. Couldn't feel his feet. Did he still have feet?

"Write," he growled. He should be angry. Why wasn't he angry? Wasn't sick, but wasn't well either.

Fear surged through him, clearing his head for a moment.

A basket on the counter full of little brushes and pots of color. Female toys. He grabbed a pencil and wrote the words that poured out of her now.

Something wrong with him. Something very wrong. But he wrote the words until her voice stopped. Then he dropped the pencil and slid to the floor.

"Meg?" He licked at the blood still flowing from her wound and whined. "Meg?"

Her eyes were glazed. When she tried to raise her hand and touch him, she couldn't do it.

"Your ears are furry," she said.

They needed help. He . . . needed . . . help.

<Henry!>

<Simon? What's wrong?>

<Sick. Meg . . . hurt. Hurry.>

Meg bleeding. Had to do something about Meg bleeding. Im . . . por . . . tant.

Simon stretched out on top of Meg, his face pressed into her sweet belly, where he could breathe in all those delicious scents.

Familiar scents and sounds, but nothing that said *Meg* to him.

Meg smelled good. Tasted even better.

"I think he's finally coming around." That voice belonged to Blair, the Courtyard's primary enforcer.

Why did hearing Blair's voice make him feel afraid?

"Simon?" That was Vlad, sounding angry. Why angry? Did Vlad also lick . . . ?

"Meg!" Simon tried to move, to sit up, but his body seemed tangled and nothing worked quite right.

Until Vlad grabbed his arms and hauled him up enough so that all he could see was the fury in the Sanguinati's dark eyes.

"What. Did. You. Do?" Vlad snarled.

Do? He . . . remembered.

"Meg was bleeding," Simon said. His voice didn't sound right. His jaw didn't move the right way for human speech. What . . . ?

Tess stepped into view next to Vlad. The hair that framed her face was black, black, black, but the rest was the red of anger. And all of it coiled and moved in a way that was mesmerizing—and terrifying.

"We know about Meg," she said. "We're asking about *you*."

To avoid her eyes and Vlad's, he looked at his surroundings. The living room in his apartment. How did he get there? Then he looked at his naked body—and the jolt of what he saw cleared the rest of the fuzziness from his mind.

One leg was human, the other was a Wolf's hind leg starting from midthigh all the way down to the foot. As he processed the scents in the room and realized how many Others were looking at him, his tail curled protectively over his human genitalia. Fur on most of his torso. Hands that weren't quite hands. He wasn't sure he wanted to know what his head and face looked like.

Between was a form that wasn't Wolf and wasn't human. Many of the *terra indigene* who lived in the wild country could take the rough shape of a human but could never pass for human, could never achieve a form that wasn't somewhat between. The Wolfman in horror stories. The Others who lived in a Courtyard made an effort not to take a *between* form around humans, but they all shifted pieces when they needed some aspect of their other form. Like ears that could hear better. Or claws and fangs. There was a symmetry to that kind of shifting, even when it was more instinct than deliberate choice. But this? This was a body out of control.

He looked up at Blair, who watched him with sympathy laced with anger.

Then Henry stepped up beside Blair. There wasn't any sympathy in the Grizzly's eyes, but there was plenty of anger.

Surrounded by Sanguinati, Wolf, Grizzly, and Tess.

Have to choose a form. He wanted to shift to full Wolf and curl up somewhere until he had time to think it through, sort it out. But he was the Courtyard's leader, and the leader couldn't hide.

It took effort to shift all the way to human, and that surprised him. It felt like he'd tumbled into something sticky, something that slowed his reflexes and hampered his ability to shift.

So hard not to show fear. Impossible not to feel fear.

He must have shifted sufficiently to human because Vlad released him and Tess tossed a blanket in his lap.

"Where is Meg?" Simon asked. He needed water. He wanted food. More than either of those things, he wanted answers.

"Meg is staying at my place," Henry said. "She's been there since this morning. Nathan, Jester, and Jake are with her now, watching movies."

"This morning?" He couldn't see the windows—too many bodies in his way—but the light wasn't much different from when he'd broken Meg's kitchen door.

"Sun's down," Henry said. "I found you and Meg in her bathroom this morning. Do you remember that?"

"Don't remember you coming in, but I asked you . . ." Simon struggled to remember. "Meg, bleeding. Long cut. Too deep. Too much blood. Words. Had to write the words."

"When Henry found you, he called Blair and me," Vlad said. "We hauled you out of the bathroom so Henry could deal with Meg." He bent over so his eyes were on a level with Simon's. "You were awake. For hours you were awake, but you didn't care. About *anything*. We could have cut off your hands and feet, and you wouldn't have done a thing to stop us. *Couldn't* have done a thing to stop us. We could have carved you into pieces or cut you until you bled out, and you would have done nothing but watch us. The drug that laced the food the humans had used as bait for the Crows got into the Courtyard, got into *you*. We need to know how that happened."

He kept his eyes on Vlad's. "It's not Meg's fault. I thought it would make me angry, like the last time. I thought it would make me stronger so I could help her."

Vlad studied him. "What isn't Meg's fault?"

"The Sanguinati don't drink the sweet blood of the *cassandra sangue*. Not because of the prophecies that swim in their blood. Erebus was wrong about that. It's because the blood prophets are Namid's creation, both wondrous and terrible."

Vlad straightened up and took a step back. "What are you talking about?"

"The drug. It's the blood of the *cassandra sangue*."

"Which drug?" Henry asked. "There are two of them affecting *terra indigene* and humans."

Simon swallowed. He really wanted some water. "Both of them."

Turning into the Bird Park Plaza's lot, Captain Burke glanced at Monty. "You hear anything more from Dr. Lorenzo about Meg Corbyn's condition?"

"No, sir. Nothing since this morning." Monty had already reported his conversation with Dominic Lorenzo. Meg Corbyn had an atypical cut—too long and too deep—but there was no indication it wasn't self-inflicted. After closing up the wound, Lorenzo's recommendation had been rest and plenty of iron-rich foods to help replenish the blood that Meg had lost. "He's planning to look in on Ms. Corbyn tomorrow morning after his shift at the hospital."

Burke made a sound between a grunt and a growl as he pulled into a parking space. "Then let's take care of *this* problem."

Monty got out of the black sedan, relieved that the drive to the plaza from the Chestnut Street station was a short one. Burke was a big man, and being stuck with him in a small space when his blue eyes were lit with controlled fury wasn't pleasant.

Of course, there was good reason for Burke's fury. As information trickled in from Talulah Falls, the Lakeside government and police force began to realize they were looking at a situation that could sweep away more than one human town if everyone wasn't very, very careful.

The town of Talulah Falls was the powder keg. It was no longer a question of *if* the humans would lose another piece of Thaisia; it was a question of how much they were going to lose.

The residents and tourists trapped in the Falls could be just the beginning of what was lost.

And that was the reason Captain Douglas Burke and Lieutenant Crispin James Montgomery were standing in the plaza's parking lot at sundown, waiting as patrol car after patrol car found a parking spot and the officers got out to meet them.

Burke must have summoned every officer under his command, Monty thought. Then he spotted Louis Gresh and wondered if the commander of the bomb squad had been summoned or if Gresh understood something about Burke's meeting with the station's chief that afternoon and decided to bring his squad to this gathering.

"Gentlemen . . ." Burke began when the men gathered around him.

Just then Michael Debany's mobile phone rang.

"Beg your pardon, Captain," Debany said. Instead of turning off the phone, he moved away and spoke to someone for a couple of minutes. When he returned to his original spot next to his partner, Lawrence MacDonald, he was sheet white.

"Debany?" Monty asked.

"That was Ms. Lee, who works at A Little Bite."

Monty nodded. He didn't need that clarification, but some of the other men might. "And?"

"She's been attacked. University students. She made it back to her apartment, but she doesn't feel safe there."

"You know where she lives?" Burke asked. When Debany said he did, Burke pointed at MacDonald. "Go with him. Pick her up. Get her to the emergency room. Use Lakeside Hospital, where Dr. Lorenzo works, unless the situation is too critical for that much delay. Go."

Debany and MacDonald ran for their vehicle.

"The rest of you." Burke looked even fiercer than he had a moment ago. He swept a hand to indicate the whole plaza. "I want the owner or manager of every one of these stores brought to Hot Crust in five minutes. Anyone gives you any lip, arrest him and take him down to the station."

Monty blinked. "On what charge, sir?"

"On the charge of being a pain in my ass," Burke growled. "And right now, that is good enough for an overnight stay in our facility."

Gods above and below, Monty thought. *He means that.*

No one questioned the order. The men simply headed for the stores.

"Mind if I tag along?" Gresh asked, approaching Monty and Burke.

"No, I don't mind," Burke replied. "Give me a minute." He pulled out his mobile phone and took a few steps away from them.

"Attacks on humans employed by the Courtyard aren't good," Gresh said quietly, his eyes scanning the people who saw all the patrol cars and hesitated. Some returned to their cars and left the plaza. Most went about their business, ignoring the evidence that something was happening.

"People are scared and they're angry. They don't always think rationally under those conditions," Monty countered. He didn't disagree with Louis. Harassment and attacks weren't good at any time. Now it was like pulling down your pants and mooning beings that already wanted you dead. Not to mention breaking the human laws dealing with assault.

"I don't know how it was when you worked on the force in Toland, but around here, the watercooler and coffeemaker are great spots to overhear a whole lot of things. And the latest gossip is that the captain now has a connection to the police department on Great Island." Gresh gave Monty an inquiring look.

Monty glanced at Burke, who was still on the phone. Then he nodded. The captain hadn't said the conversation with Roger Czerneda was to be kept confidential. And most of what had been relayed could be heard on the news or seen by anyone brainless enough to drive to the island right now. "There's fog on the river so thick you can't see your own hand. But a channel of water stayed clear long enough for ferry and barge to cross for a hurried supply run and get back to the island side of Ferryman's Landing. Now the island is completely closed in." He hesitated, then added, "And it appears that there is something in that fog that is hunting anyone desperate enough or suicidal enough to try to get out of Talulah Falls by boat."

"Sanguinati?"

"Maybe. Short of falling over them, no one is going to find any bodies until the fog lifts." Not quite a lie, but part of the report *had* been confidential—the part about the Sanguinati telling Steve Ferryman and Officer Czerneda that they had yielded the river to another kind of hunter, one that didn't live on the island but must have been drawn to Talulah Falls by the glut of prey.

What was out there that could scare vampires?

"Nothing fancy about the explosives in the trash cans," Louis said after a moment. "Whoever set the charges didn't have any regard for human life. The bastards just wanted to kill some Crows . . . and maybe start a war." A glance at Burke, who seemed to be finishing up the call. "You think that's where we're headed? War?"

Maybe, Monty thought. "I hope not."

Burke joined them just as police officers began leading the first group of store managers toward Hot Crust.

"Mark Wheatley is the patrol captain for the university station," Burke said. "Until Debany and MacDonald arrive, he'll have men standing watch at Ms. Lee's apartment to prevent any further problems. Now, let's get this done."

He started toward the pizza place, then stopped when a young man with several insulated bags came out and hustled toward a car with a HOT CRUST DELIVERS! sign secured to the roof.

"You!" Burke snapped. "Turn around and go back inside."

"But—"

"Son, if you get in that car, the penalty to you is a five-hundred-dollar fine and five days in jail. And your boss knows it."

The deliveryman, who looked barely old enough to drive, stared at Burke, then hurried back to Hot Crust.

Burke followed, pulling out his badge and pushing his coat aside so that no one would miss the gun.

Personally, seeing the expression on Burke's face, Monty didn't think anyone was going to notice the gun, but he and Louis followed the captain inside. Plenty of customers filling the tables to grab bites to eat after work or waiting for their orders so they could take pizza home for family dinners.

"May I have your attention." Burke's voice boomed, cutting through the chatter. "And someone shut off that damn music!"

Silence.

He held up his badge in one hand and pointed at the customers with the other. "All of you. Out. Now. Hot Crust is closed for the next hour. They'll box up your food so you can take it with you. You've got four minutes. And you." Now he pointed to the deliveryman. "You sit over there."

"You can't do that." A man wearing a manager's name tag came out from behind the service counter. "He has deliveries to make."

"I was told Hot Crust no longer makes deliveries. Therefore, you will not be making any deliveries. Three minutes, people. With or without the food."

Some hurried up to the counter for take-out boxes. Most simply fled.

Burke waited until the customers were gone and all the owners or managers from the other stores in the Bird Park Plaza were crowded among the tables.

"If you don't know why you're here, you should," Burke said. "I know for a fact that every business in this plaza was sent a warning about the penalties for not making deliveries—*if* you provide delivery service—and for refusing to sell merchandise to the *terra indigene*. You were told to remove the Humans Only signs from your stores and to sell and deliver merchandise in accordance with the agreements made between the city of Lakeside and the *terra indigene*. Many of you are now in violation of those agreements. As of this moment, you are all being held accountable. If you're obeying orders and not willfully breaking the law, you will provide the name of the store owner, and he or she will be the individual looking at jail time and a hefty fine."

"We have rights too," said a man wearing a shirt with a Pet Palace logo on the pocket. "We've got the right to refuse service."

"Any of you been paying attention to what's happening in Talulah Falls?" Burke asked, giving them all his fierce-friendly smile. "I've been talking to police officers in the Falls all day, so I can tell you some things the news reports aren't saying."

Monty felt his stomach lurch. He'd heard plenty in the past few hours. He wasn't sure he wanted to hear what else Burke, with all his various sources, could have discovered.

"The Talulah Falls Courtyard has been abandoned." Burke ignored the few defiant cheers. "That means that, unlike us, there is no one the government or police can talk to, no one who will sit down with them now to try to work things out. Do you understand what that means? The town of Talulah Falls is cut off. The roads are barricaded or destroyed. Hundreds of vehicles clogged all the routes before people realized they were stranded. So nothing goes out and nothing comes in. No coal, no wood, no gasoline, no food, no medicines, no supplies of any kind. Whatever the town had before the explosion yesterday morning is all they have."

"What about the tourists?" one of the managers asked. "Even this early in the year, there are tourists."

"Now, that the town has in good supply. Lots of extra people using up what's available."

Mutters and uneasy shifting of feet.

"You think it's a coincidence that the phone lines still work and the radio and television stations are still able to broadcast?" Burke asked. *"Are you hearing the message, people? Because this is the message: You humans killed some of the terra indigene, and now you're going to pay."*

"Killing a vampire is a favor to everyone," another man said.

"Tell that to the families of people who will never be found," Burke said coldly. "Tell that to the families of the four people—four *humans*—who were chopped up by the maniac who managed to kill one of the Sanguinati. Think about being locked in a town with someone running loose who has already chopped up a sixty-year-old woman and an eleven-year-old boy and filled canning jars with the pieces."

A woman and two of the men rammed their way through the crowd to reach the restrooms. The rest of the people looked like they weren't going to hold on to their stomachs much longer.

"You want more?" Burke asked. They all shook their heads, but he continued anyway. "A tornado swept through Talulah Falls University this afternoon during a Humans First and Last rally. The dormitories weren't touched. Everything else? Piles of rubble. For all intents and purposes, the university is gone. And fires swept through the other college in the Falls. Again, the dormitories weren't touched, but the rest of the buildings are gutted."

Burke stared at all of them. He suddenly looked tired. "Ladies and gentlemen, all roads travel through the woods. What is happening in Talulah Falls is a harsh lesson. We need to learn from it. Bad things are happening right now in a lot of towns and villages across Thaisia, and those bad things have the *terra indigene* wondering if they want to tolerate our existence anymore. Our ancestors traded merchandise for land and skills for resources. That exchange is no different now than it was centuries ago. So if the merchants stop providing goods that are of interest to the Others, don't be surprised if the resources we need to survive also dry up."

Uneasy looks.

"Any business that still has a Humans Only sign in the window tomorrow will be fined. The owner will go to jail. If the sign is still there the following day, the next sign on the door will be Out of Business, and the owner will be put in the back of a patrol car and taken for a long ride."

Monty glanced at Louis, who stared at Burke in shock.

"The Lakeside government won't do that," the Pet Palace manager said nervously.

"No, it won't," Burke agreed with frightening congeniality. Monty felt the floor dip and rise. People who committed heinous crimes were taken for a long ride into the wild country and left without food, water, or shoes. It was a death sentence.

Looking at Burke, Monty wondered about the man's early years as a police officer. What had he seen that made him this committed to keeping the peace, to making his own kind of law to the point where he would take a business owner for a long ride? What was it about Burke that made his superiors yield when he wanted something that in some way affected the Others?

"We're done here," Burke said. "Go back to your stores."

The first steps were hesitant, as if the owners and managers didn't think he'd really let them go. Then the rush for the door.

"Lieutenant." Burke opened his wallet and pulled out two fifties.

"Sir?"

"Order four sheet pizzas for the Courtyard. You and Kowalski can take them with you. I'm sure they'll be ready in time for you to make your meeting with the Courtyard's Business Association."

"Of course," Hot Crust's manager stammered. "What would you like on them?"

Monty put in the order.

"Can we make our deliveries?" the manager asked.

"I don't know," Burke replied with a fierce smile. "Can you?"

"Yes. There won't be any trouble with deliveries from now on."

Burke wagged a finger at Monty and Louis. "Another moment of your time, gentlemen."

They went outside. Monty drew in air that held a hint of exhaust but was a lot cleaner than the fear-laden air in the pizza place.

"We're clear here," Burke said with a nod to the officers still waiting for further orders.

The officers returned to their patrol cars and drove off. Monty noticed Kowalski waiting for him beside their car.

"Something else on your mind, Captain?" Louis asked.

"Four people were butchered along with a Sanguinati," Burke said quietly.

"The older woman and the boy," Monty said.

"And two women. Late teens or early twenties. Along with the tornado and fires, there were several very localized earthquakes—quakes just violent enough to shake the jars off pantry shelves."

Monty felt his stomach rise.

"The sick bastard who killed them had just started on the women. Have to figure he ran when his jars of specimens started breaking."

Queer look in Burke's eyes now.

"What about the women?" Monty asked.

"One of them was a resident of Talulah Falls and a student at the university. The other was a *cassandra sangue*. An investigating officer in the Falls e-mailed a photo of her. It's in my car. If the opportunity arises, Lieutenant, find out if Ms. Corbyn knows the girl."

———————

Meg took a bite out of her second piece of pizza and chewed slowly, savoring the flavors and texture. She wasn't really hungry enough for another piece, but the combination of sauce, cheese, and thick crust eased the hollowness in her belly in a way the steak and spinach salads couldn't.

Not that she wasn't grateful for the choice pieces of meat that had been cooked for her throughout the day or the salads that had been made. And she was grateful for the vitamins Dr. Lorenzo had given her and the careful way he'd used the butterfly bandages to close the long cut after he'd examined the wound and put on the ointment that would keep the wound from becoming infected.

When he'd commented about the cleanliness of the wound and looked at her with a question in his eyes, she claimed she didn't know why the wound was so clean.

She had lied, and he knew it. They all knew it.

She had made a mistake out of desperation. She should have realized the addiction to the euphoria wouldn't be shaken so easily.

No wonder so many girls died when the cutting wasn't controlled by someone else. A blood prophet didn't just *want* a cut; she *needed* a cut. And if you tried to ignore that essential truth about being a *cassandra sangue*, sooner or later something would act as the trigger that turned the need into a mindless compulsion—and that was when a girl would grab anything sharp enough to cut skin.

That was when girls made fatal mistakes.

She should have set up a schedule for cutting, should have arranged it so that someone could monitor her properly and make a record of whatever she saw. If she had done that . . .

None of the Others would tell her what happened to Simon. Was he all right? Something had gone wrong. She had cut across twice as much skin as she should have even for a long cut, and she had cut too deep. The prophecies raged through her like water rushing to embrace the emptiness before the fall. She had tried to hold in the prophecies, tried not to speak so that she could see the visions since there was no one to listen. But she saw glimpses of things so terrible and terrifying, she *had* to speak, *had* to experience the euphoria that would veil what was revealed.

Then Simon appeared, pushing at the bathroom door, banging it against her legs hard enough to bruise her. She hadn't known about the bruises and wouldn't have cared. All that mattered was having a listener.

But he had licked the cut, cleaned off some of the blood, and something happened. Simon wasn't really Simon anymore. He wasn't the leader; he wasn't the Wolf with snarling intelligence. He was . . . taffy. All soft and gooey.

But the feel of his tongue on her skin, licking her as if she was the most wonderful thing in the world. Combined with the euphoria that flowed with her words, his tongue pleased her and pleasured her and made her want . . .

"Meg?" Jester urgently whispered in her ear. "Meg? Please stop thinking about whatever you're thinking about."

Blinking, she pulled her thoughts back to her surroundings.

The Coyote eased away from her while also leaning toward her and sniffing. When Nathan growled a warning, Jester moved as far away from her as he could without falling off the sofa.

Puzzled, Meg looked at Nathan—who *blushed* and whined softly before looking away. He shifted in his chair as if he couldn't get comfortable.

Jake Crowgard, the only other individual in Henry's living room, watched her with bright-eyed intensity.

Her panties were damp. She'd been thinking about Simon, and now her panties were damp.

And at least two of the males in the room could smell the arousal and need.

"Sorry," she mumbled.

"It's all right." Jester gave her shoulder a cautious pat. "It's just . . . confusing."

Her appetite gone, Meg set the rest of the pizza slice on her plate and wiped her fingers on a napkin. In Wolf form, Simon would have licked her fingers clean.

Can't think about Simon.

Nothing else she *could* think about right now. He'd been fine when he entered her bathroom. Then he wasn't fine. Wasn't Simon. Simon would have understood the importance of remembering the prophecy. Simon would have listened, wouldn't have gotten distracted.

She had seen words written on the bathroom mirror when Henry carried her out. Was that all she'd said? So little for so much skin used? Or had there been more that was now lost?

Tess, Henry, and Vlad had told her Simon was all right, but she didn't believe them. They *wanted* Simon to be all right. That wasn't the same thing.

"Jester?" She chose her questions carefully. The Coyote was friendly but inclined toward dosing helpfulness with mischief. "Where is Simon?"

"He's in that meeting with Lieutenant Montgomery," Jester replied, glancing at Nathan. "The police came to the meeting. They brought the pizza."

"Simon hasn't been in meetings all day." And even if he had been, why hadn't he stopped by to check on her or call? Sam, who was still a puppy, had called, mostly to whine a little about having to stay at the Wolfgard Complex tonight even though they all knew he enjoyed playing with the other pups and had been sleeping with the other Wolves on the weekdays.

Meg studied the Coyote. "Would you tell me? If there was something wrong, would you tell me?"

Jester sighed. "Yes, Meg. If something was wrong with Simon, I would tell you."

Simon didn't like feeling scared. He didn't like feeling sick or shaky. And he wanted this craving that made him feel distracted and hollow to go away.

Because he knew what would fill up the hollowness.

And he wished Lieutenant Crispin James Montgomery hadn't been so helpful over the past few months, hadn't shown concern for things that mattered to the *terra indigene*. Hadn't become something more than a not-edible human.

If Montgomery had kept his distance, Simon wouldn't feel some obligation to share information.

But they were gathered in the Business Association's meeting room on the second floor of Howling Good Reads because there were decisions to be made—and not all of those decisions were about the Others. Even so, he didn't think Montgomery found it comfortable to be the only human in a room with him, Vlad, Henry, Blair, Elliot, and Tess.

Henry, Blair, and Vlad had locked down the Courtyard after they realized something unexplained had happened to him. Henry had summoned Dr. Lorenzo and escorted the doctor to the Green Complex to tend to Meg. Vlad had called Heather and Lorne to tell them the stores would be closed, but they both chose to come to work. Elizabeth Bennefeld wasn't scheduled to work in the Market Square office that day, but she called to see if anyone needed her skills as a massage therapist. Merri Lee . . .

"I appreciate you letting Ms. Lee stay in the efficiency apartment for the time being," Montgomery said.

Always quiet, always courteous. No challenges or dominance games.

"We set aside one of those apartments for our female employees," Simon said. "No reason for her not to use it."

Of course, the Others had given their employees access to the apartments as a temporary place to stay during bad weather. But Tess and Vlad had seen the young woman when Officer Debany brought her from the emergency room, and they agreed that until the unrest was dealt with one way or another, Merri Lee was too vulnerable staying in her apartment near the university. And, according to Debany, the two women Merri Lee shared the apartment with were relieved to see her go because they didn't want to be targeted for living with a Wolf lover.

"This is what Captain Burke and I know about Talulah Falls," Montgomery said.

Simon listened, a little surprised that the situation had escalated so fast. Then again, when Meg had been injured and the Lakeside Courtyard had been under attack, the Elementals and their steeds had retaliated with a storm that could have destroyed the city if humans like Montgomery, Kowalski, and Lorenzo hadn't made an effort to help.

He was surprised, but the rest of the Others nodded, indicating they were already aware of the situation in the Falls, as well as the way Great Island was cut off for the time being but prepared to wait out the fog on the river. No troubles there between humans and *terra indigene*.

Maybe that was one reason why the tension in Talulah Falls had reached the breaking point so quickly. The Others in the Falls Courtyard had voiced some resentment lately about the way the human community on Great Island cooperated with the *terra indigene*. And the Lakeside Courtyard's more recent success at receiving cooperation from at least some of the humans they dealt with just added to the resentment.

If humans weren't going to live up to their part of the agreements that allowed their cities to exist in the first place, the *terra indigene* saw no reason for those cities to continue existing.

He agreed with the leaders of the Talulah Falls Courtyard that this assumption humans made that they were entitled to whatever they wanted had to be crushed quickly and completely, but Simon sincerely hoped the humans in Lakeside would continue to help him avoid making that same decision.

"Mr. Ferryman asked me to convey his thanks for the warning this morning," Montgomery said, giving Simon a look that was clearly asking *What is
wrong with you?* "But he also wasn't sure how much had been told to him in confidence and indicated that I should talk to you about it in case you thought any of
it might be relevant to Lakeside."

Simon unfolded the piece of paper and placed it on the low round table in
the center of the ring of chairs. "You know about Meg being hurt this morning?"
He waited for Montgomery's nod. "I think some of the prophecy was lost. Maybe
some of the visions weren't written down in the right way. I was . . ." He shook
his head. "This is what we told Ferryman."

He watched Montgomery lean forward to read the list of what little he had
written on the bathroom mirror.

> Fin
> Smiling shark
> Falling water
> Hide the children
> Smoke and broken jars
> Scars
> Shaking basement
> Falling jars
> Shark
> Hide the children

"I guess this explains the earthquakes," Montgomery said softly. Then he
frowned. "But . . . shark? Are there sharks in the Talulah River?"

"No," Simon replied. "The Sharkgard don't tend any of the freshwater lakes
or rivers."

"Maybe the words are a symbol to mean something else?"

Henry nodded. "At least where the shark is concerned. But falling water indi-
cates Talulah Falls. That's clear enough."

Montgomery studied the words. "Hide the children. She said those words
and 'shark' twice."

"Maybe it means a predator that would threaten the children on Great Island," Tess said. "But it could be referring to the Falls or to Lakeside. We think
Meg was referring to herself with the scar reference."

"No, I don't think she was." Montgomery removed a color photo from an envelope and set it gently on the table. "I think Ms. Corbyn may have been referring to this girl."

Simon didn't see anything remarkable about the girl, except . . . Were those evenly spaced scars on the left side of her face?

"The Falls police found the remains of four humans in the same basement where they found the Sanguinati who was killed," Montgomery said. "One of the girls was a *cassandra sangue*."

Simon felt his canines lengthen. "You're not showing this to Meg."

"If she knows this girl . . ." Montgomery began.

"Not today," Henry said firmly when Simon and Blair snarled at the lieutenant. "Meg needs to stay quiet today. And there is something more Simon needs to tell you. We don't know if the knowledge will help anyone in Talulah Falls at this point, but the trouble is too close to Lakeside now, so we agreed that the police need to know about this."

Simon stared at the photo. A blood prophet like Meg, dead.

He was leader. He might be sick and scared today, but he was leader of the Lakeside Courtyard, and no matter what the police or other *terra indigene* thought, Meg was *not* going to be in a picture like that.

"Mr. Wolfgard?" Montgomery said.

So careful, like the man had been careful after the storm. Suspecting the truth about Simon's excessive aggression when Meg had been hurt but smart enough not to ask outright about the cause.

"When I found Meg in the bathroom, bleeding so much, I . . . licked up some of the blood to clean the wound." Simon swallowed, craving water. Craving something much richer than water. "I thought it would make me angry so I could help her, protect her." He looked into Montgomery's eyes. "Like it did before."

Montgomery nodded his understanding. "But it didn't make you angry?"

"No. Well, it did for a moment, but then it made me feel good—so good I couldn't focus on helping Meg or . . . She wanted me to write down the words, and I tried. But all I wanted was to lie there and feel good." He remembered the erection, his human form's desire for sex and something more than sex. But he couldn't remember doing anything but feeling good.

"Are you all right now?"

Something in Montgomery's voice. Simon forced himself to concentrate.

"No. I'm . . . not right yet."

"You're describing an experience that matches a drug called feel-good, so it's not surprising you reacted that way. It's as addictive as an opiate." Montgomery paused and looked at the Others. "It's addictive, and there has been at least one reported death from an overdose. The person just stopped making an effort to survive."

An uneasy silence. Then Henry said, "Simon has been in a passive haze for most of the day, unable to fend for himself or defend himself."

"I see." Montgomery took a careful breath before asking, "Are you certain you didn't ingest anything else. Are you *sure*?"

"I'm sure the drug you've been calling gone over wolf comes from the blood of the *cassandra sangue*," Simon said. "And I'm sure this feel-good also comes from the prophet's blood."

Addictive? Would this hollowness and craving go away? Or would he turn on Meg and bite her for another taste? And how could two things so different in effect come from the same source? Because his reaction to Meg's blood had changed almost between one lick and the next. How? Why?

Montgomery sat back. "I'd like to discuss this information with Dr. Lorenzo in strictest confidence."

"If anyone finds out . . ." Simon warned.

"I understand the danger, Mr. Wolfgard. I do. I also know Dr. Lorenzo is scheduled to check on Ms. Corbyn tomorrow morning. I'd like to meet with all of you then."

"Not Meg." Simon felt everyone stare at him. He picked up the paper that held the words of the prophecy, and he picked up the photo of the other blood prophet.

Was this Jean, the friend Meg often mentioned? The friend who had defied the people controlling the girls by insisting she had a name and not just a designation?

"We will listen to what you and Dr. Lorenzo have to say about these drugs, and then I'll talk to Meg."

"Very well." Montgomery stood. "Unless there is something else, I need to get back to the station."

"There's nothing," Simon said.

He waited until Montgomery went downstairs, then sprang to his feet. Or tried to. Still shaky, still . . .

He whined when he saw the fur on his hands, how the fingers were changing shape despite his effort to stop them from shifting.

"It's all right. You stayed human until he left the room," Vlad said, his voice rich with sympathy. "Simon, you need rest."

He didn't need rest. He needed Meg.

"I'm going home." He handed the photo and paper to Vlad. "Hold on to these. Lock them up. I don't want them at the Green Complex."

"I'll drive you home," Blair said.

He didn't argue. Clearly he needed to shift to Wolf, and he couldn't count on keeping enough of a human shape for the drive home.

Vlad excused himself and went across the hall to HGR's office. Elliot said he needed to check in at the consulate. No doubt the mayor had left several more messages, determined to keep the lines of communication open and avoid having his city share the fate of Talulah Falls.

Simon followed Blair to the door. Hearing a startled grunt, he looked back—and wondered what Tess wanted with Henry.

Tess's true face showed through just enough that she no longer could pass for human. And her hair—black with a few streaks of red when a moment ago it had been red-streaked green—coiled and writhed in a way that made Henry think it was reaching for him, waiting for the opportunity to wrap around his throat and squeeze.

"I mean you no harm, Beargard." Even her voice was rougher, more savage. "But I'm not the only one having trouble with control today."

Henry nodded. "Simon."

"You." She pointed at his hand.

He felt a jolt of surprise. Grizzly claws at the ends of stubby human fingers. When had he shifted?

"Meg brought some trouble with her, but she has also brought good," he said. "*She* has been good for us."

"I agree. We protected her from the humans who would harm her. Now we need to do the same for the human pack."

He didn't know of any other Courtyard in the whole of Thaisia who had a human pack. They were considered part of the Courtyard now and entitled to the same protection as the *terra indigene* living there.

But Merri Lee wasn't Meg. Meg had run away from captors and didn't have any ties to the human world beyond what she was building now. Merri Lee had friends and family. Didn't she?

He suddenly realized how little he knew about the humans who worked for them.

"What are you suggesting?" he asked.

"We go to the place where she lived," Tess replied. "Pack up her things. I don't think Merri Lee has many possessions, so she values what she has."

Something the girl had in common with the *terra indigene*. Something everyone in the human pack had in common? He would think about that on another day. "What about her schooling?"

"One thing at a time." Tess's hair stopped writhing.

"Blair can drive one of our vans. I will drive the other."

"One of the police officers should go with us to avoid misunderstandings."

Henry nodded. "I will talk to Officer Debany and Merri Lee while you call Blair and arrange for the vans."

When Tess stood, he raised a hand to stop her but didn't touch her.

"You know what I am," she said, turning her face away from him.

"I grew up in the West, near the border of the High North. I never connected you with the stories I heard until I saw the way that Asia Crane died. Then I guessed."

"And said nothing."

"You eliminated an enemy. What was there to say?" He hesitated. "But with talk of a predator on the river that even the Sanguinati were avoiding, I did wonder if there was another Harvester hunting around Talulah Falls."

"Possible. There's going to be a glut of prey there over the next few days. A lot of predators who live near Lakes Etu and Tahki are going to be drawn to the Falls."

He suspected as much. At another time in his life, he would have been one of them.

He stood, towering over Tess as he towered over everyone in this Courtyard.

"Is that all we're doing, Tess? Fetching Merri Lee's possessions?"

Her hair began writhing again. "That's all *you're* doing."

She walked out of the room, keeping her head down to prevent anyone from seeing her face, looking into her eyes.

Harvesters could take a little life energy or they could take it all. They were

Namid's most ferocious predator, Namid's most effective weapon when the world needed a species decimated.

Ferocious and effective, yes. And, thankfully, a rare form of *terra indigene*. But perhaps the Harvesters weren't Namid's most dangerous weapon after all.

Shaking off such thoughts, Henry walked over to the efficiency apartments above the seamstress/tailor's shop to talk to Merri Lee and make some arrangements with Michael Debany.

Simon knocked on Meg's kitchen door. He knew she was home. He'd listened to Jake's chatter and Jester's yipping laugh to trace their progress from Henry's apartment on the other side of the Green Complex to Meg's front door.

She was home, but would she let him in?

The door opened. Meg studied him.

"I'm sorry I broke your door." He wasn't sorry, but it was the correct human thing to say.

She stepped back. "Come in."

Trying not to appear too eager or reveal how relieved he felt to hear those words, he stepped into her kitchen.

"Would you like some pizza?" she asked. "I'm not sure how many people Lieutenant Montgomery thought were participating in movie night, but there are plenty of leftovers."

"No. Thank you." Just the scent of her was making him shaky with a need he didn't know how to fulfill without doing something unforgivable.

"Are you going to tell me what's wrong with you? Because there was something wrong with you this morning, Simon, and . . ." She began to knead her left arm. Probably trying to relieve a pins-and-needles feeling. "And you're still not right."

"I don't want to talk about that tonight. Please?"

"Then what did you want?"

The words tumbled out, making him sound like a scared, whiny puppy, which was humiliating. "Can I stay with you tonight? Sam's staying with Elliot, and I . . . It feels too lonely being by myself tonight."

She looked wary. "You want to sleep with me?"

"Yes."

Her hand moved in a vague gesture. "Like that?"

"No. As Wolf. I won't shift to human. I promise." He wasn't sure he could keep that promise, but he knew if he didn't it would be the last time she let him get close enough to cuddle.

He wasn't sure what she saw in his face, in his eyes. It wasn't the strong, dominant Wolf in charge of the Courtyard. He didn't feel strong or dominant.

"All right." She shook a finger at him. "But if you're wearing fur, don't growl about me hogging the covers."

He lowered his eyes. "Okay."

"*Simon.* I was teasing."

He didn't know how to respond to that, so he closed the kitchen door as much as it could close and followed her into the bedroom. While Meg was in the bathroom, he stripped out of the jeans, sweater, and thick socks he'd been wearing. He shifted, relieved to feel his body flow into its familiar shape. And then he stretched and rolled and did everything he could think of to confirm that *all* of him had shifted.

Finally satisfied—and out of time because the toilet flushed and Meg was running water in the sink and would be back soon—Simon leaped on the bed and made sure he wasn't taking more than his half. He never meant to take more than his share. He was just bigger than her.

Meg got into bed and pulled up the covers, her arms outside the blankets.

"I'm supposed to sleep on my back because the cut is long," she said. "How am I supposed to remember to sleep on my back once I'm sleeping? And I'm not supposed to get the cut wet for a day or two, so that means a sponge bath at best and not washing my hair. And I feel really crabby about those things, and I don't know why."

He didn't know why either, but he whined in sympathy.

Sighing, Meg reached out and burrowed her fingers into his fur. "We sure didn't do things right today, did we?"

He couldn't disagree with that. Since there was nothing he could do about the mistakes he made this morning, he wasn't going to think about how the missing pieces of Meg's prophecy might have changed the fate of Talulah Falls.

He breathed in her scent—and felt the craving recede. Warmth and comfort and friendship. If he could just stop making mistakes where Meg was concerned, he would be able to keep those things.

He felt her body relax into sleep, her fingers still buried in his fur. Stretching his neck, he gave her cheek one gentle lick.

The taste of her soothed him, like it had when she had been in the hospital and he had been so angry.

He gave her cheek one more lick, then closed his eyes and fell asleep.

CHAPTER 17

S imon raced beneath a full moon, reveling in his speed and power as he closed the distance between himself and the most delicious-tasting, succulent meat he'd ever known. His soon. All his.

He chased her until she began to tire. The pumping legs, the pumping arms. They couldn't give her enough speed to escape a Wolf.

He caught up to her, felt the rhythm of her moving limbs, closed his teeth over her elbow as it swung back—and pulled her down.

Intoxicating scent, that blood. And meat so very delicious because it was . . .

<Meg!>

Simon woke with a yelp and flung himself off the bed. Panicked and panting, he peered over the edge. The room held the faint gray of early morning, which was enough light for a Wolf. He couldn't see Meg on the bed, but . . .

He started to shift. Remembering his promise to stay in Wolf form, he shoved his head under the covers and sniffed.

Blood.

Scrambling away from the bed, he howled, filling the sound with his unhappiness and fear.

<Simon?> A startled response from Vlad, whose apartment was two doors down. Tess and Henry had apartments on the other side of the complex, but they would be demanding answers soon.

He didn't have answers. He had only the memory of his teeth . . .

Simon howled again—and Meg appeared in the doorway. She flipped on the overhead light, momentarily blinding both of them.

"Simon, what's wrong?"

<Meg!> He leaped toward her, caught the scent of blood, and backed away, whining. The delicious smell of her was right, but the taste in his mouth was all wrong, confusing him.

"What is wrong with you?" She looked frazzled. "Are you hurt? Are you sick?"

That wasn't fair! She'd made him promise not to shift, but now she was asking questions that he couldn't answer because *she* couldn't communicate in the *terra indigene* way.

He shook his head. It was the best he could do under the circumstances.

Meg sagged against the doorway for a moment. "Okay. Since you're all right, I . . . have to flush the toilet and wash my hands. I thought something was wrong, and I didn't finish things."

She hurried back to the bathroom and shut the door more firmly than she needed to.

The front door of her apartment opened and slammed shut.

"Meg!" Vlad shouted.

Simon shifted, grabbed the jeans he'd left on the floor by the bed, and pulled them on before Vlad appeared in the bedroom doorway.

"What's going on?" Vlad asked as he stepped into the room.

"I'm not sure."

"Are you still sick?"

"No." In fact, now that he was fully awake, he felt good. Confused, yes, but rested, energized.

Meg returned to the bedroom and stared at the two of them. "What is wrong with all of you this morning?"

"I smelled blood," Simon said. "It was . . . upsetting." He looked at her torso, just below the breasts. Did the cut open up? If it opened up and bled again, would Meg need to speak prophecy? Or did she have a fresh cut? Was that the reason she was in the bathroom? "Is there something I should write down?"

"No," Meg replied tightly. "It's not a cut, so there aren't any visions or prophecies with this kind of blood."

He cocked his head. "There are different kinds of blood?"

Vlad, who was standing closer to her, looked at her face and took a step back. Simon wished he hadn't put on the jeans so he could grow a tail and tuck it over his male bits.

"I'm a girl!" she shouted. "It happens!"

Simon glanced at Vlad, who looked equally puzzled.

"You're both so quick to think it's 'that time of the month' whenever a girl isn't all sweet and sunny, but it doesn't occur to you when it really *is* that time of the month?"

Probably best not to point out that she'd been living in the Courtyard for three months now and this was the first time she'd done this particular female thing. Maybe blood prophets came into season once a season? How were the Others supposed to know? The human female employees usually took those days off work to avoid being around predators who might become excited by the blood scent. So this was his first experience being around a female who was doing this and wasn't *terra indigene*—and most kinds of *terra indigene* females only came into season once or twice a year.

"Meg," Vlad finally said.

She gave Vlad a scalding look. "Since I'm not getting any more sleep, I'm going to put the kettle on and make some chamomile tea."

For a short female whose weight was appropriate to her height, she could sound as stompy as a bison.

Vlad turned to look at him. "What's going on?"

"I think Meg is in season." That wasn't what humans called it, but he was rattled and couldn't remember the right word. "I was dreaming. I must have smelled the blood and . . ."

Vlad flipped the covers back. They looked at the brownish red smear on the bottom sheet. He flipped the covers up. "I don't want Meg mad at me for poking into private things, so I didn't see that." He picked up one of the pillows and frowned. "Why is one corner of this pillow drooled on and chewed?"

That explained the taste in his mouth. Instead of answering, Simon retrieved his sweater and put it on. "You head off Henry and Tess. I'll deal with Meg." He paused in the doorway. "Human females. They're kind of crazy during this time, aren't they?"

"If you choose to believe the stories written by male writers," Vlad replied.

They heard a bang and thump from the kitchen, followed by Meg yelling at something.

Simon sighed. "That many males can't be wrong."

"This morning's top news stories. Late yesterday evening, radio and television stations in Talulah Falls stopped broadcasting. Sometime after midnight, phone lines went down. A spokesman for the Lakeside mayor's office says every effort is being made to reestablish contact. Here at home, terror and tragedy struck last night at the Lakeside University when over two hundred students living on or near the campus contracted a mysterious illness. So far four deaths have been reported, and investigating officers and medical personnel are working to identify the illness and counter its effects. When asked if this was a new kind of plague, medical personnel refused to comment. However, all classes at the university are canceled until further notice. This is Ann Hergott at WZAS, bringing you the news on the hour and half hour. And now . . ."

The man sitting in front of Monty on the Whitetail Road bus turned off his portable radio and gave his fellow passengers a self-conscious smile. "Sorry. I was hoping the investigators had identified the cause of the illness."

The investigating officers know enough about the illness not to ask what caused it, Monty thought, giving the man a distracted smile before turning to look out the window. *They'll remember the talk about people who came down with similar complaints a few weeks ago. They'll look at the students who died and remember that a woman named Asia Crane had also died in a way that gave seasoned cops and medical examiners nightmares.*

The cause of those illnesses and deaths lived in the Lakeside Courtyard— and there was nothing the police could do about it.

"Captain Burke is looking for you," Kowalski said as soon as Monty reached his desk.

"Already? I came in early because Dr. Lorenzo and I have a meeting with Simon Wolfgard this morning."

"Well, I think the captain has been here for a while." Kowalski hesitated. "Debany heard the news on the radio and called me. He's a bit freaked."

"I imagine he would be." Debany was one of the officers who'd found Asia Crane. "Where is he now?"

"At the efficiency apartments. He didn't want Ms. Lee to be alone last night. But he'll be in for his shift."

Monty studied his partner. "Is Ruthie all right?"

Kowalski gave him a strained smile. "The president of the school where she teaches suggested that she take an unpaid leave of absence."

"Why? Because the rest of the faculty don't want to be around someone who is a 'Wolf lover'?"

"Something like that. There's only a few weeks left in the school year. Ruthie wants to stick it out if she can. And, frankly, it's going to be hard to afford our new place without both incomes." Kowalski tipped his head toward the captain's office. "Not a good day to keep him waiting."

As soon as Monty walked into the captain's office, Burke said, "Close the door and have a seat, Lieutenant. Your meeting still on with the Courtyard's Business Association?"

"Yes, sir. In about thirty minutes."

"Then I'll be brief. You've heard about the university?"

"And about losing communication with Talulah Falls."

"Nothing we can do about the Falls, so let's do what we can to help Captain Wheatley contain the situation at the university."

"Yes, sir." What were they supposed to do? *Stop our own people from escalating the troubles; that's what we're supposed to do.*

Burke pushed a piece of paper across the desk.

Monty picked it up and read, "'The next time you touch what is ours, this will happen to all of you.'" He felt dizzy. "What is this?"

"That message was found with one of the bodies, written in a notebook the boy must have been carrying. I think the message is clear enough."

"Simon Wolfgard wouldn't allow that." At least Monty hoped Wolfgard wouldn't agree to senseless slaughter.

"Remember when this strange illness appeared a few weeks ago, around the time when Darrell Adams died? We suspected then that there is something in the Courtyard that can kill with a look. If that creature now wants to wipe out the entire student body of Lakeside University, I don't think Simon Wolfgard is going to get in its way." Burke's smile was fierce and friendly—and held a little pity. "You're a bit innocent, aren't you, Lieutenant?"

"Sir?"

"You were born and raised in Toland?"

"Yes. My father's family immigrated to Thaisia from Afrikah a few generations ago and settled in Toland. Most of my mother's family still live in the Storm Islands."

"But you never had any real contact with the Others until now?"

Monty shook his head. "I didn't even know that Sanguinati was the name for vampires or that they ruled the Courtyard in Toland until I came here."

"And that's why you're an innocent. The Sanguinati have ruled the Toland Courtyard for two hundred years or more." Burke blew out a breath. "Gods above and below, how many other officers in the Big City don't know something that basic?"

Stung, Monty wanted to push back, but he tried to keep his voice courteous. "We were charged with keeping the peace among our own kind. Most police officers never came in contact with the *terra indigene*. It's not that different here. This station and its personnel are the only ones who have to deal with the Others on a regular basis. It's not like there's any status in dealing with the fanged and furred."

"The fanged and furred?" Burke linked his fingers together and rested his hands on his belly. "That's quite an outburst coming from you. Why do I think this lapse has nothing to do with Talulah Falls or the students at the university?"

"I have to get to my meeting." Monty didn't want to admit that it was the call he'd received from Elayne last night that was behind the outburst. Her speech had been slurred, which made him suspect she'd been drinking steadily for a few hours before the call, and he should have hung up since there was no likelihood of him talking to Lizzy at that hour. But he'd listened to her rave about her new lover and how Nicholas Scratch was going to make things happen and how much she was looking forward to spending the summer with him at his family's estate in Cel-Romano.

Suddenly he realized he'd been thinking out loud.

"Have you found out anything about Mr. Scratch or his current plans while he's in Thaisia?" Burke asked.

Monty shook his head. "I'd be accused of being a jealous ex-lover if Elayne found out I was investigating Scratch in any way, and it's already hard getting any information out of her about my daughter's well-being."

"I'm not an ex-lover, and considering his line of work and the current tension in the cities around the Great Lakes, I have a very good reason for wanting to know more about Nicholas Scratch and his speaking engagements—

especially if he's planning to visit the area anytime soon. And if I choose to share that information with some of my officers, that's just police business."

Monty felt sick with relief. He'd take whatever help he could get to keep tabs on his little girl.

But thinking about Lizzy made him think of something else. "Captain? Why isn't anyone trying to help the people in Talulah Falls?"

Burke gave him a long look. "Say the governor of the Northeast Region orders every city, town, and village to send a percentage of its police force to the Falls to extricate the citizens who are trapped there. And we're assuming some of them are still alive. How would that armed force reach the Falls?"

"They could go by train," Monty replied, having the odd feeling that he was about to prove his innocence once again. "Or pack men and supplies into buses and . . ." He understood so many things at that moment. Why the human-controlled cities in Thaisia were so far apart. Why the police in each city were the only armed force, hired and trained to maintain order within the human population—and stop people from provoking the Others into a slaughter.

"All roads travel through the woods," Burke said gently. "The moment the *terra indigene* spotted an armed force on the move, they would do what they have always done here in Thaisia—and everywhere else in the world, for that matter. They would crush the enemy, Lieutenant. They would smash the roads, tear up the train tracks, leave no survivors. And after that, what odds would you give that the Others would allow the roads and tracks to be repaired?"

"No odds," Monty said, feeling a shiver run through him. "But it would inconvenience them too."

"Not nearly as much as it would inconvenience us, because it's a good bet they've built roads that aren't accessible to us." Burke sighed. "Hopefully the government in the Falls is doing its best to negotiate for the town's continued existence and a 'citizen swap.'"

"A what?"

"I was a boy the last time it happened, and I don't even remember which part of the continent was involved. But there was a blowup between humans and Others that was escalating toward humans being exterminated in that part of Thaisia. The Others didn't want the town to go away completely, but they weren't going to deal with the humans living there. So a few towns arranged a swap—some of their people moved to the town under siege, and the existing citizens were relocated. Fresh start for everyone. If my father had been younger and single at that time, I think he would have gone for the adventure of it. But everything was too unsettled between us and the Others, and my mother didn't want to risk her children in such a place."

"Do you think that will happen in the Falls?"

"I don't know. What I do know is the farmers in Jerzy talked to the *terra indigene* and are being allowed to return to their farms. They hadn't been part of that fight, so when they asked to stay they were given permission. None of the people living in the hamlet itself were allowed to stay. The last of them were escorted out a few days ago." Burke picked up a folder and set it in the middle of his desk. "You're going to be late for your meeting, Lieutenant."

"Yes, sir." Monty pushed out of the chair. When he reached the door, he looked back. "Do you think the Others are afraid of some of their kind?"

Burke opened the folder and didn't look up. "I think some of them are afraid sometimes. And some of them aren't afraid of anything except the end of the world itself—and maybe not even that."

"I'm going with you," Meg said. She tossed her carry bag into the back of the BOW and hoped Simon didn't see her wince. Why would moving her arm pull at the cut on her torso? She didn't remember having so many movement restrictions when she lived in the compound. On the other hand, the girls didn't do anything the day after a cut except sit quietly at their lessons.

"I know," Simon replied, giving her a wary look. "I'm driving you up to the Market Square because you wanted to meet the female who is going to work for Dr. Lorenzo. And you wanted to look at the books that came in for the library since you still need to rest for the next few days."

"Yes, I want to meet Theral MacDonald and look at the books, but I also want to find out how Merri Lee is doing. She was beat up, which is something none of you thought to tell me."

She saw something change in his face and identified the look. If she kept pushing, the dominant male would need to assert his dominance.

"I was going to tell you," he growled. "You didn't need to know yesterday, so who told you?"

"Well, maybe you were right not to tell me yesterday." She saw no reason to admit that Jenni Crowgard had told her a few minutes ago when Simon had gone to the garage to get the BOW and bring it around. As if a cut on her torso stopped her legs from working properly. On the other hand, it was foolish to slap at someone who was trying to be thoughtful, especially when being thoughtful toward a human was a new behavior. "But that's not what I meant. I'm going with you to this big meeting you're all having with Lieutenant Montgomery and Dr. Lorenzo." Which was something Jenni had also mentioned, along with the grumble that the Crows weren't invited.

Simon's canines lengthened, his amber eyes held those weird flickers of red that indicated he was angry, and fur sprang up on his cheeks.

"That meeting has something to do with what happened to both of us yesterday, doesn't it?" Meg pushed with disregard for the consequences. "It has to do with the things I saw in the prophecy, and what happened to you afterward. So I should be there too."

He stared at her while the fur receded from his cheeks. If you didn't count the red flickering in his eyes and the canines, which were still too long, he could pass for human. But she didn't think he was feeling very human, especially when he came around to her side of the vehicle and pinned her between his body and the BOW without actually touching her.

"Give me the razor," he growled.

They'd had this argument before. "It's mine."

"Maybe you should be at that meeting. But I am *not* having you there with a razor in your pocket. Not on a day when you're having a bout of female crazies."

At that moment, she wished she was as strong as some of the women in stories she'd read recently. She would really like to pick up the BOW and smack him on the head with it.

Female crazies! How dare he!

"I'm not the one who was howling his head off this morning!" she snapped. "And what were you dreaming about that you chewed on my pillow?"

He leaned forward just enough that his body brushed against hers.

"I dreamed I was biting *you*."

Okay, it had been a while since he'd threatened to eat her or even bite her. But this didn't sound the same as when he used to say it. It sounded darker, riper.

She swallowed—and his eyes followed the movement of her throat. Could he see her pulse beating, hear her heart pounding?

"We're going to be late," she whispered.

He took a step back and held out his hand. She didn't argue; she pulled the silver folding razor out of her jeans pocket and handed it to him. He shoved it into his own pocket, then walked around to the driver's side and got in.

Shaking, Meg slipped into the passenger seat and closed her door. If the rest of the Others were as stirred up as Simon, maybe she didn't want to go to this meeting after all.

Monty wasn't pleased to see Meg Corbyn walk into the meeting room with Simon. He didn't think Dominic Lorenzo was pleased either. They'd both hoped the Others would have a little time to think about Lorenzo's ideas before seeing their Human Liaison.

Henry Beargard and Tess pointed to a couple of chairs around the low table, then took their own seats. Elliot and Blair Wolfgard were also in the room, but they stood against the wall. Observers rather than participants?

"This might not be . . ." Monty began.

Simon snarled at him. "We're all looking for answers. Meg is part of this, and she wants to be here." He turned to Henry. "Where is Vlad?"

"On his way," the Grizzly replied. "He said to wait for them."

Simon froze for a moment, then sat next to Meg, who was between him and Tess.

Before anyone had a chance to feel restless, Vladimir Sanguinati walked into the room with a beautiful woman dressed in a long, old-fashioned, black velvet gown with draping sleeves. Like Vlad, she had olive skin, black hair, and dark eyes. Monty felt a tug of attraction and wondered how many men who responded to that tug survived.

But it was the old man with her who held Monty's attention. His hands were knobby and veined, with thickened nails that looked more like horn. Like the woman's gown, his clothes looked old-fashioned, but there was a smudged quality to the edges that made Monty wonder if the garments were actually made of cloth.

"Mr. Erebus," Meg said, sounding surprised and pleased.

He smiled at Meg, a benign old man. "How is our Meg today?"

Something crawled down Monty's back, something more primitive than fear. He was sure the slight accent was an affectation. It reminded him too much of the villains in the movies he used to watch as a boy for him to believe it was genuine. And it made him wonder what the voice might reveal without that affection.

"I'm fine," she replied, smiling at the old man.

"She needs to take it easy for a few more days so she heals properly," Simon said. "No lifting mailbags or heavy packages. Right?" He aimed the last word at Dr. Lorenzo.

"I'll be better able to judge after I examine the cut, but there's no harm in being careful," Lorenzo replied.

"Grandfather," Vlad said, "this is Lieutenant Crispin James Montgomery and Dr. Dominic Lorenzo. Gentlemen, this is Erebus Sanguinati."

Tess was the only one in the room who didn't seem wary of Erebus, but her hair had changed from brown and wavy to green and curling with red streaks.

As the Sanguinati took their seats around the table, the door opened and four women walked in.

Monty recognized two of them. They had created the blizzard that could have buried Lakeside. Seeing them now, Monty didn't need to be told that the outcome of this meeting could have terrible repercussions.

Simon nodded to the four women, then addressed the humans in the room. "This is Water, Air, Spring, and Winter."

Lorenzo gave Monty a startled look, as if asking, *Really?*

Monty moved his head in the barest nod. Yes, really. The Elementals were sitting in on this meeting. Were the shifters and vampires feeling as uncomfortable as the humans were because of these additional attendees? After all, a blizzard could kill Wolves as well as humans.

Finally Simon looked at Vlad. "Do you have that list from the prophecy?"

Vlad handed Simon a manila envelope. "That's everything."

Simon opened the envelope, pulled out a sheet of paper, and set it on the table in front of Meg. "This is what I could remember of what you said. I think there was more, but . . ." He stopped and just watched Meg.

"There were more images," Meg whispered. "I almost . . . remember."

The fingers of her right hand moved restlessly up and down her thigh, digging into the jeans as if trying to reach the skin. The fingers of her left hand were digging into her right forearm. When her left hand reached for her torso, the fingers a claw of tense muscles, Lorenzo made a wordless protest. Simon caught her hand and said, "No, Meg."

Tess went to one of the desks in the room and came back with a pad of paper and a pen. Leaning forward to catch Meg's attention, she said, "Speak, prophet, and we will listen."

Command and promise. Monty wasn't sure if Tess was mesmerizing Meg or if it was the phrase itself, but after staring at Tess for a long moment, Meg focused on the paper with its list of words.

Her left hand reached for her right forearm again. Simon released her but looked ready to grab her at the first sign she might dig into the cut that was healing or do some other harm to herself.

Meg leaned forward and touched the paper, her fingers moving between the words "fin" and "smiling shark."

"Donkey," she said, sounding oddly tranquil while her brow furrowed in concentration. "Not donkey but like donkey."

While Tess wrote down the words, Monty reached in his pocket for his own notebook and pen, then glanced at Simon for permission. Receiving a brusque nod of consent, he too wrote down the words.

"Car," Meg said. "Sunrise. Car. Sunset. Geese and suitcases." Her fingers moved down the list. "Fog. Water. Hide the children. Shark." She stopped scratching at her arm long enough to brush her fingers over her left cheek. "Broken jars. Lumpy smoke. Scars."

Monty shivered. Out of the corner of his eye, he noticed the slight tremor in Lorenzo's hands. They had both seen the crime scene photos that had been sent from Talulah Falls before all communication was severed. Meg's words were a vague but accurate description of what had been found in that basement in the Falls.

"Anything else?" Tess asked.

Meg stared at the list. "People-shaped cookies driving a boat." Her hands relaxed. She blinked a couple of times, then looked apologetic. "That's all I remember. I don't know what any of it means."

"Figuring out what it means is our part of the job, not yours," Tess said briskly.

Simon rested a hand on Meg's back. "You want anything?"

"Water," Meg replied. "I'm thirsty."

"I would recommend some fruit juice as well," Dr. Lorenzo said, studying Meg.

"I'll get it," Elliot said. "Is the back door to A Little Bite open?"

Tess nodded, her attention on her list. "What's a donkey but not a donkey?"

"Horse, mule, ass," Blair said. "All good to eat."

"But none of those animals have fins," Monty said.

"No, they don't." Meg seemed to shrink into herself. Then she winced.

Simon gave Monty a warning look that clearly meant *Don't upset Meg.*

A glance at the Elementals and Sanguinati who were between him and the door told Monty it wasn't the Wolves he needed to fear right now.

"It's all about images," Simon said. "The images you see can have a different meaning when combined in different ways, right?"

Meg nodded.

"You mentioned cars this time," Henry said. "Maybe there is a fin or a donkey painted on the car."

"Sunrise and sunset," Blair said. "East and west."

"Someone traveling?" Tess said. "Coming from the west and heading east?"

"And traveling . . . Meg, do you remember which way the geese were flying?"

Meg closed her eyes. "North."

"Something you see as a shark is traveling east and north," Simon said.

"But a shark wouldn't be driving a car!" Meg protested. Then she looked at the Others. "A shark wouldn't, would he?"

Henry shrugged. "It's not likely any of the Sharkgard would be around here since there isn't the right kind of water to accommodate them shifting out of human form. But if you're seeing a shark to indicate a predator that's headed our way and is a threat to children . . ."

Wondering if this was how prophecies were usually extracted from the visions seen by *cassandra sangue*, Monty continued writing his notes. He would have to pull them together in an orderly fashion while this meeting was still fresh in his mind—and he would have to receive Wolfgard's permission to distribute this information in case the Others' interpretation about a threat to children was correct.

"Fog and water hide the children," Tess said, looking at the four women who had remained near the door, listening.

"Fog needs to rest a while," Water said. "He has worked hard the past few days."

Spring looked at Air and Winter. "Fog is not the only way to discourage travelers."

There was something too alien about the Elementals to pass for human. It was more than the shape of the face and the look in their eyes. It was the sense that their connection to a tangible shape was tenuous at best—and they liked it that way.

"Yes," Winter said. "We can let Fog rest for a day or two. Thunder and Lightning would enjoy a run."

"So would Cyclone," Water said. "And Whirlpool is here with us now."

Monty shuddered. Lakeside was still recovering from the last storm. He didn't want to think about what another one would do to the area.

"Won't the flowers die if you summon a storm?" Meg asked, sounding worried.

The Elementals stared at her. Then Spring smiled, and the air in the room became warmer and fragrant. "A thin blanket of snow won't harm what blooms in this part of my season. And wind cleans away the old to make way for the new."

"And I'll keep Cyclone and Whirlpool to the river," Water said.

"We can fly with the storm at night, and let the Crows, Hawks, and humans on Great Island keep watch for the enemy during daylight hours," Winter said.

Meg smiled. "That would be good. And then the cookies can drive the . . . Mr. Ferryman! He was going to talk to people in his village about making Wolf cookies."

"Sounds like a container or two are heading our way," Simon said.

"That leaves the scars and smoke," Tess said. Black streaks suddenly appeared in her hair as she looked at Erebus Sanguinati, who returned her look.

"One of the Sanguinati died, didn't he?" Meg said. Tears shimmered in her eyes. "I'm sorry, Mr. Erebus. Maybe if I'd made the cut sooner, I could have—"

"No." Erebus looked uneasy. "The sweet blood is both wondrous and terrible. It should not be shed lightly."

"But it has to be shed," she whispered.

"That is something for you to discuss with Simon," Erebus said gently. Then he added reluctantly, "And with the human bodywalker."

Lorenzo sucked in a breath, but that was the only indication he gave that he now understood how closely the Sanguinati watched Meg Corbyn.

Simon picked up the envelope again. He pulled out the photo and set it on the table. When Meg paled, he put an arm around her.

"Her designation was *cs783*," Meg said.

"What was her name?" Simon asked.

"She didn't have one. Didn't want one. She . . . she wasn't like Jean and me. She wanted someone to take care of her and she wanted to feel the euphoria when she was cut. That's all she wanted. She *liked* being kept in the compound." Meg shuddered. "Outside was nothing but the images she had to learn to describe the visions."

"So she didn't run away like you did?"

Meg shook her head.

No one spoke. No one moved. The Others waited with eerie patience.

"The Controller must have sold her," Meg finally said. "Or sent her away for some reason."

"You can guess the reason," Simon said.

"She wasn't . . . The Walking Names weren't always careful about what they said around us. I heard them once when they were evaluating some of the girls. They said *cs783*'s prophecies were accurate but lacked range. She couldn't see prophecies the way Jean can."

"Or the way you can?"

Wolfgard was circling around what they had all originally come to discuss.

"It is time to talk about what happened yesterday morning," Henry said. "Meg, what do you remember?"

"I had a bad dream, a terrible dream, and I woke up screaming because I was so afraid." Meg said. "I was so afraid, but I didn't know why, and I had to cut so I could see the danger. I should have called someone first—"

Simon growled.

"—but I couldn't wait. It felt like my skin would split on its own, the need was so overwhelming." She touched the side of her nose. "Like my skin split the night I dreamed about the blood and black feathers in the snow."

"So you put a towel on the bathroom floor, laid down, and made a long cut," Henry said.

"I don't remember the towel or lying down. I don't remember choosing where to cut. I felt so desperate, I just . . . cut. Then I tried to swallow the words and the pain because that's the only way we can remember a prophecy."

"Pain?" It was the first time Lorenzo spoke since the meeting began.

When Meg paled and seemed unable to reply, Simon said, "There is bad pain until the prophet begins to speak. There's nothing but pain *unless* she speaks. That's how the girls are punished—they're cut and then prevented from speaking."

Monty looked at Meg's left arm, recalling the crosshatch of scars he'd seen when she'd been brought to the hospital.

"That confirms some of what I've been thinking," Lorenzo said.

"What else, Meg?" Henry asked. "What happened after the cut?"

"Simon came, and he was Simon," Meg said.

Simon looked uneasy. "What else would I be?"

"You were Simon, and then you *weren't* Simon anymore. You turned soft and gooey."

He jerked away from her. "I did not!"

"You did! You were fine, and then you licked—"

Erebus sprang to his feet, a terrible look on his face. "We do not drink the sweet blood!"

Simon sprang to *his* feet, his canines lengthening. "That rule is for *your* people, not mine."

"You licked up my blood," Meg said, her voice trembling. "You licked my blood, and it made you sick."

"Not sick!" Simon snapped.

Now Meg stood and stared at Monty. "That's why all these bad things are happening, isn't it? That's what made the Crows too sick to get away."

He's afraid for her, Monty thought, glancing at Simon. *He doesn't want her to tell the rest of them what she's figured out.*

"Not sick!" Simon shouted. "Sit down, Meg, and stop being stupid, or I'll bite you!"

"I'm not being stupid, and you can't bite me!"

"I can nip really hard!"

With fascinated horror, Monty saw Erebus's legs change to smoke, clothes as well as flesh; saw Vlad and the female vampire jump to their feet; saw Henry rise to tower over all of them, his strong fingers now ending in a Grizzly's savage claws; saw Tess's hair turn red with wide black streaks. Blair and Elliot were crowding the chairs, putting themselves between the vampires and Simon—who was totally focused on Meg.

The Elementals were the only ones who didn't seem concerned, and Monty found their curious interest more frightening than being caught in the middle of a terrible fight.

Then Simon grabbed Meg's upper arms, ignoring her startled cry of pain, and hauled her up to her toes. Even then he had to bend a little to be nose to nose with her.

"I don't know how long the crazy female mood lasts when you're in season, but *you are not doing anything stupid until you can think straight!*" Simon yelled. "And if you try being stupid then, I *will* bite you, no matter what."

She stared into Wolf eyes that had turned red with fury. Then she grabbed his sweater. Seeing the way he winced, she must have pulled a couple of fistfuls of fur along with the material.

"Meat grinder," Meg whispered. Her eyes, her face, her voice, were oddly blank.

Everyone in the room froze.

"Meat grinder dream," she said. "Need the pain, need the fear to make the best meat. Hand in the grinder, chew it all up. Keep the meat alive while you cut and grind. He'll find me! He'll . . . Simon!"

He went down with her when she collapsed, cradling her in his lap while he licked her cheek. "Meg? Meg!"

Lorenzo shoved past Henry and Tess. "Let me have a look."

One moment Lorenzo was kneeling on the other side of Meg, staring at an angry human male. The next moment, there was a man with a Wolf's head holding Meg and snarling at the doctor.

"Let me help," Lorenzo said. "That's why you agreed to let me have some office space in the Courtyard, isn't it? So I can help?"

Blair put a hand on Simon's shoulder. "He'll let you help."

Monty applauded the doctor's courage. He wasn't sure he'd have enough nerve to put his hands that close to a Wolf's teeth.

"She fainted," Lorenzo said. "Her body's way of protecting her from what she was seeing. Which explains some things about the euphoria these girls experience." He eased back. "Is there someplace nearby where she can rest?"

"There's a Wolf bed in the office," Vlad said. "It's just across the hall."

"She's coming around, but someone should stay with her," Lorenzo said.

"I'll stay with our Meg," Winter said.

Blair squeezed Simon's shoulder. "Simon." A warning.

Wolfgard looked almost human by the time Meg opened her eyes.

"Your ears are furry," she said.

Simon whined.

"Let's get her settled," Lorenzo said, getting to his feet. "Then I have some thoughts I'd like to share with all of you."

Simon rose with Meg in his arms. Vlad led the way to the office, followed by Simon, Lorenzo, Winter, and the female vampire.

Monty sagged in his chair, exhausted by the adrenaline rush of the past few minutes. He didn't meet their eyes, but he noticed the *terra indigene* were all trying to regain their balance. Erebus now looked fully human again, as did Henry. The black receded from Tess's hair, and Blair and Elliot had resumed their place against the wall.

Do any of them realize that Simon Wolfgard is falling in love with Meg Corbyn? Monty wondered. *Does Wolfgard understand his own response to the girl? What about Meg? How does she feel? What would the rest of the Others do if one of their kind did fall in love with a human?*

Another complication, but what Meg described just before she fainted was more disturbing and, most likely, more immediate.

Simon, Vlad, and Lorenzo returned and took their seats.

"What happened to Meg?" Tess asked. "She wasn't dreaming and she didn't cut. Why did she see a vision? And why didn't it sound like the visions she's had before?"

They all looked at the doctor.

"I think she moved the wrong way, and a section of yesterday's cut reopened enough to seep fresh blood," Lorenzo said. "And that, in turn, opened her to prophecy . . . or allowed her to recall the details of a dream."

"But Vladimir told me our Meg was in season and the blood scent should be politely ignored," Erebus said, staring at Vlad.

"She is in season and testy about it," Simon said.

Monty looked at all the males in the room and knew that a discussion of the human female's reproductive cycle wasn't something he wanted to have with any of them today—or any day. "Does a second source of blood explain the dreamlike vision?"

"No," Simon replied. "Meg says sometimes the visions look like a clip from a movie." He looked at Lorenzo. "If she saw prophecy from a cut and could speak, why wasn't there any euphoria?"

"I don't know. Maybe because it wasn't a new cut?" Lorenzo took a deep breath before turning to address Erebus Sanguinati. "I'm not expressing an opinion about your taboos, just making an observation about shape-shifters and *cassandra sangue* blood." He waited for Erebus's nod before continuing. "I don't think the problem was that Mr. Wolfgard consumed Ms. Corbyn's blood. I think the problem was he suffered an overdose."

It was unnerving to watch a room full of predators focus on a man.

"There is a lack of information about blood prophets, and that doesn't make sense since these girls require so much medical care," Lorenzo said. "But that's a different discussion. The point is, I have no evidence to support what I say. Maybe you have something in your histories that would confirm my guesses."

"Guesses about what?" Simon asked.

"The human body is a chemical stew. The body floods with different chemicals to respond to different situations. Flight or fight response. Fear, anger, aggression." Lorenzo looked at Simon. "Ms. Corbyn had that gash on her chin when you brought her to the hospital. You were angry and aggressive that night almost beyond reason."

Simon nodded. "I licked the blood from the gash, trying to clean the wound."

"But yesterday morning, I think she began to speak prophecy shortly after you found her, and as soon as she began speaking, her body flooded with all the chemicals that create the euphoria. When you licked *that* blood, basically you were consuming a potent tranquilizer."

"So Wolves react to Meg's blood in different ways depending on whether she's happy or scared?" Henry asked, studying Simon.

"Not just Wolves," Lorenzo said. "Whoever is using these girls to create the drugs known as gone over wolf and feel-good have targeted humans as well. I think the prophet's blood is, in a way, a wonder drug and a curse."

"Namid's creation is wondrous and terrible," Erebus said.

"Poison frogs," Monty said, thinking about a program he'd watched with Lizzy. "Not harmful if left alone, but the poison that exudes through their skin will kill anything that tries to eat them." After a look around the room, he added hastily, "Not that I think Ms. Corbyn is like a frog."

"But she is," Lorenzo said. "Attack a blood prophet, frighten her or hurt her, and her body becomes a weapon against the attacker. I imagine if any of you consumed the quantity of blood you usually would from a kill, you'd all overdose to the point of turning on each other. The girl dies, but so do the attackers.

Good reason to cross *cassandra sangue* off the list of edibles. On the other hand, you have bodywalkers, which means taking care of injuries. We use opiates to relieve pain in our hospitals. But early in our mutual history, when humans and Others first crossed paths, a girl whose blood could render someone passive to the point where a bone could be set or a wound stitched up would be, I think, a valuable asset. Something you wouldn't waste. But too much of that blood, like too much of an opiate, could be deadly. Impossible not to overdose if you're feeding while she was lost in the euphoria."

"The prophet who was found in the basement," Erebus said. "Any Sanguinati would know she is not prey and could not be touched."

"We all sensed that Meg is not prey," Simon said.

"What does all this mean?" Tess asked. "And what do we do about Meg's need to cut?"

Lorenzo sighed. "I don't know. As I said, there is very little information available about blood prophets. Maybe a girl with less ability could be weaned away from the razor. I'm not sure Ms. Corbyn can stop cutting at this point. If what I saw here is typical, cutting, and the euphoria that comes with it, might be the only safety valve her sanity has. I do feel, if she's going to stay here with you—"

"Of course she's staying with us," Simon snapped.

"Then you need to work out a schedule, or come to some agreement with her. She can't be alone when she cuts. This time the cut was deeper than it should have been, but it still wasn't a serious wound. If she's alone and slices through a vein or artery, you might not be able to get help in time to save her."

"She spent her life in a cage," Henry said. "We will not put her back in one. Not even to save her."

"But we'll take what you've said under advisement," Tess added.

A dismissal. Meeting adjourned.

Monty let out a sigh of relief when Vladimir and Erebus left the room, along with the Elementals. Lorenzo went across the hall to check on Meg. Blair, Elliot, and Tess left a minute later, leaving Monty with Henry and Simon.

"Warn your people about the shark," Simon said, sounding exhausted. "I'll warn Steve Ferryman."

"I think Captain Burke would appreciate talking to Officer Czerneda about this new information. Lakeside police can set up roadblocks if necessary."

Simon nodded. "The Intuits will know if trouble is coming."

Feeling battered, Monty excused himself and went downstairs to wait for Lorenzo. He called Kowalski, who was visiting with Debany and Merri Lee, and arranged to leave in five minutes.

Lorenzo came downstairs in four, so they walked out together.

"Quite a meeting," Monty said.

"A lot more information than I expected," Lorenzo replied.

Hearing a grim undertone, Monty stopped walking toward the patrol car. "After what you saw today, what chance do you think Meg Corbyn has?"

Lorenzo looked away. Finally he sighed. "With her sensitivity to prophecy, I think Meg Corbyn was doomed after the first cut."

CHAPTER 18

The following morning, Douglas Burke studied the notes Monty had made of the additional information from Meg Corbyn. Then he sat back and sighed. "Meat grinder. Gods above and below. And your impression was Ms. Corbyn was seeing another *cassandra sangue* being ground up alive?"

"Yes, sir," Monty replied. "That was Dr. Lorenzo's impression as well."

"It's a wonder these girls stay sane as long as they do."

Burke's observation wasn't unique. Monty had stared at the television last evening, taking in nothing. Seeing Meg in the full throes of a prophecy made him wonder if blood prophets really did need to be in some kind of supervised home. Oh, not as damaging as the place she'd run away from, but surely there had to be places in between a kind of prison and leaving these girls to flounder on their own.

"Lorenzo is dropping by the Courtyard this morning," Monty said. "He promised to call with a status report."

"You're not going to stop in?"

"Until Howling Good Reads and A Little Bite reopen to the public, dropping by is a bit more difficult. I don't want to wear out my welcome."

Burke nodded. "What about Kowalski? Or Debany or MacDonald? They have personal reasons to stop by."

"Officer Debany called a few minutes ago. The stores have Residents Only signs on the doors, but the Liaison's Office is opening for business and so is the consulate."

"I doubt opening the Liaison's Office today was Simon Wolfgard's decision."

Monty smiled at the dry observation. "No, I don't think it was." The smile faded. "Debany also said Wolfgard and Henry Beargard left yesterday evening, taking one of the Courtyard's small vans. They returned just before Debany called me."

Burke thought about that for a moment. "Well, we'll either find out where they went and why or we won't."

"No word from Talulah Falls?"

"No. Between the fog on the river and the barricades and destroyed roads, there's no way of knowing what's going on there. But I keep hoping there are human survivors." Burke pushed away from his desk. "Well. I have a meeting with the chief. Mustn't keep him waiting."

Monty walked out of Burke's office, then went to his own desk to check for messages.

"Where to, Lieutenant?" Kowalski asked.

Where had Simon Wolfgard gone yesterday, and was there any way to find out? "Nowhere yet."

Simon parked the BOW in the garage behind the Liaison's Office, then followed Meg inside.

"You sure you feel all right to do this today?" He opened her carry bag, took out a couple of containers of food, and put them in the under-the-counter fridge.

"I'll be fine," Meg replied, sounding testy.

If she would let him sniff her properly, he'd know if she was all right without having to keep asking.

She turned on the lights and picked up the key to the front door as she went through the sorting room. When she returned, he stood on one side of the sorting table while she stood on the other.

Simon took the silver folding razor out of his pocket and set it on the table. But he kept his hand over it. "This is yours." She didn't insist that he give the razor back before he left with Henry last night. Maybe she'd been as frightened by what had happened yesterday as the rest of them. Maybe that was why he felt he had to return it. "Meg . . ." What was he supposed to say?

"Until I was punished, I never understood how much the euphoria shielded blood prophets," Meg said, touching her left arm at the crosshatch of scars. "Maybe the cutting started as a defense against what we saw—a kind of pressure release—and over generations it became something else, something more."

He listened, saying nothing—an attentive silence.

"I can't stop cutting, Simon. I'm not sure any of us can." Meg pointed at herself to indicate she meant the *cassandra sangue*.

"I know. But . . . not all of you die young, Meg. Even if a thousand cuts is really the limit . . ." Simon shifted his feet and whined softly. "The first time I saw one of your kind, I was fifteen. I could hold the human form well enough to pass for human most of the time, so I was with a group of young *terra indigene* having an outing in the human world. It was actually a human settlement on the edge of one of ours, so it hardly counted, but it was a first attempt at buying food from an open stall or some small bit of merchandise from a shop.

"There was this old woman with her arms brown and bare to the sun, the scars showing white. She wore a straw hat and sat at this little table, offering to read her cards and tell our fortunes.

"There was a group of humans at the settlement about the same age as my group. Don't know what they were doing there. Maybe a field trip similar to ours. They walked past her table and laughed at her, called her names because of the scars. So did some of the Others as a way of imitating the humans. But when she looked at me, I stopped. She took out a razor, the silver dazzling in the sun, and cut her cheek. And she told me what I could be."

Simon blinked. He lifted his hand off the razor and took a step back.

They said nothing, just stared at each other.

"Do you know how she managed it?" Meg finally asked. "Do you think anyone would remember her who could tell you how she managed to survive the cutting long enough to grow old?"

"I don't know. I don't even know if there is still a settlement there, but I can try to find out if you want."

"Yes. I'd like to know." Meg pressed her hands on the table. She didn't reach for the razor. "Buying a cut on my skin was expensive. That's why I have so few scars compared to the other girls in the compound."

"You're only twenty-four," he said. "You have plenty of scars for someone your age." Too many scars. Most of the girls didn't live to see thirty-five years. "We'll find an answer. We'll find a way for you to live long enough to grow old."

Her eyes filled with tears. She blinked them away. "Until then, Mr. Wolfgard, I have work to do and so do you."

He heard teasing in her voice—and also a reminder of territory. This building was hers.

"Don't forget your appointment with Dr. Lorenzo," he said over his shoulder as he walked toward the back room.

"I won't forget."

"And don't forget to eat," he called as he opened the back door.

"I won't! Go to work, Simon!"

Grinning, he stepped outside. She sounded all right.

Wishing he could shift to Wolf and run for a few minutes, he settled for a brisk walk around the Market Square. With everything that had been going on lately, he hadn't paid attention to the stores in the Others' business district and didn't know if they'd received deliveries from any merchants. For that matter, he didn't know if the bookstore had received any shipments in the past few days. He'd have to ask Vlad.

As he entered the Market Square, he spotted a human who, while familiar, shouldn't have been there at this time of day.

"*Arrroooo!*" The sound didn't have the same quality coming from a human throat, but the female stopped and waited for him.

Ruthie Stuart. Officer Kowalski's mate. Usually a sensible female, she should have known the Courtyard was still closed to all humans except employees. Then again, she *was* part of Meg's human pack, and she *could* have been visiting Merri Lee, or even going to fetch something for the other woman.

But that didn't explain why she was here at this time of day.

He slowed down when he saw her face. She looked wounded and angry. In his experience, a wounded, angry female was a dangerous female.

"Why are you here?" he asked, watching for a sign she might attack him.

"I needed a couple of things from the grocery store. I know the Courtyard is closed, but since I have a pass, I didn't think anyone would mind."

Not a lie, but not the whole truth. "This is morning. You work in the mornings. Why are you here now?"

The answer was the cause of both wound and anger.

"I've been given an unpaid leave of absence," Ruthie said.

Simon cocked his head. "Why?" Then he considered the trouble in Talulah

Falls, the trouble at Lakeside University, and the men beating up Merri Lee. And he knew. "They don't want you because you come to the Courtyard?"

"Yes."

"Then why do you come?"

"Because I think those people are shortsighted," she replied with some bite. "Being human doesn't entitle us to grab what doesn't belong to us. And I've read some of your histories and compared them with ours."

Really? Maybe he should have paid more attention to what Ruthie was special ordering from HGR. Or taking out on loan from the Market Square Library? She could have done that too.

"From what I can see, if a human shows you a product or some invention that benefits the *terra indigene* as much as it does humans, you'll agree among yourselves to release the resources needed to make the product or build the invention. Since you value the world more than you value products or profit, you're never going to release as much raw materials as humans want, and they're always going to resent you for it. But I don't have to blame you for human shortcomings."

Her own kind had driven her out in the same way humans had driven the Intuits into making pacts with the *terra indigene*. How could he use this to benefit the Courtyard as well as Ruthie?

"What did you do?" he asked.

"I am . . . was . . . a teacher. Younger children."

"What did you teach?"

"The usual things. Arithmetic, spelling, printing and cursive writing, history, literature, the basics of using a computer."

"We already have teachers for those things," he said, more to himself than to her. Okay, they didn't have someone who could teach computer stuff to the juveniles.

"Right now I'm just looking for a job to help pay the bills," Ruthie said quickly. "It doesn't have to be a teaching job."

Would anyone in the human world hire her? Simon wondered, studying her with more interest. Not likely. Not right now. But he might have a use for a human who understood the human world and could be trusted not to deceive inexperienced *terra indigene*.

"I'll think about what you can do here," he said. He started to turn away, then paused. "For today, check with Heather. See if she needs any help filling orders or stocking shelves."

"Thank you, Mr. Wolfgard."

He walked back to HGR, thinking about last night's meeting and the possibilities that hiring Ruthie might provide.

The *terra indigene* who lived in Courtyards usually stayed for a few years before going back to the wild country and letting a fresh group come in to deal with the humans. Last night the Others who had abandoned the Talulah Falls Courtyard announced that they weren't going back. They were done with the double-dealing, lying monkeys. They were done with human government that didn't keep its promises and allowed the residents of the town to do the same. This strike against the humans should have come sooner—and left fewer survivors.

Even the Crows, who were usually enthusiastic about living in and around human places, didn't want to stay in Talulah Falls. They were all heading into the wild country. Most likely none of them would brush against anything more human than an Intuit settlement for the rest of their lives.

Too much animosity toward humans. Too much resentment. And, yes, the Others in Talulah Falls had felt some envy toward the earth natives living on Great Island. They weren't fighting with humans all the time for a share of the harvest or meat. They weren't being shorted when humans delivered the merchandise the Others were entitled to receive.

Simon had listened to the frustration that had been held in for too long. Hadn't he felt those things too when he'd arrived at Lakeside to be the leader of that Courtyard? How many humans had the Courtyard's Business Association hired—and fired—in the past few years? How many quit once they realized that not knowing about some human things didn't make the *terra indigene* stupid or gullible or easy to cheat?

Then the new leaders of the Talulah Falls Courtyard joined the meeting. Some of the leaders could pass for human and would be the ones who talked to human government. Most of them had been chosen for their ability, and willingness, to savage the monkeys the moment rules or agreements were broken.

Many of the *terra indigene* coming in with them had little or no experience with living in a Courtyard. Many had little, if any, training in dealing with humans on a day-to-day basis. The leaders had attended a *terra indigene* college to acquire an understanding of business and the basics of human government. But that wasn't the same as feeling confident that you could do simple things in the human world.

Some of the Others who lived around Lakes Etu and Tahki had visited the Lakeside Courtyard recently to see a marketplace and make a purchase without the tension that usually soured the experience. The humans they had encountered were polite and helpful, and they wanted to visit again and learn more. Would Simon be willing to let the Lakeside marketplace be used as a training ground?

Simon was willing, and as he and Henry left the meeting to return home, they both promised to talk to the Business Association about this idea of using the Lakeside Courtyard to help other *terra indigene* learn how to interact with humans.

Maybe it's just as well the human customers have stopped coming to HGR and A Little Bite, Simon thought as he opened the back door of HGR. *With the help of Meg and her human pack, the Lakeside Courtyard could become a training center for the Others—safe, trusted humans teaching earth native youngsters. Isn't that how the bargains between us began in the first place?*

He found Heather in the front of the store and told her to find something for Ruthie to do if she came looking for work. Then he went up to the office and locked the door. Vlad could get in under the door or through the keyhole. Simon wasn't worried about being overheard by the Sanguinati since Vlad already knew why these phone calls had to be made.

Taking his seat behind the desk, Simon closed his eyes for a moment. A big risk, especially when he'd told the leaders in the Midwest about the source of the drugs that had created so much trouble in their part of Thaisia. But he'd balance the Midwest participants of this meeting with some of the Others who lived in the High Northeast. The *terra indigene* there hadn't been touched by the drugs yet.

No matter what happened, no matter who else would be lost, he wouldn't let the *terra indigene* kill Meg.

The fog lifted on the Talulah River. The ferry and barge that linked the two halves of Ferryman's Landing resumed their schedule, with the crew keeping a wary eye on the weather. They transported residents who had been stuck on the wrong side of the river as well as all the supplies, packages, and mail that had stacked up.

Hawks and Eagles soared overhead, and Crows perched here and there on the vessels, a black-feathered pledge of safety for passengers and crew. But the fishing boats stayed docked, and not even the residents of Ferryman's Landing dared go out on the water. Every time a boat from Talulah Falls made a dash to escape, a whirlpool appeared on the river and pulled the boat down. Every evening as the sun went down, a storm rose—sleet, heavy snow, battering winds. For two days the storm arrived at sundown and left at sunrise, and the clear blue skies of daylight were a painful reminder of what else humans could lose if they tried to take what didn't belong to them.

On Earthday morning, James Gardner found a spotted gray pony outside his barn, expecting to be fed. So James fed the animal and opened the door of an empty stall. The pony settled in as if he'd always lived there, coming and going as he pleased, following Lorna Gardner around whenever she went outside. Finally she cut up an apple and let her children feed a few chunks to the pony, and he seemed content with the treat.

The next morning, James paid a few calls to other Simple Life folks, asking if anyone had lost a gray pony. When he passed Ming Beargard on the road, he asked the same question. Beargard said, "Fog isn't lost; he's waiting."

On his way home, James stopped at friends' houses, and they spread word throughout the Simple Life community that the Elementals weren't done yet with Great Island, the river, or Talulah Falls.

When Roger Czerneda did his patrol around the island and checked in with the farmers, James told him too.

As the storm around Talulah Falls faded on Moonsday evening, a handful of police stations in the Falls found sealed tubs on the sidewalk. The tub left outside the mayor's office contained the head and wallet, identifying the man as the owner of the house where the Sanguinati and four humans were butchered.

On Sunday morning, a sobbing man on a citizens-band radio contacted the police station at Ferryman's Landing and pleaded to have someone, anyone, deliver a message: the survivors in Talulah Falls wanted to negotiate with the *terra indigene*.

CHAPTER 19

On Windsday morning, Steve Ferryman and Jerry Sledgeman stood at the ferry's rail. They had clear skies and smooth water, and plenty of Great Island residents had been at the dock this morning to take packages to the mainland half of the village and pick up anticipated deliveries.

Lois Greene, editor of the *Great Island Reporter*, had run a special edition yesterday with Steve's list of emergency measures on the front page, guaranteeing it would command the attention of every adult in Ferryman's Landing. So he wasn't surprised to see the pile of backpacks and overnight cases at the dock, ready for the ferry's return trip to the island.

The updated prophecy Simon Wolfgard had e-mailed to him had made his skin crawl. And being told that one of the Elementals' steeds, in its chubby pony form, was staying at the Gardner farm because it was "waiting" was reason enough to figure that whatever was coming wasn't going to pass them by.

"You okay with making this delivery?" Steve asked as they walked off the ferry with three plastic containers.

"Sure," Jerry replied. "Just wish I had more cargo to justify the gasoline usage."

"If things go the way I hope they do, this will be the last light delivery you'll make to Lakeside. And at least some of the teenagers who are looking for work this summer will have jobs because the village businesses will need extra hands."

They stored the containers in the van that was parked in the delivery area of the dock.

"We'll see what we see." Jerry closed the van's back doors and went around to the driver's door. "I'll give you a shout when I return."

Steve watched Jerry drive away. Then he turned back to the ferry, figuring he'd give his brother, Will, a hand storing all that baggage before running up to the bookstore to pick up a copy of the *Lakeside News* to read on the return trip to the island. But the skin between his shoulder blades suddenly started twitching and twingeing.

He looked at the sky and the water. Still clear, still smooth.

Something's coming, he thought, seeing the way Will suddenly straightened up and looked at the sky and water.

Before he reached his brother, his mobile phone started ringing.

"So Ruthie is going to be an instructor at the Courtyard, teaching the Others how to get along in the human world," Kowalski said as they drove out of the Chestnut Street station's lot. "Like what we saw a while back in A Little Bite but more formal. It doesn't pay as much in human money as her teaching job did, but with the credits for the Market Square stores, we'll do all right."

Hearing something different under the upbeat words, Monty studied his partner. "Do you have a problem with her working in the Courtyard?"

"Me? No. But we had dinner with my folks last night, and my father said he's been hearing mutters at work about how people who help the Others are traitors to their own kind. My brother is attending the tech college, and he's heard the same thing." Kowalski hesitated. "I still think working with the *terra indigene* will pay off in the end, but . . ."

"But you're worried about Ruthie's safety?"

"Yes. More so after what happened to Merri Lee. And some of Ruthie's friends—girls she's known since grade school—don't want to be friends anymore because she spends time in the Courtyard and helps the Others. And now with everything going on in Talulah Falls . . . All the TV talk shows are going on and on about what right the *terra indigene* have to dictate who runs the government in a human town."

"They can dictate the terms because their alternative is destroying the town," Monty replied quietly. "And as I understand it, Talulah Falls is no longer a human-controlled town. The government, such as it may be, will be there to keep public services running and act as a liaison between the town's human population and the Others now in charge of the Courtyard."

"I don't think that has sunk in yet," Kowalski said. "That the Falls is now a human settlement in the Others' territory and *they're* the ones making all the rules—and dishing out the punishment if any of their rules are broken."

The radio stations barely played two songs in a row this morning without repeating the special news story: as part of the negotiations with the *terra indigene*, all the top government officials in Talulah Falls were required to resign and leave the area.

The Others weren't just taking away the status and power those people had; they were driving out anyone they considered adversaries. And all the *terra indigene* who had run that Courtyard had also left in favor of new leadership that wasn't already soured by extended contact with humans. A clean slate. A new start. A last chance for Talulah Falls to remain a place where humans could live, even if it was no longer a place where humans could do as they pleased.

The news stories didn't mention that part, just as the news stories were suddenly vague when it came to acknowledging the people who were dead or missing in the Falls.

If we're not careful, there will be a lot more humans among the dead and missing, Monty thought. "Tell me something, Karl. How many *terra indigene* living on this continent have any contact with humans? Guess at an estimate, figuring in every city, town, village, hamlet, and human settlement located deep in the wild country."

Kowalski said nothing for a full minute. "Five percent? Could be less than that."

"There have to be millions of earth natives living in Thaisia, hundreds of millions, maybe even billions, living throughout Namid. Only a small percentage of them have ever seen a human, and an even smaller percentage have any interest in seeing us as anything but meat." Monty smiled grimly. "Our ancestors showed the Others how to weave, how to build a cabin, how to farm, how to build a boat and catch fish, how to build a fire. They learned everything they really needed from us centuries ago. All our technology, all our gizmos. How much interest do the *terra indigene* living beyond easy range of human habitation really have for such things?"

"Not much interest at all when you put it that way," Kowalski said.

"I keep thinking about the Humans First and Last movement. I keep wondering if any of them have paid any attention to the history of our world and the history of Thaisia in particular."

"What about it?"

"For the most part, the Others leave humans alone—until our actions force them to become aware of us."

Not much mail, Meg thought. *Not many deliveries. Not much of anything but waiting.*

She pulled a copy of *Nature!* from the stack of magazines she'd picked up at Howling Good Reads. There wasn't anyone else supplying her with images that would help her identify what she saw in a prophecy. She didn't have access to the thick binders of pictures anymore. But she could start creating her own set of image binders. Then whoever listened to the prophecy could have a reference for what she had seen.

Besides, the color photographs taken of creatures from all over the world fascinated her. She just had to remember to limit the number of new images she absorbed each day from the magazines. She didn't have those disturbing blank spots—information overload, Merri Lee had called them—when she looked at a few new images and then switched to a magazine she had already seen. That was restful, especially since she absorbed so many new images just by going through her daily routine.

The Courtyard kept changing, dazzling her with the flowers that bloomed between one day and the next, with the bare branches of trees that were swollen with the buds of new leaves and then fuzzed with green. Every day, she drove a familiar road through a new place. It delighted her, excited her, but she had to admit that the relief of being in her own unchanging apartment was almost painful some nights.

A *cassandra sangue* could absorb only so much that was new and strange before her mind shut down. Had that always been true, or was that, like the need to cut, something that had been bred into them to keep them dependent?

Either way, she probably should mention this recent understanding about herself to Simon . . . or Henry, since the Grizzly would, most likely, simply accept the information and not make a fuss about it.

She didn't know how long she'd been staring at a picture of tiny, bright-colored frogs when she heard Nathan snarl and a man calling, "Hello?"

Opening the Private door, she stepped up to the counter in the front room. A big man stood just inside the door. He held three rectangular plastic containers and a manila envelope.

"Are you Meg Corbyn?" he asked.

Nathan snarled louder at the mention of her name. She couldn't see the Wolf, which meant he was right in front of the counter and ready to attack.

"Yes, I'm Meg." She didn't recognize the man or the van, and she hadn't placed any orders in the past few days. She didn't think anyone in the Courtyard had. Their bus had made the plaza run a couple of times, but only a handful of *terra indigene* had gone out to shop, and Henry, Vlad, or Nyx had been among the Others who made the trip—a reminder of why the humans needed to behave.

"I'm Jerry Sledgeman, of Sledgeman's Freight. Got a delivery for you, compliments of Steve Ferryman on Great Island. Okay if I put these on the counter so I can show you the paperwork?"

"Oh. Yes. Of course." When Jerry didn't move, she added, "It's all right, Nathan. I was expecting this delivery."

Nathan backed away just enough to give Jerry room at the far end of the counter.

Jerry set the containers on the counter in a stack. Giving Meg a measuring look, he shifted the two top containers to sit on the counter so she could see the printed information taped to the lids.

"Eamer's Bakery?" Meg asked.

"Two sisters, Mary and Claire, run it and do most of the baking," Jerry said. "Have another good bakery in Ferryman's Landing, but that one prefers doing breads and rolls and things like that. Good bread, but when Steve talked to some folks about making some special cookies for Wolves, Mary and Claire were the ones who wanted to give it a try. They—"

Meg slapped a hand on a container as Nathan made a lunge for it.

"Nathan!" she scolded. "If you make another grab for these cookies, you won't get so much as a crumb!"

Nathan leaped away, stared at her for a moment—and howled.

"Oh, for pity's sake," Meg said. "Don't be such a puppy."

Howl!

Another Wolf answered Nathan. And another. And another.

Watching the color drain out of Jerry's face, Meg pulled the lid off one container and grabbed a cookie. "Here. Here-here-here, have a— Oh. It's shaped like a cow. How cute." She took a moment to absorb the image.

Nathan slapped his front paws on the counter. Despite his speed, Meg noticed how carefully he took the cookie from her.

"The cow-shaped cookies are probably beef flavored," Jerry said. "Claire did say they tried different flavors. It's explained in the paperwork."

She watched Nathan prance over to the Wolf bed set up on one side of the office. She also noticed how, despite acting preoccupied with his treat, his attention stayed on Jerry Sledgeman.

Before she could open the envelope, the back door slammed and Simon shouted, "Meg!" He charged into the front room, almost knocking her into the counter as he focused on the human male.

"Everything is fine," Meg said at the same time Simon said, "Sledgeman?"

"Mr. Wolfgard," Jerry said, brushing a finger against his cap. "Brought a delivery."

Meg noticed the slight tremble in Jerry's hand and the shine of sweat on his face. And she noticed three Wolves crowded in front of the office door. She'd never seen him in Wolf form, but she'd bet Blair was the one staring at the unfamiliar human. The other two seemed younger, and a fourth Wolf, who had his paws on the window and was watching Nathan eat the cookie, was definitely a juvenile.

"*Arroooo!*" The single vocalization from the youngster at the window quickly became a chorus.

Grabbing a handful of cow-shaped cookies, Meg pushed past Simon and opened the go-through that gave her access to the rest of the front room. The Wolves outside backed up enough to let her push the front door open partway.

"Here," she said. "Have a cookie and stop making a fuss."

The juvenile Wolves took the cookies and trotted off. Blair stared at her a long moment before taking the last cookie and walking away.

As she returned to the counter, Meg narrowed her eyes at Nathan.

Crunch, crunch. There was a smug satisfaction to the sound.

Simon opened the envelope and the rest of the containers. He held up a cookie.

"Human-flavored cookies?" He sounded pleased.

Nathan pricked his ears and said, "*Arroooo?*"

What little color Jerry's face had regained drained away again.

Meg looked at the papers. "The people-shaped ones have chamomile. They're soothing."

"Soothing?" A thread of something dark and menacing in Simon's voice.

"Chamomile tea is soothing," Meg said, looking at the rest of the information the bakery had sent. "I like to drink it in the evening."

Simon studied her. "You do?"

"Yes." She peeked in the containers. "Okay, the cow-shaped cookies have beef stock for flavoring. The bars have honey. Henry might like to try one of those. The . . . what is that?"

"Turkey," Jerry and Simon said.

"That's the poultry-flavored cookies. And the people-shaped are chamomile. The bakery is asking for feedback on taste and texture." Meg went through the papers again, then looked at Jerry. "I don't see an invoice."

"These are the samples to see if we can produce what you were looking for," Jerry said. "After that, you can talk to Mary and Claire about the size of the orders and price and such." He looked at Simon. "And Steve will need to talk to you about how to increase the island's allowance for the ingredients."

"Let's see how this goes, and then I'll talk to him," Simon said.

"No." When they looked at her, Meg pointed at the front door. The three juveniles were back—and the crunching sound inside the office had stopped. "Can we have a rule that you can't use howling as a form of coercion?"

Simon stared at the juveniles, who immediately looked more subdued. Then he turned to Meg. "If they're annoying you, just bite them on the nose."

Jerry coughed.

Meg sighed. "I don't think that will work for me." Pulling out her clipboard and pen, she wrote down the information for Sledgeman's Freight and tucked the business card Jerry gave her under the clip.

"You have a minute?" Simon asked Jerry.

"Sure," Jerry replied. He brushed his cap again. "It was a pleasure to meet you, Ms. Corbyn."

"Thank you." She looked at Simon. "Am I allowed to lift things yet?"

"No," he said at the same time Nathan sprang to his feet.

She thought that would be the answer. "Then you bring the cookies into the sorting room."

"Why?"

"So I can sort them." If the containers weren't in the room that was mostly off-limits to everyone else, the floor of the front room would be littered with cookies and Wolves in minutes. Not that she would say that to the dominant Wolf—especially with a human present.

He must have known why she wanted the containers brought in because he grumbled, "I want to try some of these."

"I'll make up sample packages. If we're going to order fresh-made cookies, I need to know what flavors are preferred and how many Wolves want which kind."

He stared at the containers. "How long can these last?"

Meg shrugged. "I think I saw something in the paperwork about being able to freeze them. They won't last as long as the dog cookies I'd ordered from Pet Palace, but they should last a few days. Why?"

He whined softly. "There's going to be a gathering here in a couple of days. I'd like to have some of these for that."

A gathering that made Simon uneasy? But wouldn't he have been the one to issue the invitations? "I'll put aside enough for your meeting."

Returning to the front room, he vaulted over the counter and walked out with Jerry Sledgeman.

"What kind of meeting is he having here?" she whispered to herself.

Her back was suddenly filled with that pins-and-needles feeling that indicated the answer could be found in prophecy. Gritting her teeth, she waited until the feeling faded. Then she called a couple of the Market Square stores to find the small containers she wanted.

Steve watched another busload of children head down to the dock.

Moments after he had that uneasy feeling, the grade school and high school principals and the owners of the two day-care centers on the mainland side of Ferryman's Landing called because they, too, suddenly had a bad feeling. Then his aunt Lu called to say she was getting her boat ready for anything he needed. Then his parents called to tell him they were bringing the barge across ahead of its usual schedule. Then Roger Czerneda drove up in Great Island's new official black-and-white patrol car with its flashing lights and sirens. The other vehicles they used for police business were ordinary cars with regular horns and bubble lights that could be stuck to the roofs. Funny thing. All but one of those cars were also on the mainland side of the river that morning.

Something's coming, he thought, rubbing the back of his neck. *Hide the children.*

There wasn't any debate about where to hide them. Everything he'd been told lately indicated that the island was the only place. And just to be sure, the ferry and barge weren't giving passage to anyone who wasn't a resident of the village.

If the attack was meant to happen at Ferryman's Landing, it would have to hit the mainland half of the village. The Sanguinati were keeping watch on the north and east shorelines near the Simple Life farms. The Beargard were watching the western shoreline, while Ming Beargard guarded the docks. The Hawks and Eagles were in the air, watching the river and the roads leading into Ferryman's Landing. The Crows had spread out through the mainland half of the village to watch cars and people, ready to sound an alarm if they spotted a stranger. The Foxgard and Coyotegard had spread out to maintain a perimeter watch around the island half of the village. Even the Owlgard was out there keeping watch.

They were all as prepared as they could be.

Steve raised a hand in greeting as Jerry Sledgeman pulled into a nearby parking space. Before Jerry got out of his van, Roger Czerneda turned on to Main Street and parked on the opposite side.

"Gods above and below, what's going on?" Jerry said, gesturing toward the yellow buses on the barge.

"You see anything unusual in Lakeside?" Steve asked. With Talulah Falls still cut off, there weren't many ways to reach their village except a few dirt roads through farmland, and those weren't marked in a way a stranger could identify. If someone followed the road that ran along the shore of Lake Etu, that person would reach the city of Lakeside first. Why not stop there? A stranger could disappear more easily in a city.

Then again, the Lakeside police were aware of the potential for trouble, and a city police force had all the tools for checking license plates and drivers' licenses that a little village like Ferryman's Landing didn't have. They probably even had a few of the deluxe patrol cars with cameras that could take a picture of a vehicle for identification. Balance that against one official police officer, newly hired, and a handful of part-time peacekeepers, and Ferryman's Landing would look like an easier target.

"Simon Wolfgard asked me the same question about Great Island," Jerry replied, looking around. "Of course, I didn't know about this when he asked."

"We're moving the children to the island. Too many of us had a bad feeling just after you left."

He hadn't had time to do anything except answer questions, take phone calls, and help Will load extra supplies on the ferry. As soon as the last bus was on the barge, he'd call Wolfgard. From what he could tell, none of the Intuits had a feeling about any place beyond Great Island and their own village, but without the warning from Meg Corbyn's prophecy, they wouldn't have known *why* they were all feeling uneasy or what to do to protect their own. Seemed only fair to give the Others in Lakeside a heads-up.

"Why come to Ferryman's Landing at all?" Jerry asked. "What's here that isn't easily found anywhere else in the Northeast?"

Steve thought about the question and said grimly, "We are."

Meg didn't know what to think when Blair Wolfgard, in human form, walked into the Liaison's Office just after she returned from her midday break. He had a young Wolf with him, one of the youngsters who had responded to Nathan's howl that morning.

The moment the youngster saw her, he lunged for the counter, miscalculated the leap, and got only his front half on the countertop, his back legs scratching at the wood base in an effort to haul himself up and over.

Blair grabbed him by the scruff and pulled him off the counter. "You already had a cookie. She's not giving you another one." Then to Meg, "This is Skippy. He arrived a couple of days ago from the Wolfgard in the Addirondak Mountains and will be living with the Wolfgard here now."

As soon as Blair released him, Skippy immediately went to investigate the item that would be of most interest to a Wolf—the cushiony dog bed Meg had ordered from the Pet Palace when Nathan became the watch Wolf for the office. Skippy threw himself on the bed, rubbing and rolling. Claiming.

"You pee on that, I'll bite your tail off," Blair growled. "Or Nathan will."

Skippy, on his back with his paws in the air, just looked at the Courtyard's enforcer and wagged his intact tail.

The young Wolf had to be a juvenile, but he seemed less mature than Sam, who was still a puppy.

She didn't have any images of Wolves she could use for comparison, but there was something going on that she didn't understand.

She leaned toward Blair. "He knows about not shifting where he can be seen by humans? I don't want to explain to the police why a naked teenager was wandering around the delivery area." So far she'd avoided any calls about Nathan being outside without clothes or fur, but she didn't think she would be that lucky with Skippy.

Something in Blair's eyes. Pity? Acceptance?

"He's a skippy," Blair said. "They don't shift from the form they have at birth."

"So his name is Skippy . . ."

"Because he *is* a skippy. Their brains don't work quite right and skip over bits of what they need to learn. If they survive to adulthood, they settle down and do just fine. But most of them can't survive in the wild country long enough for their brains to catch up. A Courtyard is safer, and if a hunt is spoiled here because of a skippy, the pups in the pack won't starve."

And the pack's leaders wouldn't have to choose between driving away one youngster in order to save the rest.

"I didn't have any packages for you," Meg said.

"Wasn't expecting any right now." Blair didn't like being around humans, but he did like tinkering with things—especially the machines that could transform sunlight and wind into electrical power. She suspected his tolerance for her was in direct proportion to her diligence in delivering the parts he had ordered for his current project.

"So you came up to the office to introduce me to Skippy?"

As the Courtyard's enforcer, Blair exuded a more feral quality than Simon, and she wasn't quite sure he believed the "Meg isn't bitable" rule.

"Skippy is going to be the watch Wolf for a couple of afternoons," Blair said. "He's here to learn."

Ha! She suspected Skippy needed a minder, and she'd been elected because the Wolves in the Courtyard were busy.

"Isn't Nathan going to be here anymore?" she asked. The deliverymen had become accustomed to Nathan, and he recognized them. That meant he reacted only to someone he didn't know, like he had with Jerry Sledgeman.

"He'll still be here most of the time," Blair replied. "But I need Nathan this afternoon."

Wolves weren't usually possessive about objects, but Meg didn't think an enforcer like Nathan was going to be happy about sharing the bed with a goofball like Skippy.

Keeping her voice low, she asked, "Should I see if the Market Square general store still has one of those beds so Skippy and Nathan don't have to share?"

She watched the annoyed expression on Blair's face change into embarrassed resignation when Skippy, still on his back with his paws in the air, began a yodeling *arooeeooeeoo!*

"Yeah," Blair said. "You should do that."

By the time Steve Ferryman walked out of Bursting Burgers, he wondered if he and the other adults who'd had a bad feeling that morning had made a mistake. There were still Crows winging through the village, and Hawks and Eagles still soared overhead. Roger Czerneda had been patrolling on the mainland side of the village for hours while Flash Foxgard and Ming Beargard kept watch around the docks. Now Roger parked the patrol car and joined Steve.

"Late lunch?" Steve asked.

Roger nodded as he read the sign. "Bursting Burgers?"

"You haven't tried them yet?"

"I've been getting acquainted with the shops on the island side of the village."

"These are the best hamburgers in the Lake Etu area," Steve replied. "Can't get them on the island side because Burt has a phobia about water. And boats."

"You're kidding."

"Nope. They do a great roast beef sandwich too."

"In that case, I guess I'll give it—"

Caw, caw, caw, caw.

"—a try," Roger finished.

The two men watched the car drive up Main Street and park a few spaces down from where they stood. Steve noted the Midwest license plate on the car and the way the Crows took position in the nearby trees.

The man who got out saw them and hesitated. He started walking toward them just as Steve's mobile phone rang.

Mom always has excellent timing. "Could use some help here," he said quickly, turning away so it would look like a personal call and not in some way connected to the stranger.

"Steve, I just had the strangest feeling." A pause. "What kind of help?"

"Do you have pencil and paper handy?"

"Yes."

Of course she did. "Write this down." Keeping his voice low, Steve gave her the license plate number and the make and model of the car. "Hang on to that. I'll call back." He ended the call just as the man reached him and Roger.

Short. Dapper. Pale hair cut so short it almost wasn't there. Little glasses. A sweet smile.

Steve hated him on sight, but he put on his "tell no secrets" expression and waited. He had a feeling the man really didn't want to talk to him, and especially didn't want to attract the notice of a cop. All the more reason to make sure this stranger *did* talk to them.

"You're a long ways from home," Steve said, making a passing gesture at the car.

The man looked back at the vehicle, then focused on Steve. "Ah. Yes, I am. A business trip to several cities in the Northeast Region. I was going to visit Talulah Falls—I've heard so much about the waterfalls there. But apparently there's been some trouble, and no one but residents are allowed entrance?"

Light voice. Easy to dismiss and yet oddly mesmerizing. A voice that whispered *trust me* underneath the spoken words.

"Television news stations in the Midwest didn't report on it?" Steve asked.

"I haven't paid much attention. Sometimes such things distract one from what is important. I was hoping to speak to someone in authority. Could either of you gentlemen point me in the right direction?"

"No need to point." The space between Steve's shoulder blades twitched and twinged. "I am the mayor of this fine village, and my friend here is with the police." He waited a beat. "And who might you be?"

"Phineas Jones."

Wishing he were wearing gloves and wouldn't have to touch that skin, Steve looked at the extended hand a moment too long before completing the handshake.

"What business are you in, Mr. Jones?" Roger asked.

"I'm more a representative of a philanthropic endeavor than a business," Jones replied.

"There aren't enough people in the Midwest interested in this philanthropic endeavor, so you have to drive all the way up here? That's a lot of miles to travel and gas coupons to use for a might-be-maybe venture." Roger scratched his head, then resettled his hat. "Of course, you might have a couple of interested parties lined up already that would make the expense worthwhile."

A heavy silence. Jones's sweet smile didn't change, but it somehow seemed colder.

Right on target, Roger, Steve thought.

"I'm a specialist in a very particular field," Jones finally said. "And while I had intended to visit the Falls and see this natural wonder for myself, I'm here in Ferryman's Landing because . . . Well, to put it delicately, I had heard that a girl took her own life last year because of an addiction to cutting her skin. Some parents insist that girls will outgrow this behavior and don't take steps to get their child the professional help she needs. Studies have shown that if one girl is discovered displaying this behavior, there are several more in the community who are still successfully hiding their addiction. Parents may see symptoms without fully understanding what they're seeing. Until it's too late."

Steve didn't think Phineas Jones missed much, but he hoped the man couldn't detect his uneasiness.

"I think the incident was reported incorrectly," Steve said.

Cold, sweet smile. "Oh? How so? A girl jumped into the river and drowned last year. What can be incorrect about that?"

"Nothing, as far as it goes. Except she didn't jump into the river. She *fell* into the river. Fast current here. Lots of rapids farther up. Most people who live around the water know how to swim, but the river takes one or two a year. And at least one boat each year rides the falls down to the rocks. You may have heard on the news that some fools tried to go out during foggy weather a few days ago. There are rescue boats and volunteers still down there fishing out pieces of boats and bodies. It's a tragedy when it happens, but it does happen."

"Perhaps I should talk to the administrators of your schools. Sometimes school personnel—"

"Mr. Jones," Steve said pleasantly. "I think you should get back in your car and drive away. It doesn't matter what anyone else tells you. *I'm* telling you this is as close as you get to any child in Ferryman's Landing."

"The philanthropists I represent only want to help these girls," Jones said. "Why are you so defensive? What are you afraid of?"

Trust me. How many parents had regretted trusting that voice?

"I'm afraid of the Beargard who rule the land around here as far as Lakeside," Steve said, his own voice turning hard. "I'm afraid of them taking offense at a stranger poking his nose where it doesn't belong and tossing a human into the river for sport. You should have paid more attention to what was happening in Talulah Falls, Mr. Jones. This is the wrong time for you to be doing business anywhere around the Great Lakes. You need any help finding your way out of the village?"

Another heavy silence. "No," Jones said. "No, I think I have all the information I need. Good day, gentlemen."

They watched him walk back to his car. They watched him drive away. And Steve watched the Crows fly off to start the relay of Crowgard, Hawkgard, and Eaglegard that would track Jones's car for as long as they could.

Finally Steve said, "Officer Czerneda?"

"Mr. Ferryman?"

"Did Phineas Jones look like a smiling shark to you?"

"Yes, he did. He certainly did."

Steve nodded grimly. "I'd better give Simon Wolfgard another call."

Hearing the knock, Meg opened the back door of the Liaison's Office and stared at Merri Lee.

As part of her training, she had seen videos of women being assaulted, had studied images of battered bodies and faces. She'd even seen one of the girls in the compound punched and slapped and kicked—a girl whose skin couldn't earn enough to justify keeping her. The Controller had recorded that session and had shown it often enough that the real experience of seeing a girl beaten to death lost much of its impact.

Much, but not all.

Those images took on an additional meaning when superimposed over the face of a friend.

"Do you feel well enough to be out?" Meg asked, stepping aside.

"Dr. Lorenzo said to take it easy for the first couple of days and then use common sense," Merri Lee replied as she entered the back room. "It's been a week since . . . the assault. I lazed around, reading books and watching movies for the first few days. Even indulged in a couple of massages. Now I'm feeling restless and want to do something useful." She hesitated. "With A Little Bite still closed to everyone but Courtyard residents, Tess doesn't need me right now. I offered to help Heather fill out book orders, but she's freaked about what happened to me, and I don't think she'll be comfortable being around me until the bruises completely heal."

Meg understood why Heather would be upset. Merri Lee's face was still healing, so the black eye and bruises must have been very bad. Heather's life was in the human part of the city, and Merri Lee's injuries were a harsh reminder of what could happen to someone labeled a Wolf lover.

Unlike Heather, Meg didn't have any reason to avoid Merri Lee because she didn't have to go beyond the Courtyard and its protection.

"Do you think Tess would let us wash these containers at A Little Bite?" Meg asked, pointing to six small containers. "I'm supposed to make up sample packages of Wolf cookies, but there's just the bathroom sink here."

"I could take them over and wash them for you," Merri Lee said.

"Thanks."

A yodeling *arooeeooeeoo* came from the front room.

"What is that?" Merri Lee asked, looking startled.

"That," Meg sighed, "is Skippy."

As soon as her friend left, Meg opened the large plastic containers. Blair didn't say she *couldn't* give the youngster a cookie. She reached for a cow, then thought for a moment before taking one of the people-shaped cookies.

She walked through the office until she reached the counter in the front room. Keeping the cookie out of sight, she patted the top of the counter. "Skippy. Front paws here."

He rushed over and plopped his paws on the counter, aquiver with juvenile enthusiasm.

She held up a finger to get his attention. "Gently," she ordered. Then she held up the cookie.

He wasn't grown enough to leap on the counter or over it, and he couldn't get his brains off the cookie long enough to think about backing up to get a running start. After three failed attempts to grab the cookie, the command Meg kept giving him finally got through. The fourth time she held up the cookie, he managed to take it from her with great care.

Of course, he also managed to step on his own foot in his haste to get back to the Wolf bed and devour his treat.

Meg sighed and returned to the back room to wait for Merri Lee. One chamomile cookie wouldn't hurt Skippy. And, really, if it actually calmed him down, she'd be doing everyone a favor, because if she had to listen to another hour of that yodeling, she was going to find the heaviest box she could lift and beat Blair over the head with it.

If Skippy had nipped one of her fingers . . .

The pins-and-needles feeling suddenly filling her left hand was so fierce it burned under her skin.

Skippy . . . and teeth.

By the time Merri Lee returned, Meg had everything set up in the bathroom. Skippy was so engrossed in his cookie, he didn't pay any attention when Meg closed the Private door and locked it. Maybe it was just as well that Nathan wasn't the watch Wolf this afternoon. He'd have sounded the alarm the moment she locked the door because *he* would know why she was trying to lock him out.

"Put those down," Meg said as soon as Merri Lee walked into the back room. "I need your help."

"What's wrong with your hand?" Merri Lee asked, putting the clean containers on the small round table that functioned as a dining area. "Why are you rubbing it?"

"I need to cut. I need you to write down the prophecy."

Merri Lee took a step back. "Meg, this isn't a good idea. I'm not qualified to—"

"Something is going to happen," Meg cried.

"I'll call Tess. Or Henry."

"There's no time!" Meg panted in an effort to stay focused. "I can't explain how it works. Not now. But if I can't warn them, someone will get hurt!"

"Gods above and below," Merri Lee muttered. "Okay. All right. What do I need to do?"

"Everything is ready." Meg rushed into the bathroom, sat on the closed toilet seat, and opened the silver razor. "Just write down everything I say. And once I make the cut, say, 'Speak, prophet, and I will listen.' I don't remember the Controller saying that, but whenever Tess says it, it helps me focus."

"Gods above and below," Merri Lee muttered again.

Meg held the razor over her left hand, following the pins-and-needles feeling until it became a buzz centered in her little finger. Gritting her teeth and fighting the urge to slash the skin open, she made a precise cut. Still gritting her teeth, she set the razor on the sink and swallowed the need to scream as the agonizing pain that was the prelude of prophecy filled her. Then she heard the words that were a signal to speak, and pain changed to euphoria as she shared the visions that spilled from her mind as her blood dripped into the sink.

When she came back to herself, Merri Lee was staring at her.

"Wow," Merri Lee said. "That's fascinating to watch in a creepy sort of way."

Meg looked away.

"Sorry. It's just . . . Wow." Merri Lee blew out a breath. "Meg, we have to call someone. Bandage up the finger first?"

"You don't have to stay. Just give Henry the prophecy. He'll pass it on to Simon." It hadn't occurred to her that a human would think watching a prophecy being spoken was creepy. Maybe all the Controller's clients felt that way. Or was it different when you were paying lots of money to be told something about yourself?

"Of course I have to stay," Merri Lee said briskly. She turned on the water taps, adjusting one then the other until she had the temperature she wanted. "Put your hand under the water."

Meg let her friend wash the hand and pat it dry. Neither of them said anything while the ointment was applied and the little finger carefully bandaged.

"Call Henry or Tess," Meg said as they left the bathroom. She would clean the razor in a minute. "Simon isn't going to be happy about this."

Merri Lee gave Meg an odd look. "You don't remember anything you said, do you?"

She shook her head. "In order to remember it, the prophet has to swallow the prophecy. Not speak," she clarified.

"And that hurts."

"Yes."

Merri Lee nodded thoughtfully. "I'll call Henry." She stopped at the doorway to the sorting room. "Meg? I'm sorry I said it was creepy to watch. It is, in a way, but I'd like to understand it better. And I'd like to help." She paused. "I have an idea. I'll see if Lorne sells index cards at the Three Ps."

While Merri Lee went into the sorting room to call Henry and Lorne, Meg cleaned her razor. She wanted it out of sight before any of the Others burst through the office's back door.

Vlad walked into HGR's office. "Another meeting?"

Simon remained sitting behind the desk. "Humans have meetings all the time."

"I know. How do they get anything done?"

He didn't much care if the monkeys ever got anything done.

Tess, Henry, and Blair walked into the office.

"Close the door," Simon said.

"This can't be good," Blair muttered as he closed the door.

No reason to fluff it up. "Steve Ferryman called me earlier today, after Jerry Sledgeman made the delivery of cookies. Too many Intuits had a bad feeling this morning, so they moved all the children over to the island."

Blair nodded. "That call was the reason you wanted Nathan roaming the delivery area instead of being inside the Liaison's Office."

Simon nodded. "Ferryman called again a few minutes ago. A man named Phineas Jones showed up at Ferryman's Landing."

"Fin," Tess said. "Ass."

Simon nodded. "Ferryman called him a smiling shark."

"What did this Phineas Jones want?" Vlad asked.

"He didn't actually say it, but Ferryman thinks Jones is looking for blood prophets," Simon replied.

"Is the shark still in Ferryman's Landing?" Tess asked.

Simon shook his head. "Ferryman told him to be on his way. The Crowgard, Hawkgard, and Eaglegard kept watch on him all the way to Lakeside, then lost the car in traffic. We should figure that he's gone to ground here."

"Do we call that lieutenant?" Blair asked. "Can he hunt for Jones?"

"Doubtful," Vlad said. "Jones isn't an unusual name, and there are plenty of hotels, inns, and B and Bs in Lakeside. We don't even know what this man looks like, besides being a smiling shark, which I don't think the police will find useful."

"Ferryman gave me a basic description, and he and Czerneda are working to get a likeness of Jones's face made," Simon said. "Once they have that, they'll send the image to us and to Lieutenant Montgomery. But I don't think we'll have to do much hunting. We know he's here, and there's only one blood prophet in Lakeside." He looked at Blair. "You get Skippy settled into the Liaison's Office?"

"More or less," Blair replied. "But he's not much good as a watch Wolf."

"Nathan won't be far away. In two days we'll be meeting with leaders from the Midwest, Northeast, and High Northeast. We're going to keep the Courtyard stores closed to human customers, but I want our humans working. Marie Hawkgard will stand watch at HGR. Nathan will roam the area around the Market Square, Liaison's Office, and consulate."

"So will I," Blair growled. "Right now, Skippy's form of attack is tripping someone in his enthusiasm to see if they have anything to eat."

A frantic tapping on the door before John opened it and poked his head in the room. "Sorry to interrupt, but Merri Lee just called and said Henry or Tess should come to the Liaison's Office right away. Meg just had a prophecy."

Simon pushed past everyone in the room and knocked John aside in his haste to get down the stairs and out of the back door of HGR. But he wasn't as fast as Vlad, who had opened the upstairs window, shifted to smoke, and flowed down the outside wall and over the pavement. By the time Simon caught up to him, Vlad had shifted back to human form and was opening the office's back door.

They charged into the room together, followed by Henry, Blair, and Tess.

Merri Lee let out a startled yip and jumped away from the sitting area. She stared at the Others, then looked toward the table and said, "You weren't kidding when you said they wouldn't take this well."

Simon spun toward the table. Meg sat on one of the chairs, looking a little pale. She held up her left hand, showing all of them the neat—and small—bandage on her little finger.

He wanted to tear off that bandage, wanted to see the wound and lick it clean. Wanted . . .

A warning growl from Henry stopped him from taking a second step toward the table.

"You're making tea?" Tess said.

Merri Lee nodded. "Peppermint for me and chamomile for Meg."

"I'll finish it. You sit down."

When Merri Lee didn't move, Simon stepped back as much as he could with Blair and Henry standing behind him.

"You all right, Meg?" Vlad asked.

She nodded, then looked at Merri Lee as she touched the pad of paper on the table and the stack of index cards. "Tell them."

Merri Lee slipped into the other chair. "I wasn't sure how this is usually done, so I made extra notes."

"Words first," Henry said.

Merri Lee looked at her list. "Teeth. No! Sandwich. Skull and crossbones. Broom. Bright frogs. Arm. Shark. Teakettle."

Simon swallowed the desire to snarl, howl, and otherwise express displeasure and frustration. Cryptic nonsense. And what wasn't cryptic were the two items that had shown up in other prophecies—and at least one of them meant something lethal.

Tess brought the mugs of tea to the table. She stared at the pad of paper, then at the index cards. "What are these little drawings?"

"Associations," Merri Lee said. "It wasn't just the words. Meg made gestures that seemed connected to the words. It reminded me of a picture game I used to play as a kid. You tried to make a story out of the pictures on the cards, and you could rearrange the order three times to create the best story."

Tess spread out the index cards to reveal all the drawings. Then she took the pad of paper and brought it over to the rest of the Others.

Simon looked at the first index card and snarled at the cartoony Wolf head that had some kind of symbol over its bared teeth. He knew by the way Merri Lee hunched into herself that snarling right now wasn't helping, but he couldn't stop himself.

"No teeth?" Vlad said.

"No biting," Merri Lee replied. "The circle and line symbol means 'do not' or 'no,' and after Meg said 'teeth' and 'no!' she mimicked biting something."

"I did?" Meg looked startled.

"You said to write down the words, but I figured the gestures were important too. So that seemed like it meant no biting." Merri Lee tapped the index card that had the cartoony Wolf head with the "no" symbol drawn over its muzzle.

"Skull and crossbones means poison," Tess said, as Merri Lee put the index card with that symbol after the cartoony Wolf. "We know that from when Meg's prophecy saved the ponies." She stared at the list. "Sandwich? That doesn't sound threatening. Neither does arm."

Fur sprang up on Simon's shoulders and back. Had to stay human. Had to stay in control. Had to listen and not yell about Meg not calling *him*.

"Every time she said 'sandwich,' Meg mimicked spreading something on her arm," Merri Lee said, laying the "sandwich" and "arm" cards after the "poison" card. "But sandwich doesn't necessarily mean food. It could mean something in layers if the visions aren't always literal."

"I don't know," Meg said when they all looked at her. "I wasn't part of deciphering the visions, so I don't know how it worked."

"Frogs?" Tess asked.

Merri Lee glanced at Meg and nudged the index card with a frog into position. "When I went into the sorting room to phone Henry, I saw a magazine on the counter. It was open to a picture of frogs."

Vlad disappeared and returned with the magazine. As he quickly skimmed the article, he looked grim. "Poisonous. Lethal. A defense against predators because devouring them kills you. Montgomery mentioned poisonous frogs killing their attackers."

Leaning over the table, Henry repositioned the frog card after the skull and crossbones.

"Can't put poison on your own skin," Simon said. "You would kill yourself doing that, wouldn't you?"

"Sandwich." Tess held her hands one above the other with a little space between. "Two protective layers with poison spread in between?"

They all looked at the story made from the drawings on the index cards. Then they looked at Meg.

"The girls are tied to the chair for cutting, so I don't think I acted things out before," Meg said. "I don't remember doing it now. But the cards . . ." She touched an index card. "The Controller could have done something like this, arranging pictures until a sequence had meaning to the client."

"Maybe the shark is doing the biting and 'no' is a warning?" Merri Lee said. "Meg didn't mention a Wolf, just the shark and frog, and frogs don't bite. At least, I don't think they do."

She didn't have to mention a Wolf, Simon thought. *Meg knows who would be most likely to bite an intruder. And so does Merri Lee.* "Steve Ferryman called me. We know the shark is a human named Phineas Jones."

"We do?" Meg gasped.

Ignoring her, Simon put the simple drawing of an oval with a fin and tail after the other cards.

"What if we rearrange the pictures, see if there is another story?" Henry said.

Henry put the index cards in a different order. Merri Lee reached out, hesitated, then changed the order of a couple of them.

Henry nodded. "That's a story. Don't bite the shark who has a sandwich of poison on his arm."

"What about the broom and teakettle?" Simon asked.

Merri Lee shook her head and set those two index cards apart from the rest. "No clue. Except I think they go together somehow."

Simon hadn't noticed Blair had left the room until the enforcer returned, holding up half a cookie and scowling at Meg.

"What did you give Skippy?" Blair demanded.

"I wanted him to calm down, so I gave him a chamomile cookie," Meg said, narrowing her eyes at Blair. "It was either that or bite *you* for leaving the singing Wolf here."

If she were anyone else, she'd get nipped for sounding so uppity, Simon thought. "Something wrong?" he asked Blair.

"Damn Wolf is in the front room snoring," Blair growled. "Doesn't have any idea we're here. Which isn't helpful since he's supposed to be the watch Wolf." That last part was directed at Meg.

"I'll make a note for the bakery that the chamomile cookies are a little too strong," Meg said. "And too big. I didn't mean to knock him out, just calm him down a little."

Simon studied the two women. Meg and Merri Lee had done well working together to reveal this prophecy, and using the index cards was a clever way to share the images Meg saw in the visions. But the girls should have told him *before* Meg made the cut. After all, Meg was his friend, so he should have been told. Which was why, instead of praising them, he growled, "Can the two of you manage to stay out of trouble for the rest of the afternoon?"

"Oh, Simon," Tess muttered.

Henry's hand suddenly landed on his shoulder, almost buckling his knees.

"Our Meg did stay out of trouble," Henry said. "Her friend was with her to watch and to help. They saw much, and lives will be saved because of what we know from the visions."

"Maybe you should go home and rest," Simon told Meg. Maybe he could go home with her and they could cuddle for a while or play a game. Or she could watch a movie and pet him.

"Merri Lee is helping me make some sample packages of cookies," Meg said, sounding like the only game she wanted to play right now was whack a Wolf.

A warning rumble meant it was time to go before Henry decided he needed a friendly reminder to leave. The Grizzly's reminders tended to hurt.

Simon tore off the pages that held the prophecy, dropped the pad on the table, and walked out. Then he waited for Vlad and the others to join him outside.

"All right," Blair grumbled. "I wouldn't mind having some of those chamomile cookies to give to the youngsters when it's time to sleep, but a watch Wolf is supposed to be awake enough to watch, even if he is a skippy."

"Have Nathan come back for the last hour," Simon said.

"Those two females aren't having anyone as friendly as Nathan watching over them." Meaning the dominant enforcer planned to park himself in the office for the rest of Meg's shift.

"I don't like our Meg having this prophecy now," Henry said. "Is there a connection to so many leaders coming to Lakeside and this shark suddenly appearing in our territory?"

"If he's here hunting for a blood prophet, the connection is Meg," Vlad said. "She's the reason Simon called this meeting."

"I wonder if the enemy isn't also guided by prophecy," Vlad said. "Wouldn't you use a *cassandra sangue* to find out the best time to strike out at us?"

"When this Phineas Jones comes to the Courtyard, he'll have a defense that will kill us if we respond to a threat in the usual way," Simon said.

"Then we use human weapons instead of teeth," Henry said. "No matter how it's done, we make sure Jones doesn't leave here with Meg."

Simon nodded. "He's not taking Meg."

"Hello?"

"The Others are making free use of your property."

"Are you sure?"

"Not only using the property for themselves, but providing samples to other interested parties. I had an excellent lead and should have been able to acquire some new merchandise, but the deal was soured before I arrived. They were expecting me."

"Where was this? Lakeside?"

"No, a place called Ferryman's Landing. I'm in Lakeside now. I'll wait a couple of days and let things settle. Then I'll see what I can do about extracting your property."

CHAPTER 20

"*Mr. Smith is on the line for you.*"

The Controller picked up the phone. "What is it?"

"The scrap girls I sold you. I'd like to get them back."

"We agreed at the time of the sale that there would be no returns."

"Yes, I know, but all my best girls are suffering from breakdowns. No matter what my clients ask, all the girls talk about is a killer, a destroyer, blood and fire and death. Clients are demanding refunds since they aren't getting what they paid for."

"Prophecy is about interpretation, Mr. Smith. It's *your* job to interpret what the prophet sees. And we all know how fluid interpretation can be if one looks beyond the literal."

A pause. "What if the girls are saying what they're really seeing for my clients?"

"It's unlikely."

Another pause. "About the girls . . ."

"The scraps you sold me have already been used and are no longer available. Good day, Mr. Smith."

The Controller hung up and stared at the phone. Then he pressed the office buzzer and waited for his assistant's response.

"*Sir?*"

"Prepare *cs747* for the chair."

———

"Today's top story. A town in the Midwest is under quarantine after an outbreak of violence. There are rumors that a shipment of tainted ground beef was the cause of a series of violent attacks that ended in several deaths. Officials believe this is an isolated outbreak, but they advise caution and are recommending that citizens dispose of any ground beef bought in the past three days."

Emotionally battered and physically queasy, Monty turned off the radio and locked his apartment before hurrying to reach the bus stop. He needed to hear whatever Burke had to say to all the men this morning—and whatever Burke was willing to say in private.

He didn't think any other humans besides himself, Dominic Lorenzo, and Captain Burke were aware of what Meg Corbyn had revealed when she experienced that odd secondary prophecy from the reopened cut. So they were the only ones who had a good idea what the officials investigating the violence in the Midwest town were going to find.

The beef had been tainted with a particular kind of human flesh.

The Controller watched the attendants check the straps that secured a girl to the chair and prevented her from struggling just as the cut was made, since an imperfect cut spoiled both skin and prophecy. Like other men in his line of business, he'd lost a few valued clients recently—men who had regular appointments and were now making excuses for not wanting another prophecy.

Not want another prophecy? His clients weren't the kind of men who would leave their fortunes to chance. No, they'd gone to West Coast compounds or to one of those "charitable homes" in the Southeast and paid for a cut on an inferior girl.

If that was the depth of their loyalty for the guidance he had provided, then fuck them all. Prophecies could be read in so many ways, as he'd told that fool Smith. Until recently, his girls and his interpretations had been superior to those of anyone else in the business.

Now it was time to utilize his own resources and find out why things were going wrong. Had been going wrong since that bitch *cs759* managed to escape. If she couldn't be reacquired, she had to be destroyed.

But he wasn't here to find out about Meg Corbyn. He was here strictly for himself.

He snapped his fingers and waited until *cs747*'s eyes focused on him. "Tell me about my future. What do you see around me? Speak. Tell me what you see."

He'd ordered a cut on prime skin. Not much good skin left on this one, but the only girl superior to *cs747* when it came to prophecy was *cs759*.

"Tell me about my future. Tell me what you see," he said again when the cut was made and the blood started to flow.

She resisted. Despite the agonizing pain that flooded a prophet's body before she began to speak, this bitch always resisted for a few seconds, and he couldn't be sure she revealed everything she saw before the euphoria clouded her memory.

"A map," she said dreamily. "You're holding a map of Thaisia. It's bleeding. All the cities are bleeding. Drip, drip, drip on the floor, splashing your shoes." She paused. "They know your name."

The Controller's breath caught in his throat. *No one* knew his real name. "What do they call me?" he asked harshly.

"Killer." She smiled and looked right at him with clear eyes. "Destroyer." Then she laughed, and the sound held no sanity.

He rose, furious. "Clean her up and take her back to her cell."

The next time he needed scraps for the grinder, the bitch would be on the truck.

Jean lay on her narrow bed, drifting on the last bit of euphoria. Had the Walking Names who brought her back to her cell raped her? Or was she too scarred by the cuts and the beatings for them to keep it up long enough to get off?

Had to hold on for those moments before the pain forced her to speak. She could hold out longer, but then the Controller might start to wonder, might have the Walking Names do a more thorough check of her cell. They might find out about the little secret cuts and start wondering what she'd seen.

She'd seen enough to know she had to hold on a little while longer.

All the cities bleeding because of the Controller. That was the future for the humans in Thaisia. There was only one person who might be able to change that future, and it wasn't the Controller. It was Meg Corbyn.

"Meg," Jean whispered, smiling.

As she drifted to sleep, she wondered why, in all the recent visions, she kept seeing her scarred hand holding a jar of honey.

———

Meg drove her BOW to the Wolfgard Complex. The Green Complex, where she lived, was the only one where humans were tolerated because it was the multi-species complex. The rest were segregated by kind, and even when she made deliveries, she was careful not to intrude, going only to the area used for the delivery of mail and packages.

But today she wanted to see Sam before she started work, so she drove to the Wolfgard Complex with her container of treats—cookies she'd broken into puppy-size pieces, as well as a few cookies for the adults.

The pups were playing in front of the complex when she pulled up. Most of them remained focused on each other and the game. One stopped and watched as she got out of the BOW. Then he ran toward her, his feet still too big for the rest of him.

"Sam!" she cried happily, crouching with her arms open in welcome.

The other pups, hearing the cry and seeing Sam racing toward her, joined in the chase.

Alarmed, Meg shot upright, realizing too late that Sam might remember he had to be gentle with her but none of the other pups knew she couldn't be nipped or scraped with claws. Even if they didn't intend to hurt her, an accident could have terrible consequences for all of them.

A sharp *arrrooooo!* had them all skidding to a halt before they rammed into her.

The female striding toward her and the pups was mostly human in form but couldn't pass for human. For one thing, she had fur instead of hair and her ears were still Wolf.

"Hello," Meg said. She smiled at the female before crouching to hug Sam. He wiggled and licked and talked at her in Wolf, which started the other pups vocalizing.

Laughing, she stood up. "Sorry, I can't speak Wolf."

The female said sternly, "No shifting outside. It's still too cold to be out here in human skin without any clothes."

And it spares me from looking at a pack of naked little boys—and girls? Meg thought as she opened the passenger door. She wasn't about to look closely enough to figure out gender.

The puppy pack, spotting the containers, surged around her legs, almost knocking her off her feet.

Before the female could react, Meg said, "Enough! Polite puppies get a treat. Pushy puppies don't get anything but rocks."

There was some jostling and nipping as the pups sorted themselves out, but in short order they lined up behind Sam and looked at her expectantly. The female simply watched her.

It still amazed her that a demand for polite behavior actually got results. In their pony form, the Elementals' steeds were the Courtyard's mail carriers, coming up to the office so she could pack their baskets with mail for each complex. She also gave them treats every workday morning—carrots or apples or, on Moonsday, sugar lumps. Whenever they started pushing each other in order to be first for the treat, a reminder that only polite ponies carried mail and received treats was usually sufficient to convince them to settle down. Since they had names like Tornado and Avalanche and could easily knock the building down around her, her insistence on good behavior was as much about safety as manners.

"These are fresh-made cookies," Meg said opening the container. "So they're a special treat." She held out a piece of cookie.

Sam approached her, his exaggerated care in taking the cookie from her acting as a demonstration for the other pups. As soon as the last pup had his cookie, they all ran off to munch on the treats.

Meg focused her attention on the female again. "I'm Meg, the Human Liaison." Not that any *terra indigene* in the Courtyard didn't know that. She was not only an employee of the Courtyard; she was a major source of entertainment for the Others.

Now she hoped this female's curiosity would last long enough for Meg to carry out the other reason she'd driven to the complex.

"You're not a dominant female, but they still obeyed you," the Wolf finally said.

"They weren't going to get the cookies if they weren't polite."

The Wolf shook her head. "They're still young, but the pack of them could have taken the cookies if obeying you wasn't important to them in some way. Not dominant, but not prey. This is interesting. I'm Jane, the Wolfgard body-walker." She lightly touched one furry ear. "You aren't frightened by this?"

Meg considered the question. She'd seen Simon when he was a mixture of human and Wolf. It usually happened when he had a strong emotional response to a situation and instinctively took what he needed from both forms. Having seen him in full human form and full Wolf, seeing him between was more disturbing—or, at the very least, more distracting.

"You look balanced," Meg said honestly. She didn't know if Jane *couldn't* shift the rest of the way and look fully human or if this was a personal choice. Either way, she suddenly understood why Howling Good Reads and A Little Bite were sometimes open only to residents of the Courtyard. Humans and Others were an uneasy mix most of the time. Seeing reminders that the ones who ruled Thaisia— and most of the rest of the world—had never been and never would be human could do nothing but add more fuel to an already combustible relationship.

"I'm glad you're here." Meg reached into the BOW and brought out the other container. "Mr. Wolfgard wanted most of the cookies in this delivery for his big meeting, but I wanted some of the adult Wolves to try these. If they want to. I need to get some idea of whether it's worth ordering them from the bakery at Ferryman's Landing." She opened the container and held it out. "The cow-shaped cookies have a beef flavoring, the turkey-shaped cookies have a poultry flavoring, and . . ."

Jane held up one of the cookies. "Human-flavored?"

Meg stifled a sigh. That would be the first thing on her feedback list: don't make people-shaped cookies. The Wolves were way too interested and all of them leaped to a logical, if disturbing, expectation about the taste.

"No, those have chamomile," Meg said. "It's an herb that makes a soothing tea. I gave one of these to Skippy and he . . . Well, he went to sleep for several hours."

"I heard about that." Jane sniffed the cookie.

"I think it might be too hard for people teeth," Meg said quickly when it looked like Jane was going to take a bite. Then she wondered what a human-shaped mouth full of wolf teeth would look like and decided she didn't want to know. "Anyway, I thought you might have a use for the chamomile cookies. The instructions said the cookies can be frozen and then thawed when you need them."

"Yes, these would be useful," Jane said thoughtfully.

"The other cookies are just treats. The ones cut into bars have honey."

Jane wrinkled her nose, confirming Meg's suspicion that the Wolves weren't going to be interested in the honey bars. But Henry had taken a couple, and Jenni Crowgard had taken one to share with her sisters.

"I'd better go, or I'll be late opening the office." Meg closed the passenger door and walked around to the driver's side. "Let me know how you like the cookies."

As she got in the BOW, she saw the puppies racing toward her until they realized Jane now held the container of treats. But there was one pup who let out a mournful, squeaky-door howl as he watched her drive away.

When Monty reached Howling Good Reads, the sign on the door said RESIDENTS ONLY. He rapped on the door anyway and kept rapping until Simon turned the lock, pulling the door open but blocking entrance into the store.

"This isn't a good time, Lieutenant. The Courtyard has some guests for the next few days, and the stores aren't open to human customers."

"I have some questions, and I need answers," Monty said. "And having a few select human customers might be something you would find useful."

Simon studied him with amber eyes that held flickers of red. Then the Wolf stepped back enough for Monty to enter the store.

Turning the lock, Simon went back to the book display.

Monty followed him, putting aside the questions for a moment when he noticed the author names on the covers. He picked up a book. "Alan Wolfgard? I haven't heard of him. What does he write?" He figured the red ink splashed on the cover was a strong clue but felt it was prudent to ask.

"Thrillers and horror." Simon gave him a toothy smile. "As you must have guessed from the name, he's *terra indigene,* so you wouldn't have heard of him unless you borrowed some books from our library. You could ask Ruthie. I think she's read some of Alan's stories."

In that case, he would definitely ask Ruthie. And Kowalski.

"I've heard the Courtyard bus has been to the train station a couple of times today, picking up passengers."

"Our being able to use the trains is part of the agreement that allows humans to have the tracks between cities."

"I wasn't commenting about the Others' right to use the railway, Mr. Wolfgard. But you said you were having guests. With the current unrest here and the future of Talulah Falls not completely resolved, I'm concerned."

Simon didn't look up from the display. "Some of the *terra indigene* leaders have things to discuss. Don't human leaders meet to discuss things that concern their people?"

"Yes, they do. But when our leaders meet, cities don't usually disappear."

Simon laughed. It was a cold sound. "Wait here." He walked to the back of the store.

A gathering of *terra indigene* leaders. How long had this meeting been planned? What had been the catalyst? And why had the Lakeside Courtyard been chosen to host this particular meeting?

Simon returned to the front of the store and handed Monty a thick book.

"You have your version of the history of Thaisia since humans first came to this continent, and we have ours," Simon said. "Don't think for a moment your leaders were innocent when it came to cities disappearing. Now it's time for you to ask your questions and go."

Do I really want to know what choices we've made? Monty thought. *How many humans have ever seen this version of Thaisia's history? Why is Wolfgard showing this to me now?*

The book was a warning. That much he understood.

Forcing his thoughts back to his original purpose, Monty said, "You've heard about the quarantined town in the Midwest?"

"Heard what the radio reported," Simon replied. He cocked his head. "You're afraid to ask."

"Yes. I am." Monty blew out a breath. "Meat grinder. Still-living flesh. The ground meat was tainted with the flesh of *cassandra sangue*, wasn't it? That's why the people who ate it became violent."

"Seems likely." Nothing about Simon Wolfgard had changed physically, but Monty wouldn't mistake him for human now.

"Street drugs made with *cassandra sangue* blood will reach a limited number of people, no matter how dealers try to distribute it. But ground beef? Entire families could end up raving mad and violent without choice or warning, just by eating dinner. Who was the target, Simon? Was this the next stage of someone's attack on humans and Others?"

"Not us," Simon said thoughtfully. "Blood prophets don't smell like prey. It's not just that they aren't edible; they aren't prey. Their flesh mixed with other ground meat wouldn't smell right to us, and wouldn't taste right no matter how someone tried to disguise it. I don't think any *terra indigene* would consume enough to be influenced. Of course, we might not sense wrongness in time if we bit prey that was contaminated. That's how a lot of the Others were dosed with gone over wolf or feel-good."

"So humans are the targets," Monty said.

"It looks like someone is experimenting on using you as a way to kill shape-shifters and Sanguinati," Simon said.

"I'd say someone is after all the *terra indigene*."

Simon gave him an odd look. "Provoking the Elementals would be a mistake humans wouldn't survive."

Vlad stood by the back door of HGR and watched the pickup truck drive past the back of the Liaison's Office and park close to the wooden gate leading into Henry's yard. Even though two of the leaders from the Toland Courtyard were attending, the Sanguinati weren't happy about this meeting of leaders. The *terra indigene* sometimes quarreled among themselves—the different predators they'd absorbed over the centuries made that inevitable, especially when they had overlapping territory—but they were always united against their common adversary: humans.

This time Simon was gambling that the Midwest leaders weren't so bitter or angry that they'd already decided what needed to be done.

From what Vlad had seen as the guests arrived throughout the day, there was plenty of bitterness and anger in the *terra indigene* coming in from the Midwest, as well as the areas around the Great Lakes where humans were spewing about the Humans First and Last movement without thinking for one second about who was listening to them.

Simon might be taking a risk calling this meeting and bringing them all to Lakeside, but he'd also been smart enough to stack the deck, as humans said, by bringing in three *terra indigene* from the High Northeast—a part of Thaisia that hadn't yet been touched by the troubles—in the hope that they would provide some balance to the discussions.

Bobbie Beargard was a Black Bear who taught at one of the few *terra indigene* colleges on the continent. She had once told a visiting human professor who was spouting some nonsense about human superiority that if she wanted to handle crap, she'd shit in her own paw. Even if he hadn't been eaten on his way home, the professor wouldn't have been invited back.

Then there was Alan Wolfgard, whose thrillers were wildly popular with the *terra indigene*—especially the Others who had never seen a real human.

The last of the three stepped out of the pickup and raised a hand in greeting. Charlie Crowgard was tall and lean, with a kind face that somewhat hid the sharp intelligence in his black eyes. Like many *terra indigene*, he couldn't shift the last little bit to look completely human. But being a musician, he'd used that to advantage by tying his black hair back into a thin tail and letting the feathers that wouldn't shift hang in plain sight like an ornament.

"Why didn't you take the train?" Vlad asked.

"Couldn't," Charlie replied, cocking a thumb at the pickup's bed. "Wasn't going to try to carry that."

Vlad came around to the back of the pickup. "What is it?"

"It's wood." As the gate to Henry's yard opened, Charlie added, "Henry. Give us a hand. I think this old tree has a story to tell, so I brought it to you."

Henry studied the chunk of wood and nodded. "It's a good piece."

Vlad climbed into the bed and helped Charlie shift the wood to the tailgate— where Henry picked it up with a small grunt and took it into his studio.

"Brought the guitar," Charlie said as he jumped off the bed and closed the tailgate. "I know we're not here for fun, but . . . what's that?"

"That's a human," Vlad said, watching Theral MacDonald, Dominic Lorenzo's new . . . whatever they called her. Assistant? Phone person? Exploding fluffball?

No, that's what *he'd* taken to calling Meg's human pack. A few months ago, the humans who worked in the Courtyard just did their jobs and kept out of the way. Now they had *opinions*.

"I know that," Charlie said. "What's she carrying? It looks like a fiddle case. You have humans here who play music?"

Since Charlie sounded delighted by the prospect of meeting a music-playing human, Vlad called out, "Ms. MacDonald?"

Being very newly employed, Theral had kept her head down and her hair around her face in an attempt to walk past them without seeing them—as if not seeing them meant they couldn't see her. Typical prey mentality, but that might change once she settled in. Now she stopped and moved toward them, every step filled with reluctance. "Mr. Sanguinati?"

"What are you carrying?" Charlie asked. "Is it a fiddle?"

"Yes, it's a fiddle," Theral said.

Charlie smiled at her before turning to Vlad. "Do you all join in and perform in the Market Square? If I remember correctly from my visit a few years ago, you have a platform there that would be perfect for performing."

"Ms. MacDonald just started working for us, so I don't think anyone has mentioned playing in the square," Vlad replied. Then to Theral, "You staying here?"

Theral nodded. "Lawrence is picking me up after his shift. Mr. Wolfgard said it was okay if I stayed with Merri Lee until then."

She hurried up the stairs to the efficiency apartments and knocked on the outer door. It opened moments later, so Merri Lee must have been waiting for the other girl.

"So," Vlad said. He looked at the open area that was bordered by the garages, Henry's yard, and the backs of HGR, A Little Bite, and the Liaison's Office. Then he looked at the pickup, which was a lot bigger than the BOWs that were usually parked in the space. "How are you going to turn this thing around?"

Charlie grinned. "Very carefully." The grin faded. "Simon is going to have to move carefully too."

"I know," Vlad said. Then he added silently, *If the shifters want more blood shed than the Sanguinati will accept, Simon won't be the only one who will need to be careful.*

CHAPTER 21

"**S**ince you've figured out what's causing the sickness, let's wipe it out at the source," Joe Wolfgard snarled again.

"The source is a special kind of girl," Simon snarled back. "They're not choosing to be drugs that make us aggressive or passive. They're being used. They're being cut and bled, and that's not their fault."

"The source is *human*," Joe snapped. "The solution should be simple."

"You've had a couple of incidents in the Northeast," Jackson Wolfgard said, pointing at Simon. "And now the Northwest has seen a few cases of humans being so aggressive they've no sense of self-preservation. But the Midwest Court-yards have been hit over and over by humans who are diseased from the blood of Namid's terrible creation. If we can't stop these attacks soon, a lot more than a few humans will disappear."

Catching a warning look from Henry, Simon sat back and let the various leaders discuss and argue. The Wolfgard and Coyotegard from the Midwest had been the hardest hit. And the Crowgard had suffered losses every place the drugs gone over wolf and feel-good had been found. But they'd all become so fixed on the terrible side of Namid's creation, they didn't want to hear what he'd been trying to tell them about blood prophets.

Cheryl Hawkgard, Patty Crowgard, and Vera Owlgard wanted to know how the *terra indigene* were supposed to find a specific breed of human among a city full of humans. Simon had some thoughts about that, but he wasn't going to share them while tempers were hot.

<The Wolves and Coyotes want slaughter,> Simon said to Henry.

<Can't blame them,> Henry replied. <They've lost the most kin because of these drugs. Only the Crows have lost more. Let them talk. Eventually they'll realize they can't kill the source without poisoning themselves.>

But would they realize it in time? Simon wondered. The leaders who had come for this meeting had been in the Courtyard's library for an hour now, arguing about what should be done to eliminate the problem.

<I'm more interested in why the Sanguinati from the Toland Courtyard have offered no opinions,> Henry continued.

Vlad had offered no opinions either, and Simon began to find that silence unnerving.

Perhaps Roy Panthergard found the Sanguinati's silence unnerving as well because he said, "Stavros? Tolya? What do you have to say?"

Vlad replied quietly, "The Sanguinati will not harm the sweet blood."

Hearing the warning—and threat—beneath the words, everyone stopped talking and focused on the Sanguinati.

"You've lost one of your own because of these drugs," Jackson said.

"The Sanguinati do not drink the sweet blood," Vlad said. "We do not harm the sweet blood. And if necessary, we will stand against other *terra indigene* who try to harm the sweet blood."

No wonder Stavros and Tolya had said nothing. Vlad was the messenger, but Erebus was giving the orders—and making the threat of going to war against the shifters if they tried to eliminate the *cassandra sangue.*

Alan Wolfgard exchanged a look with Bobbie Beargard and Charlie Crow-gard, who both nodded.

"Look," Alan said. "We're just chasing our tails. We can talk about this from one sunrise to the next and not have any answers because the answer isn't in the library." He looked at Simon. "You said you have one of them here in the Lake-side Courtyard. It's time you showed us Namid's terrible creation."

Leading his guests from the library to the back door of the Liaison's Office, Si-mon reluctantly turned the doorknob. He'd wanted to tell the leaders about Meg and how her desire to actually do the work a Human Liaison was supposed to do, and more, had altered so much in just the few months she'd been here. He wanted them to see past a kind of human who was a danger to the *terra indigene* and see *Meg*. But they had already decided Meg was a fearsome creature who should be destroyed along with the rest of her kind.

Then Meg *screamed*, and the terror in that sound had him flinging the door open and running through the back room and into the sorting room with Vlad, Henry, Charlie, and the rest of the Others slamming in behind him. And then they all stopped, stumbling into each other as they stared at Meg, cowering on top of the sorting table, with envelopes and catalogs scattered on the floor around her. And Skippy, holding a mouse by the tail, his hindquarters bunched for a leap onto the table.

"Skippy!" Simon growled the word, barely able to make human sounds.

Wolf and woman turned toward his voice. Taking in the audience staring at her, Meg's fair skin turned a deep rose color, which probably looked appealing with her natural black hair but made the weird orange look weirder.

Skippy, finally realizing he might be in trouble, lowered his head to drop the mouse.

Meg shrieked, "Don't let go of it!"

Despite being in human form, Simon's ears flattened at the sound. He felt empty space at his back as everyone except Vlad and Henry took a step away from the table. And he noticed that the mouse was still alive, since it began flailing its little legs when it sensed a chance at freedom.

No longer sure he could speak, Simon switched to the *terra indigene* way of communicating. <Skippy.>

Skippy gave Simon a woeful look. <Meg wouldn't play with me.>

Vlad made a choking sound.

Henry opened the sorting room's outer delivery doors and said, "Skippy, take the mouse outside. Leave it on the grass past the Market Square."

Being a skippy meant the youngster sometimes had gaps in his thinking, but this time the juvenile Wolf knew exactly what to do. He took his mouse and fled.

Henry closed the outer doors. Charlie stepped forward and picked up some of the mail scattered on the floor. After a moment's hesitation, other *terra indigene* picked up the mail close to them and gingerly set it on the table.

Henry looked around. "Meg? Where's the step stool? How did you get on the table?"

"I don't remember," Meg said, shifting to sit on the edge. "One moment

Skippy was chasing me with that . . . *rodent* . . . and the next I was up on the table."

Before Simon could go to her, Henry hooked his big hands under her arms, lifted her off the table, and set her down.

Looking flustered, Meg linked her fingers together and tried smiling. "Hello. I'm Meg, the Human Liaison for the Lakeside Courtyard."

"It's a pleasure to meet you," Charlie said, returning the smile.

Everyone else mumbled niceties before retreating out the back door, where they all gathered except the Grizzly.

<Henry?> Simon called.

<I'll take a sniff around the rooms and make sure Skippy didn't bring in anything else to play with,> Henry said.

<We had a nest of mice in the office before.>

<I think it's better if Meg believes the mouse came from outside, don't you?>

Oh, yeah. If it occurred to her that Skippy had found the mouse in the office, Nathan would have to do a mouse check every morning, regardless of his actual assignment.

But right now, Simon was surrounded by leaders who had come to discuss the trouble and deaths that had been happening in Thaisia. He understood the confusion he saw in their eyes. They had been prepared to meet a dangerous predator, an adversary equal to themselves, not a short female with weird hair and a fear of mice.

"Simon?" Charlie finally said. "It was just a mouse."

"I know," he replied.

"A *small* mouse."

He sighed. "I know."

"So," Alan said after a long pause. "That's Namid's terrible creation?"

"Yeah. That's Meg."

Another long pause. Then Bobbie said, "Why is her fur that strange color?"

"It was a disguise."

Bobbie made a sound that was half laugh, half disbelief. "What was she pretending to be? One of those traffic cones humans put on the street when they're making repairs?"

Simon growled softly, offended on Meg's behalf. Then he noticed how they were all looking at one another, and he had an idea. "Why don't you ask some of the Courtyard residents about Meg?"

"She's known to more than the Business Association?" Jackson Wolfgard asked, sounding startled.

Vlad laughed. "I think everyone in the Lakeside Courtyard can tell you a story about Meg."

"We'll meet back in the library in a couple of hours?" Alan said, looking at everyone.

"Might as well leave the clothing there," Bobbie Beargard said. "Any chance of something to eat when we get back?"

Simon nodded. "Tess said she'll have coffee and breakfast foods available, and Meat-n-Greens is serving a variety of food throughout the day."

"Will we have a chance to observe the Courtyard's other human employees?" Bobbie asked.

"Yes."

All the guests ambled back to the library to discard their clothes and shift, leaving Simon and Vlad standing behind the Liaison's Office.

"You have enough to think about," Vlad said. "You should let Blair explain the 'no live toys' rule to Skippy."

"Let's hope he didn't find that toy in the office," Simon grumbled.

"It could have been worse."

Simon snorted. "How?"

Vlad grinned. "Skippy could have found a rat."

The guests returned to the library a couple of hours later. Most gave Simon and Vlad wary looks. Alan looked intrigued, and Charlie was clearly amused, especially when Joe and Jackson returned with their fur encrusted with snow and chunks of ice clinging to their tails.

The Elementals or the ponies must have heard those two expressing an unfavorable opinion about Meg, Simon thought.

"We all have a lot to think about," Cheryl Hawkgard said. She hesitated. "These blood prophets. They can't all be like your Meg."

"No, they can't," he replied. "But I don't think we should blame them for being a weapon when no one is giving them a choice."

CHAPTER 22

O n Watersday, Meg took the broom and dustpan out of the storage area while Merri Lee began cleaning the kitchen area in the office's back room.

"It was kind of strange this morning," Merri Lee said. "All these *terra indigene* leaders filling up the tables at A Little Bite, with Ruth, Theral, Lawrence, and Michael sitting at one table playing the part of human customers. And Lorne coming in to buy coffee and pastry to take back to the Three Ps. And Jenni Crowgard and her sisters sitting at a table, all flustered and giggling."

Meg stopped sweeping. "Why would Jenni be flustered? She has a high standing with the Crowgard here. Doesn't she?"

Merri Lee grinned. "I got the impression that Charlie Crowgard is a celebrity among the Crows. I think Jenni . . . Well, it would be like me sitting near a human film star I had a crush on."

Meg nodded. She didn't understand the feeling, but she turned the words into a kind of image that she could recall later.

"Anyway, a couple of things struck me. This was the *terra indigene* elite who deal with humans, and I don't think most of them had ever been in a coffee shop or had a meal in a restaurant like Meat-n-Greens."

Meg frowned but continued sweeping. Merri Lee's words had layers. She wanted to stop and concentrate, but she had the impression Merri was talking in order to understand, and Meg didn't want anything to shut off the words.

"For instance, they were all going to take a spoonful of honey and eat it off

the spoon instead of drizzling it on the warm scones Tess provided." Merri Lee
went into the bathroom to rinse off the cleaning cloth.

"Would just eating the honey be bad?" Meg asked, raising her voice to be
heard over the running water. She felt a tingle in her left arm. Why would men-
tioning jars of honey start the pins-and-needles feeling?

Merri Lee returned to the back room. "Not bad in itself." She opened the
wave cooker and wiped out the inside. "But it would be something snobs would
point to as proof the Others weren't really equal to humans. After all, they don't
even know how to properly eat honey." Her voice took on a condescending tone.
Then she stopped working and looked at Meg. "I thought it was kind of strange
that Mr. Wolfgard was hiring Ruth to teach *terra indigene* how to do human
things—simple things like placing an order in a restaurant or when to use a fork
and when to use a spoon. But we learn those things at home, don't we? And if
you *don't* know those things, other people think less of you."

Do they? Meg wondered. *Do you think less of me because of all the things I don't
know?* She didn't think that was true of the girls who worked in the Courtyard,
but it revealed how vulnerable she would have been outside the compound if
she had landed anywhere but here.

"It made me realize how progressive this Courtyard is compared to the other
ones that keep watch over human cities." Merri Lee pushed her hair back, then
picked up the electric teakettle. "And it made me wonder how many times a human said, 'This is how it's done,' and misled the *terra indigene* so they would look
foolish in their dealings with other humans. I began to understand how things
could have gone wrong in Talulah Falls and other towns. If the Others can't trust
us to be honest about something simple like when to use a fork or a spoon, why
would they trust what we say about anything important?" She turned and stared
at Meg. "Why are you rubbing your arm? What's wrong? Should I call Tess?"

"What?" Meg looked down and watched her right hand rub her left forearm,
trying to ease the prickling. "No. Don't call Tess."

"Meg?" Merri Lee sounded alarmed.

She stared back at her friend. Merri Lee was holding a teakettle. She was
holding a broom.

"Teakettle and broom," she whispered. She had seen a broom and teakettle
in the prophecy about sharks and poison.

"Oh, gods," Merri Lee said. "The last two images we couldn't place."

"I don't want Skippy in the front room by himself." The prickling under Meg's skin increased. She set the broom aside and went to the front room.

Skippy was tossing a ball and chasing after it. Since the ball left a wet mark every time it bounced, Meg figured he'd been at it long enough that she wouldn't want to pick up something with that much slobber on it.

"Skippy, come into the sorting room." Meg pulled back the slide bolt on the go-through's wide top, allowing him to come behind the counter and enter the sorting room through the Private door.

Skippy looked at her for a moment before tossing the ball again.

She didn't know if he was deliberately ignoring her or if this was one of those times when his brain skipped and what she'd said was forgotten so fast it left no impression.

"Want a cookie?"

That made an impression. She stepped out of the way to avoid being knocked down by his rush to find the cookie.

With Skippy safely in the sorting room, Meg closed the go-through, sliding the top bolt into place. Then, gritting her teeth as the prickling in her arm increased, she slid the two hidden bolts into place.

Returning to the back room with Skippy dancing beside her, she opened the container that held the cookies she'd set aside for him. It was tempting to give him a piece of the chamomile, but just reaching for it made her hands buzz. So she gave him a cow cookie and watched him settle on the floor near the small table and chairs.

She didn't protest when Merri Lee took her arm and led her back into the sorting room.

"What's going on?" Merri Lee said. "The broom and teakettle were clues. What does that mean?"

"Pins and needles," Meg replied.

"That's bad, right? Shouldn't we call someone?"

Meg tried to steady her breathing. "It's fading. That feeling usually means something bad is going to happen, but when it fades then the bad thing won't happen."

The pins-and-needles feeling returned with such ferocity, Meg stifled a cry. When Merri Lee turned toward the phone on the counter, Meg grabbed her arm and whispered, "No. Stay near the Private door, but stay out of sight."

"Meg, you're scaring me."

"Me too." But she stepped into the front room and stood behind the counter just as a small, dapper man pulled the door open.

Not a deliveryman. For one thing, he wasn't dressed like a deliveryman. For another, he wasn't carrying any packages.

Every scar on Meg's body began to burn as the man walked toward her. Every scar except the ones she'd acquired since coming to the Courtyard.

"Can I help you?" she asked.

"Oh, my dear," he replied in a voice ripe with kindness. "I'm here to help you." *Trust me.*

She didn't hear the words, but she would have sworn he said them. "I don't need help."

His smile was sweet, but the eyes behind the glasses were oddly blank of any emotion. "You do need help. I can see it, feel it. You're overwhelmed by the outside world, and it will chew you up. But I can take you to a safe place, a good place where you'll be looked after. Wouldn't you like that?"

Of course she would like that. Who wouldn't like to feel safe? And if the scars weren't filling her with so much burning pain, she would put her hand in the one he was holding out and follow that soft, compelling voice to . . .

A soft hiss from Merri Lee, barely heard. But it was enough to conjure the training image of a snake rising out of a basket and a man playing some kind of instrument. *Snake charmer.*

"What's your name?" she asked, struggling to ignore his voice. She took a step back to avoid being within reach of his hand.

"I'm Phineas Jones. I'm here to help you." He walked around the counter to the go-through and slid the top bolt open. But the go-through, still secured by the hidden bolts, didn't budge.

Phineas Jones, Meg thought as she heard Merri Lee whispering, "Shark, shark, shark." *No biting.*

Thank the gods Nathan wasn't the watch Wolf this morning. Skippy was too involved with the cookie to notice a stranger in the office, but Nathan wouldn't have hesitated to bite the hand that had reached for her, regardless of any warning she gave.

She backed up until she stood in the Private doorway. "The office is closing in a couple of minutes for the midday break. If you need assistance, you should call at the consulate to make an appointment."

He stared at her with those blank eyes. "You need to come with me. I can help you. I can make the hurting go away."

She still wanted to believe him, couldn't stop herself from believing him.

Then Merri Lee, hiding on the side of the doorway where she couldn't be seen, grabbed the back of Meg's sweater, a reminder that she already had help from people she could trust.

"You have to leave now," Meg said, trying to sound firm and professional but hearing the quiver in her voice. "We're closed."

He pushed at the go-through again, then reached down, feeling for the hidden bolts.

If he got in, she wouldn't be the only one in danger. "We're closed!" she shouted as she stumbled back into the sorting room. She locked the Private door, then hurried to the receiving doors to make sure those were locked too.

"Meg?" Merri Lee whispered. "I think he was trying to hypnotize you. Do you know what that is?"

"Snake charmer," she replied as she hurried to the back room. She didn't lock that outside door. The Others used it to pick up the mail for the Market Square, HGR, and A Little Bite—and there was the unspoken worry now that she might cut herself and they wouldn't be able to reach her in time if all the doors were locked.

Skippy was on his feet, watching them come into the room. Meg wasn't sure if he finally sensed something was wrong or if he'd finished the cookie and was hoping to get another one.

Whatever the reason, the Wolf stood between her and the back door when Phineas Jones walked in.

"Get out!" Merri Lee yelled. "I'm calling the police!"

She would never know if it was the tone of Merri Lee's voice or the words or a spike of fear that Skippy picked up, but something made the youngster turn on Jones, who scrambled out the door.

"No biting!" Meg yelled as Skippy rushed after Jones.

She grabbed the broom and went after the Wolf.

It was like a movie with gaps, only she was the person in the pictures. Inside the office, grabbing the broom . . . *skip* . . . outside, screaming as Phineas Jones raised an arm in a protective gesture and Skippy prepared to leap on the intruder and bite . . . *skip* . . . swinging the broom and whacking Skippy so hard she bowled him over . . . *skip* . . . Crows cawing, Wolves howling . . . *skip* . . .

screaming as she whacked Phineas Jones with the broom . . . *skip* . . . more screaming as Merri Lee beat on Jones with the teakettle . . . *skip* . . . suddenly surrounded by heads and bodies that were and weren't human . . . *skip* . . . Simon grabbing her, dragging her away and shouting something at Charlie Crowgard and . . .

They were in the back room. Merri Lee looked as sick and dizzy as Meg felt. And there was Charlie standing between them and the door, changing his position and raising his arms to prevent Merri Lee from going to the window that would give her a view of whatever was happening behind the office.

Shouts. Roars. Howls. Caws. Screams.

Silence.

Then Charlie, looking grim, said, "Simon wants you to call the police. He said you would know which one."

With their arms linked, Meg and Merri staggered into the sorting room to reach the telephone on the counter. Meg's hands shook so much she could barely lift the receiver.

"I can't remember the number," Meg said. "Lieutenant Montgomery."

"We'll call Michael. He'll reach everyone else." Merri Lee punched in the numbers while Meg held the receiver.

Just as Michael Debany answered the phone, Charlie stepped into the doorway and said, "Tell the police to bring humans who can handle dangerous things."

Having delivered the message and given Michael a shaky reassurance that she and Merri weren't hurt, the two women returned to the back room.

"I can make some tea," Merri Lee said, turning toward the counter. "It's gone. The electric teakettle is . . ." She swallowed convulsively a couple of times, then ran into the bathroom and threw up.

"Meg?" A gentle voice. Kind in a way that wasn't at all like Phineas Jones's voice. A voice she really could trust.

She focused on Charlie, who was crouched beside her on the floor.

"You have feathers in your eyebrows," she said.

He looked embarrassed. "I'm having some trouble holding the human shape."

They were all having trouble holding on to the human shape. People teeth weren't as useful as beaks and fangs, and . . . She grabbed Charlie's arm. "No biting. Poison frog. Tell Simon no biting!"

"He knows," Charlie said, patting her hand. "You told him, told all of us. Don't you remember?"

She'd been too scared to remember. Suddenly exhausted, she lay flat on the floor, releasing her grip on Charlie's arm.

"Just tired," she said when he made some inarticulate sound of distress. "Just tired. Tell Simon all the pins and needles are gone."

She heard Merri Lee return and ask a question, but she slid into sleep before she heard Charlie's reply.

Monty tried not to think about what they would find in the Courtyard. For now, it was enough that Simon Wolfgard had placed the call. Well, not Wolfgard personally, but he'd sanctioned the call.

And Wolfgard had asked for police who could handle dangerous things. Not knowing what to expect, Monty had called Louis Gresh, the bomb squad commander, figuring Louis had been seen before by Simon and Vlad, and a familiar face was a better choice no matter what they were up against.

Gods above and below, please don't let this be someone trying to assassinate the terra indigene *who came for this meeting,* Monty thought. He didn't want to consider what would happen to Lakeside if anyone started *that* kind of trouble.

Lights flashed and sirens screamed as every available police officer from the Chestnut Street station descended on the Courtyard—including Captain Douglas Burke, who was driving so close to their bumper, Monty hoped Kowalski wouldn't need to make a sudden stop.

Debany and MacDonald were already there, their patrol car poking out of the access way.

"Park . . ." Monty began, then didn't bother to finish when Kowalski pulled up in front of the street entrance, effectively blocking the delivery area.

Louis wasn't going to be pleased with being shut out. Then again, maybe he'd be relieved that he had an excuse not to bring his vehicles onto land where human law didn't apply.

But they asked for us, Monty thought as he got out of the car and hurried toward MacDonald.

"Where's Officer Debany?" Monty asked.

"In the consulate," MacDonald replied. "Ms. Corbyn sort of passed out, and Ms. Lee is real shaky. Mr. Sanguinati and Mr. Wolfgard didn't want the girls taken past . . ." He suddenly looked ill. "They're in Elliot Wolfgard's office. Michael's helping get them settled. He's not taking a statement; since he's dating Ms. Lee, we figured you should do that."

Feeling Burke approach, Monty just nodded. Then he noticed the smoke on either side of the consulate door. "Was there a fire?"

"No, sir," MacDonald whispered. "Some of the Sanguinati are standing guard, so to speak."

He heard Captain Burke suck in a breath, but no one said anything until Simon Wolfgard walked out of the access way at the same time Louis Gresh hurried to join them.

"You look first," Simon said, indicating the three men. "Then decide who else should come in. We all want answers, so we're all staying to hear what is said. Some shifted to their preferred form. Others have stayed human—mostly." He walked away, leaving them to follow.

"Brace yourselves, gentlemen," Burke said quietly.

When they reached the end of the access way and turned toward the back of the Liaison's Office, Monty was grateful for the warning. Even seeing Simon Wolfgard as a kind of wolfman when Meg Corbyn was in the hospital didn't prepare him for this.

The Others were the stuff of nightmares. If they'd been malformed or disproportioned in some way, they might have been pitiable. But these blends that married human and animal in harmony were a terrible reminder of why humans would always be meat.

Louis made a sound that might have been a quiet moan, but the man's face was set in a professional mask as they followed their captain to the *terra indigene* who had formed a circle around . . .

The Others stepped aside, revealing a human, a broom, and an electric teakettle.

"What is that?" Burke asked.

Monty looked at Burke and realized the man wasn't asking about the human or the objects. He was looking toward the back of the bookstore, where a wailing *arrrooooo!* continued almost without breath.

"That's Skippy," Simon replied. "Meg saved his life, but right now all he's absorbed is that she whacked him with a broom."

The wailing Wolf sat at HGR's back door, one hind leg lifted as if it was injured.

"Is he hurt?" Monty asked.

Simon shrugged. "Probably has a bruised leg. He managed to get out of her way to avoid getting whacked again, so I doubt the leg is broken."

"And this man?"

"Phineas Jones."

Burke let out an angry sigh. "The man who was in Ferryman's Landing a couple of days ago. He's good at covering his tracks. Even with the description we had, we couldn't locate him. Do you know why he came to the Court-yard?"

Simon snarled—and his canines lengthened. "He was after Meg." He took a moment to regain control, then continued, making a gesture that included all the *terra indigene* who were present. "We were taking a break from our talks and had just walked outside when we heard Meg and Merri Lee screaming."

"Howling," another Wolf said.

"Battle cry," a woman with black fur said with approval.

"Anyway," Simon continued, "we all ran toward the sounds and found Meg and Merri Lee whacking at this human with a broom and teakettle. We got the girls away from him, and Charlie took them inside. Meg was yelling at me about no biting. Either of the Beargard could have brought him down with a blow, but after we surrounded him, he pushed up his jacket sleeve and bit his own arm. Then he died, so I had Meg call you to bring the humans who deal with danger-ous things."

"What sort of danger do you think it is?" Louis asked.

"Poison," Simon said.

That explains why Meg Corbyn whacked the young Wolf, Monty thought.

"Okay," Louis said. "Any idea what kind of poison?"

"Frog," Simon said.

Burke stiffened, and Monty noted how many *terra indigene* suddenly focused on the captain.

"Don't ask, Commander," Burke said when Louis started to do just that. "The information came from a reliable source."

After a moment, Louis nodded.

"You have no objections to our taking the body?" Monty asked.

Simon shook his head. "It's better not to have poisoned meat on our land."

"If you could all clear the area while we work?"

"You should be careful with the broom and teakettle," the unknown Wolf said. "When we pulled the females away, I noticed the edge of the teakettle looked wet."

"What I can see of the shirtsleeve looks wet too," Louis said, crouching to study the body. "If he had some kind of container of poison taped to his arm, a blow might have caused a leak." He looked at Monty. "Would have made it a lot easier for him to ingest the poison himself."

"Might have killed a lot of us if we'd bitten poisoned meat," Henry Beargard said.

And you probably would have bitten him if Meg Corbyn hadn't warned you, Monty thought.

The Others didn't leave. They gathered in small groups in front of the garages that formed one side of the space behind the buildings. And there were Crows and Hawks and even a few Owls flying in to perch on rooftops where they could keep watch.

"I can arrange transportation of the body and the weapons," Louis said.

"I'll talk to Ms. Lee and Ms. Corbyn if they're up to it," Monty said.

"I'd like to sit in on those interviews," Burke said.

Kowalski, Debany, and MacDonald were waiting for him in front of the Liaison's Office. And they were keeping an eye on Nyx Sanguinati, who stood next to the consulate's door.

"Mr. Wolfgard thinks the man who died was after Meg Corbyn," Monty said. "He had to have transportation nearby, but I doubt it's the same car that was seen in Ferryman's Landing. Debany and MacDonald, take a look at the parked cars, especially the ones that are illegally parked on this side of the street. Kowalski, you take Officer Hilborn and check out the parking lot and the cars near the Stag and Hare. Pay special attention to cars that have a rental agency sticker on them."

"Yes, sir." When the officers headed off, Monty and Burke crossed the delivery area to the consulate.

"I'd like to get a statement from Ms. Lee and Ms. Corbyn if they're feeling up to it," Monty said.

"Vlad says they will talk to you," Nyx said just as the door opened.

Elliot Wolfgard studied them. "Follow me."

Monty hadn't seen the mayor's office, but he'd bet it didn't have furniture of the quality that filled Elliot's office. And he'd bet anyone who thought dealing with a Wolf meant dealing with someone who could be conned had an unnerving—and possibly short—epiphany when they walked into this room.

Meg and Merri Lee sat on a leather settee, looking pale and shaky. He thanked Vlad when the vampire brought him a straight-backed chair. Burke remained standing, close enough to hear everything but clearly not participating.

It didn't take long. Merri Lee had made notes, and her main concern and emphasis were on the way Meg had sensed the danger and the hypnotic quality of Phineas Jones's voice. Meg talked about prickling under her skin and wanting Skippy out of the front room.

A good choice, Monty thought as he listened to them. They'd acted rationally right up to the moment when Skippy ran after Jones. Then some other sense had taken over.

Broom and teakettle, Monty thought as a wave of dizziness swept over him. *They'd gone after a dangerous man with nothing but a broom and teakettle—to save a Wolf.* He thanked the women; then he and Burke followed Elliot Wolfgard back to the consulate's door.

"This is as much about public relations as police work," Burke said quietly as they walked back to the scene.

"You think we'll have protests or people causing trouble because Phineas Jones killed himself instead of killing *terra indigene?*"

"That's possible, but I wasn't talking about the citizens of Lakeside, Lieutenant. I was talking about the Others. How many of the ones watching us work have ever talked to a human outside of a confrontation? A leader among them called humans for assistance. I doubt the rest of them have ever considered that, let alone done it."

"I understand, sir," Monty said. An opportunity to change the dynamics between humans and Others shouldn't be wasted.

Burke stopped. "Then I'll leave you to—"

Monty had tuned out the wailing howl. Now he noticed its sudden absence.

"Gods above and below," Burke breathed, then quickly looked at the ground.

Simon and Henry, standing near Louis and the medical team who were preparing the body for transport, moved to block the men's view of the back of the stores. And every single *terra indigene* was looking in the opposite direction.

Monty leaned to one side and got a glimpse of Tess's coiling red-streaked black hair before Burke grabbed his arm and said, "Don't look," in a low, harsh voice.

For a moment, his vision blurred and his heart couldn't find the right beat. He blinked several times and everything seemed all right. "Sir?"

"They're afraid of her," Burke said. "*All* of the Others are afraid to look at her."

"But that's Tess. She's . . ." Suddenly he thought about Asia Crane's death the night the Courtyard was under attack, and the deaths of the students who had assaulted Merri Lee—and Burke telling him weeks ago that there was something in the Courtyard that could kill with a look. What was Tess? If he asked, would anyone give him an answer?

If they did give him an answer, would Tess let him live?

A BOW pulled up. Moving away from Louis, Simon said, "Nathan, take Skippy to the Wolfgard Complex. Ask Jane to look at him."

Tess strode toward them, and Monty realized Burke was right. The rest of the *terra indigene* made an effort to stay out of her way. Except Simon, who stepped out to meet her, reminding Monty of the old movies he used to love as a boy where the gunslingers met on the street of some dusty little town in order to settle some dispute.

"Here," Tess said, handing Nathan something wrapped in a paper towel as he passed her, his eyes averted. "Give this to Skippy once you get him in the BOW, and tell Jane he's eaten one of those chamomile cookies." As she turned toward Simon, the black hair changed to red, and the red streaks changed to green. She held up one of the insulated sacks that A Little Bite used to deliver food around the Market Square. "The girls should have something to eat, and I didn't think you wanted them out here yet."

Simon Wolfgard looked her in the eyes, and that was a message to everyone: Tess was no longer a danger to them.

"Thanks," Simon said, taking the sack. "We'll have to figure out what to do with the two of them this evening."

Tess laughed. "Romantic, girly movies and lots of chocolate should do the trick. And don't whine if they cry in your fur."

Louis twisted around to look at Simon and Tess. Burke choked. And even though Monty didn't see any ears change shape, he knew the Others' ears were all pricked, one way or another, to catch every word.

"Females," Simon grumbled once Tess was out of sight. He eyed Monty, as if daring the man to laugh at him. "I'll deliver the food and then be in HGR if you need anything." Still grumbling, he walked to the consulate.

Burke left to check on the officers who were looking for Jones's vehicle.

Not wanting to leave Louis and the medical techs alone, Monty stayed with them, aware of the wary approach of one of the Wolves and a Crow who had a couple of feathers tucked in his black hair. They hesitated until Vladimir Sanguinati walked up to Monty; then curiosity must have overcome wariness.

"Can I ask you something?" the Wolf said.

"You going to put this in one of your stories, Alan?" Vlad asked.

When Alan just shrugged, Monty filled the silence. "What did you want to know?"

"Is this . . . normal . . . for humans?" Alan said, sounding bewildered and intrigued.

"There is nothing normal about exploding fluffballs," Vlad muttered, which made the Crow laugh.

"I've done some research for my books and talked to a few humans, and they all said humans would use guns and knives and clubs for weapons."

The Crow nodded. "A screaming woman with a teakettle just doesn't sound sufficiently dangerous."

"But she was! They were!" Alan said. "How would a human deal with them?"

"Don't know about anyone else," Louis said, getting to his feet, "but I'd want a stout door with a strong lock between me and her before I tried talking to her."

Monty stifled a laugh. "People will use anything that comes to hand when they're fighting for their lives—or for someone else's."

"Interesting," Alan said. Then he looked at Vlad. "Are any of the other humans who work here exploding fluffballs?"

Vlad pointed to the back of Howling Good Reads. "Her name is Heather. She's more of a bunny, but she has the potential to explode. Tell her I asked you to autograph your books."

Alan frowned. "Autograph?"

"Authors sign their names in their books. Humans like having books like that."

"Why?"

"I don't know. But it should be a safe way to interact with her."

"I'll go with you," the Crow said. "This is entertaining." Then he looked at Monty and Louis. "Are there weapons in a bookstore?"

"It's a store full of books, which are objects that can be thrown as well as read," Monty replied blandly.

The Crow cocked his head. "I had no idea you humans lived with so much danger."

Monty watched the Crow hurry to catch up with the Wolf, while Vlad headed for the Market Square.

Louis cleared his throat. "Well. We're ready to transport the body. I'll send the teakettle and broom to the lab to test for poison. I'll also talk to a hazmat cleanup crew and get their recommendation for washing the poison residue off this pavement. If they feel they should handle it, I'll let you know. Oh, and I found an empty vial nearby. Don't know if it's relevant, but I bagged it for testing."

Casually mentioned. Nothing that would give anyone a reason to connect the vial with the last time someone attempted to poison members of the Courtyard. But taking the vial away before some curious youngster gave it a sniff and lick—and ended up dead—was better for all the humans in Lakeside. "Thanks," Monty said. "I appreciate it."

Louis turned a little so he wasn't facing the few *terra indigene* who were still watching them. "They look human now. You could pass most of them on the street and not know what they are."

Monty stepped out of the way. The Others had seen the police respond to a request for assistance. They'd seen his people working and following procedure. They would be given whatever information he could find about Phineas Jones.

But he suspected the thing most of them would share when they returned to their home territories was the story of the exploding fluffballs who used nothing but a teakettle and broom to save a Wolf from an evil human.

CHAPTER 23

After a quick meal at Meat-n-Greens, Simon, Vlad, Henry, and the Courtyard's guests reconvened in the Market Square Library. Tess walked in a
minute later, her hair coiling and completely red. Not good.

What also wasn't good was the way the rest of the *terra indigene* tensed as
soon as she walked into the room. Simon hadn't known Tess's true nature until
recently, but it seemed at least some of his guests had recognized the predator
who sat among them.

"We need to find a human called the Controller," Simon said, resisting the
urge to shift in his seat when Tess sat in the chair beside his. "We need to find the
place where the humans are making the drugs from *cassandra sangue* blood."

"And we need to give human government more incentive to keep better watch
over the places where the blood prophets live," Vlad added. "We need to impress
on them that *we* know what's in the drugs and that we're going to hold *them* responsible for anything that happens from now on because of those drugs."

"They'll whine and wring their hands and say there is nothing they can do,"
Cheryl Hawkgard said. "They won't want us to find those places."

"They will," Simon said quietly. "But first we need to narrow the search as
much as we can. And for that, we need Meg."

"No," Tess hissed as half the coiling hair turned black.

He wished he could move out of reach of the coils of hair that made him
think of angry snakes.

"A thousand cuts," Tess said. "Do you know how many she already has? How much of her life are you going to take for this hunt?"

Charlie Crowgard leaned forward. He looked at Tess, then at Simon. "What does she mean?"

"Each time a *cassandra sangue*'s skin is cut, she's that much closer to the cut that will either kill her or drive her insane," Vlad replied, staring hard at Simon. "But that's not what you meant. You're not going to ask Meg to cut her skin."

"Yes, I am," Simon said. He'd thought about this while they'd been having their meal break. "One cut. Before she sets that razor on her skin, we're all going to work to give her as much information as possible. She knows more about how she got here than she realizes. She sees things in images. So she saw at least some of her journey to Lakeside. We need to help her find images that match what she saw."

"She knew about the kind of poison Phineas Jones was going to use because she'd seen a picture of those frogs in a magazine," Tess said, the coils relaxing into loose curls.

Henry nodded. "This will be like a puzzle where we eliminate pieces in order to see the picture."

Now Alan Wolfgard and Charlie were both leaning forward, interested and struggling to understand. The Midwest leaders looked surly, and Simon could sympathize. He'd be less interested in circling around to find the prey if a straight path could be taken. But to them, Meg was just a human, and they didn't fully realize how the Elementals would react if she came to any harm.

"Are you all just crapping in the den?" Bobbie Beargard demanded. "If not, then say what you mean."

"How do you get from one human city to another?" Simon said. "Train, bus, car. Humans wouldn't walk to the next village, so they wouldn't walk from one region to the next. Trains have stations at specific cities. Buses travel specific routes, whether they stay inside the city or are the ones that provide transportation between human places."

"And some buses make a stop at the train station," Alan said, nodding.

"When she reached the Courtyard, Meg wasn't wearing clothing appropriate for the Northeast," Tess said.

"She could have lost a winter coat or left it somewhere," Vlad said. "Or maybe it became soiled in a way that would have called attention to her. She had to stop somewhere for a little while when she dyed her hair red."

All the guests cocked their heads. Finally Charlie said, "Her hair is red?"

Vlad waved a hand dismissively. "It was supposed to be."

"Photographers have been allowed to go into the wild country and take pictures of the land and the animals," Simon said. "And photographers take pictures of the human places. We have books in the library here and at Howling Good Reads that have pictures of the wild country and of cities in every region in Thaisia. Tomorrow we're all going to work on putting them together in a way that will help Meg narrow down where the enemy is hiding."

"If we show her the right pictures, maybe Meg will not need to cut," Henry said. He rose and stretched. "Enough. It's time to rest." He walked out of the library.

Since he should have decided when the meeting ended, Simon said, "It's time to rest."

After an awkward shuffle, the guests left the library. Which left him alone with Vlad and Tess.

"One cut," he said. "I'll ask Meg for one."

"And if we need more information in order to narrow down the hunt?" Vlad asked.

Simon gave Vlad a sharp smile. "Once Meg tells us what she knows, we'll ask our friends in the police to help."

Meg sat in her living room, turning the razor over and over. Pretty flowers on one side of the handle, *cs759* inscribed on the other side. A designation, not a name.

Were there young blood prophets in Lakeside? Girls who were just starting to show the disturbing tendency to cut? They had names, families, lives. Choices. Or were *cassandra sangue* born with this addiction, this need?

She opened the razor and stared at the blade. One-quarter inch wide—the perfect distance between cuts. Prophecies remained separated without wasting usable skin. Right now it would be so easy to justify cutting fresh skin because it would help someone else. Wouldn't it?

A slow suicide, one cut at a time, Meg thought. Except very few of the scars on her body had been created by cuts that were her choice.

Phineas Jones was dead, and that was a relief. After returning to her apartment, she'd spent an hour recalling images of death that she had absorbed during her lessons at the compound. Why did he bite the sack of poison on his arm? Did he expect that kind of death to be quick, painless? She didn't imagine being mauled by a Grizzly or torn apart by a pack of angry Wolves was painless, but . . .

He knew things he didn't want the Others to know. If he was here to take girls who lived outside, then he knew how to find the Controller or men like him. He swallowed poison so he wouldn't tell. But I want to tell. I just don't know how.

The howling right outside her door startled her enough that she almost cut her finger with the razor. Closing it, she slipped it into her pocket before going to the door.

Simon stood there in Wolf form, holding one of those lengths of soft braided rope the Wolves used as a toy. He looked at her and wagged his tail once.

"Oh, no," she said. "I know this game. It's all 'we'll just take a walk,' and then it's 'hold my rope for a minute,' and then you're chasing me all over the place because the person holding the rope gets chased."

He cocked his head as if to say, *Of course. Why are you standing there? Get your coat!*

"Wait there." She left the door open while she put on her coat and made sure she had her keys. Simon wasn't going to like her decision, so joining him in playtime might make him less snappish when she told him she was going to make a cut in an effort to find the Controller.

That much decided, Meg closed the door and walked down the stairs with Simon right beside her.

Simon walked beside Meg, growling softly. Damn clueless human female. It wasn't like she didn't know the game. He'd offered her the rope a half dozen times since they started walking toward the fork that led to the Pony Barn, but she just strolled along with her hands in her pockets! What sort of game was that?

When she finally took her hands out of her pockets, he pricked his ears, anticipating play. But she just covered her mouth and *yawned*. He enjoyed taking a walk with Meg and having time to leisurely sniff at what was around them, but he thought she'd accepted his invitation for a game and—

She grabbed the rope so suddenly, he braced and pulled without thinking. Letting out a gleeful hoot, she released the rope and shouted, "You're it!" Then she *lunged* at him. And he, being unprepared, leaped away from her. *And she chased him!*

<Wait! *I'm* the one who's supposed to chase!>

Of course, she couldn't hear *terra indigene* speech, so she chased him, trying to grab his tail!

Meg didn't hear him, but the other Wolves did.

<Simon?> Blair called. <Simon!>

Suddenly there were Wolves racing toward him and Meg—Blair, Nathan, John, Elliot, and Jane. Even Alan, Joe, and Jackson had come along for an evening romp.

He saw Joe and Alan focus on Meg, probably assuming that she had turned aggressive. He understood why Joe would think that, coming from the Midwest and dealing with all the recent problems with humans. And most of Alan's stories had deranged humans as the villains, so it wasn't a stretch for him to react as if a Wolf were under attack.

Before Simon could snap out a warning, Blair and Nathan shoulder-bumped Joe and Alan, knocking them off stride, while Jane and Elliot blocked Jackson.

That's when Meg pointed at him and shouted, "Simon has the rope!"

And that's when all the other Wolves focused on *him*.

Simon spun and ran past Meg, who laughed so hard she could barely walk. Now clear about what game they were playing, the Wolves gave chase. Since he didn't have to stay on the road to accommodate Meg's lack of night vision, he ran hard, bounding up the rises and weaving through trees until he could circle back to the sneaky female.

When he reached the road again, with the rest of the Wolves nipping at his heels, he saw Meg trotting back toward the Green Complex. Nathan trotted along with her. He wasn't sure if that was Nathan's idea or Blair's, but it was smart to have a guard with her when she might be mistaken for real prey.

<Your turn,> he said when Blair came up beside him.

Blair obligingly grabbed the rope and ran off.

<Go,> Simon told Nathan. He lunged at the other Wolf when Nathan hesitated. *My Meg!*

With a yelp of surprise, Nathan sprang out of reach and ran to catch up with the rest of the Wolves playing chase.

Not my Meg, Simon thought uneasily as he settled into a pace that kept him beside her. *My Meg* sounded like more than a friend. Didn't it? And thinking that way could be dangerous. The human form was merely a convenience since humans couldn't seem to interact with anything that didn't look like them. But absorbing too much from the human form and becoming too much like a human could alienate a *terra indigene* from his own kind and leave him with no one and no place that felt like home. He was a Wolf, would always be a Wolf. Having a human friend wouldn't change that. And he wasn't the only one with a human friend. Henry, Vlad, Tess, Jenni, Jester. Even Winter claimed Meg as a special human friend. Did Nathan . . . ? *My Meg!* Okay, he could share Meg the squeaky toy with another Wolf but not share Meg the friend with another Wolf? Except Sam, of course. Which was fair since Sam had been friends with Meg first. And he was still a puppy.

My Meg. Another confusion she'd brought into his life and something he would have to figure out later.

Panting, Meg slowed to a walk. Didn't take that long for her breathing to even out, which pleased him. She was getting stronger, fitter.

"Simon, we need to talk," she said when they turned into the Green Complex and approached his apartment. She opened his door and let him go in first.

He sighed. He needed to talk to her too, but talk meant human, so he went upstairs to his bedroom to shift and pull on a pair of jeans. When he came back down, she was waiting for him in the living room.

"Sam isn't living with you anymore?" She sounded wistful, and it struck him that she actually missed the pup. He knew Sam missed her.

"Not all the time. It's safer for him right now to be with the rest of the Wolfgard. But the next time he's here, you could come over and spend the day with us," Simon said. "We'll even let you choose one of the movies." And he and Sam would have a talk ahead of time about being polite even when you were bored silly by a movie that someone else was enjoying.

Meg smiled. "I'd like that."

When he looked human, she was wary of letting him get too close. He sort of understood that since his human form was becoming more interested in hers in ways he was pretty sure didn't fit with being a friend kind of friend. But she'd let the Wolf cuddle up next to her while they watched a movie. And getting licked by someone furry wasn't threatening but being kissed by the nonfurred male was, which made no sense when the furry and nonfurred were the same person. Wolf. Whatever.

Maybe that was just Meg, who was more like a puppy learning about the world than an adult female. She didn't smell like she was interested in kisses. Of course, he wasn't interested either because they were friends and kisses that weren't licks would cause more confusion.

Maybe he really did need to read one of those romances about humans and Wolves to figure out the inconsistencies in the female brain.

"Simon," Meg said quietly.

Her tone reminded him of why they needed to talk—and why he wanted to avoid talking. "Meg?"

"Using prophets' blood to make drugs that stir up trouble between humans and *terra indigene*. Grinding up a girl to infect meat so lots of people go temporarily insane. You have to stop those things or it will keep happening, and each time it will be worse. More anger, more hatred." Meg raised her chin. "You need a prophecy to help you find the Controller. So I'm going to make another cut."

She said exactly what he needed her to say. But that meant hurting his friend, so he bared his teeth and snarled at her. "I'm not asking you to put your foot in a trap to save the rest of us."

"No, you're not. But if one of the pack chose to do it, you'd accept her choice."

His snarl changed to a whine. He didn't like it, but she spoke truth. Then again, he didn't think Meg spoke anything else.

"I'll make the cut tomorrow morning."

"No." He shook his head. "First we're going to find out whatever you can remember about your journey to Lakeside. That way your skin won't be wasted."

"All right." She shifted her feet. "I should go home now and get some rest."

He wanted to go with her, wanted to curl up beside her tonight. Then he heard the Wolves howling, a reminder that there were guests in the Courtyard who might become uneasy if they saw evidence of him being *too* friendly with a human—especially one who was Namid's terrible creation.

CHAPTER 24

Despite Earthday usually being a day of rest for both humans and *terra indigene*, the next morning the guests crowded into the front part of Howling Good Reads. Henry and Vlad stood behind the counter while Tolya and Stavros Sanguinati floated near the ceiling in smoke form. Tess leaned against the doorway between HGR and A Little Bite. Simon waited for the four females—Merri Lee, Heather, Ruthie, and Theral—to join them.

Walking in from the stockroom, the girls hesitated when they saw the crowd of *terra indigene*, but they came forward when he wagged a finger at them. He'd called all of them last evening, telling them to come in for a full day's work and he'd explain at the meeting this morning.

Before he could say anything, they pulled notebooks and pens out of the carry sacks they seemed to haul around everywhere. Meg carried a purse when she went to the office or the Market Square, but it was small and didn't hold anything of particular interest. He knew that because he'd looked. But these sacks were big enough to contain all kinds of curious things, and he wished he'd poked his nose into one before now to find out what it held.

"Today we're all participating in a special assignment," Simon began.

The four girls opened their notebooks to a clean page, wrote the date at the top, then looked at him expectantly.

Out of the corner of his eye, he saw Bobbie Beargard hunch her shoulders, shifting her body into a preattack stance. He noticed how many of the other *terra indigene* guests also stiffened.

If only one of the girls had done it, none of them would have thought about it. But all four? Was this something that was *supposed* to be done during a meeting? Did everyone have notebooks and pens, or only females? Was this a secret human thing, a subtle indication when making a deal or trying to buy merchandise that the other person wasn't really human? If the human teachers the *terra indigene* paid—and paid well—to teach them how to interact with humans were omitting pieces of that training deliberately, what other ways had they been lying to the Others?

And most important, who could they ask when asking made them vulnerable to deceit?

Simon eyed Ruthie and thought he had the answer to that.

"Mr. Wolfgard?" Merri Lee said, glancing at all the *terra indigene*. "You were going to tell us about the special assignment?"

"The man who came here yesterday was . . ." Simon faltered, not sure how to explain since he didn't want to tell them what would happen when the Others found their prey.

"Someone hired him to procure blood prophets," Merri Lee said with a simmering anger that made everyone brace for an attack. "He tried to hypnotize Meg into believing she needed to come with him." In contrast to the simmering anger in her voice, her eyes looked haunted. *"He was a bad person."*

"Yes," Henry, the Courtyard's spirit guide, said with quiet authority. "He was a very bad person who would have brought harm to many other girls and their families. Meg's warning to hide the children stopped him from taking anyone from Ferryman's Landing."

Merri Lee hadn't killed Phineas Jones any more than Meg had. But their defensive attack had prevented the man from escaping, and being captured *had* ended with him dying by his own hand. Simon didn't think it was as simple for the human female to accept as it was for the Others.

"We need to find a man called the Controller," Simon said. "He runs the compound where Meg was held, and he keeps a lot of other girls there and treats them as property. He was the one who called Meg *cs759* because property doesn't need a name. We believe he's responsible for manufacturing the drugs gone over wolf and feel-good—and for making the tainted meat that caused so much violence and death in a Midwest town. So what we're all going to do today is help Meg figure out how she reached Lakeside and how she reached the Courtyard."

As he watched them absorb the words, he understood some things about his employees. Heather was definitely a bunny, and while she was a good worker, he didn't think she'd be staying much longer. Theral was so new he couldn't decide whether her uneasiness came from trying to understand the Courtyard as a whole or this assignment. But Merri Lee and Ruthie? He saw a bit of Wolf in them, just like he saw in Meg at times. *They* understood that the Controller wouldn't live a day after the *terra indigene* found him.

Maybe Merri Lee wasn't having as much trouble accepting Phineas Jones's death as he thought.

Before he could explain the actual assignment, Merri Lee looked at him and said, "Pictures. Meg needs photographs, drawings, maps, names of towns—images that she'll remember seeing on the journey to Lakeside." She turned to Ruthie. "She doesn't always see in a direct way. Sometimes the answer is by association."

Ruthie nodded. "So we want to start broad and then keep narrowing the focus."

The next thing Simon knew, Merri Lee and Ruthie were dividing up the tasks and scribbling notes about who was going to do what—including handing out assignments to the Others.

<Aren't you supposed to be in charge?> Vlad asked, amused.

<Shut up,> Simon growled.

The *terra indigene* were assigned land—plants, animals, water, distinctive features of each region—while the girls would check the human locations.

"What can we use for reference?" Ruthie asked.

"Any of the books in the store or in the library," Simon replied. "Just indicate in some way the books from the store if we need to reshelve them later. You can use the big tables in the library and work with Meg at the sorting room table in the Liaison's Office."

"I'll get a Lakeside map and talk to Meg," Merri Lee said.

"Can I use the computer in the library?" Ruthie asked. She continued without waiting for Simon's agreement. "I'll check the train and bus schedules and see what might have been coming into Lakeside and from where. But first I'll ask Meg if she remembers any town names."

"There can be more than one town with the same name," Theral said.

"Yes," Ruthie agreed. "But not all of those towns would have a bus or train link to Lakeside. Not directly, anyway."

The girls looked toward the rack of maps that stood opposite the checkout counter. It was usually within easy sight of whoever was at the counter. Today there was a crowd of earth natives standing in the way of anyone who wanted to reach the maps.

Smoke flowed along the ceiling, then drifted down toward the rack. An arm and hand took shape, along with enough of the face for Simon to identify Stavros when the Sanguinati selected several maps and handed them to Alan Wolfgard, who gave them to Charlie Crowgard, who passed them on to Simon, who gave them to Ruthie.

After murmuring their thanks, Merri Lee and Ruthie headed for the back of the store, followed by Theral. Heather looked over her shoulder at all of them before hurrying to catch up to the other girls.

The other humans.

<She won't be staying,> Vlad said, sounding regretful.

<I know,> Simon replied. <When the time comes, we'll do it the human way. We'll flip a coin to see who has to fill out the paperwork.>

He collected one copy of every magazine the store stocked, which wasn't many since the *terra indigene* didn't find magazines all that interesting and the human customers didn't like paying the nonrecycling fee he tacked onto the price. Now, though, he would consider whether magazines would provide a useful reference for Meg. He'd have to talk to her about that.

Should he pick up a notebook at Three Ps so he could write such things down? Why did he need to write them when he could remember them?

Damn humans. He was second-guessing himself, wondering if he'd really passed for human as well as he'd thought all these years.

Wondering why it mattered now.

After he handed out the magazines, most of the Courtyard's guests took their assignments into A Little Bite, where they could use the tables and get a drink.

Alan wandered over to the shelves of children's books and selected several before he joined Joe and Jackson at A Little Bite. Vlad went upstairs to deal with paperwork. Henry and Bobbie headed for the Market Square shops to see what might be helpful.

That left Simon alone with Charlie.

Going behind the counter, Simon reached for the stack of orders from the *terra indigene* settlements. If Heather was going to quit, he needed to get a start on these.

"Whispers from across the water," Charlie said quietly.

Simon began separating the orders into stacks that would go on the same earth native delivery truck. "Whispers of what?"

"War."

He looked up, giving Charlie his full attention. "War" was a serious word because war reshaped the world. "You think the humans over there are that foolish?"

"Enough of them are."

"If it does start over there, do you think war will come here?"

"It will touch us. But not, I hope, with the ferocity that will touch the Cel-Romano part of the world."

"How did you hear about this?"

Charlie smiled. "The Crowgard live in many parts of the world, not just Thaisia. We share what we know. But the Crows can't tell if the humans will fight to steal territory from each other, as they sometimes do, or if they are looking to take what is ours."

"I guess the *terra indigene* over there will find out soon enough and deal with it," Simon said, frowning as he read the titles being requested from the settlements supplied by the Lakeside Courtyard. It looked like everyone had finished reading the survive-the-blizzard-and-the-evil-human thrillers and had made the seasonal change to stories about surviving other kinds of storms. The evil humans didn't vary even that much.

Charlie leaned his forearms on the counter. "Simon. This Controller is your enemy, and the Midwest leaders especially are not averse to helping you with this hunt. But that human might not be the only one making the drugs. He might not be the one responsible for the bad meat."

"He might not be," Simon agreed. "So that's one of the things we'll ask Meg."

"Meg?" Ruthie asked while Merri Lee opened up the Lakeside and Northeast Region maps on the sorting table. "May I ask you something?"

"Isn't that what we're supposed to do today?" Meg replied, setting aside the *Lakeside News*. "Ask questions in order to find answers?"

Ruthie raised her notebook. "Why would the *terra indigene* be angry about us taking notes for this assignment? If they're worried about security or something, we can leave the notebooks here."

"And everyone in the Courtyard's Business Association knows Ruthie and Karl are living together and will be getting married this summer and that Michael and I are dating," Merri Lee said. "At the very least, Simon and Vlad have to figure the police will be aware that *something* is going on since Ruthie and I were called in to work on Earthday."

"So why would they be upset about the notebooks?" Ruthie asked. "Because all four of us saw it. The Others in HGR were seriously ticked off, but they didn't say anything. I know it made Heather and Theral uneasy."

Meg closed her eyes and recalled training images of notebooks. Appointment books? No, she was pretty sure Simon and Vlad used that kind of notebook to make the work schedule for the store, and Elliot must use one for his meetings with the mayor and such. Journals? No. The Others wouldn't be upset about such things. Besides, Ruthie and the other girls wouldn't have brought a journal to a meeting. So what would matter to the *terra indigene*?

Girls and boys carrying books, going to school, sitting at desks and writing, taking notes while a teacher pointed to something on the blackboard. Then she considered what she knew about the little school here in the Courtyard, about what puppies like Sam were learning and what the juveniles were learning before going off to schools that would give them the technical training or education that was supposed to match what was available to humans. According to the agreements made with the *terra indigene* in Thaisia, humans could *not* be taught anything that wasn't also available to the Others if they wanted to learn.

But what if there were less blatant ways to discourage the Others from insisting that those agreements were met to the full?

She opened her eyes and looked at her friends. "How old were you when you learned to take notes?"

"How old?" Merri Lee frowned. "Before high school. Certainly before going to the university."

Ruthie nodded. "Not the first few years of school, but definitely before high school. And I've always liked keeping track of a project, making notes for myself when I think of something or listing the things I need to do for the assignment, so I started carrying a notebook around since I learned how to write and spell. It's my way of thinking aloud. And I keep them for reference."

More images. Boy in the back of the classroom, books closed, sneering at the teacher. Or looking resentful. Or hiding confusion by looking bored? "And if someone doesn't take notes during class? What would the teacher think?" Meg asked.

"Not interested in the lesson," Merri Lee replied. "Figures the student thinks the subject is beneath him. Or her."

"What if no one ever explained to you about taking notes?" Meg asked softly, thinking of how Simon and the other *terra indigene* she considered friends treated the notebook she used as something private. Which it was. The notebook was her way to build a life, to bridge the gaps between the images she had absorbed during lessons at the compound and the full experience of living. They were curious about why she needed to write things down, but they'd assumed it was part of her being a blood prophet—until this morning when four humans pulled out notebooks and pens and showed the Others that this writing things down wasn't exclusive to the *cassandra sangue*. "What if you didn't learn about taking notes when you were young, so that when you attended classes in a human school, the teacher thought you didn't care and were wasting his time? What if you wanted to learn but thought the teacher . . ."

Fetching the copy of the *Lakeside News*, Meg opened it to the comics and pointed to one strip.

"That strip has been around for years," Merri Lee said. "When I was young, I thought it was funny, but it doesn't seem funny anymore."

One group of characters in the strip always wore elaborate hats, symbols of authority. But the other group, dressed in business suits, were always pulling tricks on the primitives who "couldn't understand civilization."

"The Others never learned about taking notes to help them remember what they heard in classes?" Ruthie said. She pressed her lips in a thin line. "Then the instructors would think they're taking up space in classrooms because they're entitled to be there but they don't really care about learning. So the instructors don't make an effort to find out why the *terra indigene* aren't doing the things that would help them get the most out of the class. And the Others realize they aren't getting what was promised even if they aren't sure what's missing, and they resent the humans they still see as intruders even though we've been living on this continent with them for centuries."

"And they express their resentment by tightening the resources we need for the way we live and the things we make, because why should they give up bits of the world that belong to them in order to make things convenient for us?" Merri Lee added. "We *all* feel a lack, and resentment keeps building. And when the humans go that one step too far . . ."

"I picked up an old book at an estate sale," Ruthie said. "Inside was a folded sheet of paper with a list of cities that don't exist anymore. I didn't realize at first that's what it was. It was just a list of city names and dates. When I looked up the cities . . . or tried to . . . that's when I realized they had been destroyed, reclaimed by the wild country." She looked sad. "How many of those cities vanished because someone couldn't be bothered to explain something as simple as taking notes?"

Meg watched Ruthie turn to a clean page in her notebook. "What are you doing?"

"Mr. Wolfgard hired me to teach the Others about human things, and that's what I'm going to do. And not just how to order from a menu or what utensil to use when in a restaurant or how to make a purchase in a store. Karl thinks we have an opportunity to interact with the Others in ways that might make a difference for all of us, and I think so too. So I'm going to teach the *terra indigene* in the Courtyard about social skills and what to do when they attend a school that employs human instructors. I'm just going to take a minute to make a note about this."

Merri Lee nodded. "While you do that, Meg and I will start working with the Lakeside map to figure out how she got here."

It sounded simple. It wasn't. Meg hadn't realized how little of the journey she had absorbed. Or, more to the point, she wasn't sure what had been real and what had been training images. She had focused on following the images that had guided her escape and somehow managed not to see anything that might have created confusion or doubt—the very things that would have helped them now to follow her journey.

There had been a train. She remembered being too scared to sleep and too tired to stay awake. Caught in that mental vagueness, the images that guided her were sharp but had no context. She'd bought a ticket for the last train leaving that night, but she couldn't remember how she'd reached the station. There must have been a vehicle that had left the compound, but . . . She remembered riding on the train a long time and seeing something that triggered the decision to get off before the stop listed on her ticket. Which city? She didn't know. And there had been buses, the kind that provided transportation between cities. And another ticket for another train? But, again, she had followed the visions, and most of what she'd seen had faded too much to recall.

Before the three of them became too frustrated, the first set of pictures was delivered for a review of region.

The pictures of alligators, panthers, and snakes fascinated her. Her training images of these creatures had been line drawings that weren't the least bit scary. *These* images were of predators. Maybe even *terra indigene*. The trees and flowers were like nothing she'd seen before, not even in training images.

"Okay," Merri Lee said, making notes. "You didn't recognize the critters or the plants, so I'd say you didn't live in the Southeast or come through there when you ran away."

"It was dark a lot of the time," Meg said. Or had that been her mind's way of protecting itself from absorbing too many images as the train sped on? There *had* been daylight at least part of the time, but not bright. Winter light and gray sky.

"You were wearing jeans, a T-shirt, a denim jacket, and sneakers," Ruthie said, making her own notes. "You didn't have a winter coat, so you came from someplace warmer than here."

Meg frowned. "No. The denim jacket was part of the outfit. The Walking Name was wearing the winter coat."

They looked at her.

"They wore white uniforms and changed out of their regular clothes. She took the coat out of her locker because she went outside for something. She didn't close the locker properly. That's why I could take the clothes and the money in her wallet."

"It was cold when you went outside?" Merri Lee asked.

Meg nodded. "Very cold. But I was so afraid. Maybe it felt cold because I was so afraid of what the Controller would do to me if I got caught. Jean . . . Jean and I were going to run away together. It was before the visions that helped me escape, so it was just talk, just wishful thinking about having a real life. But a Walking Name overheard us, and the Controller didn't think I would run away by myself, so he . . . broke one of Jean's feet. I still wanted both of us to run away, but she said if she went with me, we'd get caught. By myself, I would escape. And I did." Meg didn't realize she was crying until Merri Lee handed her a tissue. "But Jean is still there."

She wiped her eyes and blew her nose. "I've never been in the Southeast. I'm sure of that much."

They crossed off the High North next. Theral was using the library computer to check details for them, and she confirmed that the lake-effect storm that had touched Lakeside the evening Meg arrived had shut down rail and bus transportation in the High Northeast for the whole day.

Tess brought over coffee, sandwiches, and fresh-baked chocolate chip cookies, as well as another stack of pictures.

Meg, Merri Lee, and Ruthie drank the coffee, ate the sandwiches and cookies, and crossed the West Coast region off the list.

Midafternoon, Heather showed up with a handful of magazines and eyes that were puffy from crying.

"I don't think I can do this anymore," she said, setting the magazines on the sorting table. "They used to make more effort to stay human, and they don't anymore. Have you noticed that?" Heather looked at Merri Lee, who had been working at A Little Bite for over a year. "And most of the customers were human, so it wasn't too bad. And with the Market Square credit, I was making as much working part-time hours as I would make working full-time in another bookstore in the city."

"Then why can't you do this anymore?" Merri Lee asked.

"Last night my father told me he doesn't want me setting foot in his house again while I'm working in the Courtyard. He said it was hard enough to find work in Lakeside, and being tarred as a Wolf lover was the first step toward losing a job and then sleeping in a homeless shelter and begging on the streets, and how that brush spread the muck over everyone in a family. And while he was saying those things, my mom just sat there and wouldn't look at me. She didn't say anything to me until I got up to leave. Then she stopped me at the door and told me if anything happened to my younger brother or sister because I was being a whore for the Others, it would be on my head."

"That's awful," Ruthie said. "They had no right to say those things!"

"Like your family hasn't said it to you?"

Ruthie took a step back.

"You lost your job because of this place." Heather looked at Merri Lee. "And you were beaten up and can't go back to school."

"The Others didn't do those things," Merri Lee replied. "Humans did."

"Because of them! And now we're being asked . . . Do you even know what they're going to do with the information we're providing? What if we're helping them do something terrible? What happens to us if we're branded traitors to humankind?"

"I don't think anything about working with the *terra indigene* is as black-and-white as that," Ruthie said carefully. "Maybe it is that simple in places like Cel-Romano or Tokhar-Chin, where humans control a big chunk of land and only brush against the Others at the borders between human-controlled land and the wild country. But our ancestors settled on a continent that didn't belong to humans, so it's different for us. If we can't work with them, they'll turn against us."

"That doesn't change the fact that Heather has been given a choice: give up the job or lose her family," Merri Lee said.

What will happen to Heather if she makes the wrong choice? Meg thought, knocking her hand against the underside of the sorting table as she reached for the magazines. She almost cried out at the sudden stab of pain, but she swallowed pain that turned into mild agony, too surprised to speak when the cover of a magazine kept shifting into a different picture. Only pieces, so she never saw the whole image, as if she was seeing bits of several pictures. Then, struggling to focus on the vision, she saw a date—and blood soaking the paper.

When she came back to herself, she realized no one had noticed anything had happened. Ruthie and Merri Lee were still talking, still trying to offer Heather some sympathy and encouragement. But their friend didn't need sympathy and encouragement. She needed . . .

"Heather, you have to go," Meg said quietly.

They all stopped talking and looked at her.

"I'd rather stay here and work with you," Heather said. "There's too much strange fur and fang in the library."

"No." Meg walked over to the counter, picked up the phone, and dialed. "You have to hand in your notice today and go."

"Meg?" Merri Lee said. "What's going on?"

She shook her head as Vlad answered the phone at HGR. "Vlad? Can you come to the office? We need to talk to you. No, just you." She hung up before turning to look at her friends and the maps and the notebooks, but she didn't see anything else, didn't feel any warning prickles.

"Meg!" Vlad rushed into the sorting room moments later and jerked to a stop.

"Heather needs to leave," Meg said. "She can't work in the Courtyard anymore."

"I hadn't decided that!" Heather protested. Clearly frightened, she turned to Ruthie and Merri Lee for support. "I didn't say that."

"She didn't say that," Merri Lee said.

Vlad gave Heather a considering look, but Meg didn't think the decision surprised him. Then he sniffed the air and walked around the table until he stood next to her and said gently, "Let me see your hands."

"What?" Meg said.

"Your hands," Vlad repeated.

"What's going on?" Ruthie asked.

"Meg?" Merri Lee said.

She held out her hands. The gouge on the top of her right index finger was tiny, barely the size of a pinhead, but it was just enough lost skin for blood to rise in the wound.

"How did you do that?" Vlad asked.

"I hit my hand on the table when I reached for the magazines. I must have scraped something?"

"And you saw . . . ?"

She saw Merri Lee scramble for a notebook and pen. Distracting. Another image. Not the answer to Vlad's question. "I saw the cover of the magazine." She tried to point but Vlad still held her hands, so she tipped her head to indicate the stack of magazines on the table. "But the one in the vision wasn't the current issue. I saw blood. All the pages were soaked in blood."

"What does that have to do with Heather?"

"Her family wants her to stop working here. When I reached for the magazines, I was thinking about what would happen if she made the wrong choice, and then I felt pain . . . and I saw . . ." She looked at Vlad. "She has to go."

"Yes," Vlad said, giving her hands a gentle squeeze before releasing them. "I'll take care of it." To Heather he added, "Gather your personal belongings, then meet me in the store's office. I'll give you your pay."

Heather stumbled to the back room and out the door.

"I'll make sure she has enough money to take care of her bills for a couple of months," Vlad said. "That will give her time to find another job. And I'll have Blair come by to sniff out the spot where you damaged your finger and repair it so you won't get hurt again."

"But I don't even know how I did it!" Meg protested. "How can he find the exact spot?"

Vlad smiled. "He's a Wolf with an excellent sense of smell. He'll find it." The smile faded as he waved a hand to indicate Merri Lee and Ruth. "What about the rest of the human pack?"

No pins-and-needles feeling in response to the question. No other vision. "They can stay," Meg replied. Then she added silently, *They'll be safer here.*

She couldn't be certain of that, but the thought felt right.

"All right," Vlad said. "I'll have to tell Simon, so take care of that wound before he shows up howling about it."

Once Vlad left the building, Ruthie turned to Meg, wide-eyed. "Okay, that was weird. What was that?"

"That," Meg replied, "was prophecy."

Simon wasn't happy that Meg had called Vlad instead of him, but after he went off by himself for a few minutes to snarl about it, he thought he'd worked out the human logic. Since he'd summoned the *terra indigene* leaders to Lakeside, he was in charge of the big meeting, which left Vlad in charge of the bookstore. And Heather leaving and being paid was bookstore business.

Realizing Vlad would also be stuck with the employee-quitting paperwork cheered Simon up considerably. He hated filling out that paperwork.

Of course, finding new humans to work for them wasn't going to be a romp in the woods.

We'll make do, he thought as he checked the list of pictures he was supposed to look for. *Most Courtyards don't have any human employees except the Liaison. Even Lakeside didn't have other humans working for us on a regular basis until I became leader and opened a couple of stores to human customers. Most Courtyards don't have humans like Lorne running a little printing business that is strictly for us.*

Now most of those humans were gone. Would the *terra indigene* who couldn't pass for human feel more comfortable shopping in the Market Square now? Would the human employees who were left respond badly to Others who didn't look like them?

No point in chewing on a bone that wasn't there, so he focused on the task he could see.

He had found half of his list of images when he gathered up the books and magazines and headed for the Liaison's Office. He just wanted to see Meg, make sure she was all right. He deserved a reward for politely calling the office instead of rushing over when Vlad told him about Meg's vision. No reason to think Vlad would make light of anything that hurt Meg, so the injury really was nothing to howl about—just a puncture so tiny that Meg hadn't realized why she'd seen the vision until Vlad had scented blood and checked her hands.

It probably would be considered bad manners to sniff her just to make sure the Sanguinati hadn't missed another injury—especially if the other girls were still in the office.

Neither he nor Vlad understood why the prophecy meant Heather had to leave the Courtyard today, but they didn't challenge Meg. For one thing, none of the other leaders had seen a *cassandra sangue* speak prophecy. When they did witness a cut, he wanted them to have no doubts about the accuracy of what was said.

Interpretation was something else. Meg wasn't always right when it came to interpreting images. She'd thought she was going to die in the Courtyard because of the prophecy she'd seen about herself. And she had come close to dying. But she'd survived, which proved her wrong.

Not something he intended to mention.

Charlie caught up to him as he walked out of the library and headed for the Liaison's Office.

"Tess the Scary says the girls should take a break. Get some food and fresh air," Charlie said.

"That's a good idea." Too bad they couldn't play prey. Meg was a fun squeaky toy when she was the pretend prey, but there was too much risk right now of her getting hurt by a Wolf who wouldn't remember it was pretend. And seeing a human being chased might scare the other girls into resigning. Once all the guests went home and everyone settled down, there would be time to play again. "And don't call Tess names."

There was no one around them, but Charlie lowered his voice. "There are stories about her kind throughout the world, and those stories are very old." He studied Simon. "You do know what she is?"

"I have some thoughts. Henry knows for sure." He'd found and read some of those old stories, but he hadn't told anyone what he knew about Tess's kind of *terra indigene*. Not even Henry. Safer that way for all of them.

"And yet you let her stay."

"My choice," Simon said in a tone that would have warned anyone else that the conversation was done.

"Did you know they're called Plague Riders in some parts of the world?" Charlie said.

He did know. In contrast, calling them Harvesters made them sound more benign—until you saw what they could do.

"You would be wise to keep that information to yourself," Simon said. "Especially while you're here."

A beat of silence. "Wasn't intending to share it with anyone but you."

They walked into the office. The girls had taped maps on the walls and then pinned notes on the maps. Spread out on the table were photos of trains and buses and pictures Theral must have printed off the computer of signs that read WELCOME TO . . . some town or other.

Seeing the images, Charlie grinned, then said in a conductor's voice, "All aboard! Next stop, Wheatfield!"

Meg spun around so fast she stumbled into the sorting table. "What did you say?"

Charlie backed up. "I don't know. I was just—"

Merri Lee leaped at Charlie and held up a list. "Say the names of these towns, just like you did that other one."

When Charlie looked at him for some explanation, Simon just shrugged, too busy trying to keep his ears from shifting. His human ears hadn't heard whatever Merri Lee and Meg had heard, but the Wolf ears wouldn't do any better because it was the tone that had significance. Human ears could hear that just fine. His brain understood but his instincts weren't convinced.

Charlie obliged, saying the town names the way a conductor would. Meg shook her head or nodded. Merri Lee wrote in that damn notebook while Ruthie made notations on the map. When Charlie called out the last name, the girls sagged, and Simon realized Tess was right—they needed to rest.

"That's it," Merri Lee said.

"What's it?" Simon asked.

"That's what I remember of the journey to Lakeside," Meg said, sounding too weary. "It's broken up, and there are too many possibilities of how I got to the first town name I remember hearing. I'm sorry, Simon. I don't think I can get closer than that."

He looked at the map. "Nothing to be sorry about. We started with the whole continent this morning. You've narrowed it down to a region."

"That's still a lot of towns and cities," Ruthie said, sounding uneasy.

"It's fine." He tried a smile. When Ruthie and Merri Lee paled, he ran his tongue over his canines. Damn. Those were definitely not human anymore.

"We should take a break," Meg said. "Get some air. And I could use another sandwich."

There was something too deliberate about the way the girls set their notebooks on the sorting table before heading out.

"Can we look at these?" Charlie asked, reaching for Merri Lee's notebook.

"I don't know," Simon replied, wishing he knew either more or less about human females. <Henry? Gather our guests and bring them to the Liaison's Office.>

While they waited, Simon studied the map. Either Meg had been scared witless or she'd been attempting to hide her trail from a hunter. She'd been right to assume the Controller had sent men after her, but he'd seen rabbits with a Wolf on their tails zigzag less than she had. And since the bus station and the train depot were both in the downtown part of Lakeside and south of the Courtyard, how had she ended up *north* of the Courtyard in order to head back down until she reached the Liaison's Office and Howling Good Reads the night she applied for the job?

She may have been a brainless female for being out in a storm that night, and she probably arrived on the last bus or train that had reached Lakeside, but she'd gained enough time to escape capture and find the *terra indigene*.

The room usually felt like it had plenty of space, but with so many earth natives crowding around the map, he was glad he didn't have a tail right now that could get stepped on.

"So, the enemy *is* in the Midwest," Joe Wolfgard said. "That's confirmation enough for us. We know what we need to do."

"That can be the last choice," Simon said. "First, we'll try to narrow the search for the prey."

They didn't want it to be a last choice. He saw that truth in the eyes of the Midwest leaders. Humans were causing too much trouble. It was time to seriously thin the herds. He wasn't opposed to thinning if it needed to be done, but that would mean abandoning everything humans made in that part of Thaisia or asking *terra indigene* to take up those tasks. Which meant more of the Others staying in human form for hours a day in order to do the work.

Maybe the Midwest leaders were also considering what they would have to ask of their own because Cheryl Hawkgard finally said, "How do we narrow the search?"

He bared his teeth in a smile. "Now we get the police to help us."

CHAPTER 25

When Simon walked into A Little Bite the next morning, he found Meg, Merri Lee, Ruthie, and Theral sitting at a table scribbling in notebooks and talking in voices so low he'd have to shift his ears to hear them.

But it was Tess who caught his attention. Her hair was solid red and curling wildly—a sign her temper had turned savage but not yet lethal.

"Something wrong?" he asked, going behind the counter to stand beside her.

"The bakery truck didn't make a delivery this morning, and when I called to find out why . . ." Tess stopped speaking. Black threads appeared in her hair.

Simon resisted the urge to take a step back. As leader, he couldn't. As a sensible Wolf who now knew what kind of predator he faced, he wanted something more than air between him and her.

"Call that bakery in Ferryman's Landing," he suggested. "See what they can provide."

"Having some baked goods to sell here is not the point and you know it," Tess snapped. But she kept her voice low enough not to attract the girls' attention. "If humans aren't going to keep their side of the agreements, they shouldn't be allowed to live in Lakeside."

They shouldn't be allowed to live is what you really mean, Simon thought.

It was a sentiment he'd heard too many times yesterday as the leaders from other regions talked about their increasingly unsuccessful dealings with humans. Was Lieutenant Montgomery's arrival in Lakeside Namid's way of maintaining balance? If the lieutenant wasn't making an effort to work with him and keep relations between humans and the Courtyard as cordial as possible, would the businesses who refused to provide goods or services have tipped the scales sufficiently that he would have been voicing the same anger and hostility as the other leaders? Probably.

Unlike those other leaders, he did have humans like Montgomery making an effort to understand how their kind fit into the world. And he had employees like Merri Lee, Lorne, and Ruthie. Even Heather hadn't given him anything to snarl about. All of them had, in fact, given him reason to feel obliged to protect them as he did his own kind.

And then there was Meg with her strange skin and underlying sweet nature that made her not prey.

Could a few humans keep a city balanced enough to avoid a serious fight when the rest of the humans seemed to want to start trouble that would end with many of them dying? Or would these ordinary humans who wanted to live in harmony with the *terra indigene* become the next group who was persecuted by the rest of their kind? Would the Wolf lovers become like the Intuits and form their own small communities in order to survive?

Did those prejudiced humans understand what would happen if they drove out the very people who were making *their* presence tolerable?

Can't do anything about other cities, but maybe, with our pack of humans helping, Lakeside can survive.

"I'll give them one more chance," Tess said, sounding reluctant to do that much. "I'll call the bakery, give them my order, and tell them if they don't deliver—or deliver inferior goods—I'll take my business elsewhere. And if I have to take my business elsewhere, I'll send a letter to the Lakeside authorities, informing them of a breach of the agreements between the city and the Courtyard."

"Not as satisfying as biting the bakers on the leg—or in the ass—but that kind of letter will scare them just as much," Simon said.

Tess huffed out a laugh. Half her hair turned green. "You win, Wolf. Aren't you meeting with the police?"

"They'll be arriving any minute now. Montgomery and Captain Burke. And Dr. Lorenzo."

"Then go away so I can go back to eavesdropping."

Simon eyed the girls. "I thought they finished yesterday."

"They're trying to figure out what kind of building or buildings make up the compound where Meg was kept," Tess said, glancing over her shoulder. "I don't think they've succeeded in doing anything except becoming upset and angry, but they might come up with something useful."

The girls had noticed him, so it was time to retreat. He raised a hand in greeting. Meg smiled at him; Ruthie and Merri Lee looked at him warily. And a little guiltily? He wasn't concerned about Officers Kowalski and Debany knowing what the girls had worked on yesterday. He was hoping the men knew—and had told Montgomery. That would make this meeting with the police easier, especially since a handful of the Midwest leaders would be there along with Alan Wolfgard and Charlie Crowgard. Being a writer, Alan was more articulate with human speech and understood more of their odd phrases than most *terra indigene* did. And Charlie had a knack for looking curious and harmless. Charlie was always curious. Being a Crow didn't make him harmless.

As Simon stepped out of the back door of the coffee shop, a black sedan drove down the access way toward the employee parking lot.

<Two humans,> Jake said from his spot on the brick wall that divided the delivery area from Henry's yard. <We know their faces. The Montgomery and the Burke.>

<Good,> Simon replied.

Then Nathan reported, <The human bodywalker is here.>

<Let him in. Tell him to park in the employee lot.> Simon watched a white car drive past, then walked to the back door of the Liaison's Office to wait for the three men.

Until Meg began working for them, the Others hadn't allowed any humans but the Liaison to have access to the sorting room. But Meg was so efficient in delivering the mail and packages, there really wasn't anything for other humans to see if they were trying to spy on the Courtyard. And he and the rest of the Business Association had adjusted the "no other humans" rule so that Meg's human pack could be there with her without penalty. So letting police and the doctor into the sorting room wasn't that much of a step beyond the new rules.

Besides, he had a feeling the girls would strip some fur off him if he moved their maps and any of their notes fell off.

When they went inside, Simon indicated that Burke, Montgomery, and

Lorenzo should stand closest to the map of Thaisia that had been pinned over the pigeonholes that filled half of the sorting room's back wall. While the three men frowned at the map, the *terra indigene* came into the room, spreading out so they blocked every exit.

Simon wasn't sure if Lorenzo realized the humans were trapped, but Montgomery and Burke knew.

"A man called the Controller runs a compound where he keeps *cassandra sangue* and sells the cuts he makes on their skin to humans who want to know about the future," Simon said. "We believe he is responsible for the drugs called gone over wolf and feel-good, as well as the bad meat that caused so much trouble in one of your Midwest towns. We're also convinced that much, if not all, of the trouble in the Midwest that resulted in the deaths of *terra indigene*, as well as the attack in Jerzy, was instigated by this man."

Burke's face revealed nothing, although there was a hint of fear in his scent now that hadn't been there when he walked into the room. Lorenzo looked puzzled, but he was on his way home after his shift at the hospital, so maybe he was too tired to be smart right now. Montgomery, on the other hand, couldn't quite hide his alarm.

"The *terra indigene* have decided that this human is our enemy." Simon looked each man in the eyes. "We're going to put him down." A human phrase for killing what they didn't want.

He watched them. Listened to the catch in Lorenzo's breath. Saw the way Monty flinched—an indication that the man understood what was coming. Only Burke gave no outward response to the words.

He pointed at the map. "As you can see, we put a great deal of work into figuring out where this Controller lives. We've narrowed it down to the Midwest. Now you're going to help us find him."

Lorenzo sputtered, "Why would we do that?"

Joe Wolfgard stepped forward, drawing the humans' attention. "Because we'll tear apart every human town, village, city, and settlement in the Midwest if that's what it takes to find him. And if we have to do that, every human in those places will be considered an enemy and, therefore, prey—even if we have to dig them out of their dens in order to kill them."

Shocked, the three men looked at the map.

"There are dozens of cities in the Midwest Region," Burke finally said.

"And thousands of humans," Simon said. "Today, anyway. Tomorrow?" He shrugged. "That depends on your people. The *terra indigene* are going to hunt down this enemy. If you don't want us to attack all of those cities in order to find one man, give us a smaller target."

Montgomery's dark skin had lost enough color to make him look ill. Lorenzo, too, looked ill. Only Burke's face didn't change.

"We appreciate your candor, Mr. Wolfgard," Burke said. "Obviously, reaching out to fellow officers and alerting them to the existence of such a dangerous enemy will not be a quick process. How much time do you think we have before the *terra indigene* take action?"

Simon looked at Cheryl Hawkgard and Joe Wolfgard.

"The next time humans try to use either of those drugs against us will be the last time," Cheryl said.

"Clock is ticking," Montgomery said so softly Simon was sure the man hadn't meant for anyone to hear him.

Simon escorted the humans out of the building. He didn't watch them walk back to their cars; he didn't need to. Jenni Crowgard and her sisters were keeping an eye on the back of the Liaison's Office and the parking lot.

<Meg and the other girls are getting restless,> Tess told him. <Meg wants to start work and is waiting for you to finish your meeting since you're all in the way. The other girls want to use the computers in the library and find pictures of buildings.>

<We're done,> Simon replied. <Give us a couple more minutes to clear out. Then I'll be at the bookstore.>

<Good. Apparently, Nyx is thinking about working at HGR and wondered if you were going to open it again to human customers. You might want to discuss this with Vlad.>

Not a discussion he wanted to have right now. Then again, he'd rather discuss Nyx interacting with humans then have the discussions Burke and Montgomery would have to face.

"I didn't sign up for this." Standing in the parking lot next to his car, Dominic Lorenzo sounded frightened and angry. "I agreed to provide some medical services in the Courtyard, not help the Others commit mass murder. It won't be just one person who gets killed. You know it won't."

"Keep your voice down," Monty said, pretending he wasn't aware of all the Crows gathering on the roofs that overlooked the parking lot.

"You might not have signed up for helping them hunt down a man," Burke said, "but if you back out, the Others won't forget it."

"And you can live with that?" Lorenzo asked.

"I can live with that a lot easier than doing nothing and then watching the *terra indigene* destroy all the cities in the Midwest," Burke replied. "But I think you're forgetting the other side of the coin, Doctor."

"And what is that?"

"Someone put a living girl into a meat grinder in order to wreak havoc in a town. Should that man, that murderer, be granted benevolent ownership of an unknown number of girls whose affliction is being used for profit?" Burke studied the Crows for a moment, then looked at Lorenzo. "You're not the one who has to find this man. But you do need to decide if you're going to help the girls who were his victims."

Still pale, Lorenzo got into his car and drove off.

Monty and Burke didn't say anything until they were in their car and Burke was driving toward the Chestnut Street station.

"Lieutenant, the Others are going after a man who has enough juice to influence governors and start a manhunt over half of Thaisia in order to find a girl who had escaped his control. He sent a team of trained mercenaries to Lakeside. It stands to reason a lot of important people will not want him to be found." Burke looked grim. "Before I start making phone calls and shaking up police departments in the Midwest, I'd like some confirmation of just how bad the bad could be. So you know who you need to talk to."

"Yes, sir, I do," Monty replied. "But I think I'll have a better chance of talking to Ms. Corbyn alone if I wait until this afternoon."

Monty waited until late afternoon before returning to the Courtyard.

"Will you be able to get a cup of coffee at A Little Bite?" he asked Kowalski.

"If anyone has objections to me staying, Tess will give me the coffee and tell me it's to go," Kowalski replied. "Anything I should be doing there if they let me stay?"

"Keep your eyes and ears open." Monty got out of the car and went into the Liaison's Office while Kowalski drove the patrol car to the employee parking lot.

He recognized the watch Wolf, who sprang off one of the Wolf beds and blocked his approach to the counter.

"Good afternoon," he said, raising his voice enough to be heard in the next room. "I'd like to have a word with Ms. Corbyn if she's available."

Meg stepped out of the sorting room, rubbing her left hand. "Mr. Wolfgard thought you'd be back. Come inside." She opened the go-through.

When Monty took a step toward the opening, the Wolf blocked him again and snarled.

"Nathan, I know Simon told you Lieutenant Montgomery was here this morning and has permission to enter the sorting room," Meg said.

Another deeper, wetter snarl.

"Nathan!"

He backed away, watching Monty and still snarling. As Monty slipped behind the counter, Meg pointed at the Wolf.

"If you start howling just to rile up the other Wolves, I'm going to forget where I put the order for the Wolf cookies," Meg said sternly.

"*Arrroooo!*"

Monty noticed that Meg didn't lock the go-through, and she didn't close the Private door all the way.

"I don't want to cause trouble," Monty said.

"You're not. Nathan is just being . . ."

"Thorough?" he suggested.

Meg smiled. "Yes."

Monty returned the smile. "Can't fault a security guard for doing his job."

"*Arrooooo!*"

"This is as private as it gets," Meg said, huffing out a breath.

He eyed the door and considered the question he'd come to ask. No help for it. Simon Wolfgard might have given permission for him to be in a room with Meg, but the chaperone with teeth was going to hear everything that was said— and report it.

Well, wasn't that why he'd asked Kowalski to have a coffee at A Little Bite? To listen and report whatever was overheard? Right now trust was a fragile commodity.

It suddenly occurred to him that Wolfgard wasn't granting this privacy for his sake; it was for Meg.

"I have a question," Monty said.

"Simon thought you would."

Meg looked at him with eyes that were older than when he'd first met her a few months ago. Someone else used to make all the decisions for her. Now she wasn't shielded from seeing the results of the prophecies she spoke, and the weight of that knowledge showed.

"I told Simon I was going to make one cut to help find the Controller, but after all of us spent a lot of time narrowing down the possibilities of where I was held, the Others didn't think I would be able to tell them anything more that would be useful right now. Simon, Tess, Henry, Vlad, and I talked it over, and we agreed that if the police needed that one cut to help you search, then I would make the cut."

That makes me responsible for the next scar. Monty didn't want to take that responsibility. Why would anyone want to take that responsibility? But someone had to, and this time, he was that someone.

"We need an answer," he said.

"Wait a moment." She went into the back room. When she returned, she placed several paper towels, folded to make a thick pad, on the table, and set another one off to the side. Then she removed a folding razor from her jeans pocket and set that on the table.

"Is there something wrong with your left hand?" he asked, watching her.

"It's been prickling since you arrived," she replied, rubbing it. "The feeling has been getting stronger. I'll need to cut soon, so ask your question, Lieutenant." Holding up a hand to stop him, she opened the Private door and stared at Nathan, who had his forelegs on the counter and was leaning in as far as he could.

"Go out now," she said. "Tell Tess to come in a few minutes. She knows why."

Monty didn't think the Wolf would obey, but apparently the danger of being around a *cassandra sangue* when her skin was cut was sufficient motivation. Or else Meg was simply confirming an order Simon had given already.

"Why have him leave?" he asked.

"Nathan would want to lick the wound, and that wouldn't be good for him," Meg said. "And it wouldn't be good for you."

Monty nodded. Whether the Wolf reacted aggressively or passively, the Others wouldn't respond well to a human being present.

Once Nathan went out the front door, Meg said, "Ask your question."

"The police have been asked to help the *terra indigene* find the Controller. Our concern is that the Others might go in and eradicate an entire town in order to eliminate a single enemy. My question is this: what will happen if the police *don't* help the *terra indigene* find this man?"

Meg picked up the razor and opened it. "Do you remember the words that Tess used at the meeting? It's not what was said in the compound, but the first time Tess said them when I made a cut, it helped bring everything into focus."

"I remember the words."

"Then ask your question again and say the words." She turned her left hand and braced it on the table before resting the width of the razor against her skin.

Monty swallowed hard. Seeing her hold the razor, he wanted to tell her to forget it, wanted to walk away before she sliced her skin. But she was the only one who could tell him what the future might look like.

"What will happen if the police don't help the *terra indigene* find the Controller? Speak, prophet, and I will listen."

Meg turned the razor so the edge rested on skin and cut the side of her left hand. Monty slipped the razor out of her hand and set it aside, unnerved by the agony he saw on her face before it became filled with a blank sensuality that was even more disturbing.

She looked at the table. Her right hand moved as if she were unrolling something.

"Map of Thaisia," she said. Her hand moved up and down. "Midwest."

"What do you see?" he whispered, not sure she could hear him now.

"Twisting wind. Fire. Broken buildings. Ash." Her hand moved up and down again. "Bones."

Monty shivered. "Do you see any people? Where are the people?"

"Ash and bones."

Meg took a deep breath, then let it out in an orgasmic sigh. She blinked and looked at him. "Did you get your answer?"

She really doesn't know, he thought. *Doesn't know what she said, doesn't know how wanton she looks. When she speaks prophecy, she becomes a vessel and forfeits the person, the personality. Not that big a leap to think of her as property, as something that can justifiably be used.*

"Lieutenant?"

And then she was Meg Corbyn again, with that childlike sweetness that was inherent to her.

"Yes. Yes, I did. Thank you." Disturbed by his thoughts, Monty focused on Meg's hand, resting on the pad of paper towels that was stained red. "Do you want some help bandaging the cut?"

He heard a door open. Tess walked into the sorting room, coming in from the back.

"I'll take care of it, Lieutenant," Tess said.

Her hair was green and loosely coiled. Since she sounded brusque rather than angry, he made a mental note of the color and degree of curl. It had been brown and straight the first time he'd met her. From what he'd gleaned from Kowalski's and Debany's observations, brown and straight meant relaxed or at least not anxious about anything. Green was the first sign of annoyance. Red indicated anger. And no one, *no one*, talked about her hair turning pure black.

Having looked at the crime scene photos of the four Lakeside University students who died after the attack on Merri Lee, Monty thought he had a good idea of what happened when Tess's hair turned black.

He nodded to Tess, then turned to Meg. "I appreciate your help, Ms. Corbyn." She gave him a wan smile.

"Officer Kowalski is in HGR, talking with Alan Wolfgard," Tess said. "They were discussing a story about a girl who gets swallowed by a wolf and then rescued by a hunter. Apparently, whether you see it as a story of love and courage overcoming danger or a horror story about devious humans depends on whether or not you have fur."

"Ah." Monty took his leave and hurried over to Howling Good Reads. He trusted Karl to be cautious when engaging in this kind of discussion, but he thought it prudent to avoid reminders of devious humans for the foreseeable future.

Retrieving his partner, they drove back to the Chestnut Street station, where he told his captain about the prophecy.

"Pete? It's Douglas Burke."

Silence. Then a too-hearty "Doug! It's been a long time."

"Yes, it has. Haven't seen you since we took that long ride into the wild country."

"You looking for a lawyer? My clients are usually located in town, but . . ."

"I don't need a lawyer. Not exactly."

Another silence. "I guess you're calling in the IOU." A sigh. "Burke's Justice doesn't come without cost, but it can save a man's life. What do you need?"

"Information about a man called the Controller. He runs a compound where *cassandra sangue* are held. I know he's in the Midwest."

"The Midwest is a big region."

"That's why I need help from people who live in that part of Thaisia."

"'Where *cassandra sangue* are held'? You make it sound like a prison."

"Prisons have rules about how inmates can be treated. No one is monitoring what happens to those girls."

Uneasy silence. "Look, Doug. I've never gone to one of those places. Gods, I have a wife and two kids, not to mention a car payment, and we're hoping to buy a house. I couldn't afford it. But this might not be a good time to be spending your money on a prophecy."

"Why is that?"

"Client of mine. He's not guilty of all the charges against him, but he's not innocent either. I haven't been able or willing to guarantee he won't go to prison for a while, so he went to visit a man called Mr. Smith who has ways of predicting such things. But when I met him after that very expensive meeting, all my client did was complain that he'd been cheated, that the girl hadn't told him anything about himself or his spot of trouble, had just screamed about wind and fire. Mr. Smith tried to pass it off as metaphor for a heated debate in court, but when my client threatened to raise a fuss, Mr. Smith returned half the fee. Lately there have been whispers that the places claiming to have girls who can see the future are just scams."

"Has it occurred to anyone that the girls *are* seeing the future? That the wind and fire are an accurate prophecy?"

"Oh, now, that's . . . Doug? What are you saying?"

"I'm saying if the man known as the Controller isn't found very soon, those prophecies will be accurate. The Midwest will burn, Pete, and the Others aren't interested in leaving survivors."

Gasps. "Why?"

"You've heard about the troubles? About the drugs called gone over wolf and feel-good? About that town that went crazy because of the tainted ground beef?"

"Sure, I . . . The police suspect *him*? Is there any proof?"

"Human law does not apply in this case. The *terra indigene* consider him an enemy, and they are going to hunt him down. How much of the Midwest survives that hunt will depend on how quickly they find him. Help me find him, Pete."

"I . . . How much time do we have?"

"When was your client going to trial?"

"Two weeks."

"Then we have less than that."

Another silence. "Is it just me, or are you calling in other IOUs for this?"

"I'm calling in all of them."

CHAPTER 26

On Sunday morning, the guests of the Lakeside Courtyard gathered behind the Liaison's Office, waiting for the bus that would take them to the train station for the journey home.

Moments after Blair drove up and opened the bus door, Meg stepped out of the office.

Something's wrong, Simon thought as he hurried toward her. Not a big wrong; she hadn't sounded an alarm. But something was bothering Meg.

Henry and Charlie noticed moments after he did, and moments after that, all the *terra indigene* leaders were watching her.

Meg trembled, but she faced the Others and said in a quiet voice, "We were taught a lot of things in the compound in order to provide accurate prophecies that could be understood by the Controller's clients. But we weren't taught about ourselves, and I think most of what we were taught was a lie. But the Walking Names weren't always careful about what they said around us. That's how I know that buying a cut of my skin is very expensive."

Simon looked at the bandage on the side of her left hand. The Others hadn't asked for the cut; the police had. But whatever she'd told Lieutenant Montgomery was the reason the police were working hard to locate the Controller.

<We're going to miss the train,> Blair warned.

Simon ignored him.

Joe Wolfgard looked at the other leaders before turning back to Meg. "We have some human money. We can harvest other things that humans covet to get more."

Meg shook her head. "I don't want money or things." She paused. "We're told we can't have a life like other humans. We're told we can't survive outside the compound. If it wasn't for my friend Jean, I would have believed the Walking Names. But Jean wasn't born in one of the compounds. She came from outside. She had a mother and a father and a baby brother. Someone like Phineas Jones took her away from her family and tried to turn her into property. But she never forgot, wouldn't let *them* forget that she'd had a name once, had a family just like they have families. She was my only friend. She told me about outside. And she used up some of her skin to help me escape. So this is what I want from you. You're going to find the Controller, one way or another. That's not prophecy, just . . . belief. You're going to find him and you're going to find that place. And when you do, I want you to save Jean, if you can. I want you to find a new place for her where she'll be safe and can have a life."

"You want her to come here?" Simon asked. Wasn't that what Meg wanted? To bring her friend to Lakeside? After all, *she* was safe here, had a life here.

"Only if Lakeside is the right place," Meg replied after a moment's thought. "It's the right place for me, but it might not be for her."

The *terra indigene* studied her, this human who didn't want gold or silver or gemstones or money. Finally Cheryl Hawkgard said, "We will try to save your friend."

"Thank you," Meg said. She went into the office and quietly closed the door.

The *terra indigene* hustled to load their carryalls into the bus. Blair took off for the train station as soon as he could close the bus door. After a brief discussion, Alan Wolfgard and Bobbie Beargard decided to ride back to the High Northeast with Charlie, so they loaded their gear in the back of the pickup. Alan wanted a last quick browse through Howling Good Reads and Bobbie went with him, leaving Simon alone with Charlie.

Smiling gently, the Crow said, "Don't absorb so much of what is human that you forget who you are. But if you must, do it for your own sake rather than for the benefit of the rest of us." He looked around. "This is a good place. Can I come back and visit again?"

"You will be welcome," Simon replied.

Alan returned with another bag of books. Even Bobbie had a couple she tucked in her carryall before he could see the covers.

After they were gone, Simon returned to Howling Good Reads and looked around. All the guests had taken advantage of shopping in a bookstore—and interacting with humans who chatted with them and recommended books—so there were a lot of empty spaces on the shelves. He and Vlad were going to have some work ahead of them to restock. Maybe he should get a cloth and wipe the shelves now that he could see them.

Was that too human?

He understood Charlie's warning, but he was a Wolf and always would be.

But would it be such a bad thing to be just a *little* more human? Just enough more?

Don't get too comfortable in this skin, he thought as he went into the stockroom and rolled a cart to the shelves. *Especially when there's no certainty you'll still want it a decade from now.*

Monty flipped the folder closed when Louis Gresh walked up to his desk.

The two men studied each other. Then Louis said, "Yesterday you and Captain Burke went to a meeting at the Courtyard. Since then, he's been on the phone and you've been working at your desk instead of being out on patrol. Burke's not always easy to read, but you've got the look of a man who knows there's a bomb and is trying to find it before the clock gives that final tick."

Monty said nothing.

"Not only that," Louis continued, "you're keeping your partner out of it with the captain's blessing, which means he knows how bad this will be if things go sideways."

"Something you want, Louis?"

"Let me help on the QT."

"Did Burke okay it?"

Louis smiled. "Okay what?"

Monty hesitated. The fewer people who knew the ultimatum the Others had given, the fewer people who might tell the wrong person. The Controller had clout with people in government and business. What if someone warned him as a way of garnering favor? What would happen to the Midwest—and the rest of Thaisia—if the man managed to escape and go to ground somewhere else?

But they weren't going to narrow down the target without taking chances. Not in the window of time Burke figured they had before the *terra indigene* began destroying the Midwest.

He wrote down the names of a dozen villages, towns, and cities, then handed the paper to Louis. "We're looking for private schools, institutions, or any other kind of place where blood prophets might be kept."

Louis gave the paper a little wave. "These located around the Great Lakes?"

"Lower Midwest."

Louis looked at him for a long time. "If this bomb goes off before you find what you're looking for, how much of Thaisia do we lose?"

"The whole Midwest Region."

"Gods above and below."

Monty watched Louis carefully fold the paper and put it in a pocket. The Midwest wasn't their jurisdiction. Government officials should be informed of the threat, and the rest should be up to the Midwest's governor to locate the Controller and stop the actions that were adding to the ever-present tension between humans and Others.

But that assumed the Midwest's governor wasn't a client of the man the *terra indigene* wanted killed. That wasn't an assumption the humans who would get caught in the destruction could afford to make. It wasn't an assumption *he* could afford to make.

Clock is ticking, Monty thought. He hoped Dominic Lorenzo would come through and give him the list of private hospitals or other medical institutions that could hide a compound that matched the description Meg had provided. He hoped that what he was doing would give all of them the chance at a better future.

He hoped he found the answer before the bomb made of wind and fire destroyed the Midwest.

CHAPTER 27

On Firesday morning, Monty waited at the bus stop and listened to the people around him.

"Crows gathering around schools and medical facilities in the Midwest. Why would they do that?"

"Spying. That's what I heard."

"Spying on what? Looking to snatch food from the children or pick through the trash is more like it."

"All those people arrested for shooting *birds*. It's not right."

Not wanting to get entangled in the discussion by pointing out that killing crows was against the law, Monty felt relieved when the bus arrived.

Gods above and below. Shooting crows. Those Midwest towns might as well paint a target in the town square and have the government stand there shouting, *We have something to hide!*

The police force grapevine could be an effective tool. However, in this case, some people who shouldn't have had gotten wind of the hunt. But the Lakeside police were discovering the grapevine had also revealed unexpected allies in other regions. Much of what Captain Burke received was speculation or rumor about halfway houses for girls with addictions, but it was becoming clear that many police stations across Thaisia were looking at Lakeside and wondering if the Chestnut Street station might provide a new model for working with the *terra indigene*. After all, Lakeside had come through that recent conflict with the Others with minimal casualties and damage to property.

It won't mean anything if the east and west of Thaisia are divided by a scorched hole where the Midwest used to be, Monty thought. *But we'll keep trying. Clock is ticking, so we have to keep trying.*

"Gods, Doug. What did you get me into?"

"Problem, Pete?"

"You're damn right there's a fucking problem! Someone e-mailed my wife's itinerary to me to show they can find her at any hour of the day. Someone sent me a photo of my children's school and a close-up of children on the playground during recess, with a black X over my kids! Someone doesn't want me asking questions."

"You want to back out?"

"The time to back out was when you called. But I don't want to come home one day and find my wife and kids . . ." A choking sound. Then a shuddering effort to regain control. "I'm pretty sure I located Mr. Smith's compound. It's not in my town. It's in the nearest city, which is on the main rail line."

"We've been looking at the towns with railway access too."

"I sent you an e-mail with all the information I have about Mr. Smith and his business. Here in town, there's a facility that specializes in group housing for 'those who can't live on their own.' It looks legitimate, but the administrator became 'very busy, must dash' as soon as I asked about blood prophets. In one of the farming hamlets nearby, there's a government-run orphanage. It has a small medical facility attached to it and is the place girls who get themselves in trouble go when they're giving up the babies."

"Sounds like a good place to run a breeding program for *cassandra sangue.*"

Stunned silence. "What did you say?"

"Nothing you heard." A long pause. "Pete? How are you set with gas coupons?"

A hesitation. "Eve and I have been conserving fuel since I got your call earlier in the week. I can spare a few gallons of gas from the family budget if you need me to drive somewhere and take a look around."

"No, I want you to pack up your family and come to Lakeside. Now."

"You said we had time. Doug, there's still time—"

"To find someone waiting for you when you get home?"

"I . . . I need to cancel the newspaper, put a hold on the mail, hand off my cases or at least contact—"

"Someone who will tell the people who sent you your wife's itinerary and pictures of your children at recess that you're going to disappear?"

"Gods." Rough breathing. "Will . . . Will we be able to come back here?"

"Hopefully I'll be able to answer that by the time you get here. And Pete? Keep your eyes open. If you think you're being followed, head into the wild country and make enough racket to draw the attention of whatever is out there. Right now, your wife and kids have a better chance with the Others than they do with whoever knows you were asking questions."

"I'll call you when we get to Lakeside."

"Check in along the way. And before you leave, send me an e-mail with the make and license number of your car."

"All right." A pause. "Doug? Do you think it's all worth it?"

"I think we'll know in a few days, one way or the other."

CHAPTER 28

The following Windsday morning, Monty entered Burke's office and closed the door. "I think we found the compound owned by the Controller."

Burke gave him a long look. "Call Dr. Lorenzo. Tell him it's time for whatever input he's willing to give. And send a car around to pick up Simon Wolfgard. This time he needs to come to us."

Monty went back to his desk, made the call to Dominic Lorenzo, and sent Kowalski to pick up the Wolf. Then he sat back, almost swaying with fatigue despite the early hour.

For several days he, Louis Gresh, and Burke had been running on strong coffee, sketchy meals, and little sleep as they tried to narrow down the possible places where the Controller's compound could be located. An incident room had been set up at the station and was kept locked. Not that a lock was needed. The sign that read RESERVED FOR DOUGLAS BURKE was enough to make other officers in the Chestnut Street station avoid that corridor as much as possible.

Everyone at the station knew something was going on and it was something big, something dangerous. Everyone knew he and Louis were involved and their respective teams were not. Everyone knew it somehow involved the *terra indigene*.

Everyone knew something bad was about to happen, but not even the station's chief had asked Captain Burke for an explanation—especially after the report came in that Burke's friends were run off the road on their way to Lakeside. The two adults and two children suffered minor injuries and were now in some undisclosed location. The assailants, however, suffered fatal injuries when the roadway suddenly turned to quicksand and buried them up to the chest before hardening again.

It was understood that the local wildlife didn't find the unexpected feast until after Burke's friends had been taken from the area.

Louis sat on the corner of Monty's desk and leaned toward him. "Do you think we defused this bomb?"

"Not completely," Monty replied, rubbing his eyes. "But it will be a smaller one because of what we've done."

Hearing the soft scuff of a shoe, Meg spun away from the front counter and hurried into the sorting room, hoping Simon finally had some news. But it was Jane, the Wolfgard bodywalker, who stood in a spot where she wouldn't be seen by someone entering the office.

"Hello, Jane. Is there something I can do for you?" Then she thought of one reason why Jane would come up to the office. "Sam! Is he sick? Is he hurt?"

Jane shook her head. "Sam is fine. Did you . . . have an itch?"

Meg sagged against the sorting table. "No. When I saw you, it was the first thing that popped into my head."

"Prairie dog thoughts. They can pop up right under your nose."

The image made her smile.

It felt like she hadn't smiled in days. It felt like all she'd done was wait for news, for answers, for . . . something. The *terra indigene*, on the other hand, had worked and played and hunted as if nothing was happening. Sure, more of the Wolves were patrolling the Courtyard's boundary, more Crows were on lookout, more Hawks were soaring, but the Others weren't waiting the way the humans were waiting. They were ready. Until it was time to act, they would simply live.

"I was wondering about the Wolf cookies," Jane said.

"Did you want something in particular?" Meg asked. "Tess is going to e-mail the order to Eamer's Bakery today. I've asked for smaller cookies for the puppies. The beef-flavored cookies were the most popular, and—"

"The people-shaped cookies," Jane said.

"Oh." Meg hesitated. "I don't think it's a good idea to have people-shaped cookies anymore."

Jane looked disappointed. "They were useful."

"Oh. They could still make chamomile cookies in a different shape," Meg said.

"Small cookies? I've been giving Skippy a little piece each morning, and it calms him down just enough for his brain to work properly. We've all noticed the difference."

"I'll put in the request."

"Thank you." Jane shifted from one foot to the other. "Are there any humans working in the bookstore today?"

"I don't know. But Merri Lee is working at A Little Bite. Did you want to talk to her?"

"No." The word was snapped out too quickly, followed by a little whine. "No, I just thought, while I was up here . . ."

Merri Lee, Ruthie, and Theral had grown up watching scary "wolfman" movies, and they all agreed the real thing was a lot more terrifying. But they also agreed that the Others shouldn't feel reluctant to shop in their own Market Square just because a few humans worked there—especially the *terra indigene* who *couldn't* go to the human stores because they couldn't pass for human and would likely cause a panic if people saw them.

Having someone like Jane Wolfgard, a respected bodywalker, go into Howling Good Reads and purchase a book when Merri Lee or Ruthie was at the checkout counter, or sit in A Little Bite to have a drink and a snack, might make other *terra indigene* feel easier about doing the same thing.

And anything that helped each side accept the other had to be a good thing. Especially now.

Meg touched the side of her head. "No one will mind furry ears."

Jane studied her, then nodded and went out the back door.

Hearing the Crows who were on watch *caw*ing at someone's arrival, Meg returned to the counter in time to see a patrol car pull in and continue up the access way. Then she heard someone come in from the back and turned, thinking it was Jane needing a little more reassurance.

Not Jane. Simon crossed the sorting room and stopped at the Private doorway.

"They found the enemy," he said. "I'm going to the Chestnut Street station to talk to Montgomery and the other police."

"All right." Suddenly cold, Meg hugged herself. "Will you tell me . . ."

Simon cocked his head. "Tell you what?"

"I don't know."

He waited a moment, then said, "I have to go."

Gone.

She waited and watched until the patrol car pulled out of the delivery area and turned right on Main Street, heading toward the Chestnut Street station.

She held out her hands, studied her arms—and wondered if she should be relieved or alarmed that she didn't feel even the faintest prickle anywhere.

Caught in an uneasy sleep, Jean grimaced, and a split on her lower lip reopened, turning dream into a prophecy that flowed like a movie clip.

The ground shook. The wind roared. The Walking Names shouted and pleaded and screamed. Walls were sprayed with blood, and limbs ripped from bodies littered the corridors.

The girls, locked in their cells, shivered and cried.

Then her door slammed open and she saw . . .

Jean opened her eyes—and she smiled.

Dominic Lorenzo looked haggard when he walked into the incident room at the Chestnut Street station. He studied Monty, Louis, and Burke before sagging into a chair. "Do you realize what we've stirred up? How many influential people have called to rattle the hospital administrators about my suitability to practice medicine?"

Burke sat down opposite Lorenzo and gave the man a fierce-friendly smile. "Oh, I wouldn't worry too much about that, Doctor. Lakeside's police commissioner has been dealing with similar calls about me and mine. I think the people complaining about you now will be singing a different tune very shortly."

"Why?"

Burke's smile became fiercer. "Benevolent ownership."

"A necessary evil."

"What about breeding farms? What about breeding girls with an eye to enhancing their ability to see prophecy? What about breeding them until the offspring are so sensitive they *can't* survive without that benevolent ownership?"

Lorenzo stared at Burke. "That's monstrous."

Monty studied the doctor. "But it also confirms something you've begun to suspect, doesn't it?"

Lorenzo opened his briefcase, pulled out a thick stack of papers, and didn't reply for a minute. Finally, "The people who use these compounds and buy prophecies aren't going to let that kind of information come to light. Breeding farms for those girls? None of those people would survive the firestorm of *that* kind of scandal."

"Which is why I'm not planning to give the information to other humans," Burke said. "I'm going to give it to the *terra indigene*."

"Give what to the *terra indigene*?" Simon Wolfgard asked as he and Vlad Sanguinati walked into the room.

"We'll get to that," Burke said. "Lieutenant?"

"We're reasonably sure we've found the city where the Controller's estate and the compound are located," Monty said, walking over to the map on one of the incident boards.

Can't pass for human today, Monty thought, glancing at Simon and Vlad. *Neither of them. There's just too much predator showing through.*

"What about you?" Simon said, looking at Lorenzo.

The doctor hesitated, then pulled out his own map and unfolded it. "I've talked to colleagues, acquaintances, and hospital administrators. I've marked the places where blood prophets have been given some medical care. I want to point out that most of the facilities who brought the girls in for treatment are known in their communities and are run openly."

Simon and Vlad said nothing. They just looked at each map. Then Simon opened up another map and set it on the table next to Lorenzo's.

"What have you marked?" Monty asked, noting the same towns that were marked on each map.

"Crows talk to the Crowgard," Vlad said. "So they obliged when asked to look at human places. We made note of the places where humans shot them."

"The towns where people shot the crows are the same towns we suspect of having compounds that hold *cassandra sangue*," Monty said.

Simon nodded. "Your maps confirm the conclusions reached by the *terra indigene* in the Midwest."

"Now what?" Burke asked.

"Now Lieutenant Montgomery, Dr. Lorenzo, and I will board the westbound train that leaves at two thirty this afternoon and meet up with the *terra indigene* who will settle things with the enemy."

Lorenzo shot to his feet. "I'm not going anywhere!"

Simon and Vlad both smiled, showing their fangs.

"You'll go because you're a human bodywalker who is interested in blood prophets, and you'll want to help the ones who survive," Simon said.

"The ones who—"

"And the lieutenant will go because the police will want to talk to one of their own instead of the earth natives who will be present in that town," Simon continued.

"And you?" Monty asked. "Why will you be going?"

"To keep a promise."

Lorenzo shook his head. "No. It's hard enough to have gathered this information, knowing what—"

"Have you heard about the other shipment of tainted meat?" Vlad asked. His voice was friendly; his eyes were dark ice. "Two delivery trucks full of the stuff. One had an odd accident and managed to tip over in such a way that the driver wasn't hurt but the back door popped open. The driver got into the other vehicle and it drove off, leaving all that tempting meat just lying on the road. Funny thing about the Sanguinati. About all the *terra indigene*, but my people in particular. We recognize the blood prophets as not prey. The *cassandra sangue* are Namid's creation, both wondrous and terrible. We don't drink their blood. Other earth natives don't eat their flesh. And we can recognize it even when it's ground up and mixed with beef in an attempt to hide what it is."

Louis groaned. Lorenzo sat down heavily. Monty braced his hands on the table, feeling sick. Burke stared at Simon and Vlad.

"Are you sure more girls were used to make that meat?" Burke asked.

"We're sure," Vlad said. He folded up the map Simon had brought and tucked it under his arm.

"Train leaves at two thirty," Simon said. "If you want humans to have any say in what comes next, don't be late." He and Vlad walked out of the room.

Silence. Then Burke said, "Lieutenant? You and Dr. Lorenzo should go home and pack a bag. Doctor, Commander Gresh will drive you home and take you to the train station. Lieutenant, have Kowalski drive you. I'll clean up here." After a moment, he added quietly, "May Mikhos watch over all of us."

Mikhos was the guardian spirit for police, firefighters, and medical personnel. Monty suspected his name would be invoked many times over the next few days.

———

Simon reached for the carryall but didn't pick it up.

He didn't want to go. It was important and necessary, and a few months ago, he'd gone to the Midwest Region to meet with leaders and had dumped Meg and Sam together with barely a second thought. Now he wouldn't hear her voice for days, wouldn't have the comfort of her scent. Now he would miss her.

He picked up the carryall, walked out of his apartment, got into the van, and looked at Vlad, who was driving him to the train station.

"You'll keep an eye on everything?" he said.

"She'll be fine, Simon," Vlad replied. "Meg won't come to harm while you're away."

He sighed. "How did things get so stirred up?"

"It's not the first time. Won't be the last. If the shifters and Sanguinati who live around humans can't get things settled, the older forms of *terra indigene* and the Elementals will. They always do." Vlad pulled up near the back door of the Liaison's Office. "Go inside and say good-bye. Give her a hug."

Simon hesitated. "That wouldn't be too human?"

"No," Vlad replied quietly. "That would be a friend in any skin."

He went inside. Meg was in the sorting room turning the pages of the *Lakeside News*. But he didn't think she was absorbing any images because when she saw him she looked preoccupied—and scared.

"It will be dangerous for you to be on a train now," she said.

He cocked his head. "Are you sensing something?"

"Nothing. Maybe I've been drinking too much chamomile tea. Jane said the chamomile cookies have helped Skippy's brain not to skip. Maybe the tea is blocking my ability to feel . . . something."

"Or maybe there's nothing to feel." Had to get moving and get to the station. "Meg? Want a hug? It's a friend thing to do when someone is leaving."

When she nodded, he put his arms around her, pulling her against him. Her arms went around him and held on.

He breathed in the scent of her until Vlad said, <Simon? Time to go.>

He eased back and looked into her gray eyes. "Don't cause too much trouble for Vlad and Henry."

She sputtered. "I don't cause trouble!"

That made him laugh. He walked out with her still sputtering. And the scent of her on his clothes was a comfort.

———

Monty's phone rang.

He hesitated, almost let the answering machine pick up. But habit made him reach for the phone. "Hello?"

"You did it on purpose, didn't you?" Elayne's voice, tearful and strident.

"Did what?"

"You sabotaged Nicholas's speaking engagements in Talulah Falls and Lakeside—that's what you did!"

Monty rocked back on his heels. He couldn't be hearing what he was hearing. "Elayne, have you paid any attention to what's been happening in Talulah Falls? No one is getting in or out of there yet. And considering the problems they're having and the trouble the Humans First and Last movement has already caused in Lakeside, it's not surprising your boyfriend's speaking engagements were canceled."

"Because *you* didn't want to be shown up for the jealous, small-time man you are!"

"Is Lizzy there?" He didn't have time for this nonsense, but he'd like to hear his daughter's voice.

"No, she is not here!"

More and more strident, which made Monty wonder if Elayne thought Nicholas Scratch was as wonderful as he'd first appeared to be.

"Elayne, I have to go."

"By trying to ruin Nicholas, you're also ruining Lizzy's chance to have something better. You realize that, don't you?"

He felt a pang in his heart, even if he didn't believe for a minute that Scratch could offer Lizzy a better home than he could.

"I have to go," he said again. As he hung up, he heard Elayne screaming, "What's so important that you can't give me a minute to talk about your daughter?"

His hand hovered over the phone. They wouldn't have talked about Lizzy. Whenever Elayne claimed that she wanted to talk about their daughter, the conversation quickly became the list of what Elayne couldn't have because of his inadequacies.

"What's so important?" He repeated her words as he stared at the phone. "I have to go help the Others murder a town full of people."

CHAPTER 29

Throughout the Midwest, the Elementals moved toward the town that held the enemy's lair.

Air flirted with Earth, tickling and teasing until Earth twitched—and left humans trembling in their insignificant houses.

In the towns where crows had been shot, Fire embraced the utility poles as he passed by, silencing electricity and telephones by the time Water arrived to deliver a punishing rain.

Tornados chased cars and trucks, sometimes catching them and tossing them high in the air, sometimes letting them go with nothing more than the lightest brush of warning.

Lightning struck with vicious accuracy, and Fire and Air danced in the houses of the men with guns before galloping away on steeds who shattered the roads as they ran.

Finally the Elementals arrived at the place that held the enemy. Once they had the town surrounded, they stopped playing.

And the world held its breath while the Elementals and their steeds waited for the rest of the *terra indigene* to arrive.

The conductor escorting Monty, Dominic Lorenzo, and Simon said, "Our executive car isn't being used at the moment, so we thought you would appreciate the privacy."

Meaning the railway didn't want too many human passengers to realize a Wolf was on board, not when everyone was already stirred up and a minor conflict could swiftly become violent.

Monty looked at the leather chairs and the tables with padded bench seats. "Very nice. Who usually rides in this car?"

The conductor glanced nervously at Simon, who was poking around in the back of the car. "Men who do a lot of traveling and use the hours they commute to keep up with their work. Over here is a small kitchen area, stocked with sandwiches and some other foods and drinks. There is also a bar."

"People pay on the honor system?" Monty asked.

"Oh, no. Food and drink are included in the ticket for this car."

Monty thanked the conductor and went to the back of the car to find out what intrigued Simon.

"Toilet and sink," Simon said, pointing to one door. He opened the door on the opposite side. "What is that?" He pointed to something that looked like a porcelain half-barrel with a seat. Water taps and a handheld shower attachment were secured to the wall behind it.

Dominic joined them. "It's a little shower stall."

Monty returned to the front of the car. Food, drinks, comfortable seats, and workplaces. Even an adequate washroom so a man traveling overnight could arrive fresh to a morning meeting. And privacy. "How much do you think it costs to ride in this car?"

"More than you or I would want to pay," Lorenzo replied as he and Simon joined Monty. "Better take our seats. Feels like the train is leaving the station."

They stowed their bags on the overhead racks and found seats.

Once the train reached the open land beyond Lakeside, Simon said thoughtfully, "What kind of humans would use this car?"

"The conductor said it was men who needed to work while they're traveling, so I imagine it's mostly businessmen and government officials," Monty said.

Simon nodded. "Businessmen and officials. And humans who don't want too many other people to notice where they're going?"

"Why would they care if someone noticed . . ." Dominic looked at his companions and didn't finish the question.

Monty stared at Simon. "You think that someone who can afford to purchase a ticket for this car can also afford to buy a prophecy?"

"Just because a person uses the executive car doesn't mean he or she also goes to one of the compounds for a prophecy," Dominic protested.

"No, but I don't think the people going to those compounds do so openly," Monty replied. "So while not every person who uses the executive car buys prophecies, it's a safe bet that most people who buy prophecies would use the executive car." He looked at Simon. "What do you think?"

Simon stood. "I think I'm hungry, and I want to see if those sandwiches are worth eating. And I think the railroad wouldn't waste fuel to pull an empty car, so I'm wondering where the humans who had tickets for this trip were heading."

Simon didn't think the sandwiches were any better than what could be bought in the dining car, but maybe it was the convenience of not having to wait in line that made the food special.

Or maybe the fancy food had been replaced when the humans who had tickets for this car didn't show up. Didn't matter to him. Montgomery and Lorenzo had insisted they preferred the chicken sandwiches, leaving the beef ones for him, so they'd all eaten their fill.

No, it didn't matter to him if there was a fancy car, but someone was going to feel Elliot's wrath—and his teeth—when Lakeside's consul found out he'd been relegated to regular passenger cars with all the stinky smells while human government officials rode in this special car that had the pleasing scent of leather and food whenever you wanted it.

As far as Simon was concerned, the value of this private car was the fact that the passengers would be easy for the *terra indigene* to track even if they tried to hide their faces or lied about who they were. You might get away with lying to some kinds of earth natives, but that just gave the rest of them more reason to pay attention.

Couldn't always ask the Crows to keep watch. That would be too obvious, and they were more vulnerable—and easily distracted by shiny. The Sanguinati? Definite possibility. After all, train stations were good hunting grounds for Vlad's kin.

After the meal, all three of them pulled books out of their bags. Simon noticed that Montgomery had a book by Alan Wolfgard. Considering where they were going, he wasn't sure that was the best choice of story for a human, but he offered no opinion. Humans had remarkably shallow memories. Whenever the *terra indigene* destroyed a city and reclaimed the land, humans wailed and claimed they didn't understand. How could they not understand something so simple? If you break the agreements with the *terra indigene*, the *terra indigene* will strike back and strike hard. When would humans realize they always started the fights that would kill them?

He glanced at the two men sitting on the other side of the aisle. He didn't think either of them had shallow memories, so maybe it was good that they would see what the Others could do. Maybe it was smart to let them see exactly what stood against them if their people started a fight.

Meg stared at the silver razor she'd placed on the sorting room table. *Cs759*. A designation for disposable property. Except *cassandra sangue* shouldn't be property, shouldn't be disposable.

"Meg?"

She looked up when Merri Lee walked into the sorting room.

"All this trouble started because I didn't want to go back to the compound, because I wanted to be more than property," Meg said.

"What, nobody made any choices but you? You know better than that." Merri Lee pointed at the razor. "What choice are you making now?"

"I don't know. I want to help Simon."

"Do you need to cut? Is there some prophecy pushing at you that you think is about him?"

"No, but . . ." Simon wouldn't want her to cut, not without a reason. Was being worried that her friend might get hurt enough of a reason?

Merri Lee walked over to the phone and picked up the receiver. "Do you know the number for his mobile phone?"

"Yes."

"Call him, Meg. Leave a message on his voice mail. Then come over to the apartment. I'll show you how to make spaghetti. That will help distract both of us. Ruth and Theral are bringing ice cream and chocolate to my place this evening, and we'll all watch movies that give us an excuse to cry."

Meg took the receiver. "What do I say?"

"Tell him you called because you were thinking about him. I think he would like that." Merri Lee smiled. "I'll wait outside."

When she heard the back door close, Meg dialed Simon's number. She knew she'd gotten his voice mail when she heard the growled order to leave a message.

So she left her message, closed up the office, and joined Merri Lee for an evening of distraction.

Lorenzo was asleep on one of the padded benches that folded out to a bed. Simon had spent the past few hours staring out the window and occasionally pretending to read. And Monty, halfway through the thriller by Alan Wolfgard, wondered how many humans had read *terra indigene* books. If nothing else, the story, with its devious, murderous human villains, provided insight into how the Others perceived people. After meeting the humans who worked in the Courtyard, would a different kind of human appear in some of Alan's stories? How many times would a human female beat off an attacker with a broom or a teakettle?

At a station about an hour away from the Midwest border, a man entered the executive car. Three-piece suit and briefcase. A little portly and very well groomed. He jerked to a stop when he saw Monty and Simon.

"I think you're in the wrong part of the train," the man said. The pompous tone produced a growl from Simon. Instead of backing down, the sound seemed to goad the man into adding, "*This* is a *private* car."

"Yes, sir, we're aware of that," Monty said courteously. "And we are in the correct car."

"Are you? Are you indeed! Let's see your tickets."

Monty stood, stepped into the aisle, took out his ID holder, and opened it. And watched the man pale. "Now, sir. I'd like to see your ticket."

"Mine?" the man blustered. "Why should I show you mine?"

"Because I'm a police officer, and I asked. Or I can request that the train be held while I make inquiries at the ticket station and confirm that you are, in fact, entitled to use this car."

"You can't do that!"

"If he can't, I can," Simon growled.

Monty didn't have to look at the Wolf to know Simon no longer passed for human. He could see the fear in the man's eyes.

The man pulled out a ticket, waved it in front of Monty, and put it away before anyone could take a good look at it.

Monty didn't insist on seeing the ticket again, and he didn't ask the man to provide a name and home address. He didn't think either of those things would be important today.

He put away his ID and sat down, allowing the man to put his luggage on the rack and take a seat.

Simon didn't like the human who had invaded the private car. Didn't like the look of him, the feel of him, the smell of him. He couldn't put a paw on why letting this human live offended him so much, but if such a man got near any member of Lakeside's human pack, and especially Meg, he wouldn't hesitate to rip into him and tear out the liver before the heart took its last beat.

<*Caw!* Message for the Lakeside Wolfgard.>

He looked out the window, but he didn't see the Crow. <I'm the Wolfgard.>

<Train will stop soon. Wolves will meet you and your humans, drive you the rest of the way.>

<Is the track broken?> he asked.

<Not if the train stops and goes home. Air is riding Tornado and will be watching.>

Wouldn't just be this train or this station. The *terra indigene* would have closed off all escape from the Midwest until the enemy had been hunted down and destroyed. And in their own way, the Others were protecting the humans who might otherwise be caught up in the killing.

The conductor came into the car a few minutes later. "Last stop, gentlemen. Please prepare to depart."

"Last stop?" the businessman said, leaning into the aisle. "What do you mean last stop? I have a ticket for—" He stopped, as if reluctant to have a policeman and a Wolf overhear his destination.

"Uncertain weather conditions have made it inadvisable to continue," the conductor said. "You or your company will be credited for the part of the ticket not used."

"So this is the railway's decision?" The man sounded angry. "What happens if the train continues on to its original destination?"

"The vultures will feast for days," Simon said.

The conductor moved with control as he retreated from the car. The businessman stank of fear.

Moving carefully to avoid exciting a predator was a sensible response from the conductor. The fear of being turned into carrion was an understandable, and pleasing, reaction from the businessman.

The train pulled into the station. Simon looked at Monty and shook his head. When Monty resumed his seat, he said, <Crows?>

<Here.>

<There is a human who will leave the car I'm in.>

<There are many humans leaving.>

<But there will be only one from this car. Watch him.>

<We cannot follow him far. We will ask other *terra indigene* for help.>

<Good. And tell your leaders about him. Let all the Crows know this human should not be trusted.>

<We will tell them.>

Satisfied with that, Simon pulled his carryall off the rack as soon as the businessman left the car.

"Unless I totally misread the map, we still have a ways to go," Monty said. "Hours of travel, in fact."

"Yes," Simon replied. "But this is as far as the train will go. Come on. We're being met."

As soon as they stepped off the train, they heard the cawing. The Crows weren't making any effort to hide their interest in the businessman, which was drawing the attention of other humans. Flustered, the man hurried into the station, where the Crows couldn't follow. But at the doorway, dust and debris suddenly swirled and resettled.

Simon, Monty, and Lorenzo joined the passengers flowing into the station, but Simon immediately led the two men out the other set of doors to the parking lot. The minivan wasn't any different from other vehicles, but the two males standing beside it looked too dangerous to be human, despite a clear effort to hold that shape.

He nodded to the Wolves.

<We don't need to know your humans,> they said.

He thought Montgomery and Lorenzo would have liked knowing the names of their new companions, but the Wolves didn't want to be that sociable, so he said nothing.

"Looks like the businessman evaded the Crows," Lorenzo said, stalling a moment before getting into the minivan.

Simon wasn't sure if he heard concern or relief in the doctor's voice. Humans understood so little. "It doesn't matter now if he evades the Crows," he told Lorenzo. "Until he stops breathing, he can't hide from Air."

CHAPTER 30

They drove for several hours before they turned onto an access road that wasn't used by humans. A short time later, the minivan pulled up within sight of the compound, at a spot where Joe Wolfgard waited for them.

The Wolves who had been their drivers and escorts got out and joined their leader.

"Stay here," Simon told Montgomery and Lorenzo. Then he got out of the minivan and approached Joe.

"This isn't your territory," Joe said. "We appreciate the help you gave us to locate the enemy, but this isn't your fight."

"Not my territory, not my fight," Simon agreed. "But a common enemy."

"Yes," Joe said. He hesitated, as if trying to decide what should be said. "I was one of the leaders who made a promise to your Meg."

"I made a promise too."

Joe nodded. "When the enemy is dead, you can come in and hunt for the promise. Will that satisfy your Meg?"

That will depend on the outcome, Simon thought. But he said, "That will satisfy her."

Needing to know what was happening, Monty stepped down from the minivan. The Wolves had left the van's parking lights on. That probably wasn't for the Others' benefit, since they all seemed to have excellent night vision. He thought it was considerate of them to provide light for their human guests. Then he saw them and wished they hadn't been considerate.

Three of the Wolves had stripped off jackets and shirts and then shifted their torsos into a furred and muscled shape that accommodated heads that were fully Wolf. They looked at Monty and growled. Then they ran toward the compound.

"Gods above and below," Lorenzo breathed as he stepped down beside Monty.

"I'm not sure the gods are going to listen to us today," Monty said as Simon tipped his head back and howled.

Earth, riding Twister, smashed through a part of the compound's wall, and the Wolves followed, slaughtering everyone in their path. Water followed on Fog, blinding the humans who guarded the gates of the enemy's lair, leaving them vulnerable to the Crows, Hawks, and Owls. Air shook the buildings and rattled all the windows, finding the tiniest openings. The Sanguinati, in smoke form, followed Air. They surrounded the security guards armed with guns, drinking enough blood to render them unconscious. Shifting into human form, they opened the doors for the Wolves.

And then things got messy.

The ground shook. The wind roared.

Jean sat up in bed. Her cell wasn't near any of the main corridors of the building, but she could still hear the Walking Names shouting and pleading and screaming.

She reached out and pushed the light switch on the wall. Once her eyes adjusted, she studied the dresser.

Most of the drawers held clothing or items for personal hygiene. But one drawer had a lock, and the Walking Names kept the key. It was just another way to tease and torment the girls.

She stood, then waited a moment to let her damaged foot accept her weight. A few shuffled steps took her from bed to dresser. She ignored the screams outside her cell and pulled the drawer open. Then she picked up the folding razor.

Pretty flowers on one side of the silver handle. A lie.

The plain designation, *cs747*, on the other side. Truth.

The ground shaking, the wind roaring, the screams, and the drawer that should have been locked but wasn't. She knew what they meant.

"It's the end," she whispered.

Holding the razor, Jean went back to her bed and sat down to wait.

The Controller swallowed another dose of gone over wolf, slapped a fresh magazine into his pistol, then ran through a corridor filled with nightmares that would make the dark gods rejoice.

A Wolf turned toward him. He fired into its mouth and kept running, barely able to restrain his own howl of triumph as his enemy fell.

Had to get to the special room. Had more weapons there. Had *victory* there. It had taken three cuts on that bitch *cs747* to get enough useful images to ensure his escape. He hadn't told his staff about the attack; the chaos and slaughter were necessary for his own survival. Staff, like prophets, could be replaced. But the knowledge and skill he could offer the Humans First and Last movement were irreplaceable.

He fired again and again, hitting his own people, hitting the Others. What did it matter? He was glorious, invincible. He was the answer humans had been waiting for!

He rushed into the room that held the key to his freedom. As he stumbled over a smoldering body, he saw the automatic rifle nearby, saw the spent casings littering the floor. The weapon he'd counted on was useless!

Movement at the corner of his eye. He turned, firing his pistol at the blaze that suddenly surrounded his torso. Smoke covered his face and acquired fangs that sank into his neck. Released by Fire, the Controller stumbled forward before being knocked back when something with a Panther's head swiped at his belly, ripping it open. As he fell, a Wolf grabbed his wrist, biting through bone and charred flesh while the Panther bit through his other arm.

Then the vampire, Wolf, and Panther screamed in rage and ran out of the room, juiced with a double dose of gone over wolf, while the Controller lay on the floor, burned, bleeding, broken. Dying.

Understanding.

That bitch *cs747*. Somehow she'd managed to tell him only part of what she'd seen. Instead of showing him how to escape the attack, she'd identified images that would lead him into a trap.

That . . . bitch . . . *lied to him.*

———

Monty couldn't see much from where he stood with Lorenzo and Simon Wolf-gard. But he heard more than enough.

Gunfire, quickly silenced.

Screams, prolonged and terrible.

And all of it over too fast to give a human any hope.

Then the Wolves howled, and the fog vanished as if it had never been.

"Time for us to go in," Simon said as he started walking toward the compound.

Sirens in the distance, coming closer. Horses and riders moving toward the smashed gates of the compound.

"Should I wait at the gate and talk to the police?" Monty asked.

"The Elementals are going to deal with the police," Simon replied. "The Midwest *terra indigene* want all three of us over here." He pointed at one of the buildings.

Monty figured Dominic Lorenzo had seen some bad things as an emergency room doctor. As a police officer, he had seen some too. But neither of them had ever seen anything like what the *terra indigene* could—and would—do to humans they hated.

Walls splashed with blood. Floors slick with gore. But as he stood there, too stunned to move, he watched a Wolfman tear off the sleeves of a white medical coat and the shirt underneath, rip the arm off at the shoulder, and take a bite while another Wolf . . .

"He's eating that man's liver," Lorenzo said in a voice that had the calm of someone too shocked to feel.

One of the Wolves shifted back to a mostly human head and stood up. As he gave his bloody paws a couple of licks, Monty realized it was Joe Wolfgard.

Joe said, "It's good meat." Then he looked at Simon. "Do you hear them?"

"I hear them."

Monty suddenly noticed that Simon's ears were Wolf-shaped and furry. That change struck him as almost comical compared to everything around them. "What do you hear?" he asked.

"The girls."

<Let these humans have some of the girls,> Simon said.

<Why? > Joe protested. <We're taking these weapons away from humans. Why give some of them back?>

<Humans would call it a show of good faith. We can't let these girls loose in the wild, so we're going to need help. Give these humans a reason to help. I'll make sure the girls aren't used as weapons against us—even if I have to kill them.>

<Much will change in Thaisia because of this. We will want some help in return.>

<Yes,> Simon said. <Lakeside will help.> There would be plenty of time to explain to Lieutenant Montgomery and Dr. Lorenzo that he had included police and doctors in that promise. It was the only way to give the two men a reward for standing witness to the destruction of the enemy called the Controller.

Monty watched Joe's paws shift into something resembling hands. The Wolf held up two digits. "You can each take two girls."

"Six girls?" Monty said. "There are only six girls in the compound?" *Left alive?* he added silently.

"You can take six," Joe repeated.

"What about the other girls?" Lorenzo asked. "They'll need . . ."

"Six or none," Joe snarled. "That is five more than we promised the Lakeside Wolfgard."

"We'll take six," Simon said. He turned and walked away, his ears pricked toward a sound the humans couldn't hear.

Monty hesitated; then he and Lorenzo hurried past the Wolves who were feeding on one of the bodies and caught up to Simon. The Lakeside Wolf probably wanted to feed like the rest of the Others, but Simon, at least, recognized Monty and Lorenzo as more than meat, so it was safer to stay close to him.

A stairway led down. They followed it to more corridors. Simon stopped and looked at them. Red flickered in his amber eyes, and Monty wondered how much longer he would stay in control.

"I'm only here for one," Simon said. "The Lieutenant can choose three."

"What will happen to the rest of the girls?" Monty asked.

"That is for the Midwest *terra indigene* to decide."

"They think these girls are poison," Lorenzo protested.

"If you try to take more than five, the *terra indigene* will kill them all," Simon said. He stepped away from them and howled. Then his ears pricked and he strode down the corridor, slipping a little in the blood. He turned a corner and disappeared, leaving Monty and Lorenzo facing a corridor of locked doors.

"Gods above and below, how do we choose?" Lorenzo asked.

Monty picked up a set of keys lying next to a body and opened the door in front of him. The girl trying to hide in a corner of the room was maybe a year or two older than his daughter, Lizzy.

He thought about Meg Corbyn, struggling with an addiction to cutting that would most likely kill her while she was still young. Would she have felt compelled to cut if she'd lived in a place where she could receive some support, where her skin wasn't a commodity?

"We choose the young," he said, looking back at Lorenzo. "We choose the girls who will have the best chance of learning how to live in the world."

Handing the keys to Lorenzo, he walked into the cell and crouched in front of the girl.

"Hello," he said. "I'm Lieutenant Montgomery. I can help you leave this place. Would you like that?" He held out his hand and waited.

She stared at him for a long moment. Then she put her hand in his . . . and broke his heart.

Simon smashed the door open, then stopped.

They would have done this to Meg, he thought, baring his teeth in a snarl.

Instead of showing fear, which would have been sensible since he'd just smashed through a door and was showing his fangs, the female smiled and said, "You're Meg's Wolf."

Battered and scarred, she sat quietly on the narrow bed, her hands in her lap. One foot didn't look right, and he wondered if she could walk on her own. She smelled foul, as if the humans had stopped caring for her and didn't even let her try to care for herself.

"Jean?" He hoped she would deny it. How could he bring this creature back to Lakeside?

"Yes, I'm Jean. How is Meg?"

"She's fine." Reluctant, he stepped into the cell. "Meg is fine."

"I helped her escape."

"I know."

"I'd like to ask you for a favor."

He cocked his head to indicate he was listening.

"Don't kill me in this room. Take me beyond these walls that I've hated for as long as I can remember. Beyond the compound. And use this." She turned over her hands to reveal the silver razor. "They kept this locked in a drawer, so close yet out of reach, as a torment. But I knew that there would be a day when the Walking Names would forget to lock the drawer, and the next day Meg's Wolf would come." She brushed a finger over the razor. "So this is mine again. You should use it to kill me. If you bite me, it will make you sick."

He took a step closer, then sank down to sit on his heels. "I didn't come here to kill you. Meg asked me to take you away from here, to save you." When she didn't respond, he said what he thought Meg would want him to say. "She lives with us in the Lakeside Courtyard. You could come live—"

"No," she said quickly.

He puzzled over that for a moment. "You don't want to see Meg?" *He* wanted to see Meg.

"See her, yes, but not live in the same place." Jean leaned toward him. "Meg is a kind of pioneer. Do you know that word, Wolf?"

He nodded. "The first humans to invade our land. Our first taste of the new meat." He bared his teeth. "Meg *is not* a pioneer."

Jean had a distant look in her eyes. Meg had that look when she was recalling images.

"Trailblazer," Jean said. "Pathfinder. Someone who goes first, creating a path so that others can follow. Are those better words?"

"Better," he agreed. At least those words didn't mean an edible human.

"Meg needs to let go of the past." Jean waved a hand to indicate her body. "I'm too much of a reminder, and she'll think this happened to me because of her."

"Did it?"

"Some of it, but it would have happened anyway. When she looks in a mirror, she has enough reminders of the past. She doesn't need more."

"Then what would you like?" he asked. Strange female. Crazy female? No, not really. The eyes that looked back at him didn't belong to crazy.

"I don't know. The images don't make sense. Water falling. Mist rising. A sound that is a roar but not a roar. A jar of honey."

"That's where you're supposed to go?"

"Yes. If I didn't die here, that's what I saw as my future."

"Then it does make sense." Simon stood and held out his hand. "I know that place. The people who live there are called Intuits. They can help you—and I think you can help them too."

She held out the razor. "Hold on to that."

He took the razor and shoved it into his pocket, not asking why she would let it go now that she'd just regained possession of it. Meg got nervous when she didn't have control of her razor.

Meg the Pathfinder. The one who could show all of them the new path toward Thaisia's future? That was a large burden for one short female, but he would help her. Somehow. He just hoped Meg leading the way didn't mean all the blood prophets would do strange things to their hair.

"Time to go," he said.

Jean struggled to her feet. She could walk, but she couldn't have run away. Pity stirred in him. Had she seen what would happen to her after she helped Meg escape? Probably. And she'd said nothing so that Meg would run and not look back.

He let her hold his arm to help her walk. But he stopped at the doorway. "It's bad out there. Maybe you should close your eyes."

"Wolf," she said gently, "I've already seen it."

CHAPTER 31

Two Hawks drove them back to the train station. The Wolves and the Sanguinati had other tasks right now that took priority. That's what Monty and Lorenzo were told when they loaded the five terrified girls into the minivan, followed by Simon and the battered woman he'd rescued.

Monty had the impression that Simon knew exactly what tasks the Midwest Wolves and Sanguinati were performing, but the Wolf didn't volunteer any information and Monty didn't ask. He wasn't sure he could deal with anything else at the moment—and he knew he was going to have to deal with a lot more.

They boarded the same train, which had been held at the Midwest border and was now making the return trip to Lakeside. The conductor escorted them to the private car and assured them several times that *no one* would be permitted to join them for this trip.

Simon Wolfgard's doing. Monty hadn't thought beyond selecting the five *cassandra sangue* they could take with them and getting the girls away from the compound and the slaughter. Neither had Dominic Lorenzo. But the Wolf had realized that privacy would be vital for the return to Lakeside.

And when the train pulled out of the station and the girls began to scream, it was Simon who did the simple thing of lowering the blinds on the windows so the girls had to deal with new experiences only inside the private car.

———

"*Simon, it's Meg. I'm closing up the office now and . . . It's not the first time you've had to go away, but it feels . . . different . . . this time. Empty. I don't know. I want my friend to come home. I'm going over to Merri Lee's to watch movies that we can cry about, but I'd rather be able to hide behind you and watch a scary movie. When you're there, I don't see too much of the scary. Anyway, see you soon.*"

Simon put the mobile phone back in his pocket and left the toilet. He'd found the messages when they reached the train station—one from Vlad, assuring him that everything was fine at the Courtyard, and this one from Meg. The sound of her voice. Not as good as cuddling next to her and being petted, but close. And her comment about hiding from the scary had provided the clue he needed when the girls began screaming. He couldn't hide them from the scary—too many of them for that—so he closed the blinds to hide the scary from them.

As he returned to the front of the car, he glanced at Montgomery and Lorenzo. Damn humans were floundering like deer in deep snow, and that puzzled and annoyed him. He was the only one with decent teeth here, so he needed to be on guard, and *they* should be looking after the prophet pups. But they didn't seem to know how to do anything helpful.

Too much blood and half-eaten bodies at the compound? Had they seen too much? Lorenzo had grumbled about not being allowed to take more of the girls. By the time they arrived at the train station, he wasn't grumbling anymore. He looked sick and scared. So did Montgomery.

Simon watched the men as they moved to the back of the car. Maybe they were still worried about the girls they left behind and wondering what would happen to them. Joe Wolfgard and the other Midwest leaders had been concerned about allowing humans to take away some of Namid's terrible creations. After seeing the horrible things humans had done to some of the blood prophets, they didn't want to release any of the girls into the care of humans. But Simon had assured the Others that Montgomery and Lorenzo were dependable, even almost Wolflike in the way they cared about pups.

Now he wasn't so sure. Not that it mattered. Seeing the two men flounder, he'd made his own decisions about the girls and had spent the trip working out the details. By the time they reached Lakeside, there wouldn't be much for Montgomery and Lorenzo to do.

But there was one thing he could do now that might help Montgomery later.

Slipping out of his seat, Simon approached the table where Jean was laboring to write a letter.

"Could I have a sheet of paper and an envelope?" he asked.

She handed them over, along with the extra pen.

He took them and retreated. It was hard to be around Jean because he looked at her and saw what Meg's future would have been if she hadn't been brave enough to run away—and if Jean hadn't been brave enough to stay.

Standing at the back of the car with Lorenzo, Monty watched Simon fetch paper and pen from Jean before retreating to the counter in the kitchen area.

He'd disappointed the Wolf, and that stung. But he'd been too stunned by what he'd seen in the compound to function well. Now, nearing the end of the journey, he realized he'd left Simon to deal with all the practical care for six *cassandra sangue*.

It wasn't the slaughter that disturbed him so much, although he'd never forget it. It was the girls. All those girls. The young ones who were being trained but were yet unmarked and untried. The older teenagers who already had scars over entire areas of their bodies. The fourteen-year-old who had held out her arm and shown him her first scar—and looked as if she wasn't sure if she should be proud or ashamed of it.

Walking away from her had damn near killed him, but in the end, he and Lorenzo had chosen five girls between the ages of eight and eleven who had not been cut yet.

"What are we going to do with the girls?" Lorenzo asked, keeping his voice low. "I wasn't thinking past getting them out of that place, but now . . ."

"I wasn't thinking past that either," Monty replied.

"We can't put them into foster care. We can't put them into a city-run home either. If word got out—and you know it will—that *cassandra sangue* were living in a place like that, they'd be abducted before the staff knew what happened. We can't have twenty-four-hour security at foster homes. And do we need weekly checks to make sure no one cuts the girls for a prophecy?"

Monty looked at Simon, who had just licked the envelope and obviously didn't like the taste of the glue. The Wolf had gone outside to make a phone call every time the train stopped at a station. In between, he watched the girls and he watched Jean, who was writing on the paper Simon had picked up at a kiosk in one of the stations. He'd also dashed out at the next stop to pick up coloring books and crayons for the girls.

It hurt Monty's heart when he realized the girls were turning the pages of the coloring books to absorb the images and studying the colors of the crayons but didn't understand how to use them. It worried Lorenzo that the girls went in and out of a catatonic state, their senses overloaded by the journey despite efforts to limit their visual input.

That had shown Monty and Lorenzo what caretakers would be facing. And it gave them some understanding of what Meg Corbyn had faced when she ran away from the compound—and what she still faced daily by living with the stimulation of a place like the Courtyard.

"A sealed ward in a hospital wouldn't be much better than what they've known," Lorenzo said bitterly.

"Do you think that's what it will come to?"

"I don't see much alternative, do you?"

"No, I don't." Monty studied Simon for a moment before adding, "But I think he does."

When they reached the Lakeside train station, the Courtyard's small bus was waiting for them. Monty called Captain Burke to let him know they were back.

He'd expected the bus to go to the Courtyard, where he and Lorenzo would have to decide what to do with the girls. But Blair Wolfgard left the train station and headed north on River Road.

"Mr. Wolfgard?" Monty said. "Where are we going?"

Simon, sitting up front with Blair, just looked at him for a long moment before turning away.

Uneasy, Monty sat back, not sure what he could do if the Wolf had stopped trusting him. The girls looked frozen in place. Even Jean, who had maintained some ability to function throughout the journey, looked as if she'd reached her limit of new experiences. And he didn't think he and Lorenzo could stop whatever the Others decided to do.

When they reached the mainland half of Ferryman's Landing, Monty suddenly realized what Simon intended. The barge waited for them, and they left for Great Island as soon as the bus was secured on deck.

They didn't stop at the docks. They drove to a bed-and-breakfast and pulled into the lot.

Simon pointed to the five girls, then at the building. "Look at that place. Could you stay there for a while? This is outside, so you have to mind the adults looking after you or you could get hurt."

After some hesitation, the girls moved to look out the windows where they could see the B and B. Monty watched them rub their arms the way Meg did when a potential prophecy prickled her skin. But after a minute, they looked at Simon and nodded.

"Jean?" Simon asked.

She wrapped her arms around herself, shook her head, and closed her eyes. "Too much," she whispered.

Nodding as if that wasn't a surprise, Simon herded the girls off the bus. They were met by Steve Ferryman, who introduced everyone to Margaret Seely and Lara Herrera, the owners of the B and B.

Lorenzo made one effort to maintain control, but a warning look from Steve Ferryman silenced him, and Monty was well aware of the Crows gathering in the trees around the B and B—and Blair Wolfgard standing at the bus's open door, on guard. So it was only the two women and Simon Wolfgard who escorted the girls into the building.

Steve made a "follow me" motion at Monty and Lorenzo before walking to the other side of the parking lot.

"You have a problem with this?" Steve asked. "Because I can tell you, you won't be taking those girls off the island. Not right now, anyway."

"You're not equipped to deal with *cassandra sangue*," Lorenzo said.

Steve snorted. "Are you?"

"No, we're not," Monty said before Lorenzo could argue. "But I don't think you realize how difficult this will be."

"Namid's creation, both wondrous and terrible," Steve said softly. "You could say the Intuits were the original breeding stock that produced the blood prophets. And, no, we aren't any better equipped than you to deal with them. If we were, we wouldn't have lost a girl last year. But we're all going to have to think hard and fast about what can be done."

"I'm not easy about the girls being taken out of our hands," Lorenzo said. He wagged a finger between himself and Monty. "We brought those five girls out of the compound. We had to leave dozens behind, dozens of girls who . . ." He shook his head. "We'll find someplace for the girls."

Steve gave them a strange look. "You don't understand how the *terra indigene* work, do you? They've taken this out of your hands—and I'm not just talking about the girls you brought back to Lakeside. Now that they know what to look for, you can bet the Others are out there now, hunting for *cassandra sangue* in every human settlement."

We showed the Others the likeliest places for the girls to be kept, Monty thought, feeling chilled by the amount of blood that was about to be shed. "All of those children, killed."

Another strange look. "It's possible that whoever runs the compounds will kill the girls rather than let someone else have them. But that's not what you meant, is it?"

He hadn't considered that. As a police officer, he should have considered it. "No, that's not what I meant."

Steve said nothing for a minute. "I expect a lot of people are going to die over the next few weeks because of this. And I have to figure that not all the girls will be able to survive when their lives are no longer so restricted. But I can tell you that Intuits have coexisted with the Others ever since humans set foot on this continent, and we have never known them to harm a child."

Monty watched Simon walk out of the B and B alone. "So we let them go."

"The Others aren't going to let you keep the weapons, so, yes, you have to let the girls go."

Jean kept her eyes closed, sufficiently overwhelmed by the quiet sounds of the Wolves and men returning to the bus. Engine turning over. Movement. Where were they going now? Could it matter? Did anyone else on this bus understand what was coming?

The *terra indigene* would move fast and strike hard—and Thaisia would never be the same. As for the *cassandra sangue* who would be caught in the whirling images of these fights . . .

Blood. Desperation. Terror. The flash of razors as a way to silence fear of the future, only to see the truth in a prophecy that comes moments too late.

Not for me to know, Jean thought. *Not much of me left to use.*

She had lived too long in that restricted life. She had yearned to be outside since the day she'd been taken from her parents, a little girl who had held on to memories as proof that there was something more than the cells and the lessons and the men and women who looked at all of them and saw nothing but the value of skin.

Now that was over. But outside was too big, too much. She'd sent Meg outside with nothing but her childhood memories as proof that the *cassandra sangue* could survive. And yet, Meg had survived and would make things better for all of them.

She must have dozed off, because when Simon Wolfgard said, "We're here," she opened her eyes and realized the bus had stopped moving.

She slowly made her way down the steps, assisted by Simon and Lieutenant Montgomery and followed by Dr. Lorenzo and Steve Ferryman. A man and woman waited for them in front of a comfortable-looking house. There were other buildings nearby—a barn and . . . chicken coop . . . and another, smaller building that looked similar to the house. Cottage? Guesthouse? She couldn't recall an image that quite fit the look of the structure.

"This is James and Lorna Gardner," Steve Ferryman said. "They're Simple Life folks. That means they make use of some practical technology, but they prefer to keep their lives uncluttered."

"The guest cottage is empty," James said. "We had a cousin living there for a while, but she met someone at our last gathering and went to live in his community. Mr. Ferryman sent word that you might be needing some quiet, so you're welcome to stay if it suits you."

Jean looked at the cottage and the land and the two people waiting for her answer.

Then Lorna stepped forward and handed her a jar. "You can take your meals with us, of course, but this is our traditional welcoming gift."

Jean looked at her own scarred hand, holding the jar of honey.

"Could you stay here for a while, Jean?" Simon asked.

She swallowed tears and smiled. "Yes, I'd like to stay."

Monty sat in the visitor's chair in front of Captain Burke's desk and waited.

"Choosing the lesser of two evils is never easy, Lieutenant," Burke said quietly. "If we hadn't provided assistance in locating that compound, the *terra indigene* would have torn the Midwest apart. Make no mistake about that. And now the Others throughout Thaisia have grabbed the human governments by the balls with an ultimatum: voluntarily reveal the places where *cassandra sangue* are sheltered or lose that human settlement—the whole village, town, or city reclaimed immediately if the Others go in and find even a single girl hidden away."

"What about all the politicians and businessmen and whoever else bought prophecies?" Monty asked.

"As I understand it, the *terra indigene* aren't going to stop anyone from buying a prophecy. At least, not immediately. I think the compounds will have new staff to look after the girls and the security will be handled by the Others. So they're going to know everyone who goes in or out of those places. They'll know if anyone tries to smuggle out blood or a girl—and may the gods help anyone foolish enough to try it."

"So even with the compounds revealed, nothing will change for the girls."

"Everything will change, Lieutenant. The breeding farms will be shut down. The girls living in the compounds now won't be forced to leave a familiar place, but those places will be run more like supervised housing. And if they want to leave, they can. The blood prophets will make their own choices, live their own lives. And that will include deciding to make a cut for someone who wants a prophecy."

"With the *terra indigene* watching and knowing exactly who is buying prophecies." Monty sighed. "That will give power brokers more reason to support the Humans First and Last movement."

"Probably," Burke agreed. "We'll just deal with one problem at a time."

"Sir? How do you know all this?" It didn't surprise him that Burke knew. He just wondered how the man had found out before anyone else.

"I stopped at the Courtyard, intending to give you a lift home and get your report. But you were on your way to Ferryman's Landing, so I had a brief chat with Elliot Wolfgard. I think he was so forthcoming because he wanted to see how humans might react to the news. The next few weeks should be interesting."

I could do with a little less interesting for a while, Monty thought as he pushed out of the chair. "I'm not sure Dr. Lorenzo is going to keep his office in the Market Square. Realizing the Others don't let you pick and choose how you help them . . . I'm not sure he's going to get past what he saw in that compound."

"Are you?" Burke asked.

He didn't know, so he said, "Good night, sir."

"Have someone drive you home, Lieutenant."

"Yes, sir." Monty called MacDonald and Debany since they were on duty and arranged for the ride home. Then he sat at his desk to wait for them to return to the station.

He looked at the book about Thaisia's history that Simon had given to him and wondered how much the Others' version of recent events would differ from the human account. Then he pulled an envelope out of his pocket and opened it. Simon had given it to him when they got off the train.

The single sentence read: "Unlike humans, the *terra indigene* do not harm the sweet blood."

He suddenly understood the task the Midwest Wolves and Sanguinati had undertaken. They wouldn't leave the girls in that compound. Not that one. No, they would scatter those girls among the small human settlements under their control, most likely the Intuit villages. The Others would give the girls a chance to live—or allow them to die if they were too wounded in mind and heart to survive. Not all of them would have Meg Corbyn's strength and will to live, but he hoped enough of them would.

Monty folded the paper, put it back in the envelope, and tucked it in his desk drawer. Then he opened the history book and began to read while he waited for Debany and MacDonald.

You couldn't choose to step away once you got entangled with the Others. He just hoped that humans would gain something from the bloodshed that was coming.

Simon looked at the windows of his dark, empty apartment and wanted to howl with loneliness. He wanted company, companionship, but not . . . Wolves. Yes, he wanted them too, but being around his own kind wouldn't take away this particular feeling of lonely.

He wanted his friend. His Meg. Her phone message had meant something. Hadn't it?

He'd found her cell in the compound, the place those *humans* had kept her for all those years. It still held her scent and looked untouched, as if they'd been waiting to lock her back in that place. That had horrified him in a way the slaughter of the adult humans in the compound never could.

Even with the Sanguinati on the inside to open the doors for the rest of them, the Others hadn't been able to save all the girls. The Controller and his people had seen to that. But that wasn't something Lieutenant Montgomery or Dr. Lorenzo had needed to know then or now. It was enough that they had seen what the *terra indigene* could do. Now he would wait and see what they did with that knowledge.

"If you keep standing there, you won't find the note I left for you." Meg's voice came out of the darkness, a light that banished the shadows of lonely.

He walked over to the stairs that led to her porch. "What note?"

"The one that said to drop off your carryall and come up for dinner."

"Oh." He climbed the stairs, bringing the carryall with him. "You have food?"

She smiled at him, a glee that invited him to play. "I made spaghetti."

That didn't sound right, but he'd caught the scent of something tasty, so he followed her to the kitchen, leaving his carryall by the door.

"Merri Lee taught me," Meg said as she lifted the lid on a pot and carefully stirred. "The sauce has ground beef and some vegetables. The beef was thoroughly sniffed before Boone Hawkgard ground it fresh for me, so it's fine. And the pasta is almost ready."

He felt like his paws weren't on firm ground, and he didn't know how to move. The food scents were too strong, so he couldn't tell if she'd cut herself recently. "How did you know when to . . . ?" He trailed off, certain he would spoil things if he asked.

The look in her clear gray eyes was equal parts annoyed and amused. "Blair promised to call when he dropped you off so that I would know when to put the pasta in, and he did."

"Oh." He yelped in surprise when the timer buzzed, and that made her laugh.

"Here." She shut off the heat and handed him two potholders. "Pour the pasta into the colander in the sink. Be careful. It's boiling water and the pot is heavy."

It was boiling and it was heavy, and he realized that was the reason she let him do this—to protect her skin. While he followed her directions and transferred the spaghetti to a plate, Meg ladled some of the sauce out of the other pot.

"You're supposed to have bread and salad and other things with it," Meg said. "At least that's how it's served at the Saucy Plate, but this was all I could do today."

"It's a lot," he said, and meant it. A train ride with five young girls who

couldn't cope with even the smallest personal experience and a severely damaged Jean had shown him how much effort it took for Meg to do simple things
without being overwhelmed by the images and stimulation of doing.

He was hungry and wanted to gulp the food, but he ate slowly, appreciating
the tastes and the effort. And . . .

He was sure now that she hadn't cut herself, but there was a little bit of her
flavor woven through the rest of the scents. She had touched the food, and that
contact had retained a hint of her. He enjoyed the meal even more because of it.

When they'd eaten enough, they stored the rest of the food and did the dishes
together. He worried for a moment that he was acting too human, but he liked
the closeness, the company, the companionship.

She didn't ask about the girls or the compound or Jean until they were sitting on the sofa in her living room. That's when he gave her the letter Jean had
written on the train.

"You got her out," Meg said, turning the envelope over and over. "You
saved her."

He wasn't sure of that. He wasn't sure anyone that scarred and battered
could be saved.

"She's living on Great Island, so you can visit her," he said. "But not yet.
She's . . . damaged, Meg, and doesn't want to see you for a while. That's why she
gave me this letter."

"She needs to settle into a routine before coping with something else that's
new." Meg turned the letter over and over. "But I could write to her. I could buy
stationery at the Three Ps and send her a letter telling her about my life in the
Courtyard. Receiving a letter could be part of the routine."

"Yes, it could. Meg? I'd really like to get out of this skin."

"Okay. I picked up a movie to watch tonight. You can watch it with me if you
like. It's a chick movie. Merri Lee said that means girls like it, not that there are
small birds in it."

Since watching a movie about small birds didn't appeal to him either, he had
no objections to a movie without them. While Meg put the movie in the player,
he went into her bedroom to strip and shift. He gave himself a good shake—and
then wondered if he should offer to vacuum the carpet.

Maybe in the morning.

He returned to the living room and climbed onto the sofa with her.

Either she didn't find the story interesting or the past few days had exhausted her, because she fell asleep halfway through the movie.

He wasn't quite sure how she managed to end up halfway on top of him, but he didn't mind feeling the weight of her or her breath ruffling his fur or being surrounded by the comforting scent of her skin. He didn't mind it at all.